CONFORM

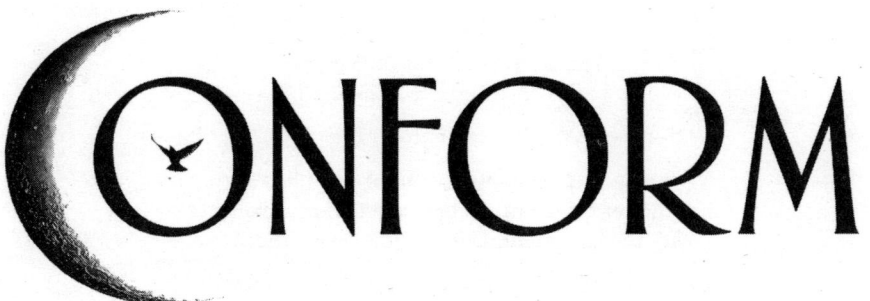

ARIEL SULLIVAN

BRAMBLE

First published in the US 2025 by Ballantine Books
an imprint of Random House

First published in the UK 2025 by Tor Bramble
an imprint of Pan Macmillan
The Smithson, 6 Briset Street, London EC1M 5NR
EU representative: Macmillan Publishers Ireland Ltd, 1st Floor,
The Liffey Trust Centre, 117–126 Sheriff Street Upper,
Dublin 1 D01 YC43
Associated companies throughout the world

ISBN 978-1-0350-7225-5 HB
ISBN 978-1-0350-7226-2 TPB

Copyright © Mermaid Reform Press LLC 2025

The right of Ariel Sullivan to be identified as the author of this work has been asserted in accordance with the Copyright, Designs and Patents Act 1988.

Chapter-opening art: Dinara/Adobe Stock

Map by Francesca Baerald

Book design by Elizabeth Rendfleisch

All rights reserved. No part of this publication may be reproduced, stored in a retrieval system, or transmitted, in any form, or by any means (including, without limitation, electronic, mechanical, photocopying, recording or otherwise) without the prior written permission of the publisher.

Pan Macmillan does not have any control over, or any responsibility for, any author or third-party websites (including, without limitation, URLs, emails and QR codes) referred to in or on this book.

1 3 5 7 9 8 6 4 2

A CIP catalogue record for this book is available from the British Library.

Printed and bound in the UK using 100% Renewable Electricity by CPI Group (UK) Ltd

This book is sold subject to the condition that it shall not, by way of trade or otherwise, be lent, hired out, or otherwise circulated without the publisher's prior consent in any form of binding or cover other than that in which it is published and without a similar condition including this condition being imposed on the subsequent purchaser. The publisher does not authorize the use or reproduction of any part of this book in any manner for the purpose of training artificial intelligence technologies or systems. The publisher expressly reserves this book from the Text and Data Mining exception in accordance with Article 4(3) of the European Union Digital Single Market Directive 2019/790.

Visit **www.panmacmillan.com** to read more about
all our books and to buy them.

*To little me,
who was constantly told to get her head out of the clouds
but made a world in them instead,
thank you for never giving in.*

This is for you.

CONFORM

I've never been good at anything. Or that's what I've been told my whole life. I disagree, though. I've always been good at fucking things up.

This is one of those things.

CHAPTER ONE

IDENTIFICATION NUMBER: **F13463233**
AGE: **27**
SEX: **Female**
WEIGHT: **58.2 kg**
HEIGHT: **176 cm**
GENETIC DEFECTS: **Minor, Hereditary**
PROCREATION STATUS: ***Approved***

A HOLOGRAM FILLED THE CENTER OF MY OFFICE WITH A painting. Simple, small. Just a woman, a hint of a smile on her face.

As usual, I was alone in the Ancient Art section of the Archives, buried deep underground. My job was to destroy, piece by piece, the remnants of the world ancient humans had laid waste to in the Last War. Elsewhere in the Archives, my friend Lo sat in the Books section, and there were others who sorted ancient tools, documents, and relics from before the war. Our screens dictated what was saved, reassigned, or—like this one—destroyed. A push of a button, and the ties to the past disappeared.

The title on the screen read *Mona Lisa*. Her eyes captivated me like she held a secret. I couldn't look away. Her smile, over a millennium old, taunted my curiosity. For a moment, it drowned out the word that has haunted me ever since that morning: *Approved.*

I was one of the many women in gray who had trained for this, waiting until our fertility was determined optimal and matched to an Elite male to fulfill our role for the Greater Good. Thoughts, hopes, wants: They were unnecessary. A distraction. The Illum that ran the city provided the Minor Defects, myself included, with everything we needed. What was left to think about?

I tore my eyes from the hologram projection, its glow illuminating my dimly lit office and my foolish desires. I could finally be chosen by an Elite for a Procreation Agreement—attend their balls and enter their towering buildings in the clouds. I would see their secret life above. Be a part of it. At least while they let me. While I was usable.

For years alone in this office, I had thought about a Procreation Agreement, wondering if the beauty the ancient humans captured in paint strokes still existed Above. Fantasies found me in my bed as my purpose was drilled into me every day. A moment in a delicate gown. A kind Elite man, spinning me on a dance floor until I was free of the horrors of the last twenty-seven years.

He'd dance with me like I was special, whisper my name in my ear: *Emeline.* Chasing away the words of inadequacy that had followed me my entire life. He'd capture me in his arms and bring our faces close . . . until our eyes would meet, and he'd deem me unworthy as every Elite had done.

The light fixture's eternal drone overhead mixed with words I could never outrun.

That offspring ruined everything.
She should be in blue.
I don't care what you do with her.
Get her out of my sight.

The smiling woman kept me steady, her power seeping into the room. My spiraling thoughts fell silent in the wake of her reserved beauty, as if she could see to my core, all of my secrets laid bare.

I hit *delete*. Her smile clung to me as she disappeared. My office became a morgue once again, barren of color, of light, of choice. A place for destruction. Four white walls, a metal desk, screens that obscured the doorway, and a single hanging light.

The city had remarkable technology. I often wondered why the Illum had us doing tasks their technology could easily perform. Why they allowed us to see what came before. It was as if sorting these relics showed us how easily they were willing to toss aside the things they saw no value in. Reminding all the women of procreation age what would await us if we failed the Greater Good.

The next painting depicted a man in a blue outfit, not unlike my daily gray, sitting on a simple wooden chair. He held his face, his pain somehow palpable even after all these moons had passed. It felt almost indecent, like I was intruding on something private. Maybe the Illum were right to rid the new world of the old world if it had caused this much trepidation. *At Eternity's Gate* read the title.

"What do you think happened to him?" a smooth, unmistakably male voice said, and I jumped.

Past the screens and projected hologram, a man stood in the shadows of my doorway, his frame blocking the hall beyond. He had a rugged beauty about him, and he peered into my office as if he belonged, wavy dark blond hair falling casually into his face.

"I—I don't know," I stammered. His lips pulled up in a half smile, a dimple appearing on the left side, and heat rushed to my cheeks.

No one came down here, ever. I had spent every day here for ten years and never had a visitor. My gaze remained locked on his handsome face, unable to look away.

"I think he lost someone, someone he cared for." He leaned against the doorframe, staring at the hologram.

I could have asked a million questions—*Who are you? What are you doing here? Are you authorized to be here? Why are you so handsome?*—but I asked a question that mattered more to me than all the others, one that was dangerous.

"You're . . . curious about art?"

"Yes. Aren't you?"

For one wild moment, I wondered if an Elite had come to evaluate me for the mating contract. Could he even be my proposed Mate? Suddenly, I found myself desperate, like Lo, to be accepted. The man looked toward me, but my eyes flew to my lap, unable to meet his gaze. I couldn't risk the rejection of being *seen*. Not yet.

"All the time," I finally admitted, and my pulse turned painful at my honesty. I took a steadying breath. "Have you always been interested in art?"

"No, but lately I am," the man told me.

"Is art common there?" I asked. Would I see real art in the clouds?

"I can't give you our secrets," he said smoothly, "but maybe one day I could show you."

My insides twisted in anticipation or apprehension; I didn't know. Maybe both. I had been told since my earliest years that I was beneath the Elite. The Academy preached this every day, intermingling with the harshness of my birth father's teachings. Were they wrong? It was a traitorous thought, one that could condemn me. We weren't permitted to question the Illum.

Frustration coursed through me at how little they told us. Perhaps the Elite had lessons that consisted of more than how to be a compliant vessel for offspring. If we weren't learning how to get to the clouds by being the perfect Mate, we learned horrifying lessons on the Last War. Endless hologram lectures warned us of all the risks to life without the Illum to guide us. How ancient humans had torn themselves apart and wiped themselves out. Their conflicting beliefs and ideologies created an irreparable divide that had resulted in near extinction. The Illum had knitted it all back together, saving humanity. The Illum had seen to the rebirth of society, illuminating the best way forward with their superior intellect. The Academy portrayed the Illum as saviors of mankind. Gods and religion had no place here. We could only trust in the Illum, unseen yet always watching.

"Would you like me to leave?" the man asked, interrupting my busy mind.

"No," I exclaimed, too quickly, standing. I didn't want to be alone again, not yet.

"All right . . ." The man cleared his throat. "I don't know your name."

"Emeline," I told him as I got a look at all of him, still partially concealed in the shadows. There was a mysterious ease to him. The man stepped into my office, and my eyes flew to my desk. This was a trap of some kind, a test. Another lesson from the Academy found me.

Should you be successful in your dedication to the Greater Good and matched with an Elite Mate, you will find your true work has just begun. Every meeting with your proposed Mate will be watched by the Elite collective. Your ability to perform publicly is as critical to your success as your ability to carry an offspring.

If your behavior is unsatisfactory or displeasing, you will be among the fallen in blue. Follow the Illum's protocol, abide by the rules of the Minor Defect population, and constantly seek self-improvement, and you will rise, fulfilling your use for the Greater Good.

"Are you going to look at me, Emeline?" the man asked, his voice closer now. "I swear I won't bite."

Never look at the Elite, Emeline, my birth mother had warned. I had been only four years old, boarding the Pod for the Academy. My only memory of her speaking to me. *Just look down and they will leave you be. You must look down.*

But I couldn't displease the Elite. I took a deep breath, lifted my chin slowly, and sealed my fate as my eyes collided with his. His light brown irises had a ring of amber along the inside, as if a star had burst from the pupil. They were beautiful.

I held his gaze, my throat too tight. I waited for his rejection, disgust, and cruel words. But he didn't flinch. His eyes went wide for a single breath, yet he didn't look away.

"It's nice to meet you, Emeline," the man said, his dimple appearing. He approached my desk, extending his hand across it. "My name's Hal."

I raised my hand to his, disbelief flooding my veins. The light from the hologram cast his features into sharp relief, heightening his beauty and large frame.

And that he was dressed in blue.

I dropped my hand instantly. "You're a Major Defect?" How had I missed that? Weren't they not allowed to leave their sector?

An unsettling realization slammed into my chest: I agreed with someone in blue. I stepped away, my back colliding with the wall. It had been a relief just moments ago to think I agreed with someone from the clouds, sharing something dangerous I kept locked away.

"Guilty." Hal smirked, thrusting his hands into his pockets. "You going to run away?" I looked toward the door behind him. I was cornered. "Call for someone to save you?"

"There's no one down here," I confessed.

"I know," Hal said as he watched me. "Your kind calls us monsters."

"Are you a monster?" I whispered, too curious for my own good.

Hal's smirk spread. "Would you like to find out?"

Before I could think better, I admitted, "I don't understand. You don't look . . ."

Those starburst eyes danced with mirth. "Tell me, Emeline, how do I look?"

"I think you know the answer to that," I muttered, glancing down once more as my cheeks burned, giving me away.

"Maybe, but it would sound better coming from your lips." He chuckled, and the sound danced along my skin.

"I—I didn't mean . . . I simply meant you don't seem as terrible as the Illum say."

"Right, that's all you meant." His eyes ran over me. "And do you believe everything the blessed Illum tell you?"

"Doesn't everyone?" I might be brave enough to discuss art, but I wasn't dumb enough to question the Illum with a man I did not know.

"Perhaps," Hal drawled, stepping back as he looked toward the hologram of the grieving man. "Perhaps not."

"The Illum's rules aren't to be taken lightly. The Illum are the reason we are all here," I told him, hating how I sounded.

"They certainly are," Hal agreed.

"I only meant, why keep you hidden?" I confessed. The Illum valued things of beauty, the world above a glittering display of it. The spaces and the people. The man before me fit in their world.

"Are you implying you like looking at me?" Hal asked, his gaze seeking mine.

My cheeks grew warmer. "I did not say that."

"You didn't have to. It's written all over your face," he said smugly. "If it makes you feel better, the feeling is mutual."

My heart fluttered. He liked looking at me. I tried to brush it off—he was in blue, I should keep my distance—but no one had ever told me I was worthy of being seen, let alone enjoyable to look at. I couldn't stop the warmth that grew in my chest, regardless of the source.

"So, are you here because you like looking at me?" I asked.

"And what if I was?" Hal stepped toward me, and I sank farther into the wall. Raking a hand through his hair, he scoffed. "Right. It's the blue, isn't it?"

I shook my head, pulse hammering against my skin. Was it the blue? My approved status? My conditioning? Hal nodded at whatever he found on my face, turning toward the door.

"It isn't," I confessed, halting him. I trembled but held his gaze. "It isn't the blue, not entirely. I've never had a visitor here. Ever."

"How long have you worked down here?" Hal asked.

"Ten years," I admitted.

Something shifted in his eyes. He blew out a breath. "That's a long time to be alone. But I should get going; the sun's up. I should be beneath."

"Beneath? Don't you mean Low Town?"

Hal grinned. "Like I said, I can't give you all our secrets."

"If you ever—" I pushed off the wall, my blood pounding at my daring. "If you ever want to come back and talk about art . . . I'm always here."

The corner of his mouth pulled up, a dimple appearing. "I might do that. See you around, Emeline."

He left.

I stared at the empty doorway as if it were one of the ancient art pieces, filling me with more questions than answers. What secrets did he have? Hal had said *beneath,* not *Low Town.* It didn't measure up to what I had been told about the Major Defects who wore blue.

I glanced at the man in blue in the painting and his eternal struggle. I hesitated, then hit *delete,* and he disappeared.

I worked through the remaining twenty-two items on the list and found myself staring at the empty doorway as much as the art. Many of the pieces were landscapes, bursting with colorful flowers, lush trees, and sparkling bodies of water. I cherished these glimpses of the world the ancient humans felt compelled to capture, one that looked completely unlike ours. The city the Illum had built was shiny and paved, at least within the city limits. Was that why there was no new art? Nothing left to inspire new art? In all my time down here, I had never seen a piece of art dated post–Last War.

The final painting was of a woman holding an offspring. A third figure, cloaked in white, bowed toward the offspring. I don't know how long I stared at it before hitting *delete* without checking where it was meant to go. I would have to come up with a reason in my report for why I deleted it. We were all given a report log in the Archives—a running record of any unusual findings. I didn't know how to encapsulate that every detail was unusual, extraordinary. My reports morphing into elegies. Lo claimed she turned hers in empty most days.

The usual beep from my scanner by the door finally signaled, and I finished typing notes in my report before the screens went black. I gathered my things; then another jarring beep sounded as I scanned my wrist and ran from the ghosts of the paintings I had destroyed.

On my ascent to the surface, other women in gray filed in from the other floors of the Archives. No hellos were shared among us. The elevator doors opened to the main lobby, light and the sounds of life spilling in. I blew out a breath I hadn't realized I had been holding as I approached the large glass doors, where I spotted Lo waiting for me. The ornate chandeliers overhead cast tiny rainbows throughout the marble hall from the sun's dying rays. Every surface sparkled and shined.

"Hey, how was work?" I asked.

"Fine, sent lots of books to their doom," Lo told me. "Not a single one was saved today."

We exited the building, and I paused in a patch of sunlight, tilting my face up and closing my eyes. "Does it ever bother you that you're destroying things that might be important?"

"Nope," Lo said. "If it was important the Illum would keep it."

I cracked an eye open, peering at Lo on her Comm Device and her absolute trust in the Illum. Sometimes, I wondered how daily hellos on our synced commutes had turned into this sort-of friendship. Lo didn't share any of my concerns. She had accepted the Illum's world and her role. Her main goal of achieving a life in the clouds kept her content.

More so, I wondered how I had found myself bending their rules yet again. I had sworn after my only other friendship was taken from me that I would never do this again. Friendships weren't permitted among those in gray. Most women in gray only saw competition thanks to the Academy. The same lesson burned into us, over and over.

Now that we have removed the males, look around. The women around you are vying for your position in the clouds. Only a select few, the very best, shall be selected. If the woman next to you trounces you, she will be a contributing factor in the color you wear. Follow the Illum's protocol, abide by the rules of the Minor Defect population, and constantly seek self-improvement, and you will rise, fulfilling your use for the Greater Good.

Things had permanently shifted after that lesson. Derision and contention had taken root and only deepened from there.

"How was your art?" she asked. "Have you sunned enough? Can we go?"

"I barely finished my list," I said, breathing in the warmth, hoarding it until I saw the sun again, then followed Lo toward the line for the Pods.

"Have you ever thought about not looking at the pictures and focusing on the screen? You could just push the buttons. It'd be more productive."

As we joined the sea of gray, I bit my tongue from saying how the beauty was impossible to ignore. "I don't think I could do that."

"It'd make the time go quicker," Lo told me, unbraiding her long plait until a sheet of golden hair tumbled free. She trailed her hands through the waves. "Plus, none of that matters now. You're approved."

My stomach swooped as her words stole the warmth I had relished moments ago. I had told her this morning that I'd been approved, and she had squealed with delight before bombarding me with questions I didn't have answers to.

"Have you heard anything more yet?" Lo asked.

"No."

"What are they going to do about your—" Lo hesitated, and my gaze flew to her. "Those."

"Probably what everyone else does," I muttered. "Stare." The unspoken fear that I would be rejected hung heavy between us, and I changed topics. "Has anyone ever come to your office below?"

"No, why?" Her brows pinched.

Could I tell her about Hal? A ding sounded from the depths of my bag. I fished out my Comm Device as Lo pushed closer to me.

"Is it from them?" she hissed. We shuttled forward in the line. "What's it say?"

I reread the message several times, the Illum's insignia at the top: A golden circle with one of their impossibly tall buildings erupting from the clouds. The sharp tip was a perch for a gleaming sun, casting its illuminating light upon us all.

> F13463233—It has come to our attention that you have been approved for procreation. Congratulations. The initial meeting with M17292834 has been set for 8:00 this evening following your preparation appointment at 6:00. All travel information has been loaded to your MIND chip. If you are deemed acceptable, you will receive the Procreation Contract, which is to be completed and signed prior to your following meeting. Fertile Blessings.

I wrapped a hand around my left wrist, where the miraculous technology from the Illum lay hidden. Each offspring had a MIND—Monitoring Intelligence Nanochip Device—inserted into the left wrist at birth, providing the Illum's systems with constant updates on our health, down to our genetic makeup. I had to scan the chip everywhere: for the hovering transportation Pods, for meals, for work, even for our living quarters. The Illum gathered vital information from each scan, evaluating our ability to be of use to the Greater Good.

I stared at the last words of the message. *Fertile Blessings*. From whatever information they gathered from the device in my wrist, I was finally fertile enough. I was useful. *Approved*. My stomach twisted painfully as I glanced at the time on my Comm Device. I had ten minutes. Ten years of waiting diminished to ten minutes. I would need to take the Pod straight to the clouds. My heartbeat became a death march.

"What's it say?" Lo urged, leaning over my shoulder. I turned the screen toward her so she could read for herself. Tilting my head back, I took in the skyscrapers that soared into the sky until they disappeared into the clouds. The Elite were up there, my potential Mate among them. Would he hold my defective gaze as the man in blue had? Would he be disgusted? Would he shout the words my birth father had tossed my way?

"Tonight?" she exclaimed. "That's so quick, Emeline. It's happening."

"Yeah, right in the middle of the transition," I said, looking at the fellow Defects around us. "They're all going to see. Maybe I should wait until it thins out." The Pod, a sleek oblong hovering transportation vehicle, would make a loud announcement the moment I scanned, alerting everyone in gray.

Lo looked at the others. "You don't want to be late, though. It might count against you."

The line before us dwindled. A crammed Pod zoomed away.

"Your future depends on your ability to comply with your Mate's desires," Lo whispered. Goosebumps erupted down my arms at her repetition of the words the Academy had uttered throughout our education.

What if . . . what if I couldn't?

There were gowns, balls, and luxury up there, but they hid more than beauty beyond the clouds. It was dangerous in the clouds for people like me. I would be watched and judged. I had to comply with my Mate's wishes and the Illum. Fail to do so and I would be thrown in blue—or eliminated entirely.

Lo pressed into my back, ushering me toward the open doors of the Pod. It was almost full. I stuck out a shaking arm, scanning my chip.

A loud horn blared through the Pod, followed by an automated female voice.

"ALL DEFECTS, PLEASE EXIT THE TRANSPORTATION POD IMMEDIATELY."

Groans accompanied the disgruntled women exiting the Pod,

pushing past me. Seething words slipped from their mouths as angry eyes ran up and down the length of me. "She'll be cast down soon enough," one muttered. "Look at her eyes."

My heart slammed in my throat. I stepped onto the Pod, the divide taking hold. A location I had never seen appeared on the Pod transport screen, the lights softening.

"F13463233 APPROVED FOR AUTHORIZED TRANSPORT."

Approved. Approved. Approved. Approved. Approved. Approved. Approved. Approved. Approved. Approved. The word merged with my raging heart.

I was approved, not accepted. My gaze snagged on the firm line of Lo's mouth as she remained with the others and the doors closed. The Pod shot up into the sky, leaving behind everything I knew.

The Pod ascended, and my stomach dipped. The surface sprawled in all directions. From this vantage point, I could see the five sectors: the Wastelands, a flat stretch of land devoid of anything but rows of squat brick housing, home to female Minors; the Banks, buildings identical to ours that ran along the opposite side of the river, home to the male Minors who served the Illum on the surface; High Town, below me, the ground floor of all their towering skyscrapers; the split black and white pyramid of the Academy to the south; the Sanctuary, where pregnant women outside of Cohabitation Agreements were sent, cloistered behind a large stone wall on the eastern side of the city; and farthest away, to the west, across the river where it splits, the archaic, dilapidated buildings of Low Town. Home of the Majors.

As the clouds engulfed the Pod, my reflection stared back at me, blurring out everything else. The thing no one could bear to look at, myself included. A mark against the Elite's beauty and perfection—my defect.

I barely registered the slightly angular face, creamy pale skin, high cheekbones, straight nose, and full mouth, all surrounded by a mess of long, curly brown hair. A rather alluring face, beautiful even, if I could look past my flaw. I had my birth father's symmetry and my birth mother's delicate grace, but it was wasted.

My left eye was crystal blue as if made of ice chips, and my right eye a deep, rich brown, almost depthless.

That girl is a disgrace to our genes. Our legacy.

The Pod broke through the clouds, leaving my reflection below and replacing it with the world of the Elite.

CHAPTER TWO

Countless pods whizzed freely in all directions, weaving between the towering glass structures at a dizzying pace. I stared out the windows, breathless, my fear loosening its hold on me. The tall buildings glinted in the last rays of the sun, revealing the secrets we couldn't see from below. Large metal panels were fastened along many of the buildings, pointed toward the sun.

Mesmerized, I clutched the seat as the Pod flew between glass skyscrapers, almost brushing against them, before coming to a halt against the side of a building in a gap in the clouds.

The doors opened, and a middle-aged man dressed in a dark gray suit stood stiffly just outside. He was a Minor Defect, like me—we all wore gray. The shade varied based on the role assigned after graduating the Academy. Those of us waiting for Procreation Agreements wore a dingy gray that almost looked dirty. Men were separated in the Academy after their eighth year and trained to serve the Elite in the clouds, signified by donning a darker hue. The men who didn't qualify for the clouds ran maintenance on the surface, their gray akin to ours.

"Good evening, ma'am," he said with a bow. "If you would please exit the Pod, I will scan your MIND and escort you."

I stepped forward, my eyes glued to where the Pod touched the entrance. Would my MIND alert them of my defect, making it clear there was some mistake? Would the Pod drop out from under my feet, sending me free-falling to the ground below? To my birthright?

"Promptness and obedience are celebrated in the clouds," the man stated.

Swallowing my fear, I stepped past the glass doors, my gray shoes meeting the intricate marble tile. A delicate glass light fixture cast a warm glow around the space.

The man led me to a rivet stand decorated with an arrangement of stunning white flowers. "Your arm, please," he prompted, holding out a small scanner. "Ms. Emeline, welcome."

I looked up at him, shocked. My birth name had never appeared upon scanning. MINDs always identified us by a set of numbers. Among fellow Defects names were used. Everywhere else in the city it had always been a nameless set of numbers. His eyes widened, and he looked pointedly over my shoulder, unable to meet my mismatched gaze.

"Is something amiss, Ms. Emeline?" he inquired, stepping around the stand.

"I was surprised you knew my birth name. Usually the scanner gives my identification number," I told my dull shoes, unwilling to look at him again—to see the judgment.

His heavy footsteps echoed down the quiet hall, and I hurried to follow him. "The Elite believe it is barbaric and disrespectful to reduce someone of their ilk to just their identification number. This way."

Barbaric. The word reverberated through me until it settled in my soul. The man in front of me wore gray, making him a Defect just like me, even in the clouds. Yet, he repeated what the Elite believed. Did his allotted time in the clouds obscure more than his ground view? Had he forgotten it was my people, *his* people, whose identities had been diminished to just numbers?

After tonight, I would either gain a name among the Elite or return to the surface as another number, depending on whether I pleased my potential Mate enough and whether he could look past my defect. I pressed forward, unsure which fate would be worse.

The man deposited me in a circular room painted a glossy black, causing the chandelier's light to ricochet off the shiny surfaces, creating a glimmering display. It was easy to get lost in the beauty of these rooms. Maybe that was the whole point.

"The Starlings will tend to you from here," the man said with a little bow.

"The Starlings?"

He gave a terse smile, pausing by the door. "Oh yes, it's what they call themselves. Like the ancient birds. Fertile blessings, Ms. Emeline." With that, he closed the door with a snap.

A chill snaked down my spine. The room instantly felt too small, oppressive, the dancing lights disorienting. Each panel looked identical as I spun around. My skin grew clammy. It suddenly felt like a cage.

I heard them before I saw them, two voices through the darkness.

"Well, well, what do we have today, Violet?" a tinkling voice rang out.

"A Defect, Rose. Hopefully better than the one from last week," another woman answered, her voice deeper, silkier. Who had been chosen last week?

"Even we can't fix some things," the other chided.

Two women entered the room. One was tall with rich brown skin, long jet-black hair that fell past her waist, and heavily lined eyes. The other was short with curly, flaming red hair, pale white skin, and an hourglass shape. A clash of contrasting features, but they wore uniform quicksilver long dresses that shimmered in the low light. Was it a shade of gray, or were they Elite? The Academy had never said Defect women could work in the clouds. What had they done to be among the Elite without a Mate?

Hands ran along my body, pulling me from my thoughts. I stiffened against the touch. The intimacy of it.

"Oh, how scrumptious," Rose cawed.

"Yes, it's promising," Violet crooned, her hands in my hair, releasing the tight bun and combing out the long strands with her fingers.

"Oh, how terribly ghastly." Rose stood on the tips of her toes, peering into my eyes. "I can't bear to look at it."

You knew this would be their reaction, I told myself. I was born in the clouds. It could have been my home, if not for my heterochromia. Though I didn't have any memories of what their world looked like, I did remember the words shot my way.

"Let me see," Violet said, pulling my face toward her. My eyes stung as their judgment tangled with my conditioning. I tried to look down, but Violet held me firmly. Her dark eyes met mine, and she smiled as she took in my defect. "A *visual* defect. I haven't seen one in some time."

"The one with the—" Rose gestured to her arms like she couldn't bear to speak of it. "Remember her?"

"Yes, well, she stood no chance. She should have been in blue from birth," Violet responded, taking in my broken gaze.

"There are others like me?" I asked quietly. I hadn't seen another visual defect in the Academy or working in the Archives. The Minor women all looked from the outside to be unflawed, whatever defect they had invisible. No one ever spoke of what had landed them in gray. I had assumed, without any confirmation from the Academy, that I had somehow been able to maintain a Minor status based on my Elite family and the impeccable genetic history my birth father had spoken of.

"Not anymore. The Illum have weeded your kind out with their Procreation Program," Rose said.

Violet's dark eyes met mine. "You're a dying breed, Fledgling. The Illum must see something in you to bring you into view."

My shoulders went rigid. What could the Illum want with a *dying breed*?

"Come, little Fledgling," called Rose, revealing a hidden door in the panels. "If we do our part right and you do yours, we will have three moons together for your Courting Phase."

Three lunar cycles, or what we called moons. Our physicals took place once a year, on the day we were born. In the monotony of my life—wake, eat, work, eat, sleep—three moons, eighty-seven days, felt endless. With my approval it became impossibly short.

"Come. We will fix you for him." Rose beckoned me toward tendrils of lavender-scented steam that twirled into the black cage of a room.

"Or try to," Violet added behind me.

Firm hands pressed against my back, and the Academy lessons chased me into the steam.

Throughout your Courting Phase, public appearances shall be required. Before each outing, you shall be stripped of your gray and made palatable for Elite society. You are to follow your Elite Mate's guidance. Your future depends on your ability to comply with your Mate's desires, which we shall cover in your final year. Until then follow the Illum's protocol, abide by the rules of the Minor Defect population, and constantly seek self-improvement, and you will rise, fulfilling your use for the Greater Good.

Fail to do so, and your Public Courting and Cohabitation Rights shall be revoked, resulting in living quarters in the Sanctuary on the city's outskirts until your offspring is brought here. You will then be deposited among those in blue, far from the Illum's light. You will expire there as a disappointment to the Illum and humanity.

"We must move swiftly." The Starlings tugged the gray from my body without permission, leaving me naked before them. My arms wrapped around my exposed chest.

"Don't be shy," Rose squawked as my pulse raced. Besides my physical, where men in white coats ran exams that determined our usefulness, I had never been naked in front of anyone. We were covered at all times.

"He won't care about the eyes when he sees this." Violet smiled knowingly, pulling at my arm. "Fledgling, we cannot work if you cover yourself. You don't want to disappoint the Illum, do you?" Her dark eyes bored into mine.

I shook my head, slowly dropping my arms until I was trembling, fully exposed to them.

"The modesty," Rose huffed, holding a jar of a black substance as Violet tied my hair in a knot above my head. "You should be using all of this." Rose gestured to my naked body. "You are a vessel for humanity. You would do well to remember that. This is a blessing from the Illum, to be chosen. Arms out."

I obeyed, shivering despite the heat from the room. Rose took a large scoop of the substance in the jar, passed it to Violet, and dropped to her knees before me. I gasped loudly as the two began coating my body with the gritty substance, rubbing hard enough to remove a layer of skin. They worked methodically in tandem, leaving nothing untouched.

Rose stood and made her way to the wall, pushing a button. Behind her, a shower with countless heads came to life.

"Wash off the grime of the life below."

The shower felt like an assault as my raw skin was pelted with varying pressure of scalding water, spraying my face, shooting up my nose, bombarding me from above. Sputtering, I stumbled out of the shower.

"This way, little Fledgling," Violet said. "In the tub now."

A towel was pressed into my hands. I wiped wildly at my face before giving it back to them. The Starlings perched on the edge of a small pool, and once I eased in, their hands dived into my curls. A floral scent drifted toward me only for them to shove my head underwater. They repeated the process, washing and drowning me until they were satisfied.

"Now out," Rose commanded as they pulled me out of the tub. Violet shoved a towel into my hands, and I wrapped it tightly around my raw skin, following them into a paneled room, bare except for a silver rolling tray and a black table. The resemblance to the medical rooms I had visited for my physical caused my spine to go rigid.

For the space of several terrified heartbeats I was in the examination room, standing in a flimsy gray gauzy gown that opened in the front before three men in white coats.

Lie down and be quiet.

I had—again and again, the men never saying another word as they scanned my chip, then poked and prodded me until content.

"Towel off, little Fledgling," Violet called, wheeling the metal tray to the table. "Lie down."

Rose tugged my towel, and I clutched it against my body in a vise grip. "Not until you tell me what you're about to do," I demanded, mouth dry.

"As if you have a say," Rose told me. I gripped the towel tighter.

"You're livelier than your file made you out to be, Defect." Violet's eyes danced as she looked at me. "We are going to remove the hair from your body," she explained. My hand flew to my long, dark strands.

"Not the hair on your head, daft one." Rose chuckled. "Just everywhere else." Her smile became feline as she tugged hard on the towel again. Reluctantly, I released it, naked before them once more, and climbed onto the table.

The cold metal bit into me. Within seconds, they slathered my shin with hot paste that didn't burn. I relaxed slightly as Rose rubbed paper against the cooled substance.

"Don't scream," Rose warned before mercilessly ripping it off. I suppressed a cry at the flash of pain. They continued slowly, working up my legs, contorting my body to reach everything. I sucked in deep breaths as they reached the most sensitive parts. It felt endless as I closed my eyes and held my breath, only releasing it when they tore the hair from my body. Again and again and again.

I opened my eyes hesitantly when the torture stopped. "I'm impressed," Violet said, carrying another mystery jar. "Most from below yell and cry the first time. You barely flinched."

I scowled at her. It had not felt like I barely flinched. A woodsy, floral scent hit me, and I eyed the jar suspiciously. "It's a balm to soothe the skin and decrease redness," Violet clarified, applying some to my legs. The relief was instant.

I began to rise without prompting, assuming more was to be done. "She's learning," Rose said, tossing me a thin robe and taking me to another room, sitting me in front of a large vanity littered with different jars, vials, and cases. "Be still while we fix you," Rose told me as they bustled into action. I closed my eyes and sat silently as they touched and pulled, thankful no one asked for my robe. Violet brushed my hair before drying it with a small handheld device. Rose crouched before me, attacking my feet, clipping and painting.

A freckled face with flaming red hair rose to my memory. Alice.

"When we get out of here we can find a way to run away," she had told me. We had been fifteen, at the Academy. "The world was big before the Last War. We can go somewhere else where they don't treat us like this, or if we can't find anyone it can just be us, alone, forever. We can change our fate. Wouldn't that be wonderful, Em?"

I had stared at her bright eyes, gleaming with hope, in the communal sleeping area. The others all slept around us. I found the moon through the window above my small bed. If only we had that power.

"It would be wonderful," I had whispered.

I missed her so much. It was strange missing something that wasn't meant to exist. The Academy forbade friendships and connections of any kind. Alice hadn't cared about any of their rules. Whispered conversations after lights-out had become our routine. A secret friendship. Stranger still, mourning something I didn't know the ending to. Deep down a part of me knew she had disregarded one too many rules. That I would never see her again. She was gone.

"I think it's for her eyes," Violet was saying, bringing me back to the room.

"Have you ever seen anything like it, though?" Rose asked, clutching Violet's arm as she peered at something Violet held.

"I have not," Violet answered. "Her file . . . the Mate's identity was blank, right?"

Rose nodded. "No number or preferences were listed for her."

Violet turned toward me, a small black box in her hands. "Strange, is it not?"

"What's strange?" I asked.

"You've received a gift," Rose told me, laying a small scrap of paper upon the counter. It was too far away for me to read the meticulous penmanship on the note.

"What kind of gift?" I asked, leaning forward.

Violet grabbed my shoulders and pulled me back against the chair. "A very generous one. They sent you a film—"

"They call it a lens," Rose interjected as she placed something on her finger. It was tiny and impossibly thin. "It says to place it over the blue one."

"Who sent it?" I asked, my palms sweaty.

"The Illum," they told me together.

"We aren't often surprised, Fledgling. What have you done to win the Illum's favor with a visual defect?" Violet asked, her eyes narrowed.

"I haven't done anything," I told them honestly.

The two shared a glance before Rose approached me. Violet gripped my shoulders tighter, tilting my head back until she hovered over me. "Shame they want to cover the blue. If she had two of them, it would be quite lovely. Brown will have to do."

"It says to hold open the eye to place it," Rose told Violet.

Her hands left my shoulders, holding open my blue eye. "Don't move." My pulse fluttered fitfully as a strange film obstructed my vision. I blinked rapidly as the film moved and my sight came back.

"It works. How bizarre," Violet exclaimed, peering at my face, inches from me. "Let's paint."

Rose grabbed brushes, different jars, and vials from the vanity. I blinked incessantly, my eye watering. "Stop that," Rose demanded.

Moments later, I was being pushed into another room with a small raised platform and a garment rack bursting with breathtaking fabrics and colors. Despite myself, a small thrill raced through me. I had always hated the drab, shapeless gray garments I was forced to wear.

"This is the fun part," Violet whispered, and I jumped. "Here. On the platform, robe off," she instructed, cramming something in my hands. Ivory lace panties. If you could call the small scraps that. Dropping the robe, I shimmied into them, breasts still exposed. I stood on the platform, clutching my chest, as the two squabbled. They clearly had a deep understanding of each other. A closeness as foreign to me as the procreation phase.

"The gold," Violet claimed forcefully. "The neckline will distract her Mate, ensuring a successful contract."

"She is going to dinner, not the bedroom, tonight," Rose argued. "She should wear the pink gown. It will look beautiful among the blooms in the Garden."

"And hide all our hard work with a frilly skirt and a high neckline? Absolutely not! They sent her a lens, which the Illum have never done. We make her stand out."

Violet gently held a shimmering golden dress in her hands. The fabric was akin to liquid gold. It was magnificent. Rose gave in, and they raised the dress up my legs, leaving goosebumps in its silky wake.

"I hate when you're right, Violet," Rose said, rolling her eyes. She strapped my feet into simple golden heels, leaving me instantly off-balance.

"Last touches," Violet said. Rose painted my lips one last time and sprayed me with a sweet-smelling substance while Violet combed my curls.

"There, that is acceptable," Rose declared, turning me toward a full-length mirror. "Walked in as unremarkable as trash, and now look at you." She grinned like she had just given me the world's finest compliment. "Are you going to look or not?"

The dress was clearly picked to display all of my physical attributes. Two thin straps fell over my shoulders, plunging into identical deep Vs in the front and back. The silk bodice lay flush against my skin, as soft as a lover's caress, and cinched tightly at my waist before sheets of silk cascaded gracefully to the floor. The lush gold color brought out the matching undertones I hadn't noticed in my hair. Beautiful, unbound curls fell around me. My lips were stained pink, and my lids shimmered slightly, light eyeliner lifting my eyes, and my lashes were darker and longer.

Two brown irises. Matching.

I didn't know what would come next in the procreation phase, where I was going, or who my Mate might be. Dread filled me at the task ahead—that I was about to be deemed worthy or unworthy. But tears gathered in my identical eyes. I would be able to meet the gazes of the Elite. To look up, not down.

"Beautiful, right?" Violet stood with her arms crossed, smirking proudly.

"Here, take this. It has your Comm Device in it. Your bag will be sent back to your living quarters," Rose instructed, shoving a golden oval purse into my hand. I took it from her, glancing back at the woman in the mirror one last time, my throat tight at what I saw.

Elite. I saw a girl who knew nothing of the surface and the Archives. A girl who had done this countless times. A girl her birth family would be proud of. A girl her birth father accepted.

A hard swat to my shoulder startled me.

"Quit slouching, women of polite society never slouch," Rose scolded. "Shoulders back, head up, chest out. Poise. You're dining with the Elite. Act like it."

"I remember their lessons," I snapped. Anger and nerves twisted in my chest.

Violet's eyes went wide as a grin graced her features. "I'd watch who you speak to like that. Two phased-out Defects is one thing, Fledgling. Speak like that among the Elite, before your Mate"—Violet stepped closer, her voice dropping—"you'll be eliminated before you even begin the game. Head up." She lifted my chin.

"Come now, let's see if you can fly." Rose cackled wickedly.

The lecture from the Academy slithered in.

Welcome to the Grooming, your final year at the Academy. After this year, you might find yourself Approved to be among the Elite in the clouds to attempt to produce an Elite offspring. If chosen and the Elite male accepts this proposed mating, your status will remain the same. You rise merely due to the compatibility of your genes with that of a male Elite. The Illum uses these matches to eradicate the progression of your defects with the help of Elite genes. Fail to follow these rules and you shall be in blue. You will fall from Minor to Major, cast aside away from the Illum's blessed light, or, depending on the severity of your misdeed, eliminated.

Would I fulfill my use? Even if I did, would I not fall right back to the ground, into the Sanctuary or even Low Town across the river? The only real certainty was that my time in the Wastelands was numbered. There was no real winning for me, only different levels of survival. My insides trembled as I ran my nervous hands down the soft glimmering fabric.

I had only one choice before me: to fly or die trying.

CHAPTER THREE

The pod zoomed through the Elite City. The stars twinkled brightly just beyond the glass ceiling in a glittering array. From the ground, the clouds and lights from the tall buildings hid the stars. I gazed at their celestial dance, letting myself be captivated. For the first time, I understood why those ancient humans needed to create art. If I could, I'd capture the stars' unwillingness to dim their brilliance in the face of unending darkness.

I leaned closer to the glass, my brown irises glinting back at me. Two of them. My gift from the Illum. I didn't understand why I would be given something from them; my status hadn't changed. I didn't expect a miracle. Alone, I felt, for the first time, as if I stood a chance. A star directly above me winked. Was it to encourage or taunt me?

The Pod stopped and the doors opened. I was lightheaded from the bubble of hope intertwining with my fear for what awaited. I sucked in a shaky breath. The Elite would notice. They would know what I hid—that I didn't belong. I glanced at the stars one last time, and one of my earliest memories swarmed me, unlocking a door I never visited. My birth father's voice filled my head.

"Send her away already. She is not welcome in our house. The fact that you see her at all is a disgrace."

"What would you have me do with her?" my birth mother asked

delicately. She was always delicate. "She will be taken away in two moons."

"It is not soon enough," my birth father spat viciously from outside my small room. "I told you to dispose of her when she was deemed defective. Our good standing could falter even more from the ignominy of her very existence. I have dedicated my life to the Illum. She will not take that from me."

"I have kept her hidden," my birth mother said tightly.

"It is not enough. You taint yourself by seeing her. Stop your pitying, or you will leave me no choice but to handle this the way it should have been moons ago."

"She is—"

"She is of no value. She is the system's problem. She is to go to the Academy and rot on the surface with her kind," he declared cruelly, a loud thud reverberating through the hall. "I forbid you from seeing that—*thing* again. Do I make myself clear?"

"As you wish," she said shakily, and the door to my room snapped closed. I hadn't seen either of them again until my birth mother accompanied me to a Pod to be taken away.

Would I see my mother tonight among her kind? Would I recognize the fragile woman who had stood outside my door, intercepting furious footsteps? I had been too young when I went to the Academy, and my memories of her were murky at best.

As I stepped into the atrium, I understood Rose's push for a pink gown. I would have blended in perfectly. Hanging over the entrance were thousands of fluffy pale pink roses that trailed to the polished deep green tile floor. The central lighting fixture, resembling a gilded branch, dappled the space in soft light. Lush lavender curtains blocked the view of the room beyond, muffling the noise. The blooms perfumed the air.

"Good evening, ma'am," an attendant in dark gray said, stepping out from behind an oak stand. He looked around my age. Had we been in the same classes before all the males were taken away for service training? How did they decide which males were fit for the sky and which remained on the ground? Was it his aptitude for their training or his genes that granted him a position in the clouds?

"May I?"

I extended my wrist, fighting the shake, and the scanner beeped, no report given. "This way, Ms. Emeline. He is waiting."

My heart began an erratic dance. Not trusting myself to speak, I nodded. As we approached the curtains, they pulled back automatically.

A magnificent secret garden unlike anything I had ever seen sprawled before me, stealing my breath. Flowers of all kinds exploded everywhere—large white hydrangeas, amethyst wisteria, honeysuckle, buttercups, and orange lilies—spilling onto the tile, climbing the walls, and hanging from the ceiling. Small glowing orbs swayed from the ceiling among the wisteria, almost like stars. In the very center of the room stood a beautiful willow. A tree in the sky. It was art. Did the Elite see it? They destroyed ancient art, yet created their own. Why?

Hesitantly, I followed the attendant into the hidden paradise. I didn't know where to look first, every step revealing more beauty. Alone, I might have run my hands along the flowers and stopped to smell each one.

Life below, my life, was primitive and barren in comparison. I had been living a bleak existence, waiting in perpetual solitude. We all just accepted it.

Lo didn't. I understood her constant nagging and dedication to improving her social standing. But the sweet perfume of the flowers turned sour at the truth that Minors were given the bare minimum while the Elite surrounded themselves with luxuries. Maybe a part of me wanted to be beguiled by the beauty surrounding me. Another part—the part that didn't fit—couldn't stand the divide.

Bright colors and sparkling jewels adorned the Elites sitting at every table we passed. The glittering observers whispered behind heavily ringed hands or elaborate embroidered fans. My breath became too quick as more leaned in like a swarm of bees, lined eyes watching my every step.

The rules from the Grooming slithered into my mind.

Rule One: Remember your place. Although you are in the clouds, your MIND has deemed you defective. You are until your last breath a Minor Defect.

I looked straight ahead, unable to meet anyone's eyes, even with the lens. My golden dress was a stark, unsettling difference in a rainbow sea of colorful flowers and gowns. I was the antithesis of the delicate blooms. It was as if I were the sun shining brightly, and all the flowers and people revolved around my presence. Never had I felt so seen. I wasn't entirely sure it was a good thing.

The attendant finally stopped at a small table below the willow, its branches swaying gently. The man blocked the person waiting for me at the table. A chair scraped against the ground, and my stomach twisted viciously, heartbeats turned violent, slamming into my chest like it might bolt, and I fought the urge to follow it all the way back to the surface forever below.

"Your guest, sir." The man in gray stepped to the side, gesturing to me before disappearing in the throng of flowers and people.

My heart stopped. The buzzing of conversation, the blooms, and even the tree fell away. Silence found me as the most beautiful man I had ever seen waited—for me.

"Hello, Emeline." His voice was deep, powerful.

My breath caught. There had been a mistake. A catastrophic error in the system. I had always focused on the Procreation Agreement and its implications. A scary, unpleasant thing. The man standing in front of me wasn't unpleasant at all. I hadn't considered what my Mate might look like. He would be Elite; I knew that. He would be attractive; it was what they valued. Seeing it in person, though . . . I hadn't considered this. Him.

The Elite, my proposed Mate, watched me. Did he see my weakness? Could he see past the captivating façade the Starlings had created? Did he know the Defect that was hidden? The stunning man extended his hand toward me. "I'm Collin. It's an honor to finally meet you."

Honor? The word clanged through me.

He stood patiently, waiting. The first example of my wrongness. I hastily attempted a curtsy, placing my hand in his. It was clumsy, missing his confident elegance. His large hand flipped mine before raising it to his mouth. His lips, warm and soft, brushed the back of my hand. An involuntary shudder engulfed me. "Please, sit."

Rule Two: The mark of a suitable Minor Mate is obedience, above all else. Always remember it is an honor for you to be among the Elite.

Collin walked to my chair, pulling it out for me. His black suit was immaculately tailored, displaying his muscular frame. I took a step, realizing I still hadn't uttered a word.

"Thank you," I muttered hastily before taking a seat, my back to the room. Collin pushed my chair in before returning to his, unbuttoning his jacket as he looked at me with calculating eyes. *Polished* was the first word that came to mind. An elegant, meticulous beauty like the ancient marble statues I had seen in the Archives. Nothing out of place, his midnight black hair perfectly styled.

"I hope I am not a disappointment," Collin said in my silence. All rational thoughts scattered about the room to play with the flowers.

My mouth hung open, and his keen sapphire gaze traced the outlines of my lips before finding my eyes once more. I fought the urge to look away, to hide. I expected to be treated like a vessel, a means to further humanity. Yet I was asked if he, an Elite, was a disappointment to me, a Minor. As if my interest in this agreement mattered, as if *I* mattered. Shaking my head, I snapped my mouth closed.

Rule Three: The most desirable trait will be your ability to be seen and not heard among proper society. You are to be but a decorative piece, a silent accessory to your Mate. Your ability to be trained and tamed is vital to your success.

"No, not at all. You aren't a disappointment"—I fumbled—"sir." I looked down miserably at my hands twisting in my lap.

"Sir?" he inquired, amused. "You can call me Collin. I have no desire for titles."

I glanced up, his eyes still on me like the room behind me held no interest. "Is something wrong?" he asked.

Rule Four: Respect is demanded at all times. Failure to show respect will risk your usefulness to the Greater Good. Without use there is no purpose for you. Without a purpose there is no place for you.

"I'm confused," I admitted, my voice small. Those lecture hall rules conflicted with the man before me.

He leaned toward me, concern mixing with his assessment. "Why is that?"

"Your kindness," I said before I could stop myself. "I didn't expect it." His impressive jaw bulged as a man in dark gray approached us.

"Good evening," the man interrupted, holding a silver portable scanner. "May I have your arm, please, for our nutrient system?" he inquired, his device directed at me. I raised my left arm across the table, balling my fist to ease the trembling. The man scanned me before leaving us alone with my confession between us.

"Was your birth family unkind to you?" Collin asked. "You were born to Elites."

Rule Five: You are obligated to answer any questions your Elite Mate may have. The truth is expected at all times. Lying is not permitted.

"They were unsatisfied with my status," I told him quietly, "which is to be expected."

"All of them?" Collin inquired, his eyes snagging on my curly hair.

I knew I had Elite brothers based on my birth father's need to compare me to them. I had never met them. I was confined to a small room cared for by those in gray who served my family. But more than once, growing up, I swore I had seen hair like mine upon the lawn at the Academy. "I've never met any of them. Only my birth parents."

Collin nodded, then cleared his throat. "On their behalf, I am sorry for their unkindness. It was unwarranted."

"Why?" slipped from my mouth before I could stop myself. My cheeks grew warm at my daring. "I'm sorry," I muttered quickly. "I just meant you do not owe me an apology, nor do they."

His jaw sat tight, and his fingers drummed along the edge of his glass. "I disagree," he said, and disbelief left me off-balance. His eyes found mine. "They had no right to be unkind for something you did not ask for."

I stared, unnerved, at the man before me. His kindness felt like daggers destroying my own façade. I should not speak—should not think. Perhaps my defect ran deeper than heterochromia because I couldn't follow the rules. I never had.

"Why bother with the pretenses?" I whispered, carefully controlling my expression to avoid attracting the attention of nearby Elites, whose eyes I felt burning holes into my back. "I am a Defect, a vessel."

He leaned forward, his eyes becoming twin crystal beams, piercing straight through me. Danger and awareness prickled along my skin.

"Don't believe everything you see up here, Emeline," he said, his voice dangerously soft. "You aren't what I expected either."

There it was. The first thing that made sense. I looked down at my hands folded in my lap, clenching the fine silk between my fingers. "I am a disappointment."

I knew what would come. Next, he would tell me there would be no need for a Cohabitation Agreement. Maybe he would reject the entire match. They had that power. To deny a proposed Mate. I had no such thing. I was made to wait for his judgment.

It was easy to say I didn't care. All of it was easy to say with my feet on the ground. From there, it felt safe. Yet, from up here, the fall would be lethal.

"You misunderstand me." He raked his eyes over me, lifting his glass to his lips. His gaze never left mine, calculating. "You seem to think so poorly of the Elite that you would assume I'd pass judgment so nonchalantly."

"None of you have ever given me a reason to think otherwise." The words left me before I could think better. I swallowed a groan.

His brows threatened to disappear, a glint in his sapphire eyes. "So it seems. Maybe it is time someone remedies that. And I am not disappointed, Emeline. You are simply different from the Minors I have encountered."

Encountered? "Have you Mated with a Minor before?"

"I have not. This is my first mating," Collin told me as the man in gray returned with plates of food. He placed Collin's dish, a bowl of red liquid, before placing a plate before me. I stared at it, confused, the conversation falling away.

Every meal I had ever had was the same, never varying in texture, taste, or appearance. It was nutritional mush and a shake, dictated by MIND nutrient measurements. Before me was a colorful array of different foods and textures and strange, beckoning aromas. My mouth watered.

"Is something wrong with your dish?" Collin asked.

"Does food always look like this?"

"No, our nutrient system provides us with a varied offering that is best for each individual based on the information collected from the MIND."

I grabbed the fork next to the plate and took a small bite. Freshness burst across my tongue, and my eyes slid closed. I wasted no time taking another and another.

"Your salad and beets are satisfactory, I take it?" Collin asked, jarring me. Embarrassment flushed up my neck. It was like I was trying to sabotage myself into losing this agreement.

"I'm sorry, I didn't realize how hungry I was." I put my fork down, attempting to act civilized. He took another small bite, and his mouth pulled tight. "Do you not like your food?"

"I don't particularly enjoy tomatoes. The dish becomes quite irksome when made to eat them every day."

"Are those important for you?"

"Yes, they contain lycopene, a nutrient that boosts my"—he quirked a brow—"quality."

"Quality of what?" I asked.

"I don't believe it is an appropriate dinner conversation, Emeline."

My brows pulled in. Oh—oh.

My face flushed even hotter, matching his soup. The lessons from the Academy hit me. Diagrams and the science behind mating. My fork hit the table, leaving a ruby stain on the white tablecloth.

Rule Six: If your Mate wishes to practice prior to the three-moon courtship, you are to indulge your Mate's wants.

The attendant returned, as if knowing exactly when I needed him to save me from my constant embarrassment. If that were the case, he would have a long night ahead. My stomach protested longingly as I watched my half-eaten dish disappear. The price of being saved.

"There will be more courses," Collin assured me. I nodded, feeling too exposed. I looked around the Garden and caught the eye of several women and men, their noses turned up in disgust. I cast my attention back to Collin. "Do you like the Garden?" he asked, his eyes sweeping the room coldly.

"It is beautiful. It reminds me of paintings I've cataloged at my job."

He watched me, something in those depths. "I'd like to talk plainly before you have more food to eat so enthusiastically." His lips tugged up slightly. I nodded, nervous.

"About our Procreation Agreement, I had a contract drawn up. I will have a copy sent to you tomorrow morning. You may, of course, look it over," Collin said. We both knew I didn't have a say in this. "If everything is in order, we shall sign, commencing our official Courting Phase. When we reach the three-moon minimum, we can commence cohabitation. When our efforts are successful"—Collin cleared his throat before continuing—"I feel it is in the best interest to have a four-year Cohabitation Agreement in place to be present for our offspring. You will remain with me until the offspring goes to the Academy," Collin finished, grabbing his drink.

I did as well, just to do something with my shaking hands. Most women in my position would say yes to this instantly. It was the ideal outcome, a proper public Courting and cohabitation. There wasn't a single mention of the Sanctuary or Low Town. There was no talk of the steps and rules required to impress your Mate. The man before me had yet to act or say anything I had been made to believe. I didn't understand.

"Am I not to be judged throughout our Courting Phase?" I asked him.

"Would you prefer to, what is it, anticipate my needs and successfully fulfill them?" Collin retorted, reciting Rule Seven as his eyes bored into mine. "Would you *like* to be judged?"

"I was unaware I had a say," I challenged, feeling that familiar fire rise in my chest.

Collin leaned back in his chair. "Are you unsatisfied with my offer?"

"What would you do if I said I was?"

I knew, *I knew* I was being too bold. But it was like I couldn't control myself in the face of his consideration.

Collin shook his head slightly. "I would tell you, *Our next three moons will be eventful, Emeline.*"

"Forgive me; I'm trying to understand. You seem rather okay with this pairing. Collin, I . . ." I took a steadying breath. "I am a Defect."

"I'm aware of your status," he assured me, his eyes on mine. "I knew your status when I chose you."

"Chose me?"

"I prolonged my bachelorhood as long as I could. I was told to take a Mate. I was not given an option, at least not one I was willing to take. The system paired us as an excellent match. I accepted."

"Did you not wish for a Mate of your status?" I asked, again too boldly.

Collin's eyes slid over my shoulder before returning to me. "If the

Illum's procreation matching system declared us a worthy match, should that not be enough?"

"Won't they—" I stopped, working to swallow. "Won't the Elite have something to say about this?"

Collin's eyes locked on mine. He seemed to exude power into the room. "I stopped caring about the Elite's opinions long ago."

"I—" I began, but the attendant returned, placing another beautiful plate in front of me. This new revelation that food could be art thrilled me.

"Your main courses," he informed us.

"Thank you," I said as the server made to leave the table. Shock flashed in his eyes before he hurried away.

"I would be careful who hears you speak to them like that," Collin said. "The Elite will take offense."

"The Elite take offense to everything."

I swore I saw a smirk flash across his face. My stomach fluttered despite myself, and I quickly looked at my plate, perplexed again at another different-looking food.

"It's salmon," Collin told me.

Digging my fork into the salmon, I placed a small piece in my mouth. A sound escaped me. I snapped up at Collin's deep chuckle, his sapphire eyes sparkling.

"So we have moved on from scarfing down the food without breathing to—" He paused. "What would you call that indecent sound?"

I caught my lip between my teeth. He tracked the movement. I opened my mouth to reply, only to be interrupted once more.

"Why, Collin, how nice it is to see you this evening. Not locked away at work for once," boomed a lean man with bright blond hair, pulling Collin's searing gaze from my mouth, the glint in his eyes disappearing.

"Edward," Collin said and nodded politely. "I took an evening off to attend to an important matter."

"Forgive me. I do not know your friend," Edward remarked. His eyes slid over me, marking my deep neckline and ample cleavage on display. My body recoiled.

"You wouldn't." Collin's mouth was a tight line. "Emeline is my intended Mate and is not a member of high society."

I whipped my head toward Collin. At the information he gave up unabashedly.

"A Defect," Edward blurted, shocked, looking me over again. His gaze made me long for the showerheads from earlier. The so-called grime from life below was nothing compared to the filth I felt coating everywhere his eyes roamed.

"My intended Mate," Collin corrected, his voice a lethal calm. I sat up straighter at the sound.

"Yes, of course, of course. I'm shocked that even you are made to stoop so low. To take a pet, forced to socialize with their kind. Barbaric, but it is for the Greater Good. And if they look like this, why not bring them out in public for some entertainment. A beauty, regardless of status." My body locked up at his comment, as greasy as his gaze.

"I believe your Mate is waiting for you," Collin said coldly. "Good evening, Edward."

Edward bowed his head. "Of course, of course. Good evening, Collin. Sweet Emeline." Edward slunk away to a gaggle of Elite standing by the lavender curtain. Gasps abounded and they glanced my way, and it was clear what news Edward had shared with them. Collin watched them with unnatural stillness.

"I apologize for his rudeness. The Elite are nosy and insufferable," Collin said and began on his meal.

"You say that like you aren't one of them," I commented, following his lead, taking small bites and keeping my indecent noises to myself.

Collin glanced away from me. Confused, I placed my fork back on the table. He had referred to the Elite as an entity all night; he hadn't once said *we*. "You are Elite, right?" I asked, my pulse quickening.

"No, I am not." His handsome face yielded nothing.

You can't be a—" I paused, not wanting to offend him. "You can't be like me," I finished lamely.

"No, I am not that either." He took several more bites of his food. I just stared. Who was I to be Mated to? Glancing up, he noticed my hesitation. "After the Academy, I showed great promise for our cause." He laid his fork on his plate, clasping his hands over his meal. "I am the youngest member of the Illum."

The few bites I had eaten flopped in my stomach as my insides free-fell back to the ground. I had never heard of a Defect mating with an Illum. Come to think of it, I had never heard of an Illum mating at all, but then again I lived beneath this. I had spoken against everything the Illum taught us at the Academy—to one of them. Why hadn't I already been eliminated? I should stay quiet and count my blessings. But I had never been good at acting appropriately.

"Surely—surely, you could have had your pick of the Elite. Of anyone. Why did you choose me?"

"The list of possible Mates was extensive."

I should be thankful and say nothing, and yet . . . "So why me?"

"I have my reasons," Collin said, his sapphire eyes on mine. "I had no intentions of taking a Mate at all. Tabitha advised I take one. There is hierarchy even among the Illum, and she is our leader. I have taken you. Therefore, I do not intend to reject you. My work is demanding. The Press is forever interested in my life. They will be watching us. Edward will have told the entire Elite community come sunrise. I do not have the time or patience to construct a trial for you. If that is what you desire, you will find yourself disappointed." Collin straightened the front of his jacket as he leaned toward me. "We are tied together for the foreseeable future." His eyes flickered over my shoulder for the space of a breath before finding mine once more. "For the Greater Good."

"And my defect?" I asked, barely audible.

His piercing gaze left me as bare as I had been with the Starlings.

He smiled tightly once more, like he knew precisely what lay hidden.

"Let me worry about that, Emeline," Collin said. "We have many moons ahead of us."

"And the Press and the Elite?" I whispered, leaning toward the youngest member of the Illum, my soon-to-be Mate. "Should I be worried about them?"

"Yes." Collin stared behind me, watching the Elite. "You should be."

CHAPTER FOUR

Loud knocking jolted me awake. Drool covered my pillow, sticking my nest of tangled curls to my face. I had never been late for my shift. One night in the clouds, and I had overslept, fully dressed in my gown. There had been none of my usual dreams or restlessness—despite everything I had learned and experienced.

"Emeline," Lo called.

"Coming." I shot up only to trip on the golden fabric. Cursing the gown, I ripped it off, tossing it unceremoniously onto my bed before pulling on my usual gray attire, mundane in comparison. I scanned my wrist quickly and opened the door. Lo pushed her way in as the automated voice we were all forced to listen to every day began its usual report about the information the Illum's system had gleaned from my MIND scans.

"What happened?" Lo greeted me, holding two steaming cups. She stared at the discarded gown before glancing back at me, her fear obvious. "You weren't down there with everyone for the Pod. I got worried. I thought something had gone wrong."

"I just overslept." The rising sun painted my white walls in my solitary living quarters with soft pinks and yellows. I made my way to the bathroom mirror, revealing smeared makeup and a knotted mess of hair. Somehow, I had dined with an Illum last night. I turned on the water and began washing my face.

The rest of dinner had proceeded with minimal embarrassing moments. We sat in poignant silence after Collin's warning. I ate every bite of my dinner, practicing restraint in not licking the leftover sauce off the plate. Collin's eyes flickered between my plate and mouth like he half expected me to. The server had swept in once again, saving me. He brought us tea, a bitter concoction, and a small piece of something Collin informed me was chocolate cake.

"Before you take a bite, I am going to warn you," Collin had advised. "This is going to make everything else you've eaten tonight obsolete."

"You didn't have what I had," I claimed before taking a small bite. He had been right, so very right. After I devoured the cake, Collin led me back to the entrance and summoned a Pod. Promising to be in touch soon and thanking me for a memorable evening, he kissed my hand again. I had almost been able to block out the Elite necks craned in our direction.

Only when the Pod doors shut had I breathed out my relief. I had survived. Now I had to wait to see whether the contract would come through.

I toweled off my face. My matching brown eyes captured my attention. I didn't know how long the lens would stay, but I had no intention of removing it. I attempted to tame my hair just as the automated voice finished her report.

Procreation Contract pending.

Even with Collin's assurance he would reach out, I half expected to be informed I had been rejected. I had been brash last night, spoken out against the Illum to one of its members.

"Come here," Lo said, taking the brush from me and gently working through my curls.

"What are you doing here? You'll get in trouble for being late," I said.

"Doubtful. I don't have a Mate. They don't watch the Mateless like they now watch you. There are too many of us to monitor all the time." She began braiding my hair. I didn't know if I bought her theory, but she might have a point. We didn't know the extent of the Illum's technology, but to track everyone all the time would be difficult. However, I knew from experience what happened to those who stepped out of line.

"Still, you have your yearly soon," I reminded her.

She tied the ends of my hair. "I'm aware. If we grab your stuff and run, we can catch the last Pod. We'll barely be late." She spun me. "Let's—" She stopped, her blue eyes wide. "Your eyes! What did they do? Is it permanent?"

"They put a lens device to cover it." The lens itched as I said it.

"I have so many questions," she said as the black box that delivered my nutrients dinged. I had no appetite for the mush after last night. She peered out the window. "Pod's here. Grab your stuff."

I grabbed my bag and followed Lo. My eyes snagged on the golden heap on my bed and the wrongness of it in the sterile white room—as out of place as I felt last night seated before Collin. I shook off my insecurities and chased after her.

Minutes later, we zipped through the city alone in our Pod. The buildings shifted from squat rudimentary brick complexes to soaring glass skyscrapers as we entered High Town. The Archives were housed beneath the tallest one.

The megastructure had columns of shiny metal and glass weaving together in a dance that threatened to touch the sun at its tip. The base, where we entered, was impossibly wide, metal pillars piercing the ground connected by sweeping arches with towering doors. I always felt they resembled the trees in old art pieces I had cataloged. There was an unyielding beauty to them. There were six others, slightly smaller yet otherwise identical to our building.

"Here," Lo said, handing me a cup. "It's a stimulant drink—the Majors drink it for energy."

The aroma was a heady mix. "How do you have a drink that's for Majors?"

"You remember Becca? The Minor with dark hair who was rejected four moons ago and cast down to blue?"

I nodded; I didn't know her really, but I had heard the story from Lo. I took a small sip and shuddered against the bitterness.

"I saw her near the river last moon. I had hoped she could tell me what she did wrong. So I could, we could, you know—not end up like her."

"Why was she out in public?"

Majors weren't supposed to be seen. Their work was completed during curfew for the rest of us.

"She said she missed fresh air. Please don't lecture me; I know I could get in trouble." Lo sighed as my brows shot up. We weren't permitted to talk to anyone outside the Minor population, but I was in no position to remind Lo of that after meeting Hal. "I just don't want to end up like her," she continued. "I don't want *us* to end up in blue. Anyway, she was drinking one of these. She gave me the rest of it. It gives you so much energy. Now I've been sort of seeking her out for them. She's there every morning following her shift. I went looking for her when you didn't show up. Thought she might know if you ended up there."

"You thought I'd mess up?"

Lo threw me a reproachful look. "I didn't think you'd mess up. I know you, though. You don't like the way things are. You get upset easily."

She was right. I had done exactly that—not only with the Starlings but with the youngest member of the Illum.

"Did Becca give you any information?" I asked, shying away from the accuracy.

"Oh, no." Lo downed the rest of her drink. "She told me they aren't permitted to talk about it or Low Town or they're eliminated. Enough about that. Tell me about last night. What happened? How did you do?"

Sapphire eyes flashed before me. I bit my lip, thinking of how Collin had watched me all night. He had been so accepting. Taking a deep breath, I told Lo everything: about the Starlings—"They sound creepy"—to the dress I wore—"Was that what was on your bed?"—and finally, the dinner. I explained the Garden, the food, and the décor.

"*And?*" Lo probed as the Pod came to a stop. Lo grabbed my cup, downing the rest without a word before shoving my cup and hers into her bag.

"And what?" I asked, following her off the Pod.

"Your proposed Mate," Lo exclaimed. "You haven't mentioned him once!"

My cheeks flushed. "He was . . . very nice." I tilted my head toward the sun's warmth.

"Very nice! Oh, come on, Emeline! Tell me more than that," Lo demanded, pulling me toward the building.

We entered the large glass doors, and the chandeliers and their beauty normally dazzled me. But now they were lackluster compared to Collin.

We scanned into the elevator, and as it descended, I admitted, "He didn't treat me like I was below him."

"Did he say anything about your defect? Was he pleased with your behavior? Did he say anything about the way you looked?"

"He didn't say anything about my defect, but it was covered," I said as the door opened to her floor. "He seemed fine with my behavior, I think."

Lo stepped into the hall, identical to mine. "I'm happy for you, Emeline," she said with a smile.

"Thanks. He's not an Elite." My heart pounded. The one thing I was afraid to say out loud. The door began to close. "He's a member of the Illum," I spat out.

Lo's jaw dropped, her utter shock following me down.

Yesterday morning, my life had been consistent, predictable. Now I had a proposed Mate who accepted my status. Who had already offered me a contract. Lo was talking to a Major Defect in her attempt to be approved. A different Major Defect drifted back to me. The moment the Pod sent me to the clouds I had pushed away the encounter with Hal completely. In the dark, beneath the surface, the mysterious man in blue returned to my mind.

I opened the door to my office, ignoring the dings from my Comm Device as Lo bombarded me with questions. An ostentatious display of flowers ate up half of my desk, the delicate perfumes engulfing me. As if Collin had gathered the very essence of the Garden and deposited it here just like I had imagined doing last night. My desk had been moved, now centered in the room, facing the wall to the left of the door directly below the hanging light.

"Ah, there you are."

Sitting in my chair, his feet crossed on my desk, looking entirely at home, was Hal.

He lazily flipped a small notecard between his fingers. "Good morning, or should I say afternoon? For me, it's almost the middle of the night. Nocturnal life."

"Can I help you?" I asked, feeling jittery all over. Was it because he was in the room or was it the stimulant drink?

"No," he said simply, remaining in my chair. "I don't need any help."

"Then, what are you doing here?" I asked. "Why move my desk?"

"I moved the desk so you weren't caged in the corner. You're welcome. As to why I'm here—you offered." His gaze shifted to the flowers before landing on the card in his hand. "Unless the offer has changed now that you're in a Procreation Contract?"

I glanced at the clock. "How long have you been here?"

"About an hour," he told me, glancing at the card once more. "But who's counting. Not me. The Illum probably is. They do love numbers and monitoring everything."

I cursed, bringing my wrist up to the wall to scan in. I was late. The ding clanged through me.

"I assume that card came with the flowers," I said, tossing my bag loudly on my desk, "and that you read it."

"I did. It's the most exciting thing to happen to a guy like me.

Care to hear it?" he asked, standing, his impressive frame eating up all the space in the room.

"I can read it myself," I gritted out, attempting to grab it from him. He was too quick, lifting the card high in the air, out of my reach. "Are you fucking kidding me!"

Hal chuckled. "Swears and late to work. I am shocked." I made a futile swipe at the card, my chest brushing against his. He stood casually, his arm still over his head, looking down at me, those starburst eyes staring at my matching ones.

"Emeline, these flowers pale in comparison to your beauty."

I stared up at him, blinking rapidly. Heat blossomed deep in my core.

"Something befitting the most beautiful thing in the room. To more indecent sounds." I recoiled, realizing my mistake. He was reciting the card. They were Collin's words. "'Indecent sounds'?" Hal asked, handing me the card as he stepped away.

"The food was really good," I blurted out.

Footsteps scuffed across the floor outside my room. One moment, Hal stood before me. The next, I turned to find him crammed between the open door and the wall. I hadn't even heard him move.

A man in dark gray came to my open door, holding a stack of papers. "I have an urgent delivery for Ms. Emeline."

"Yes, that's me." I took the papers from him. The man's eyes flickered around the room.

"I shall return in an hour to collect the signed documents," he stated, then left.

I glanced at the first paper, the Illum's golden insignia at the top. *Procreation Agreement between M17292834 and F13463233.*

"Is that your Procreation Contract?" Hal asked a moment later, leaning against the empty doorway. I nodded, fishing around in my bag for a pen. "Are you going to sign it without reading through it?" he asked incredulously.

"We discussed it last night," I answered, flipping through the pages, looking for the signature line.

"So you don't care to read the steps you agree to take if you are unsuccessful in three moons? You don't care to know what happens after six moons of being barren or if a pregnancy doesn't extend to ten moons and it results in fetal demise?" Hal asked, his voice dark.

I looked up at him, my pen poised to sign. "Why do you know any of that?"

"The Elite's horror stories filter their way down, even to us."

I glanced between him and the contract. "Then you know that it doesn't matter what this says. I have no say," I told him, signing it.

Hal just looked at me as if he were seeing me plainly. "I see the Academy did its job on you."

"You don't even know me," I fired back, fuming.

"Yes, I do," Hal stated. "They have made thousands of women just like you. Brainwashed and compliant to a cause you know nothing about. You're a plaything."

His words landed squarely in my chest, knocking the air from me. "I am a Minor Defect," I bit out. "You act like I have a choice in any of this. It doesn't matter what this says. I have to sign. If I don't sign this, if I am unsuccessful in any way, I'll be in blue—"

"And that's the worst thing that could happen, right?" Hal interjected, crossing his arms.

Was it the worst? They made it out to be. "I didn't say that."

"You didn't have to; it's written all over your desperate face." A humorless chuckle escaped him.

I lost my hold on my anger. "Maybe I am desperate. I could be eliminated if I mess this up. I have no purpose if I cannot fulfill my use to the Greater Good. Without a purpose there is no place for women like me. I don't expect you to understand, nor am I interested in your approval."

"Only the Illum's approval," Hal declared.

"Why are you here?" I demanded. He didn't know me. He didn't understand. He was a man. He wore blue. He had not been conditioned as I had been. He had no right to judge me. I signed the contract willingly. Collin had been kind. It was more than most received.

"Beats me," Hal said, reaching the door. He gripped the doorway tightly. "He's wrong."

"Excuse me?"

"I said he's wrong. Your proposed *Mate*." Hal spat the word like it tasted bad. "You weren't the most beautiful thing in the room."

"You didn't see me last night," I interjected, thinking of the woman I had beheld in the mirror. Being the most beautiful might have been a stretch, but with my defect covered, I had felt beautiful.

"Were you wearing that thing?" He gestured to my matching gaze.

"Of course."

"Then he was wrong. You were covering what makes you beautiful."

My eyes collided with his. Shock hollowed me out. No one had ever called my defect beautiful. People couldn't even look at it.

Hal shook his head as he walked out, leaving me more confused than ever.

I hurled the pen at the empty doorway.

CHAPTER FIVE

Ninety-six hours had passed. Four full days. Had it not been for the flowers that had slowly begun to wilt on my desk and Lo's constant badgering for updates, I might have believed I had made it all up. There had been nothing from Collin, no message, no other gifts. At this point, I would have welcomed a visit from Hal. Our parting words had been unkind, but fighting with him would at least provide a distraction. Nothing. I did find the pen I had chucked after him on my desk the following morning. It could have been anyone from the janitorial staff that put it back.

Maybe Collin *had* been judging me. Maybe it had all been a test and I had failed spectacularly. Maybe my defect that knew no bounds had won yet again. Perhaps the Starlings' efforts and the lens hadn't been adequate.

Four days in, the lens felt like sandpaper in my eye. A part of me was desperate to take it out. Call it stubbornness, perhaps just stupidity, but I couldn't. Even as my eye burned incessantly, I wouldn't remove it. I had taken to squinting or keeping my left eye fully closed. If I took it out, then this silence might actually mean I had failed. For some reason the idea of being rejected by Collin bothered me.

I racked my brain again for the proper procedures for the Procreation Agreement I learned at the Academy. There was the initial meeting, which could be conducted in private or public. Collin had opted for a public initial meeting with a Defect.

Then there was the contract. Several different contracts were well used. We all feared the Procreation Contract with no public Courting Phase, no cohabitation, and no support. Just breeding. It was a ticket straight to the Sanctuary. Then there was the contract with public Courting and cohabitation for the procreation phase. Once you were pregnant, you moved to the Sanctuary. Then there was the one everyone hoped for, but only a few got. The one Collin had proposed to me freely—public Courting, cohabitation for procreation, and the postpartum period when the offspring dwelled in the living quarters before going to the Academy. Those contracts usually led to a continuation for a second offspring if you produced an Elite offspring. If approved by the Illum.

By him, I reminded myself. Collin was an Illum.

A chill crept down my spine at the thought. Was this different because Collin was an Illum? Was that why he didn't see the point in the normal trials? Did he think being an Illum would easily eradicate my defect in our offspring? Questions and thoughts swirled in my head at a dizzying rate.

I laid my head against the cool surface of my desk. I couldn't stand the game of it. But I hated myself for caring about something I had so fervently detested just days ago.

Here I was at the whim of the Illum and the Elite. Was this what they wanted?

"Do you ever work normally?" a smooth voice asked. Startled, I turned to find Hal leaning against my doorframe with that damn dimple of his.

"Would it bother you if I said no?" I asked. He had an uncanny knack for finding me in my difficult moments.

He chuckled. "No, I would say I had finally found—" He paused, his brow furrowing. "What's wrong with your eye?"

"Nothing is wrong with my eye."

"Your left eye is closed."

"It's nothing." I turned toward my screen. "My lens is bothering me."

"Take it out then."

"No." I would do no such thing. He didn't understand.

"Adding *stubborn* to your list of personality traits," Hal said, pushing off the doorframe.

"I didn't realize you were taking notes," I retorted snidely.

Hal ran a hand through his hair. "You need to take it out."

"No, I do not."

"You look ridiculous," Hal stated. "Just take it out, Emeline. It's bad for your eye."

"The Illum monitor everything. If something comes up, my MIND will take care of it," I snapped, attempting to open my eye. Every time I tried, it burned viciously and blurred my vision.

"So you're going to act like your eye isn't bright red and clearly irritated, just to keep that thing? To adhere to your dear Mate's demands?"

"He didn't demand it, and he isn't my Mate."

"You signed, though," Hal said quietly.

"I did. I haven't heard from him since. I think . . . I think I messed it up somehow." There it was. In saying it, I felt so small.

Hal sighed. "I doubt you messed it up. The Elite live life by their own rules, on their own time. He'd be stupid to reject a woman like you. I am sure there's a reason."

"What if I'm the reason?" Even as his comment sent my pulse fluttering, the dam broke open, and all the horrible thoughts threatened to spill onto the floor around us until we both drowned in my self-pity. Why was I telling him this? The things we had said to each other four days ago found me. I must seem crazy.

"You don't have to worry," Hal reassured me. "I am a Major Defect, Emeline. Nothing you say is crazy." I whipped my head toward him, unnerved. "You wear all your feelings on your face," he clarified. "Now take the lens out. Please."

It would be nice to be able to see fully again. Still, I didn't move.

"I'll even apologize first for the other day," Hal said. "I am sorry."

I stared at him, huffing a breath, and he crossed his arms expectantly. Finally, I attempted to fish the lens out. It took several tries until I felt it release from my eye. Immediate relief flooded me.

"Better?" Hal asked, walking into the room. "Would it kill you to admit I was right?"

I rolled my eyes, the lens still on my finger. "I'm not willing to find out."

He *was* right, though. My eye was still sore, but I could keep it open again.

"The red will go away soon." He peered into my eyes. I stiffened at his proximity, the fluttering turning savage. "The blue and brown combination is striking," Hal confessed, and he leaned closer, his warm breath caressing my face. "I'm still waiting on your apology." I shot him a glare even as my pulse danced, and he pulled back, smiling widely. "I'm patient. Take your time."

"I will."

His gaze shifted toward the dying flowers. "So you're possibly in a contract."

"I am, or I think I am. He said we were."

"Does that change your offer?" Hal asked, hesitation lacing his words. "You said you're always here if I wanted to come and look at art. If your invitation remains . . ." Hal shifted, tugging at the sleeve of his blue jumpsuit. "I would like to look at art with you."

I stared at the man before me, at his hesitancy and the blue.

"All right," I said, turning toward my work. I sent a landscape to reassignment. A new piece appeared, marked to be destroyed.

A man and a woman embraced fiercely in the art piece. They gazed at each other, her face pleading as she clutched the ends of a white band wrapped around his arm. He cupped her face tenderly with one hand, but the other pulled against the band. The title read *A Huguenot, on St. Bartholomew's Day*. Was the white band an identification of some kind? Did they use colors to declare status before the Last War?

"Do you think they are saying hello or goodbye?" Hal asked, moving beside me, bracing his arms upon my desk for a better look.

"I wouldn't know," I said. "I have never had a hello or a goodbye resemble whatever that is. Have you?"

"I have," he told me, his voice tight. "I think they are saying goodbye."

"Why do you think that?"

"Because there is a desperation in their embrace. See how she clings to him, how he's holding her face? When you embrace hello, there's hope. There's a future. You don't cling because you know there will be more to come. The finality in a goodbye embrace—when you let go, it might never happen again. So you cling to the person, the feeling, the moment. You hold on longer because it's doomed to be nothing but a memory."

I looked up at Hal, but he was lost in the painting or some goodbye. I had been down here for ten years, dissecting works of art by myself. I had always thought my rumination made me an outlier. Finally, I was not alone.

"What are the Illum doing with it?" Hal asked, breaking my thoughts.

"They're destroying it," I told him, hitting the *delete* button. The image disappeared—now just a memory. I clicked for the next one, a landscape. I shook my head.

"What?" Hal asked, but it came out like a hiss. His hand flew to his side as he leaned closer to the screen.

"They'll keep this one," I said. "Are you okay?"

"Yeah. The Elite are running me ragged." Hal grimaced slightly before glancing to my screen, and sure enough, the verdict said *reassigned*. "How did you know that?"

"I have a theory," I said, catching my lip between my teeth. My heart raced at my boldness. It was one thing to have these thoughts.

Telling them to another person terrified me, but Hal had just confided in me. Maybe I could do the same.

He tugged at the collar of his dark blue jumpsuit. "Major Defect, remember. You're safe."

I took a deep breath. "I think they get rid of all the ones with people to erase what life was like before the war. I think anything that makes the viewer feel is—is a threat. Like we might want more, and that would be the end of everything. Or maybe the beginning." I bit my lip harder.

Hal looked at me. He smiled slyly like he saw something more.

"I underestimated you," Hal confided. "Until our next meeting, Emeline."

He made to leave. "Wait." I stood, walking up to him. "Did I say something wrong?"

"No, not at all. It's just late." Some of his smugness seemed to falter. His smile didn't meet his eyes this time. I hadn't noticed the blue smudges under his eyes before. He looked exhausted.

"Okay," I said, turning back to my screen. Hal walked to the door, then stopped.

"Emeline," Hal said over his shoulder. "Can I come back tomorrow? You know, to see the art."

Our eyes met, starburst meeting blue and brown.

"I'd like that," I responded, surprising myself.

Hal smiled at me, a genuine smile. I'd be damned if it wasn't one of the most stunning things I'd ever seen. A work of art in its own way.

"Until tomorrow," he said.

I smiled back, and his eyes roved over every inch of my face. "Okay, until tomorrow."

I watched him go.

I got through several more items, wishing I could talk to Hal about a painting of several warped melting clocks and see if he had any insight into its meaning. *The Persistence of Memory* was reassigned. Maybe it would come back around again, which happened sometimes. We could discuss it then, if we had the time. I was convinced a lot of the items circulated endlessly.

My Comm Device dinged. I grabbed it, assuming it would be Lo. It wasn't. I had two messages, the first from an unknown device.

Communications will reach out shortly. Look forward to seeing you again. —Collin

My stomach swooped. The second was an official message.

F13463233 It has come to our attention that your next meeting with M17292834 has been set for 5:30 this evening following your preparation appointment at 3:00. All travel information has been loaded to your MIND chip. Fertile Blessings.

A million thoughts hit me all at once. The main one: I hadn't messed it up. I checked the time. I needed to go now if I was going to make my three o'clock meeting with the Starlings. I quickly packed my bag, typed some notes into my report, and darted out.

As I ascended, I pulled out my Comm Device and quickly updated Lo. In the atrium, the chandeliers glittered even more splendidly from the afternoon sun's rays. Mesmerized, I took a minute to register the cacophony of voices.

The atrium was full of people dressed in gowns and suits in extraordinary colors—no shades of gray or blue among them. There was only one group that was allowed to wear colors of their choosing.

The Elite.

Panic engulfed me. I couldn't breathe. *Just move,* a voice yelled at me. *Just keep moving.* I ducked my head, beelining for the door, my heart thundering.

I had never seen Elite here, but I had never ventured to the surface other than to move to and from my living quarters during designated transition hours. Were they always here at this time? The glass doors loomed closer. Twenty more feet and I would be free.

I weaved among the Elite, close to running. Ten feet. I lowered my head even more, focusing on my dull gray shoes as sweat coated my body. Why did I remove the lens?

Five feet. *I can make it.*

I collided with someone. Steadying hands grabbed my shoulders.

"I'm sorry," I muttered, dipping my head more as I tried to step away.

"I didn't see you," the man said.

I glanced up at his odd tone to find features that were familiar. I shared some of them, my blue eye the same crystal shade as his, the same straight nose, and he shook brown curls, a shade lighter than mine, out of his face.

I knew, without having to ask, that we shared blood. He was one of my Elite birth brothers. His face went completely blank.

"Is that a Defect?" someone exclaimed.

"Truly disgusting how they think they can be here," a male voice rang out. My cheeks burned fiercely.

"Did you see her eyes?" another whispered. "They aren't the same. A Defect out in the sun."

"I want to see." Several people began to push to the front as if I were an exhibit.

"You may proceed to the Defect-designated Pod pickup area," my birth brother told me, pocketing something before turning away from me. "They're ready for us," he told the others, leading the sea of colors away from me. Whispers filled the air as I fled.

What were the ramifications of this? What would Collin say?

I began to jog. I had a birth brother. He was real.

The jog turned into a run. My lungs burned in a gloriously familiar way. I had loved going for daily runs before my MIND forbade it. Each pounding footstep into the earth cleared my head, washed out the fear.

I arrived at the Pods too quickly, taking deep gulps of air. Perspiration dripped down my neck, chilling me despite the afternoon sun.

I had felt seen in the Garden, or I thought I had. But I had looked like one of them. They had seen a crafted façade. They hadn't truly seen me, until now. The Elite and my birth brother saw me for what I was, a Defect. A disgrace.

An empty Pod stood open, waiting. I scanned in and took a seat, trapped with my thoughts, pushing the walls in, suffocating me.

This time, I didn't even bother to fight the hopelessness that threatened to consume me whole.

CHAPTER SIX

The starlings swarmed me the moment I stepped into the room, squawking about my horrid appearance and my missing lens. They pelted me with their questions while they led me into the bathing chamber.

"Why did you take it out?" Rose demanded. *It hurt,* I stopped myself from saying. "Why is it so red?" she carried on. "And why are you *damp*?"

"It's sweat, Rose," Violet twittered. "Why are you sweaty, Fledgling?"

"I ran."

"Why would you run?"

I hurt. The peering eyes and judgment and indifference from my own birth brother—it hurt and no one cared.

The Elite's constant scrutiny toward anything that could be seen as a flaw had followed me my entire life. Time hadn't dulled the cruelty, sharper than any blade. The moment I had opened my eyes, I was damned.

Don't go there. Do not go there.

The Starlings continued squawking at me. I just let them as I held the vicious thoughts at bay—barricading myself against my earliest memories.

They began their degrading process, tearing me apart to make me acceptable. I let them, tuning them out through the shower, the bath, and the removal of all the hair on my body. It wasn't until Rose began painting my nails that their hushed twittering dragged me from my numbed state.

"Well, I heard from Eve that it was close this time," Rose muttered in a hushed voice. "They made it into the Capitol building again. They might have gotten away with it if it wasn't for the extra measures they put in from their last attempt."

"Was the one they all whisper about there?" Violet asked quietly, her dark eyes sliding to me. My gaze found my lap as her hands weaved my curls into an intricate braid.

I glanced up in time to see Rose nod.

"They are growing more daring," Violet muttered, pulling pieces of hair from the braid to frame my face. "Did they get any of them this time?"

"No," Rose said, her face grave. "But Eve said six Elite were killed. She said the Illum are a mess over it. They blocked all sky travel into the Capitol for now. They're making the Elite enter the building from the surface."

My mind churned. Was that why all those Elite had been in the atrium? I had never seen them there before. Did I work in the Capitol building?

"I'm sure the Elite are thrilled about that," Violet retorted.

"They're all in a tither over the disrespect," Rose said, shaking her head. "There's a big meeting today before the Illum."

"You seem to have a great deal of intel," Violet shot toward Rose. "You and Eve have grown rather close as of late. Is that why she summoned you this morning before dawn?"

Rose dropped my left hand, moving to my right. "It is. I've been dressing Eve since she left the Academy."

"She's an Elite," Violet told her sternly.

"I know that, as much as I know my own status," Rose snapped, her face fierce. "I don't need another lecture, Violet."

"It isn't a lecture," Violet said.

Curiosity got the best of me. "When was the meeting?"

"How long have you been listening, Fledgling? You've been unresponsive for over an hour," Rose cawed, finishing my nails. They were filed into long ovals and painted a pearly white.

"Is the Capitol the tallest building?"

"It is," Violet confirmed, her eyes gleaming. "What time was the meeting today, Rose?"

"Three," Rose told us begrudgingly.

I took a deep breath. That *was* why those Elite had all been there.

"They saw you, didn't they? That's why you were a mess when you arrived," Violet stated, watching me closely.

"I saw my Elite birth brother and he didn't care." Surely my birth brother had seen the similarities too. Had he known about me? Did he see me like my—*our*—birth father did?

"Didn't care because you were in gray?" Violet asked.

I nodded.

"The Elite don't see people like us. Not even Defects who live in High Town and serve them," Violet said coldly.

"You live in High Town?" I asked.

"Everyone in gray who works in the clouds lives in High Town beneath the cloud level. It's easier for them to beckon us at any given hour when we are close but out of sight," Violet explained. My brows pulled in. "What is it, Fledgling?"

"I—no one has ever answered any of my questions."

"For good reason. Questions mean trouble," Rose said.

"True, but we all wear gray, right?" Violet added, watching me closely.

I nodded. "You said something happened?"

"Well—"

"Violet, we ought not discuss this with her," Rose interjected. "There is a reason questions go unanswered. Answering them can result in elimination."

"She's a Defect," Violet snapped. "Fledgling, are you close with your Mate?"

"I don't know what you mean," I said. "I've met him once."

"Yes, but were you a person to him or an obligation?"

My heart sank. Had we discussed anything of substance, really?

Violet smiled, knowing the answer. "See?"

"It is on you if this gets back to us," Rose warned, pulling out a small vial. "It's too dangerous, Violet."

"Now who is lecturing? You have chosen to trust an Elite. I choose my own kind." Violet shook her head. "There's been trouble in the clouds. There are some who are tired of being told what to do by the Illum, and they are letting them know."

Rose swore under her breath. "Tilt your head back so I can get rid of the redness," she instructed and opened my eye, applying several drops of a liquid solution. A sigh escaped as instantaneous relief flooded me.

"Letting them know how? What are they doing?" I asked breathlessly.

"We don't know everything. The Illum isn't giving any details, which means the Press isn't either," Violet said from the vanity while Rose worked. "Rumors are flying, though. It's the perk of serving them. We hear everything from the women. The Illum seem to have crossed a line. Some are finally done with the Illum's illuminating rules. They found others who are as well. Things have escalated. Those are the rumors, anyway."

"They've gone too far with the offspring. The Academy should be left alone," Rose whispered. "Nestor just allows it."

The dual Academy buildings were identical looking, two halves of a whole, placed several hundred yards away from each other, as if something had cleaved them apart. If pushed together, the halves would form a pyramid. The Elite side was a flawless, gleaming white. The Minor side was a black that swallowed all light. A giant lawn sat between them, where the Elite offspring were permitted to lounge in between lessons while the Minors watched, cloistered inside, never to cross paths.

"Rose, Nestor is an Illum. Of course he allows it."

"I know, but he seemed different," Rose claimed as Violet rolled her eyes.

Nestor was the headmaster, an impossibly tall man. He didn't interfere with the Minors' education often. Occasionally he graced Minor students with his presence, usually only to read out names on visiting day and to welcome incoming offspring.

"What did the Illum do to the offspring?" I asked.

"Minor offspring are being downgraded."

"Eve said an Elite offspring was downgraded to Minor last week," Rose said, sweeping a brush across my cheeks.

"I still do not believe that," Violet said.

"What do you mean, 'downgraded'?" I turned the hem of my robe over in my hands repeatedly. Would that be my offspring's destiny? Would I condemn them with my defect?

Rose pulled the brush back from my face, glaring. "No more talking. You'll ruin my work."

Violet crossed her arms, a vicious glint in her dark eyes. "The Illum are changing offsprings' status. But the truth is murky, concealed in the rumors."

"But why? Where do they go?" My heart fell in rhythm with my whirling thoughts. Why would that be happening if the "defects" were seemingly determined from birth?

"Those aren't truths the Illum are illuminating for anyone," Violet continued. "That isn't the important part. The important part, the dangerous part, is that people are rising up."

"Enough, Violet," Rose snapped, her face furious before me. "They are calling the Elite Force to handle this. If these people do not stop and follow the Elite, treacherous times are ahead."

"Did Eve tell you that as well?" Violet probed. "You didn't mention any of this earlier."

Rose didn't deign to answer her partner as she moved toward the vanity littered with vials, putting away brushes. Her face in the mirror looked fearful.

"Why is it that Eve is so informed? I thought she was avoiding society," Violet said, stepping closer. Eve must be an important Elite member to have been seeing the Starlings for so long.

"Things change," Rose claimed. "We have said too much. If the Elite Force is involved at all, we should hold our tongue."

"What's the Elite Force?" I asked.

Rose crossed her arms.

"They're—" Violet began.

"Enough," Rose demanded. "Stay silent or there will be trouble. Let's get you dressed and be done with you." Rose practically sprinted from the room. I glanced in the mirror, and two brown eyes stared back.

Violet walked toward the door, peering out before turning toward me. Her words were hushed and quick. "They are a group of highly trained men that claim to maintain the peace. They actually carry out the Illum's will with force—physical force."

"Why are you telling me all of this?" Everything they had said left me dizzy. Surely they knew the dangers of voicing dissent to a near stranger. Did they not fear the consequences?

Violet stood straighter, fierce determination on her face. "I was once like you. As was she. Every woman since the Last War has been an obligation and a vessel. I see a lot of your kind. Many do not have a care in the world. They do not think, simply pleased to be chosen. Not you. You questioned us, pushed back during your initial meeting. I want more for us. Maybe I am done being powerless. I think you might be too."

"There are consequences. You could be eliminated."

"I have seen enough to know there are worse things, Fledgling." Her face was grave as she disappeared into the black room beyond.

A few minutes later, I stepped up on the dais. Violet handed me a pair of panties that were the exact color of my skin as Rose carried over what looked like a cloud. A sheer cloud. I slipped on the scraps of lace before she ushered me into the chiffon silk fabric. Violet wrapped two impossibly thin strings around my neck several times before securing them as Rose fluffed out the dress. A heavy silence hung between the two.

I caught my appearance in the mirror. The dress was completely sheer and featherlight, floating in layers to the ground. Diagonal seams bunched new layers of fabric together strategically, providing me the slightest amount of modesty. The dress was delicately beautiful, the thin fabric shifting with the lightest movement.

Violet kneeled, tying cream heels to my feet. They wrapped around my ankle much like the dress wrapped around my neck, the only places I felt any security in the outfit. As I shifted, the seams went askew, leaving my breasts fully exposed.

"I'm naked," I protested, tugging the gown back into place.

"You are not; I've dressed many in less," Rose informed me. "The Elite view the human body as a reflection of their superior genes. They relish exposed skin."

"Fine, I'm *practically* naked."

Rose ignored me as she continued fluffing the dress insistently.

"Rose, it's beautiful. Some of your best work. They will love it," Violet reassured her, her tone gentle.

Rose paused her fussing to smile. "Thank you."

"You make these?" I asked, looking at the tiny details. It must have taken her days.

"If you have exhausted your Procreation Abilities, you must convince the Elite that you have value. An Elite vouched for me to the Illum years ago. She showed me a great kindness." Rose stepped back, looking over the ensemble one last time. "They are all my creations. Your Mate requested the best after your first meeting. So make them look good," she warned.

As she grabbed something from beside the rack of gowns, I took in the layers. I would fit in among the clouds. Even with all their talk of treacherous times, the beauty of the gown delighted me. With both Starlings distracted, I twirled, and the dress floated around me. My eyes snagged on a faint glowing. Did the gown glow?

It wasn't the gown. My left wrist glowed brightly, encircled in rich gold. The color imprinted on my skin. I brought my wrist up to my face, perplexed.

"I see your Procreation Agreement has been officially approved," Rose announced, staring at the golden band.

Violet approached me, grabbing my wrist. "It is gold." Her eyes narrowed in disbelief. I swore fear flickered there. "So an Illum has actually taken a Mate? A Minor Mate? I didn't believe the Press."

Rose gasped, eyes flying between Violet and my wrist. "I—I must get started on your first ball gown." She thrust a small black box into Violet's hands and hurried off.

"Seems odd," Violet muttered as she opened the small box, extracting two dangling pearl earrings. "There's trouble afoot and an Illum has chosen a Minor with a visual defect. It's almost as if they need the Elite's focus elsewhere."

She fastened the pearls to my ears before handing me a small white bag. I stepped off the dais, my hands clammy.

"Welcome to their game, little Fledgling," Violet whispered, steel determination upon her face. "There's no way out now."

Fear choked me as I followed Violet toward the hall. She held the door open for me, her hand capturing my chin, lifting it. "Chin up. The Elite will now watch your every breath."

I stepped into the hall, my insides trembling. Violet slowly closed the door, her last words floating through the crack and down the hall. "You must fly now, Emeline. There is no other option."

When I reached the podium, the attendant bowed. "Your Pod, Ms. Emeline. Fertile blessings." The juxtaposition in his demeanor, when I entered in gray versus when I left in a dress, was unsettling, as if a garment and some paint on my face somehow made me worthy of respect. Was I not the exact same person?

I stopped on the threshold. "What's your name?" I asked, turning toward him.

The man's eyes darted around the room. "My name?"

"Yes, your name. You said last time that reducing someone to a set of numbers was barbaric and disrespectful. Right?"

He wrung his hands, eyes locked on my glowing wrist. "My name is Harold."

"Thank you, Harold."

Harold held the door open as he sputtered, "I don't want any trouble."

"What?"

"If I offended you in some way, or they're asking questions. I just do my job, Ms. Emeline. I am loyal to the Illum." His fear was poignant.

"I just wanted to thank you, Harold. That's all."

Harold's face grew pale. Beads of sweat peppered his clammy complexion as he released the door. "Good day, Ms. Emeline." He strode over to his desk, unwilling to look my way.

Everyone beneath the Elite had fear. It was as much a part of our genetic makeup as our defects. And we had reason to be afraid.

I knew what happened when a Minor Defect attempted to change their fate. When they refused to conform and follow the Illum's protocol.

Alice. Together, we had dreamed. Crafted elaborate ideas for life after the Academy, spun stories of the lost history of those bygone humans. Alone in the dark, everyone else asleep, we had built something that went against everything we were taught. The Illum's lessons cited us against each other. It wasn't enough for the Illum to forbid socializing. Urging us to outperform the Minors around us, resulting in fulfilling our use for the Greater Good. Warping any idea of camaraderie among Minors.

Over the years, Alice grew angrier and more outspoken, until one night she was called into the headmaster's office. I waited and waited for her to return, but she never did, and no one bothered to tell me where she'd gone. No one told me why my friend had seemingly disappeared. Until a lecture a moon later, the hologram floating in the center of the large room, the seat next to me empty.

As we continue the most vital portion of your education, it is crucial to the Illum's success, and all human life, that we preserve this way of life. The Illum have always cherished the education of all offspring, Minor and Elite alike. The Illum view the proper care of these formative years as essential to our peace while pruning rotten genes that risk diseasing everything. Distractions from the Greater Good threaten our progress and peace. Fail to adhere to the rules of your status and risk elimination.

For the longest time I refused to accept it. That a force like Alice could just be eliminated. Even now I didn't fully accept it. I liked to believe she had found that place where she was free. I just wish she had taken me with her.

My thoughts carried me through the soaring buildings until the Pod slowed next to a cylindrical glass building. Thin strips of metal ran up the sides, connecting the glass panes and meeting at the domed top. A large sphere sat precariously on top of the dome. It seemed as if one strong wind might send the sphere soaring from its perch and hurtling to the ground below.

The Pod took me straight to the sphere of doom.

As the Pod stopped and the doors opened, I attempted to fluff my dress the way Rose had. There was no atrium this time, just a long transparent bridge leading to a suspended platform. I stood, dumbstruck. A gleaming golden disc hovered in the center of the sphere, a podium upon it, the bridge tethering it to the entrance. A Defect in dark gray waited.

My entire body trembled. There wasn't enough substance around me. How did they live like this, with no foundation beneath their feet? My words from earlier found me. *Just move. You can do this*, I told myself. *Walk across the transparent bridge in the glass ball of death thousands of feet above the ground.*

I took my first step onto the bridge. Clouds drifted lazily under my feet. My pulse left me unsteady until I reached the center platform. I clung to the solid edge of the podium, scarcely hearing the man in gray welcoming me to the Sphere. The beep from his scanner caused me to jump.

He directed me toward the edge behind him, and I glanced around to see several other floating platforms. The man extended a hand, helping me onto the floating ferry, piloted by another attendant in gray. He steered the platform off into the Sphere as I clutched the railing in a death grip.

How much fear could my body handle before I would vomit or faint? I knew I was approaching my threshold. But my fear fell silent as the rest of the Sphere came into view. My breath caught at the beauty of the Elite's world.

White landings wove around the curved glass walls of the Sphere, coming together before gliding apart in a twisted dance that created a wavelike effect. In each dip of the swells were intimate alcoves, booths of varying sizes nestled securely within. It was marvelous.

The platform slowed, arriving at a smaller nook. The entire back of the alcove was glass. I had a perfect view of the sun, still making its evening descent. My beguilement was shaken by only one thing—that smooth, powerful voice.

"Hello again, Emeline."

CHAPTER SEVEN

I TORE MY EYES FROM THE VIEW TO FIND ANOTHER THAT left me equally mesmerized. Collin reclined along the low-back curved booth. His midnight black suit matched his dark hair, a stark difference from the booth's lush cream velvet. The dripping crystal chandelier's delicate lights reflected in his sapphire eyes as they ran up the length of me before settling on my concealed defect.

He was breathtaking, so at home among all the Elite's beauty.

I exited the floating platform and tried to ignore the drop that awaited anyone who got too close. All the Academy training of grace thrown aside, I scooted away from the edge and farther into the booth, my dress catching on the velvet, until my bare arm met solid warmth. I froze, glancing up to find that my fear had driven me right into my Mate's very firm body.

My breath caught, and I suddenly felt too warm even though I was dressed in practically nothing.

"Here," he suggested and voluntarily moved closer to the perilous end of our table, giving me space in the middle of the booth.

"Aren't you afraid of the edge?" I asked.

His lips tugged up. "I haven't feared the fall in a long time."

I turned to the sky outside, the ground forever below. "I think I might never get over it," I admitted. "I might always fear the fall."

"It will take some time getting used to," Collin told me. His eyes locked on my glowing wrist where I gripped the table, then skated over me before he cleared his throat and looked toward the rest of the Sphere.

I followed his gaze. All around, Elite socialized, unperturbed by how close their dining arrangements were to death. I didn't understand how the Elite lived life so exposed, how they walked in the clouds as if it were normal. How they didn't fear the height.

"Your gown has gone askew," Collin said thickly, his eyes fixed on the brightly colored Elite all around us.

A flush swept up my neck, and I quickly adjusted the fabric, clinging to any modesty I could find. It wouldn't last between us. I had signed the paperwork. The Academy had taught me what to expect about the Procreation Agreement, and he would see everything soon enough . . .

"Did you know you bite your lip when you're thinking?" Collin said, interrupting my thoughts.

"I didn't realize," I said, releasing my lip. "I'm sorry."

"I didn't make the observation to elicit an apology."

I nodded, my hands finding my lap, and I stared at the golden glow. The alcove was much more secluded than our initial meeting in the Garden had been, but the Elite's judgment from earlier still haunted me.

The look of disbelief on my birth brother's face. The first time meeting him and the Elite's stark reminder of our divide.

Truly disgusting how they think they can be here. . . . A Defect out in the sun.

The Starlings' whispers of rebellion rang in my ears.

The Illum seem to have crossed a line. Some are finally done with the Illum's illuminating rules. They found others who are as well.

My thoughts tangled with the Grooming at the Academy.

Rule Nine: You are an obligation to your Mate. He is free to do as he wishes at all times. His loyalty is to the Illum, not to you.

Violet's face swam before me.

Every woman since the Last War has been an obligation and a vessel. . . . Maybe I am done being powerless. I think you might be too.

Was she right?

"Are you okay, Emeline?" Collin asked.

"I am fine," I lied, tearing my gaze from my glowing wrist.

"Is it the atrium?"

My eyes flew to his, my heart thumping uncomfortably. "You know about that?"

"Very little happens in this city that I am not aware of," Collin told me, leaning toward me. "When it comes to you, I am aware of everything." Goosebumps erupted across my body. "Especially now." His eyes slid back to my wrist.

I captured my lip once more, and Collin's eyes found mine, amusement there.

"You are free to speak plainly. We are alone," Collin said. "It was why I chose to meet here, unlike the more . . . public outing of our initial meeting. No one can get to us. We will see them coming."

The disdain for the Elite bled into his tone, and again I found myself wondering at this man who seemed to hate the very people he partially ruled. I knew I couldn't trust him, and yet . . .

"I have questions," I admitted. Collin held my gaze, quirking a brow in silent invitation.

I wanted to know why he had chosen me, defect and all. I wanted to know more about the trouble I had heard about from the Starlings. But most of all, I wanted to know more about my birth brother. I had felt alone for so long.

"There was a man, an Elite, with curly hair, like mine, and blue eyes, in the atrium. He's—he's my . . ."

"Phillip is your brother," Collin confirmed. A lump formed in my throat, and his gaze softened. "I work with him. He is the one who informed me of the incident."

My birth brother's name was Phillip. "Is he an Illum?"

"He isn't."

"So Elite work for the Illum?" I asked.

"Only a select few, those who show potential."

"Okay," I said, more to myself. I knew being in the clouds would change things. That I might come face-to-face with people who shared blood with me. I pressed on. "I have others, right? I have more birth siblings in the clouds."

Collin took a deep breath. "You have two others, Gregory and Richard."

I nodded again, glancing away from him as my mind made room for the information. I should have been quiet, but another desperate question escaped. "Do they know?" I couldn't look at Collin. "Do they know I am your Mate?"

"Phillip knows. The others, the rest of the Elite, have heard rumors of me taking a Minor Mate, thanks to Edward's meddling in the Garden. The Press knows but your identity is still undiscovered. I am afraid that will end soon, possibly tonight. Which brings me to another issue." Collin shifted in his seat. "It was decided today that there will be a dinner in six days with some of the High Council Elite to provide a united power against the rising unrest. I have been told you are to attend."

Surprise flickered through me. "Me?"

"Yes, Tabitha said it was wise for you to be there. I think it is to counter the rumors the Elite seem determined to spread."

I found myself nodding once more, even though none of it made sense. "Can you tell me more about Tabitha?"

Collin stared at me for a moment like he was debating his next words. "Tabitha is the head of the Illum. She is responsible for the entire city."

"A woman?" I asked.

"A woman," Collin confirmed. "She has held her position for over fifty years. Tabitha is . . . different." Collin looked toward the Elite as he tugged on his jacket sleeve, and I knew he would say no more on the subject. "Another thing that will change for you. Now that you are officially my Mate and we have agreed upon a public Courting, an HI is being installed in your living quarters."

"A Hologram Instructor? Like the ones from the Academy?" I asked, my spine straightening.

"Yes. Every morning, you will have an hour-long session. It will instruct you on the Elite protocol. It will also provide dance lessons before we attend our first ball, which will take place at the end of the moon. A public Courting requires fresh lessons. It was all in the contract."

Right, the contract I hadn't even read. I glanced toward the sky again, the sun sinking away slowly.

"Did you look over the contract?" Collin asked.

"I didn't," I admitted, glancing his way. "Was there any reason to? I couldn't reject you."

My stomach hit my feet as I snapped my mouth closed, my eyes finding his. He simply watched me curiously.

"Emeline, I—" Collin cleared his throat as he straightened his jacket. "Today," he began again, his jaw tight, "you should have been able to leave unseen. It was unfair to you. I have ensured that issue won't arise again."

"Right. No one wants to see someone in gray."

One day a year, birth parents were permitted to visit their offspring at the Academy. Standing in the entrance hall, I remembered adults, mostly in gray, coming through the grand doors to greet their defective offspring. Not many Elite showed up, but a few did. I stood in that hall every single year, waiting for my name to be called. I drifted toward the back of the crowd as the years passed. After Alice disappeared, I stopped going altogether. My name was never called. No Elite wanted to see me, even when I was young.

Why would that change now?

"Usually, that area is clear of the Elite," Collin continued. "However, things are difficult right now. The Elite are being made to use the ground entrance. I have spoken to the Comm Department, ensuring that they will not mess up again."

"Why are things difficult?" I asked quietly. Would he tell me what Violet had shared?

"It is a complicated answer," Collin said. It wasn't an answer, but it didn't shut down the conversation either.

I bit my lip, attempting to silence the vicious war at play, that burning desire to understand eating me alive.

I glanced up to find Collin solely focused on my lip between my teeth.

Maybe it was simply to prove Violet wrong, that I was a person to him—to someone. Maybe being told to talk plainly made me too bold. Or perhaps my defect knew no bounds.

"Is it because of the people going against the Illum?"

Collin didn't move, seconds stretching until they felt like minutes, hours, days. He tilted his head, watching me with an intensity that set my skin ablaze. "I did not realize the happenings in the clouds had reached the ground so quickly."

"They haven't. I . . ." Mind racing, I cursed myself. I had talked too plainly. Too freely.

It is on you if this gets back to us. Rose's warnings echoed through me. *Questions mean trouble.*

Collin looked at me like he saw something entirely different, that he had miscalculated something. "The Starlings were talking about it?"

My frantic pulse pushed against my skin. How had he guessed? I hesitated, but I had to answer him. "I only asked why the Elite were at the atrium. They just said an Elite told them there was trouble. That's all."

"An Elite shared the information?"

"Yes, someone named Eve."

Collin shifted in his seat. "Have you mentioned this to anyone else?"

"I have only seen them and you," I said, taking a steadying breath. "Is it bad?"

"It's nothing the Illum will not see an end to," Collin told me, adjusting the sleeve of his jacket. I opened my mouth, but Collin cut me off. "It is why we had to wait four days for our second meeting. The Illum will stop at nothing to silence those who speak about it."

My questioning had come to an end.

A heavy silence fell upon us. I scanned the Elite but too many looked our way. The Sphere filled with a symphony of colors as the setting sun met the horizon. From this vantage point, its bloodred blaze seemed endless, illuminating the clouds around us in shades of vibrant purples, blushing pinks, and golden yellows.

The beauty stole my breath, chasing away all the terrible thoughts running rampant and making me forget the Elite who continued to stare and whisper. If only I could watch the sunset here forever, or even just a few more moments. It was fleeting, the ending already in sight. The night was not far off now, waiting to cloak the sky.

I realized the sun's final moments painted not only the clouds. My dress was no longer ivory but all the colors around us. Rose had dressed me to reflect the sunset. I smiled, relishing the small moment of joy, letting it chase everything else away.

I leaned onto the edge of the booth, watching the night finally stake its claim on the sky. Stars slowly winked awake, and the lights from the buildings all around began flicking on. "It's beautiful, isn't it?" I said. My eyes shifted toward my Mate to find him watching me again.

"Yes, it is," Collin agreed quietly.

I pushed away from the booth, straightening my dress as I turned back toward Collin and, to my surprise, a hovering podium. A Defect placed an assortment of plates, cups, teapots, and tiered arrangements of colorful foods.

With the sun gone, all the alcoves were aglow. Couples and groups chatted like tiny glittering gems on display for everyone else to see.

"Enjoy," the Defect told us as he drifted away. Other podiums floated to and from the alcoves like little worker bees. Collin reached across the table, grabbing my teapot and filling my cup with ease, lifting the sleeve of his jacket. The outside of his wrist wasn't glowing.

"Thank you." I blew on the steaming cup. "Does your wrist not glow with our contract?"

"It does not. Even among two Elites, the male's wrist will not glow."

"Why?"

"It's always been that way," Collin said. "If you're concerned about people knowing about us, I can assure you the Elite will know you are my Mate and, in turn, that I am yours." His sapphire eyes met my matching gaze. "There will be no hiding you."

My stomach made a little swooping motion. Why did Collin say such things? He was an Illum. I was a Minor. I was beneath him. Everything I had ever been told said this should not be happening. I was a vessel, right?

Collin selected a food item from the bottom tier. We each had our own tiered array of food, and the number of options was overwhelming. It seemed we had some of the same items, while others varied. The lowest level contained different shapes. The middle held round, golden things with jars, and the top displayed things that resembled chocolate cake.

"We usually start at the bottom. It contains different savory items. Then work our way up to the scones and finally the sweets," Collin informed me, drinking his tea.

"If I want to start at the top?" I eyed a particularly mouthwatering piece of chocolate dusted in gold.

The corner of his mouth tugged. "Well, in polite society, it would be unheard of."

Crestfallen, I tore my eyes from the top tier. A small sigh left my lips. Collin reached across, picking up the gold-dusted chocolate and placing it upon my plate before returning to his tea.

I stared at him. "I thought it was unheard of?"

Collin leaned back, his gaze gleaming. "What is the point in being a member of the Illum if I do not bend their rules to suit my needs? Have the chocolate."

"And my eating chocolate is your need?" I flushed at the unintended heat in my voice.

"Yes, your needs are now my needs," Collin stated. My heart skipped in my chest.

"But they can see us," I said, my eyes sliding to all the Elite.

"They know better than to question the Illum—to question me."

His eyes sparkled at me, and I snatched the chocolate and ate the entire thing in a single bite. Rich, smoky sweetness burst across my tongue. I swallowed my moan.

"Pity, I only said yes in hopes of more indecent sounds." Collin smirked behind his teacup. My blush deepened.

"You broke the rules in hopes of indecent sounds?" I asked incredulously, fighting a smile.

"No," Collin said, replacing his teacup. "I broke the rules in hopes of hearing *your* indecent sounds." His words snaked across my skin, and heat pooled low in my stomach.

"Your final tea, spiced mint," the attendant announced, startling me. I hadn't noticed his return. He placed two glass mugs with rich tan tea that smelled delicious, then removed our teapots, cups, and plates and made to remove our stands of food. A wave of regret swept through me. I wouldn't get to eat the cake.

Collin halted the Defect. "My Mate isn't done with her food."

"My apologies, Mr. Collin," the attendant said hastily. "Ma'am." He bowed his head in my direction.

"Her name is Emeline." Collin reached toward my stand, removed the top plate completely, and placed it in front of me. "This is all she really wants." He pushed the stand toward the man.

His eyes grew. Before taking my stand, he began to reach for Collin's, then hesitated. "May I remove yours, Mr. Collin?"

Collin grabbed an identical gold-dusted chocolate from his plate and placed it on mine. "You can now." The attendant grabbed his stand, uttering a quick goodbye before departing.

The tea spread warmth through my limbs, its spice blending with the sweetness of the chocolate. It was my favorite of the evening. I hummed appreciatively. Collin's chuckle caused me to look up. A small smile played at his mouth, and his eyes were on me. "Did I do something?"

"The Elite never allow themselves to enjoy anything," he said.

"Why not?"

"Real enjoyment is not crafted. It does not fit their image. They are more concerned with being proper."

"Is this considered proper?" I asked, biting into the cake. It was divine, so light and moist that it melted on my tongue.

"No. Polite society would be a mess over it," Collin stated.

"Oh," I muttered.

"No one has ever accused me of being polite," Collin assured me.

My brows pulled in. "Is this all a test?"

"No, I meant what I said. I have neither time nor patience for it. Work is demanding. The Elite will be enough of a test for you."

"*Are* the Elite testing me?" I asked.

"Not in a way that matters. They cannot overstep their position, they can only report what they see. But surviving their judgment will be a more difficult task than any I could construct."

I opened my mouth to respond, but a small ding sounded.

"Apologies," Collin said, taking his Comm Device out of his jacket pocket. His demeanor shifted completely. His brow furrowed and his mouth tightened before he replaced the device and turned his attention back to me. "How's the cake?"

"It's amazing," I said, taking the last bite. "Is everything okay?"

Collin smiled tightly at me. "Yes, everything is fine. Try the nougat," Collin suggested, gesturing toward a small square. It was like biting into a fluffy cloud.

"You like the chocolate more, don't you?" Collin asked.

"I do," I admitted, and he smiled tightly, running his hands down his jacket again. "Do you need to go?"

"Not until you are done."

I pushed the plate away from me. "I am finished."

"Are you sure?" he asked, gesturing to the last gold-dusted chocolate. I grinned and popped it into my mouth. His mouth tugged up as he leaned over, pressing a small button I hadn't noticed. A podium changed directions, heading toward us. I watched the others in the Sphere, and I swore they all looked in our direction. Maybe I was paranoid.

"Mr. Collin, *Ms. Emeline.*" The attendant stopped before our table, shifting to the side to make room. Collin nodded at the man, tucking away his Comm Device and making his way out of the booth.

I shimmied around the booth, and Collin moved to block the attendant entirely. A muscle feathered in his jaw as he waited for me, hand extended. I placed my hand in his as I entered the podium. Collin pulled me in close, our bodies meeting. The thin fabric did nothing to diminish the feel of his body against mine.

"Please, grab the railing."

Collin boxed me in, grasping the railing on both sides of me, encasing me as we moved. My heart hammered at his proximity.

"May I?" he asked, his eyes traveling down. I followed his gaze to find that the diagonal lines had gone askew, revealing everything to him. A hot flush raced up my body, and I nodded, cheeks blazing.

He gently pinched the thin fabric between two fingers, adjusting the gown, careful not to touch my skin. When he was satisfied, he leaned in, his warm breath brushing the side of my neck. I was instantly too warm and cold all at once.

"You're biting your lip again, Emeline," Collin informed me quietly as we floated toward the platform below.

"I was thinking," I said, breathier than I intended.

"I figured as much. What were you thinking about this time?"

"It's just—" I began as he leaned back from me. "Nothing, never mind."

His eyes collided with mine. "But I do mind, Emeline. I mind a great deal."

I took a shaky breath. "I just assumed it would be different. I had prepared for . . . a private contract. I didn't think anyone would want to be seen with me in public. I didn't expect you," I finished, and I couldn't deny how my body wanted him closer, despite how I felt about the Illum.

"I do not hide. I do not have to adhere to the Elite's standards. And"—his lips brushed my ear, and I shivered—"I wasn't expecting you either."

Collin pulled away, cold air swarming me as he stepped off the platform, jarring me. When had we reached the landing? He waited once more, his hand extended toward me.

I took it and something that felt like hope blossomed inside me. Everything the Starlings had said still haunted me, but maybe he truly was different. I smiled as I stepped onto the landing. His eyes flared.

"Emeline." My spine stiffened. Dread swept in, washing away that moment of hope. "Yes, it is her. Emeline." Only one woman among the Elite knew my name.

Never look at the Elite, Emeline. Just look down and they will leave you be. You must look down.

But I looked up.

Another platform drifted right toward us. The only members of the Elite I hoped to never see.

My birth family. In all their Elite perfection.

CHAPTER EIGHT

Families shared a last name before the war. We don't now. The Procreation Act focused on genetic histories to repopulate the world. Without a family name, it was easier to sever ties with genetically defective offspring.

My heart swelled painfully, hollowing out the rest of my insides as my birth family arrived on the landing. Even if there were family names, I would never choose to share one with them.

Collin turned in their direction, his hand warm around mine. The landing immediately felt too small. My eyes flew to the transparent bridge that had felt like a death sentence upon my arrival, and I debated sprinting down it to get away from the people who had ensured I knew my place in the world before I could speak.

"Emeline," my birth mother repeated in her beautiful voice, her blue eyes running over my face. Helen looked the same as the day I left for the Academy twenty-three years ago. She was slightly shorter than I was, with the same deep brown hair tied up in an elegant twist. She wore a long-sleeve red dress, and a diamond necklace sparkled at her throat. I tried to step away, but Collin's hand tightened around mine, keeping me there.

Collin nodded toward the man with the curly hair and blue eyes from the atrium. "Phillip."

Phillip tipped his head. "Collin, Emeline."

My stomach bottomed out, and I looked to the other two men, who must be Richard and Gregory. One stared me down, while the other looked bored.

"I thought Edward was making things up when he was running his mouth all over the sky," Vincent drawled. "But it appears for once the fool was reporting the truth."

His disapproval slid down my spine. The urge to run was overwhelming. I stepped back only to meet warmth. Collin released my hand to touch my lower back, his hand brushing gently against my skin, reminding me I was not in gray—I was in a gown with a Mate, a Mate who was a member of the group my birth father cared about more than anything else.

I swallowed thickly as my birth mother's eyes went wide, landing on my glowing wrist. "Collin, we are honored to be blessed by the Illum. You're—"

My ears rang, muffling her words. Of course now she spoke. She had been delicate and quiet in the few hazy memories I had of her. Her light footsteps outside my door were my only real tie to her—always outside but never inside the room. But now that I had obtained a momentary place in their clouds, now that I could breed, she suddenly saw me. My throat threatened to close.

"Mated, yes," Collin informed her, an edge to his voice. One of my birth brothers, the bored one with brutally short hair, snorted. His crystal blue gaze skated over us.

"You'll be silent, Gregory," Vincent ordered. Gregory rolled his eyes and blew out a breath.

"Fertile blessings," Phillip said, his face yielding nothing.

"It would seem some topics weren't covered today," Vincent said. My birth father had been at the meeting.

Vincent remained strong in his advanced age, with his high cheekbones, straight nose, and full mouth. Our resemblance was uncanny. The similarities tortured him, I assumed. His hateful gaze narrowed at my matching eyes. The same immovable disappointment and hatred I had always known stared back at me. I couldn't breathe beneath his stare, reduced once again to a powerless little girl.

"You talk as if the Elite are privy to all of the Illum's choices," Collin stated, no warmth to his voice. "The Elite are not worthy of input into our inner workings. Even the council."

His sapphire eyes resembled ice. Perhaps he was being honest when he claimed no one had ever accused him of being polite. In other company maybe I would have given pause to the viciousness permeating the air around us. Maybe he was as terrifying as the people whispered the Illum to be, but I couldn't find it in me to be anything except relieved for the strength behind me.

Vincent's eyes narrowed for a heartbeat, but a moment later, he smiled tightly, clapping his hands together. "You misunderstand; I am simply shocked that a decision tied so close to me would remain unknown." Vincent's cold stare conflicted with his smile. Collin's hand clenched the fabric of my dress.

"I was unaware she was close to you," Collin told my birth father.

"We would be honored to host you at our home this week. This is a blessing and should be celebrated," Helen chimed in, a delicate smile on her ageless face.

My mind ran off the rails completely. An honor? A blessing? *We?* I couldn't stand the sound of the words. Now I was worthy of celebrating, worthy of her attention. I had never been invited to their home. I had never been visited by them. I hadn't even known how many genetically Elite siblings I had. I should have run.

The hand fisted at my back released the fabric, falling flat against my skin. "You may reach out with the details. Now, after you." Collin gestured to the bridge, dismissing them. "I have a few more things to discuss with my Mate, and you are holding up the Elite."

The shock radiating from them was sickly satisfying. Collin had stepped even closer, his stable presence seeping through the thin fabric of my dress. Several platforms hovered, waiting, filled with colorfully dressed Elite all craning their necks to see the holdup.

"Yes, of course." Helen bowed her head slightly, the others following suit. Richard extended his arm, leading Helen down the bridge. "We will be in contact soon," she said over her shoulder, recapturing her superior grace as she glided down the path to the Pods. Phillip and Gregory followed. I swore one of them laughed as they passed us.

"See you tomorrow," Vincent said, barely bowing his head before following them out. I watched them go, a family.

I whirled around, my dress fanning out all around me as I faced Collin. There was no space between us. His arms found my hips, steadying me. I tilted my head up to see his face. My heart dove off the platform, unafraid of the fall, racing as I took him in up close. His sapphire eyes met mine, stealing my breath at the intensity shining back at me.

Words failed me. He had dismissed the people who had always seen me as worthless, who had denied me since birth. *Thank you* didn't seem to be enough.

One of Collin's hands left my hip. The man who had silenced the Elite, with unwavering ferociousness, tucked a wayward curl behind my ear with painstaking gentleness. My entire body ignited under his piercing gaze. I felt eyes on us but for the first time I didn't care that I was being observed.

"You are an extension of me now," he said, his voice low and rough. "They will do well to remember that. They'll regret their unkindness. They all will."

I glanced up to find everyone in the Sphere looking toward us, some even leaning over the edge. Collin's other hand drifted to my waist, a hesitation there.

"They are all watching us," I whispered. The fabric of my dress caught on his suit. Had I moved closer to him or had he moved closer to me?

"Let them," he told me, his thumb brushing against my cheek. I leaned into the warmth, my pulse fluttering beneath his touch. His gentleness was so at odds with the viciousness he had shown moments before. "Do you trust me, Emeline?"

Did I trust him? Did I want to?

Collin's eyes swept the Sphere, and his hand gripped my waist. I sucked in a shaky breath. My mouth went dry.

"Do you remember Rule Ten?" he asked, his voice lower. Those sapphire pools found me—and I willingly drowned in them.

Rule Ten: You are not permitted under any circumstances to tell your Mate no regarding public appearances, attire, or desires. If your Mate asks, you are to oblige him.

I nodded, confused. "I can't tell you no."

Something shifted in Collin's eyes, the icy depths churning with an unnamed emotion. "Forgive me."

His lips collided with mine. Gentle, delicate—hesitating.

My mind went blissfully quiet, and I was falling. His lips were soft as silk. Heart racing against the new sensation, I pressed a trembling hand to his chest, something foreign consuming me. I pushed closer, standing on tiptoes. His hold on my waist tightened, sweeping an arm around my lower back, his fingers trailing a burning path across my bare skin. I gasped, and Collin sucked in a sharp breath, his lips hovering over mine, as if ready to pull away.

But I wasn't ready for this to end.

I tightened my hold on his shirt. A low sound escaped him as his hand slid to the back of my neck and brought my mouth to his once more, the pressure shifting, the need different. I let go in the unknown, trusting him. The rest of the world fell away.

His tongue traced my bottom lip and tangled with mine when I opened. He tasted of mint tea, and I breathed him in, flattening my hand against his chest. A frenzied beat raged beneath his crafted exterior. I sighed into his mouth, pressing myself entirely against him. He froze, then his mouth left mine, the hand on my waist pushing me away.

I opened my eyes to find his gaze untamed and wild as he turned away from me completely.

CHAPTER NINE

"So, how was it?" Lo asked from my bed, dressed in a gray sleep shirt and socks.

I had messaged Lo after leaving the Sphere in a daze. The phantom feel of Collin's lips against mine lingered, and I traced my now bare lips. I had ditched the gown and doused myself in a cold shower, but my skin remained too hot. The feel of Collin's racing heart beneath my hand where I had clutched him. The flood of disappointment when he had pulled away too soon. The burn of desire that scorched me from the inside out. It all remained. Maybe it always would.

"Em?" Lo prompted again.

"It was good," I confessed as my hand dropped away from my searing lips and I started toying with the hem of my shirt. "He kissed me."

Lo squealed and yanked me onto the bed next to her.

"When? How?" Lo demanded, grinning. "Please, please, please tell me it's better than those diagrams."

During our Grooming at the Academy, our education had consisted of sterile, often intimidating diagrams and lessons detailing the procreation phase. I had always found it unappealing, even frightening. What I had experienced tonight had been frightening . . . but in a way I had never felt before. The kiss had finished almost as quickly as it had started, and the night had ended immediately, early enough that I could still catch up with Lo before curfew. Yet something had coiled deep in my gut, something endless and unabated.

"Before we left. In front of everyone. And yes, it's better than the diagrams." I smiled.

"All the Elite saw?" Lo gushed. "So you're officially in an agreement, right?"

I held up my left wrist, the sleeve of my nightshirt cascading down my arm. My living quarters filled with a golden glow.

"Why is it gold?" Lo asked, turning my wrist over. "Isn't it supposed to be silver?"

Usually, a Minor Mate's MIND turned silver when their Procreation Contract went into effect. Most women hid it from their fellow Defects. It had a way of turning the others in gray against you.

"I think it's gold because he's an Illum. That's what the Starlings said."

"Emeline," Lo exclaimed, scooting closer until our knees touched. "An Illum kissed a Minor in front of the Elite. Do you understand what this could mean for the Minors? Surely this has never happened. Maybe more of us will get public Courtings. Maybe fewer of us will go to the Sanctuary!"

"I don't think it's that simple," I said.

"What do you mean?" Lo asked.

I told Lo about seeing Phillip and the Elite in the atrium and the hideous things the Elite had said. "And I met my other two birth brothers tonight. And saw my birth parents."

Lo's eyes went wide. "They're all up there? You're the only one down here?" Lo inquired, shock radiating from her. "Are you the only Defect in your line?"

I nodded, feeling myself unraveling. Defects didn't discuss birth parents or siblings. Technically we weren't permitted to discuss anything with one another and the need for self-preservation made the topic taboo.

Lo shook her head. "I haven't been able to figure out why you hated the program so much. Well, besides your eyes," Lo said nonchalantly. "It makes so much sense now."

The comment was like a physical blow. I smiled tightly at her, not trusting any words that might come out.

"Why were all the Elite on the ground?" Lo asked.

I blew out a breath. "The Elite have to enter the Capitol from the ground right now."

"Really? Like us?"

"Yeah, there was an issue at the Capitol," I told her.

Lo sat up straighter. "What kind of issue? Is that why you didn't hear from Collin for four days?"

"It is. Apparently, some group broke in, and six Elite were killed." I shuddered at the thought.

Lo's hands found her hair, mindlessly twisting it. "Did he tell you why?"

"The Starlings didn't say." I shook my head, my eyes catching on the scanner by the door. I was surprised to see it blinking yellow. A warning that curfew was approaching. I had scanned my MIND upon my return, but the automated voice never sounded. It had remained quiet. Lo followed my gaze.

"Shit, curfew is about to start. I can't afford to get into any trouble with tomorrow and all," Lo said, some of her usual confidence faltering. "You know, my yearly."

"Oh, Lo, I'm sorry. I completely forgot."

Lo went to the door. "It's okay. You have a lot going on now. It's not like before."

I slipped off my bed. "It's not like that. I just lost track of things."

"A Mate will do that," Lo responded, opening the door. "I'll see you on the ride after our shifts tomorrow. Meet in the atrium? I still want to hear all about the tea and that thing." She pointed to my open wardrobe, where the white gown hung next to the golden one—beautiful tokens from the clouds.

"I'll tell you everything tomorrow. Good luck at your yearly."

Lo smiled at me. "I have one more question."

"What is it?"

"Was it good?" Lo asked. "The kiss?"

"Oh." I suddenly felt too warm. "Yeah, it was."

Lo's grin spread. "Good. See you tomorrow."

The door clicked closed, and I walked toward the window and stared at the night sky. I had nothing to measure my first kiss by, but it *had* been good. His lips against mine. The way Collin had sucked in a breath seconds before his fingertips had pressed into my skin, pulling me in closer. I had gone willingly, eagerly. His lips pressing harder into mine. My hand finding his chest, a wild desperate beat akin to my own. The first sign something might dwell beneath his polished exterior. Then he had loosened his hold, pushing me away, ending the kiss.

Had Collin enjoyed it?

The Sphere had been an excited mess. Voices bounced around the space, blending into one another, making their words too muddled to hear.

"Don't look at them" had been the only words Collin had said to me. He led me to a Pod, seeing me inside in complete silence, features unreadable. Polished once more. As the doors closed, I swore I heard those two words again.

Forgive me.

My door barred shut, locking me in, and the lights turned off, plunging my living quarters into total darkness. Curfew had begun. I shifted my gaze, but the glow of the moon was missing. A new moon. A new Procreation Agreement. New Mates. I lifted my hand to my lips. The golden glow broke through the darkness that surrounded me. A new want.

Forgive me.

Why did he need my forgiveness?

"GOOD MORNING, EMELINE. I AM YOUR PERSONAL HOLOGRAM Instructor."

I shot out of bed, frantically searching for the source. A female form stood near my bed. A round black orb sat on the counter, projecting the woman into my room.

I had forgotten about the session Collin had mentioned. I massaged my chest, willing my heart to slow. The sky outside was still dark, dawn a ways off. I flipped my Comm Device over, groaning. Four-thirty in the morning. I went to rub the sleep from my eyes but stopped. I didn't want to jeopardize the lens that felt dry again.

"Please scan your MIND prior to the start of our lesson."

I made my way to the scanner, shoving my golden wrist under it. A small beep and a minute later, the HI began talking instead of the automated voice I was accustomed to. I attempted to follow the woman's words while my body urged my brain to function.

"Today is the second day of the tenth lunar cycle. It will be partly cloudy with a high of forty-five degrees. You are currently in a Procreation Agreement with M17292834. You are in the Courting Phase."

I stumbled to my sink for a glass of water as she continued her report. Our scanner never told us the date or the weather.

"According to your most recent scans, you are on day fourteen of your menstrual cycle." I spit my water into the sink. "I have adjusted your foods accordingly to provide the best nutrition for your ovulation phase."

I cringed. I knew being approved for a Procreation Contract meant the end of the supplements that discontinued my cycle. All Defect women's supplements contained something that stopped our cycles until we were Mated.

"According to your morning scan, your vitamin D levels are low." I rolled my eyes. So instead of an automated voice, I now had a projected person to illuminate all my inadequacies. I downed my water.

"This is most likely due to lack of sunlight. I have increased your vitamin D dosage."

That was different. The automated voice never gave reasons. If I needed sunshine, why was I kept underground all day? Wouldn't that ensure that Defects stayed . . . well, defective?

"Your progesterone levels are also inadequate for procreation. I have adjusted your supplements. Your MIND indicates you got six and a half hours of sleep. However, your heart rate and cortisol levels were elevated upon waking."

"Obviously," I muttered. A person had been in my room—or a projected person. Hologram. Whatever she was.

The use of holograms wasn't novel. My education had been solely conducted by holograms. No one dared waste human breath on the Defects' education. Except when Nestor, the Academy headmaster, spoke to us. I didn't know if you could call him human. He was always so still, almost lifeless. Perhaps being surrounded by holograms and offspring had sapped the life from him.

Even my work now was hologram based. I had never actually seen any of the art I cataloged, just realistic projections of the pieces. This hologram was different, though. She seemed more solid than the others, more lifelike. It was unsettling.

"High cortisol levels are counterproductive to your fertility. I shall play some relaxing sounds to bring your levels down before beginning our lesson. Your food shall arrive shortly. Please relax and enjoy."

The hologram stood with her arms folded behind her back as the sound of running water filled my living quarters. Did all Elites have personal HIs and need to deal with them every day?

I padded across my living quarters and pulled on my daily gray attire. A ding filled the dark room, indicating my meal was ready. I made my way over to the first of three black boxes built into the wall of my living quarters, one each for food delivery, trash, and laundry. They functioned like an elevator, bringing food up to me and dropping away my garbage, too small for me to fit in but big enough to take away my soiled sheets and trays of food.

I glanced over my shoulder to find the HI staring at me.

The usual plastic containers sat waiting inside the food delivery box, but my everyday indistinguishable mush had been replaced by a vibrant pink nutrient shake and a food that smelled sweet. The only familiar thing was the container of supplements, but even they looked different. Lastly, next to the containers was a steaming cup of hot tea.

"What is this?" I asked, withdrawing the tray.

"Your morning meal," my HI answered. I gripped the tray tightly as I turned toward her. "You will find all of your approved supplements." The hologram began describing my food, but I became lost in all the words I didn't know, such as grains, dragon fruit, banana, and chia seeds. Whatever those were. "Your tea is a green tea."

"Thank you," I said.

"There is no need to thank me, Emeline. I have been programmed to serve you. It has been noted that you enjoy chocolate. Please enjoy your nutrients." The hologram stood there with her hands crossed behind her back once again.

My stomach gave an annoyed grumble. I slowly took a sip of tea, and she watched me, unmoving. I waved my hand before her, and I swore she nodded at me.

I turned away, unnerved, glancing around my room, bare except for a bed, the counter with a sink, a door to my small bathroom, and a wardrobe, which I had left open, the shimmering dresses the only color in the room. I stood at the counter with a sink, next to the three black boxes. There were no comforts to be found.

I wished I had a table and chair. Usually, the mush wasn't enjoyable enough to warrant a seated meal, but this—it deserved a table, real plates, and cutlery, like in the clouds. I wanted a delicate teacup and pot. I wished . . .

I wished I wasn't in gray.

It was one thing to be afflicted by the unknown. Daydreams and fantasy only held so much power. Now, knowing, even just a glimpse of the luxuries in the sky—it was addictive. That was the issue. I had wants. Wants and desires I had buried deep within. Things I had been suffocating from my earliest memories.

I knew these wants were just the beginning. I was terrified. Terrified that if I continued to want—if I released what I had repressed—I would be the one who suffocated under the deluge of unmet desires.

What about the injustice of it—that those in the sky had access to such things while the rest of us didn't? Why were they permitted luxuries while the rest of us were denied basic human needs? Did they withhold it until we became desperate and compliant?

I shook away the thoughts vigorously. I wore gray. I was a Defect, contract or not. Today my food looked appetizing. I should be thankful.

Hovering over the counter, I began to eat, not bothering to swallow my moan. I had never had a breakfast like this. It was a symphony of flavors and textures. I almost missed when the hologram began.

"In Elite society, it is impolite to make noises while eating. Please watch this video on etiquette while you eat," the HI said before disappearing. A video projected onto my white walls.

As the sun rose, the greenish hue giving way to pastels, I listened to the rules of basic etiquette, from who sits first to correct seating arrangements, to which utensil to use, to curtsies and bows, and so on. I learned I should have been curtsying to Collin this entire time. I might have worried about my lack of etiquette, but the lesson kept putting my teeth on edge.

Your actions preserve the Elite way of life.

To be the example that all Defects can admire from afar.

Elite manners are the great distinguishing factor between a civilized mind and a defective one.

Anger welled deep within me at the demeaning reminder that

the Illum and the Elite saw us as less than. I tried not to let the video ruin the taste of my meal.

After I finished, the HI returned. "I hope your morning meal was satisfactory. For your Courting Phase: You have completed your initial meeting and first tea with your Elite Mate. Your Mate has submitted his observations regarding your ability to maintain composure among the Elite and your desirability for procreation. You are to await your Mate's next needs."

My stomach bottomed out. Collin had claimed he hadn't been testing me, yet he *had* been observing me. My skin crawled at the thought. *Why?* Why did the Illum make everything a game?

"Do you have any questions regarding your first lesson?"

"No, it was insightful," I mumbled, pushing aside the countless things I wanted to ask.

"I am happy to hear that. I will see you tomorrow. Fertile blessings, Emeline." She disappeared.

I placed my tray in the removal box before grabbing my Comm Device, a gray wool jacket and gray bag, and leaving my living quarters. Any peace I had ever found there had been eradicated in one morning.

The elevator was full when it reached the ground level. In the Pods queue, I looked for Lo's sunshine hair, but she wasn't there. She had probably left early to avoid the looks and whispers that accompanied the stops at the medical building where our yearly was performed. It might be the only time the women around you showed any sign that they understood—that they knew what they took from you in those sterile rooms.

The morning sun ricocheted off the departing Pods as droves of gray clambered on. I stared at the tall stone wall across the street hiding what lay within. Unease stole the sun's warmth at the large dented steel doors that never opened. In ten years I had never seen anyone go in or come out.

The Sanctuary—a place Minor Defect women and their offspring ended up if they could not maintain their composure or whatever the hologram had claimed Collin was assessing. Placed directly across the street from us, like the two Academy buildings: one an ever-present reminder of what was out of your reach, the other a looming threat of what was waiting should you fail. It was enough to leave us desperate and terrified.

A woman bumped into me, shuffling me along. I tore my eyes away as I scanned, scrambling to find a seat.

"Look," one of the other Defects uttered. "She's glowing."

A golden glow lit up the Pod. I hastily tugged on my gray sleeve. Several Defects shot wary glances my way. I stared out the window, but even the city's beauty didn't mute their whispers about why it was gold and what that meant.

Their fervent looks followed me off the Pod. I didn't stop for the sun's rays as I hurried across the pavement that led to the Capitol's entrance, my fingers curled tightly around the sleeve of my jacket, keeping it in place.

The doors opened as a low whistle ripped through the endless gray. I stopped at the base of the building, its unfathomable height looming over me. The whistle pierced the air again, and I turned to find a group of women in gray huddled close to a group of gray-clad men—some of the fraction of men who didn't qualify for work in the clouds, running maintenance on the ground instead. One of the men stared at me, his face hateful as he whistled loudly, sending others in gray scuttling off.

The whistling came to an end, and in its silence my mind ran rampant.

The important part, the dangerous part, is that people are rising up.

I ducked my head, running toward the safety of my office. How many people were actually upset with the Illum?

I shouldn't have been surprised to see Hal lounging in my chair. Only yesterday he had asked to come back, and I had agreed. With everything that had happened, it felt like forever ago.

"Morning, Moonlight," he said, propping his legs on my desk.

"What did you say?" I scanned my wrist and the screens came to life. I leaned against the wall, willing my heart to slow.

He laced his hands behind his head. "I called you Moonlight."

"Can I ask why?"

"Well, since I met you, I find myself watching the moon while I work." Hal shot me one of his smiles that made his dimple appear.

"What does watching the moon have to do with me?"

"The moon rules our time, does it not?"

"It does."

Hal raked a hand through his hair. "Since meeting you, you seem to rule mine."

"Why?" I asked, my cheeks heating.

He chuckled. "You can't just take the nickname? I just told you I think about you when you're not around, and you need an explanation?"

I opened my mouth to reply when Hal grabbed something off my desk, something dusted in gold, and popped it into his mouth.

He hummed appreciatively, his starburst eyes alight. "These are delicious."

I leaned over to see an entire box of gold-dusted chocolates. The same exact ones from last night. Another gift from Collin. Three were missing, as were my flowers. I shot a glare at Hal. "Where are my flowers?"

"Darnedest thing, they died. So I threw them out," Hal said, eating another chocolate.

"Give me that." I lunged for the chocolate as he went for a fifth, but he caught my wrist. "You are insufferable. Do you know that?"

"I have been told that a time or two, but I've also been called charming, handsome, unforgettable." He grinned broadly. I could smell the sweetness of the chocolate on his breath, my right wrist still in his grasp. "Here." He held the chocolate between us. I snatched it with my free hand, glaring at him. He smiled like he was enjoying himself and released my wrist.

Hal walked to the door, and I popped the chocolate into my mouth, the rich sweetness dancing across my tongue. He grabbed the empty metal trash can and brought it close to the desk, flipping it over, creating a makeshift stool for himself.

"Should we get started?" Hal asked. He looked comical, his hulking frame crouching on the small metal bin.

"There's no way that's comfortable," I commented, swiping another chocolate. "You can have the chair."

"No, it's fine," Hal said.

"Honestly, I don't mind. I'm smaller than you."

"I'm a Major Defect. I can handle some discomfort," he assured me, resting his elbows on his knees. I turned around to hide my smile, pulling my chair back to the desk. "But another chocolate would definitely make it more tolerable."

"Would it?" I retorted, pushing the box toward him, revealing a small note card that had been placed directly under the box as if on purpose. "Only one," I warned as I read the card. In meticulously neat handwriting it read, *To being impolite. Collin.* I slipped the note into my back pocket.

Hal stretched his legs out before resuming his crouched position. "Long night?"

"Not really."

"Did you have another meeting with this Collin guy?" Hal asked, his left leg bouncing a bit.

"I did."

"So you didn't mess it all up then?" Hal asked somewhat tightly. I glanced over at him to find him staring at me.

"I did not," I told him. "It had nothing to do with me. There was an issue."

Hal's eyes darkened as he leaned forward. "What kind of issue?"

"I don't know. Elite got hurt though," I said, logging in to the system and pulling up the first piece of art to catalog for the day.

His eyes churned, but he simply nodded, turning toward the hologram. "Do you see a lot of cubist art like this?"

It was of a woman, but there was no realistic aspect to her. It was made up of warm geometric shapes, distorting all humanlike elements of her, and yet the woman was beautiful. The sharp angular depiction created a fragmented image, an imperfect woman. She held a book in her hands. One half of the book was light, the other dark. I felt captivated by her, drawn to the juxtaposition of each side of her.

Cubist. Was that the term for it? How did Hal know the word?

"I have seen a few like it," I said, staring at the woman. "She's beautiful, isn't she?" Hal chuckled next to me. "What?"

"Nothing," Hal said, knocking my chair with his knee. I shot him a stern look. "It's just, you see her, fragmented and all, and you say she's beautiful. But you believe them when they tell you your eyes are a defect. Why is she beautiful, and yet the same doesn't apply to you?"

"She's a painting. It's different," I said, knocking back into him.

I returned to the screen, trying to sound out the words. It was in one of the many forgotten languages that had been lost after the Last War. Leaving us with just one.

"*Femme au Corset Tesant un Livre,*" Hal corrected.

I swung my chair to face him head-on, shock coursing through me. "How do you know that?"

He shrugged. "The Illum have their secrets. We have ours."

"We?" I asked. Hal simply gestured to his blue jumpsuit. "You're saying Major Defects know about things like this?" I demanded wildly, gesturing to the painting.

"Someone has to take out their trash," Hal said quietly, his left dimple making an appearance.

"I don't understand," I confessed.

I hated how much I meant that. There were so many things that I didn't know about the Illum, the Elite, and now the Major Defects. I had become so compliant in my monotonous existence. Everyone else held secrets, even Rose, Violet, Harold, and all the other Defects serving them up in their world. They knew things that I did not.

Hal's words from a week ago rang out in my mind. *They have made thousands of women just like you. Brainwashed and compliant to a cause you know nothing about. You're a plaything.* The room felt too small, the rage burning too hot.

"I would wager that's their goal." Hal's warm voice filled the space.

"What if I want to understand?" I asked. Would knowing rob me of life in the clouds? A temporary one, but a life all the same.

Hal leaned in, tugging my chair closer to him until I could see the amber bleeding into his light brown irises. "You'd have to come to the Underworld to find out, Moonlight."

"Underworld?"

Hal lowered his voice. "Can I trust you with a secret?" I nodded, leaning toward him. "Low Town is just for looks. We don't live there."

"Where do you live?" I asked breathlessly.

"Beneath." His gaze collided with mine. "We live in tunnels beneath the surface."

I bit my lip, my curiosity racing, my thoughts desperate. Desperate not to be silenced. I had signed a contract legally binding me to Collin, an agreement that was a matter of survival, even if my body felt otherwise. It didn't seem like I was at risk for elimination, but there was an expiration date on the contract, no matter how successful I was.

And when Collin had kissed me, for a moment I had forgotten a world existed on the surface at all.

Yet what if the thing I had been taught to fear—being phased out and condemned to a life in blue—wasn't what I had thought? What else did the Majors hide?

I couldn't help the next question. "How do you get here?"

"I could show you," Hal whispered. "You just have to ask."

My head felt too full. Collin had been nothing but kind and thoughtful. He was part of the Illum, though. I stared at the painting of the woman and her book.

"What are they doing with her?" Hal asked quietly.

I looked at my screen, my heart breaking. "They're destroying her." My voice was thicker than I intended.

I hovered over the *delete* button. Hal's leg bounced. "Of course they are. They destroy everything beautiful and different." His voice was laced with something that sounded like pain.

I turned my chair toward him again, unable to stop myself. A rogue curl fell across my face. Hal reached up at the same time I did, our hands colliding. Hal recoiled, his eyes on my wrist.

"So, the contract is official, then?"

I tugged my sleeve down, concealing the glow. "It became official yesterday afternoon."

"I guess congratulations are in order," Hal said. My heart picked up its pace at the coldness permeating his words. He slowly stood, setting the trash bin back in its usual place. "Or maybe condolences."

"Don't be cruel."

Hal laughed, but it didn't meet his eyes. "Forgive me, congratulations. Didn't realize that's the type of life you want up there, being his fertile vessel." He shook his head in disgust.

"You don't know him," I shot back. Maybe that was how most Defects were treated, but this was different. Collin treated me like more than a vessel. Didn't he?

Hal opened his mouth before closing it again. "He's an Illum. I don't have to know him to know exactly what he is. You're a vessel. An obligation."

"I am not merely a vessel. He's different."

Hal stepped back. "He's *different*?" he asked incredulously.

"Yes, I think he is."

Hal snorted. "Ask your dear Mate what they call him among the Elite. Have you ever bothered asking him what he does up in his clouds? What about when they send him to the surface?" Hal stepped toward me as my brows pulled in. "That's right, you can't. That'd require you to have rights up there. To be more than a *vessel*."

"What are you talking about? How do you know any of this?" I demanded.

"Like I told you, their horror stories slither all the way down to us."

"You're wrong," I snapped.

"Am I? He's hiding you. The only reason you're in the clouds is because he's got you hidden."

"I'm not hiding anything," I exclaimed, shoving my chair back. Anger coursed through my veins.

"You're wearing that stupid lens."

"You don't understand." A contract was how I survived. If I found joy in their beautiful places in the clouds while I continued surviving, that was mine alone to make amends for.

"Try me," Hal challenged.

"This is what I am supposed to do. This is my role. I can cover my defect if that's what's required of me. I want more than this."

"Right," Hal said, stepping back, his hands fisted tightly at his sides. "You want more than this. Just like all the others. I should have known."

My skin stretched too tight across my bones as I warped myself in an attempt to be understood—to be seen. Collin and the Elite were to judge me. I had always known that, but the judgment of the man in blue before me shredded me apart, leaving me fuming and wretched.

"Is it wrong to want more?" I asked, a note of desperation in my voice, filling the space he had just retreated from.

Hal raked his hands through his hair, sighing as he stared at the ceiling. "No. It's not."

"Then why are you acting like it is?" I demanded. I had never talked to another human so openly. I hated how it made me feel, the things it gave life to.

Hal blew out a long breath and shook his head. "This is clearly what you want. I should want this for you too."

"Hal—" My Comm Device dinged several times.

"Life above calls," he muttered, turning to leave.

"Wait, Hal—"

"Don't worry about it. I was the one who said you rule my time. You made no such claims." Hal knocked on the doorframe. "I'll see you around."

His eyes met mine one last time before he walked away. A lump in my throat choked me. I could chase him down, demand that he understand. This was the life for people like me.

I fell back into my chair, defeated. I had wanted to look at art with Hal. I looked up at the woman with her book and committed her beauty to memory before hitting *delete*. I felt her demise in my soul. I blinked rapidly at the death sentence I had signed, the destruction of something beautiful and different I agreed to.

My Comm Device dinged again. I grabbed it, finding two messages from Collin.

> Vincent and Helen reached out. We are dining at their living quarters tonight. Updating your MIND chip now. Sooner we get it out of the way the better. The Starlings will be expecting you. See you at 8:00.

My insides hollowed out. The second message read:

> Hope you enjoyed the chocolates.

CHAPTER TEN

"Good evening, Ms. Emeline," Harold greeted me stiffly from behind the stand a few hours later. He stared fixedly at the ground, his shoulders tight.

I extended my glowing wrist. "Is everything okay, Harold?"

"This way." He took off down the hall without answering me. I hurried after him, my anxiety hot on my tail in the impenetrable silence. Harold held the door for me.

"Is something wrong?" I asked, unease thick upon my skin.

"I told you, I don't want any trouble, Ms. Emeline." He looked pointedly over my shoulder as I stepped into the black room. "She'll be with you shortly." He turned and fled.

The door snapped shut. What did he mean just *she*? An answer came as a door creaked open and Rose entered the room. Her quicksilver gown was wrinkled, her hair slightly askew.

"This way, come," Rose instructed, leading me into the bathing chamber—her haughty, bossy demeanor missing. Tension bracketed her full mouth. "We must move swiftly."

"Where's Violet?" I asked, rooted to the spot.

"That's none of your concern," Rose bit out harshly, jaw trembling. "Now come. I will not pretend I am as efficient on my own."

Rose disappeared into the steaming room, leaving me with no choice but to follow her.

"Undress. There's the exfoliant." She gestured to the jar of the black gritty substance. Rose pushed the button igniting the showerheads to life, thickening the steam in the room. She leaned her head back against the tile wall as her shoulders shook.

I stripped and worked the gritty paste against my skin. I moved quickly, not nearly as thoroughly as Rose and Violet usually did. Violet was missing, and Harold had been distant, almost afraid. I rinsed hastily before making my way to the tub. Rose crouched down, groaning as she washed my hair, her breathing slightly labored.

"Are you hurt?" I asked, attempting to turn toward her. Her hands held my head in place. "Rose, what's happened?"

"Do not act as if you care," Rose seethed venomously as she shoved my head under the water. The unease grew with my anxiety, leaving me dizzy.

"Finished, let's go," Rose ordered. "There is no need to wax. You were here yesterday." Rose entered the cream room with the chair and vanity, and I hurried after her. "I do not have adequate time to change your nails," she said, thrusting a robe into my hands. I slipped it on, making my way to the chair.

"Rose—" I started, but the loud humming from the blower as she dried my hair drowned me out. In the mirror I watched silent tears run down Rose's face. When the humming stopped, she pulled my hair back in a low bun. "This is the best I can do." She shifted through the vials on the vanity, one of her hands gripping the edge, knuckles white. "Is your lens dry?" she asked, voice quivering.

"A little," I told her. "But—"

"Tilt your head back," Rose ordered, silencing me again. I did as much as possible without hitting the bun. The soothing effect was instant. "Did that help, or do you need a new lens?"

"It helped."

"Good. Now sit still while I paint your face."

"Where is Violet, Rose?" I asked again.

"She is unwell," Rose responded, her tone flat.

"We don't get unwell," I answered. Our MIND had eradicated all illness and disease generations ago.

"She is unwell, Fledgling."

"I don't—"

"I guess I shouldn't call you that anymore," she stated. "You learned to fly quite quickly. Didn't you?" She shot me a seething look before storming from the room.

It is on you if this gets back to us. Wasn't that what Rose had told Violet yesterday? Fear found me, brutal and all-encompassing. I had naïvely asked Collin, a member of the Illum, about the uprising. I had thought the playful glint in his eyes and kindness were real.

I found her in the final room, hunched over a large black box like the one my lens came in. A cackle ripped from Rose as she turned toward me. My questions died on my tongue.

"There are always those willing to clip your wings." She lifted from the box a long silk gown. Deep blue silk. Major Defect blue.

"What is that?" I asked. Panic sent my pulse hammering against my skin.

"Your dress for tonight. Your number is on the box. Another gift from the Illum, perhaps? Did you fail one of their trials?" She held the gown as if it might poison her. "Horrible things happen to those who can't conform. Did you fly too high?" She didn't bother to hide her ruthless smirk.

Your Mate has submitted his observations regarding your ability to maintain composure among the Elite and your desirability for procreation. Had I failed to maintain my composure? Had I asked too many questions? Collin had assured me he had no time for a trial. If that was true, why did the Illum send me this?

I stepped into the dress. If the gown was any other color, it would be stunning. It was sleeveless, with no slits in the skirt, just a waterfall of deep blue silk, held together by a delicate gold collar that encircled my neck snugly. A thin chain snaked down my bare back, connecting to the silk just above the base of my spine. Delicate chains branched from the main strip, creating a cage of cold metal that brushed against my skin with every breath.

"Give me a moment." Rose rushed off, returning a moment later with several brushes and jars. She attacked my face before stepping back, appraising me.

My eyes locked on the woman in the mirror. Rose had exaggerated my eye makeup. There were vicious winged black tips with deep blue dusted on my eyelids. My lips were a simple nude. Under different circumstances, I would have felt dazzling, possibly even powerful.

The metal collar bit into my neck, suffocating me.

Was this my punishment for discussing what was wrong at the Capitol? For breathing a word about the rebellion to a member of the Illum? Hal had been right: I didn't know the first thing about my Mate.

"D-did you make this?" I stammered, dread blazing in my chest.

"I have no desire to sign my own elimination," Rose scoffed.

"Then why am I wearing it? I'm a—" I tugged at the too-tight collar. "I'm an Illum's Mate."

Her eyes widened mockingly. "Do you think that makes you special?"

"That's not what I said."

"I'll share a secret," she said as if I hadn't spoken. "It doesn't. Mates send their playthings little gifts. It isn't my job to question the Illum. I simply play my role."

"Did Collin send this?" I asked.

"I do not know. It only had your identification number," Rose told me, walking away.

Collin had stood up to my birth family, defended me. He had treated me as though my voice mattered. He had *kissed* me. That meant something. Right?

I couldn't imagine the version of him I had seen doing anything like this. And yet, had he known this blue dress trial was coming? Was that why he needed my forgiveness?

"Here." Rose returned with simple gold slip-on heels and an envelope chain-mail clutch that matched the collar. I slipped on the heels, holding the clutch close to me. Rose came up behind me and pulled my shoulders back.

"Remember, you're dining with the Elite. Act like it. Because whoever sent you this dress is praying you fail. I have to say I might be on their side." She pushed me toward the exit, slamming the door behind me.

Clearly, something horrible had happened to Violet and Rose. What had I done?

The question chased me into the Pod and farther into the sky, where storm clouds gathered, thunder rumbling in their dark depths. My collar felt too tight, anxiety constricting my ability to breath. I wondered if I might pass out.

My Comm Device dinged inside my clutch. I pulled it out, reading the message. Then I read it again—the message that spelled my undoing.

A work requirement came up and it's running late. I can't make it.
Forgive me. Collin

CHAPTER ELEVEN

This couldn't be happening. I sucked in deep, desperate breaths as the Pod slowed to a stop, trapping me. I had no way out of this. I couldn't face them without Collin at my side. Vincent's unwavering support of the Illum would keep his viciousness in check if Collin were present. I felt more comfortable jumping from the Pod than entering their living quarters without him.

The blue silk wrinkled in my fist. I had been a fool—a brainwashed, naïve fool—to have trusted an Illum for even one moment.

The doors to the Pod opened, and my heart plunged to the ground below, smashing on the earth's surface. I was entering my birth home at the top of one of the tallest towers dressed in Major Defect blue.

It belongs with the Majors, with those like it. Mark my words, she will end up there. When my heels clicked against luxurious tile, my birth father's words escorted me instead of a Mate.

"Good evening, Ms. Emeline," a male Defect said, bowing. "May I scan your wrist for dinner? Then I shall escort you."

I extended my wrist, and he took in the deep blue dress. Quickly, he stepped away from me. A knot formed in my throat as I followed him through my birth family's living quarters.

Floor-to-ceiling windows covered the entire wall, and the rest of the room was adorned with varying white and cream furniture, an ode to the fluffy clouds, swollen with the oncoming storm, that drifted by the expansive windows. Light danced upon the white marble tiles from the largest chandelier I had ever seen, a swirling brass structure embellished with hundreds of delicate white ceramic petals. A black fountain rested below the petals, as if waiting to catch any that fell. Trickling water fell from the edges, filling the space with a soothing sound. It looked more like a sculpture than a chandelier—alive, free, and so at odds with those who lived here. I wondered why my birth father allowed it.

The place should have felt familiar. I had lived here once. Yet I recognized nothing except the shame and loneliness that had been my only companions.

My pulse quickened as male voices drifted from the room the attendant disappeared into. I swallowed around the lump lodged beneath my metal collar and followed.

The room was darker, and for once the beauty was lost on me as three members of my birth family waited for me.

Richard, the oldest birth brother, sat on the sofa. My middle brother, Gregory, lounged in a chair, swirling a drink. And an impressive and immovable man stood in front of a marble mantel, staring at a glowing-hot rod in the hearth.

"Mr. Vincent, Ms. Emeline has arrived," the attendant stated.

"And Mr. Collin?" my birth father drawled, not even acknowledging me.

"He has yet to arrive." The man bowed. "I shall fetch Ms. Emeline a drink."

"There's no need, not until Mr. Collin arrives," Vincent ordered as a way of dismissal, looking away from me to converse with Richard, who was almost his spitting image, except, like me, he had our birth mother's deep brown hair. But his eyes were the same shade of deep brown as Vincent's. More than that, he carried himself the same haughty way.

With my lens, I would assume we looked remarkably alike.

Maybe that was why he couldn't look at me. My heart quaked at the dismissal.

How bizarre it felt to share blood and features and yet be a complete stranger. To be hated in a way only strangers could.

"Do tell me, is this color in rebellion to your mating, or are you just partial to the color of trash?" Gregory taunted lazily. He was my mother's spitting image, from the crystal blue eyes to the immaculate bone structure. He was handsome, almost beautiful. His hair color was the only link to our birth father—lighter than mine—and shaved brutally short. His full mouth smirked at me, his legs propped over the arm of the chair, his shirt unbuttoned at the top.

"I didn't choose the dress," I said quietly.

"Your Mate must have more of a sense of humor than I gave him credit for," Gregory drawled, and his smile grew as he slyly glanced at Vincent, who watched me with satisfaction gleaming in his hateful eyes. "Did you know . . ." Gregory continued, swinging his feet off the arm of the chair and coming to stand, approaching me like he was cornering prey. Despite being ten years older than I was, he was tall and lean, a boyish charm about him. ". . . that I didn't believe them when they told me the girl in the sheer white dress was my birth sister? That I had a sister?" He cocked his head to the side. The confirmation that he hadn't known of my existence jarred me. My birth brothers had already been sent to the Elite Academy by the time I was born.

Shock radiated through me as he pulled my hand up to his mouth, quickly pecking it. He was greeting me, even in blue. He smirked as he held my hand tighter, pulling me closer. "Tell me, dear sister. What horrors are you hiding beneath?"

I recoiled, my hand still in his grasp. He didn't know about my eyes. He greeted me to taunt me. An emptiness settled deep, deep in my chest.

"Gregory," Vincent thundered, "do not entertain her."

Gregory let go of my hand, glancing over his shoulder at our birth father. He shot me a quick wink before retrieving his drink and downing it in one gulp.

"How much longer are we to wait for Collin?" Vincent inquired impatiently.

They did not know. My pulse turned unruly. I was going to have to tell them he wasn't coming. Instead of an Illum, they got me. A Minor in blue. The daughter they hadn't bothered to know or even discuss.

I hesitated, catching my lip between my teeth. Richard watched me as Gregory's light blue eyes caught mine. He smiled like he was about to receive a treat.

"My Mate had something come up. He can't join us."

There was a terrible pause. Vincent glared at me before walking from the room without a word. Richard followed, muttering under his breath. A click made me jump as Gregory opened a hidden cabinet and refilled his glass, draining it in one go before refilling it. He walked over to me, shoving the glass into my hand.

"Best to drink it quickly," Gregory suggested, and I hesitated. "Trust me, you'll need it. The only way to get through these family dinners is a stiff drink."

I lifted the glass to my lips. The contents had a strong aroma that was smoky and slightly off-putting. Gregory tipped it back for me, leaving me no choice but to drink it all. I lowered the glass, sputtering, my insides on fire.

"What *is* that?" I rasped, massaging my metal-clad throat.

"Does it matter?" Gregory mocked, replenishing the glass again. "It's a wonderful thing called alcohol. It befuddles the mind."

"Gregory," a clipped voice reprimanded. "What are you doing?" My youngest brother, Phillip, stood in the doorway, glowering.

Gregory shrugged in false innocence and fell back into his chair. "Baby brother, how splendid of you to join us. Do tell us how things fare at the Capitol. Have you kissed enough asses to be an Illum yet? Sold your soul?"

Phillip ignored him. He was only slightly taller than I was. He was an odd combination of our birth parents; he had curls like mine, but they were light like our birth father's. He had our birth mother's face, making him classically beautiful like Gregory. His crystal blue eyes assessed me, but not in the poisonous way that Richard's had. He looked at me like you would a puzzle, evaluating the pieces. He shook his curls out of his face and grasped my hand quickly before releasing it.

"Collin sends his regards. Things are busy right now," Phillip told me tightly.

"You work with him, right?" I asked. I had nearly forgotten in the chaos of the last few days.

"I—" Phillip began, but Gregory cut him off.

"He does. Phillip, our little pride and joy, trying to be just like his dear friend Collin. Rejecting mating contracts, leaving all the mothers distraught, all to sell himself to the Illum like a pet."

"You're always such a pleasure after a couple of drinks, Gregory," Phillip commented dryly.

Gregory stood, stretching before strutting to the exit. "Someone has to keep it interesting around here. However, I assume our little sister is about to make things *very* interesting."

He left, and I stood awkwardly, a death grip on my clutch. My hands ached; I was sure the metal would cut into my palms if I continued to hold it so tightly. I felt flushed, and my body tingled, throat still raw from the burn of the alcohol.

"The Starlings dressed you?" Phillip asked as he looked at my gown, his brow furrowed. He didn't cringe from the blue color. Maybe being so close to the Illum gave him some protection from such things. Instead, he stared at the gown like he did me, like it was a problem only he could solve.

"Yes," I said uncomfortably, smoothing the front of the gown. "It was addressed to me. Did Collin—"

Gregory popped his head back in, cutting me off. "Mother's coming."

Phillip pinched the bridge of his nose. "Let's go." He led the way into the next room. "The gown will have to wait. Thankfully, it is only family tonight. The insult is minimal. We'll just need to make sure the Press doesn't get wind of this."

I couldn't breathe around the word *family*—and how easily he said it. My mind raced by their evident familiarity with one another, the intimacy. *Mother, brother, sister.* These were familial terms, ancient terms that I thought had died out.

Everything in the Defects' education used words like *birth father, birth mother,* and *birth sibling*—acknowledging a tie, but it was formal and detached. They meant nothing to the Defect community. The clicks of my heels reverberated through me as I walked in to meet a family, *my* family.

A family I did not know.

The dining room was as exquisite as the others, but I couldn't focus on anything other than the five people in the room and the dark clouds outside that swirled as viciously as my thoughts.

Vincent stood at the head of the large table, which was big enough for twenty. The seat to his right sat empty. Next to it, Richard, then Gregory. On Vincent's left was Helen, followed by Phillip. Next to Phillip was another open place setting, most likely my intended seat. They all stood waiting for me.

In no world would I ever be next to my birth father. Guests of honor sat next to the host, my HI had informed me this morning. I would never be that important, not to him. I could just remain quiet at the end.

I looked at the end seat. Gregory sucked his tooth, looking at me like he would allow no such thing. It was odd that Gregory sat so far from my birth father when he was second born.

Helen's tinkling voice rang out. "Emeline, since Collin cannot make it, come sit across from me,"

"It is fine. I can sit here," I said.

"Honestly, no manners." Richard sneered at me. "Do Defects often insult their hosts?"

Helen gasped loudly, not at Richard's words but at me. She stood in her rich burgundy bell-sleeved dress, staring at me. "Your gown. Why are you in that color?"

"I was told to wear it."

"Have we insulted the Illum? Is Collin angry with this match?" Helen demanded of Phillip next to her.

A laugh escaped Gregory that he instantly contorted into a cough. Vincent gripped the back of his chair almost as fiercely as I held my clutch.

Phillip simply shrugged. "The Illum do not explain themselves. We should take this and be cognizant of our actions and any that might have offended them." His eyes swept the table before landing on Gregory, who nodded somberly.

"Helen, this insult is to her alone. She should get used to the color," Vincent drawled, pulling out his chair. "It will be permanent when she messes up."

When, not *if*, like my fate was a foregone conclusion.

"I believe you meant *if*," Gregory contradicted.

"No. I spoke correctly," Vincent said coldly.

Everyone stood waiting, watching me.

"By all means, take the entire moon to sit, sister. We all enjoy being made to wait," Gregory said dryly.

"Apologies," I muttered quietly, making my way around the table to the chair on Vincent's right.

"You shall learn," Helen encouraged, her elegant eyes on the blue once more.

I swallowed tightly, instantly wishing for another mind-befuddling drink. I waited until the others were fully seated before pulling my own out. A hidden door opened before I fully sat, and several dark-gray-clad Defects waltzed in, setting down beautiful plates laden with delicious smells and enticing displays of food. My stomach growled at the rich aroma. Everyone's plate was different, each clearly tailored to our nutritional needs.

Phillip flipped out his napkin and placed it in his lap. I glanced down at mine, still on the table. I hastily swiped it, putting it in my lap as I heard Gregory say to one of the gray-clad men, "The good stuff," before starting on his food.

Richard cleared his throat. "I wanted to let you all know Poppy is with offspring again."

"A male?" Vincent asked, cutting his food.

I took a bite, hiding any indication that I enjoyed it. I glanced up to find Gregory watching me from behind his cup as if he knew.

"It is still too new," Richard informed us.

"Regardless, what wonderful news," Helen exclaimed as a worker filled the glasses with a deep-red liquid. "Four offspring, what fertile blessings."

"Oh, yes, how smashing," Gregory added snidely. "Have you not tired of her, though?"

"Poppy and I have had great success together. She is of strong genes. We have three Elite offspring. So no, I have not."

"Let us hope your fourth is of better stock than that." Vincent jabbed his fork in my direction. "I should have switched Mates after three."

My birth mother took a long drink as silence fell. Gregory's mouth became a hard line. I stared at my plate, unseeing. Phillip recovered first.

"What of your new match, Gregory?" Phillip retorted, taking a small sip of the red liquid.

Gregory drained his glass. "I assume I have you to thank for my Defect mating, little brother."

"Well, when you opt out of another offspring contract with an Elite member, you have fewer options," Phillip responded.

"I wish you and Katherine had agreed to another Offspring Agreement," Helen expressed quietly. "Why did you end it with her?"

"Because Katherine was a bore," Gregory responded, "and, quite frankly, the sex was terrible, Mother."

I choked on my food, grabbed the glass of red liquid, and took a sip. It was rich and heady and didn't burn like the drink Gregory gave me. Warmth pooled in my stomach. I took another deep drink, washing down my shock.

"Enough, Gregory," Vincent snapped.

"Apologies, Father," Gregory retorted, mockingly bowing his head. "Forgot virgin ears."

"Phillip," Helen exclaimed, trying to redirect the conversation. "Have you heard anything about an impending Mate for yourself?"

Phillip looked up from his food. "I have. Given my success in the eyes of the Illum, they will wait. My contributions are more important."

"The Illum still view you as a success?" Vincent asked as I sipped my drink again. Phillip nodded, weathering whatever Vincent carried in his eyes.

Gregory opened his mouth, but Helen cut him off.

"Emeline, your match. How has it gone? How is Collin?" Helen asked, placing her silverware down. I followed her lead, even though I wanted another bite.

"Collin is very kind," I said woodenly. I didn't know what to believe about him anymore.

"Are we discussing the same Collin?" Gregory asked, shaking his empty glass at a Defect. Richard shook his head.

"Collin is a wonderful member of the Illum," Helen chimed.

"He didn't become the youngest member of the Illum by being wonderful and kind," Gregory scoffed, sipping his newly filled glass. I grabbed mine just for something to do with my hands. "Did he, little brother?"

"You have had enough," Vincent thundered, then snapped at a worker. "Take her wine away. Bring her water."

My cheeks heated as the man took my glass. A moment later, our plates were cleared. "If you were serious about this match, you would ensure you were a suitable vessel," Vincent scolded.

A cup of water was placed before me as I blinked rapidly. "Thank you," I told the Defect, my equal.

A ringing silence followed my words as he disappeared.

"What did you say to that Defect?" Vincent demanded.

Dread filled me at my mistake. "I said thank you," I mumbled, my voice small.

"They do not need your thanks. They owe us thanks for the ability to be graced by our presence. Do you find yourself unwilling to outgrow your status? Do you still see yourself as one of them? If you do, you're smarter than I thought."

His words hollowed me out completely. *Why?* I wanted to scream at him. *Why do you hate me?* Was I nothing but my defect? The metal collar became a noose as I contemplated demanding an answer.

Workers came out of the hidden door, bringing more food. I didn't look at my plate, even as pleasant aromas drifted toward me. I heard the noise of cutlery being used. I swallowed, trying to alleviate the tightness in my throat.

"Did you know," Vincent drawled, when I finally reached for my fork, "that the Defects should be thanking the Elite for their ability to breathe?"

Lightning flashed in the tops of the clouds outside, and a rumbling boom of thunder shook the place ever so slightly. I met his stare for the first time that evening as apprehension settled in my gut. His meal sat untouched.

"There was a petition to fully eliminate every Defect, both Minor and Major. The Elimination Act," he said casually, taking a sip of his drink.

"Eliminate?" I asked. The energy around the table shifted. Even Gregory remained quiet.

"Yes, eliminate them completely. They have no use for our goal of repopulating this world. We would be better off without them. They are leeches." His brown eyes found mine, conveying what he hadn't said: The world would be better off without me.

"Who would clean our cities and dispose of our waste if they were eliminated?" Richard commented.

"They do have their purposes, I suppose, among the trash," Vincent said, downing his drink.

"We need them for more than trash. Without their genes our procreation pool would bottleneck, resulting in inbreeding," Phillip stated. "Inbreeding results in weaker genes."

My first course turned leaden in my stomach, crawling up my throat. I shared blood with these people. I had hoped that, meeting my birth family, I might feel less alone, but I didn't. They were calmly discussing murdering people, eliminating people for something those people had no control over, and the only reason they didn't was to avoid *inbreeding*. I thought I might be sick.

Gregory shook his once-again empty glass, tension lining his face.

"Emeline, with this contract with Collin, it wouldn't pertain to you," Phillip told me, cutting into his food. "In the eyes of the system, you wouldn't be eligible for elimination."

They all resumed eating in silence. I just stared at my plate of food, provided to plump me up, priming me for breeding another one of *them*.

That was my life's purpose: to break myself apart within the cage they created for the Minor women. A meek, compliant woman. Either produce an Elite offspring and be thrust into the next mating contract, or produce someone like me and be cast aside. My heart slammed against my chest, raging.

"Murdered," I said, not looking up from my plate.

"Emeline," Helen said delicately—a warning.

"They are *people*. Living, breathing people. It is not just elimination. It is murder." I trembled, my heart refusing to slow. The room felt too small as twenty-seven years of anger clawed to the surface, desperate for release—a rage I had hidden my entire life. My skin was too tight, my chest too warm.

"We could always reinstate the Core Act," one of my brothers suggested, but I couldn't focus, the blood pounding painfully in my ears.

"Would you have me eliminated?" I demanded, my voice a whisper.

"What did you say?" Vincent asked.

"*Emeline.*" Helen's blue eyes were wide and scared. Her warning fueled my anger. She had only ever *warned* me. She had never come for me. She had never comforted me. She had just stood outside my door arguing with my birth father on the other side. Warning me the day they took me away.

Never look at the Elite, Emeline. Just look down and they will leave you be. You must look down.

But now I was looking directly at the Elite, and I couldn't stomach what I saw. I could never be like her. I couldn't follow their rules. I couldn't ignore the things they hid behind their beauty. And I knew—as they did—that I couldn't be Elite. No matter the dresses. The lessons. The lens. I wasn't one of them.

I wouldn't look down.

If that condemned me to the blue color I wore . . . maybe—maybe that wasn't the worst thing.

"What did you say, Minor?" Vincent's tone was dangerously mild.

"Would you have me eliminated?"

My birth father's eyes locked with mine. He stared into them like he could see right past the lens, his hatred for my defect obvious. His hatred for me.

"There is nothing I wouldn't do for the Greater Good, for our people. Collin can cover you up, make you his little plaything, but you'll never be one of us. You were a disgrace to this family the moment you opened those hideous eyes. All of my hard work damned. You ruined centuries of success. Both our lineages were perfect, generations of Elite. Until you."

I broke. My chair scraped loudly across the floor as I thrust back from the table, shifting it under my force, and the sound of breaking glass filled the room.

I did not care about the scene I was making, the mess. The red liquid seeping across the white tablecloth. A reflection of the brokenness in me. None of it mattered as I held that hateful man's stare.

"Easier to eliminate a mistake than admit you carry any responsibility for it. It's *your* genes that created this," I snarled.

His eyes widened. I didn't bother to wait for a reply as I sent my chair clattering to the ground. I grabbed my clutch, my grip painful. My frantic heart urged me forward.

"I knew I'd like you," Gregory cooed. He placed his glass in my free hand. I didn't need help throwing it back. I downed it, letting the burning sensation replace the ache in my throat.

"Emeline," Helen started, but I was already at the door.

"Do you finally see what I mean? They are defective to their core, uncivilized." Vincent drawled.

"Who made us uncivilized?" I practically growled.

"And you wanted to save her, Helen," Vincent taunted. I spun, facing them, as his words pierced my chest.

Helen sat utterly still, her eyes on her plate. Meek and compliant like they wanted me to be. "I was wrong, Vincent."

She *had* wanted to save me. No longer, clearly. I was shaking as I stormed from the room. My heart outpaced my steps as my pulse hammered against my clammy skin.

"A Pod, please, now," I demanded tersely to one of the fellow Defects. The Elite—they weren't what I thought. All the beauty they surrounded themselves with was a façade to hide the wickedness within.

And you wanted to save her, Helen.

I didn't hear what the worker said as I kicked off my heels, shedding anything I could that made me like them, and ran into the Pod. The door shut as I scanned my wrist, and I was racing through the stormy clouds as fast as my mind spiraled.

I couldn't get air in. The chain collar was too tight. I clawed at it as my heart beat faster and faster. I needed air. The back of my throat ached with the urge to scream.

The walls of the Pod pressed in, weighing me down. I couldn't breathe. I searched the Pod desperately. There was an emergency button somewhere. They had shown us at the end of our education.

Think, Emeline, think.

My pleas were in time with my heart's hysterical pace. I sucked in a breath but choked on the knot in my throat. The Pod was closing in on me. I clawed at the Pod, running my hands along the doors. I didn't care how high I was. Where was it? A cold sweat coated my skin, making the fabric cling.

Let me out. Let me out.

Finally, I found it, a small button directly below the scanner. I pressed it blindly—desperately. My heart beat wildly against my ribs in desperation to get out. I tried to breathe again. I couldn't.

The Pod plummeted to the ground. Rain streaked the windows. I didn't care that it sent me flying back into the seat. I didn't care that my head hit the glass. I needed out.

Moments later, the Pod slowed to a stop, hovering just above the ground as the doors opened. I threw myself out the door, taking greedy gulps of air.

The Elite's towering buildings surrounded me as their clouds pelted me with raindrops, the soft patter cooling my too-hot skin. I was still in High Town. Thankfully, the street was near-empty, most workers having returned to their living quarters before the oncoming curfew. I whirled, finding where the buildings grew squat and dull—made from bricks. The Wastelands. It was a ways off.

I clawed at the collar, the gold cutting into my skin. I swore it was leaving a brand just as my birth father's words had. Thunder clapped in the distance. Years of wanting a way out of the Wastelands—now it was all I saw.

I gathered my skirt in my hands. Barefoot, I began to run.

I swore I heard my name, but I didn't look back. My feet slammed into the pavement, putting distance between me and the people who had birthed me.

My heart beat harder, but in encouragement now. I took deep gulps of air. With each step, my mind cleared. I could breathe. My raging mind went silent. I tore through the city in blue as rain pelted me, but I welcomed it, willing it to wash it all away.

The buildings slowly grew shorter, closer to the earth, less ornate. I wasn't far from my building now. I'd have to stop soon. The wounds slowly reopened as my building came into view.

My mind begged me to run more, but my body couldn't. I was too out of shape. I began to slow, the forty-eight windows and bricks just ahead on the right. I gasped for breath, my lungs ravaged, but my heart refused to settle. Little stars popped into my vision. I hadn't run in over a year.

They had taken that from me too.

"Emeline?" I heard a deep voice say behind me.

Collin had come. My legs trembled, threatening to give way. I needed to sit for a minute, just inside. I could make it inside. My soaking gown slipped from my grasp, and strong arms grabbed me, keeping me upright. I leaned my head back into a hard chest, looking for sapphire eyes, only to find starburst ones instead.

"It's okay. I've got you, Moonlight."

CHAPTER TWELVE

Hal brought one arm under my knees and the other around my shoulders, lifting me off the ground and pulling me in close. I felt the world shake, or perhaps I was shaking. He held me tightly, making small, calming noises while he rubbed his thumb in reassuring circles on my arm. The collar was too tight.

"I want it off," I begged, my chest aching. "I need it off."

"Okay, we'll get it off," he reassured me. A buzzing sound filled my ears, drowning everything out. "I need help," Hal stated, readjusting me in his arms. "Give me your wrist."

I dropped my glowing wrist as he shifted until I heard the beep and the familiar click of the glass door. "We're in," Hal said quietly. I shivered viciously, my wet gown chilling me to the bone even as we entered the empty lobby of my building.

"Give me your wrist again," Hal's warm voice coaxed. I felt the elevator lurch upward. Hal tucked me in closer against his chest. "Almost to the floor." A heaviness settled over me, the thundering in my ears too loud as I began clawing at the collar again. "Which room?"

"On the right," I croaked, my throat dry. I clutched the metal, my breathing still too shallow, too fast.

"Almost inside. Give me your wrist one more time," Hal whispered. "And we'll get this off of you." I dropped my wrist again.

"That's it," Hal encouraged before opening my door and stepping into my living quarters.

I heard the door shut.

"We're in," Hal reassured me, but his arms remained wrapped around me as he leaned against the door—pulling me in closer still. Our bodies melded. I rested my head against his chest, listening to his steady heartbeat. The firm beats caressed my nerves. I didn't know how long we stayed there, how long he held me, giving me space and time to come back until my panic finally released me. My breaths became deeper, longer, until the shaking turned into a mere shiver from the wet silk. Still, Hal held me quietly.

"I—" My voice cracked. I cleared my throat. "I can stand now."

"Okay," Hal said, slowly lowering me to the ground.

My feet ached as they met the floor. My legs wobbled under my weight. Hal kept his hands on my sides. Something poked me. In his right hand, the one that had been under my legs, he held my clutch.

I glanced up at him, taking him in. He was soaked; his jumpsuit was tied around his waist like he had become too hot while he ran. His blue undershirt was also drenched, revealing his muscular chest and torso.

My throat ached in an entirely different way. "You followed me all the way here?"

"It's not every day you see a woman in a blue gown run through High Town. I wanted to make sure you were okay." Our eyes met. I didn't look away. Hal cleared his throat. "Do you still need the dress off?"

I nodded, my hand flying to my metal collar. I heard the bag thump on the bed before he approached me. A foreign panic found me. I had never been alone in my living quarters with a man.

"I need you to move your hair," Hal instructed quietly, his breath warm on my neck.

I lifted my hands to my wet hair, untangling it from the low bun. "What were you doing in High Town?"

Hal hesitated for a moment. "I was walking to work. I wanted fresh air and to see the moon's light. The ground is usually empty at that hour, but then I saw you. That was an impressive run."

"I used to love to run," I told him, my hair finally free. I pulled it over my shoulder.

"Used to?" Hal asked, his strong hand brushing a stray hair away. His calluses scraped lightly against my skin. A shudder ran through me that had nothing to do with the wet gown. His hands began to work on the clasp.

"MIND said it made me less fertile," I said quietly. "Fertile vessel, remember?" I felt the collar give way. A sigh escaped my lips. Hal's hands stilled at the sound.

"Do you have the dress?" Hal asked. I nodded, and he released the gown. I heard him step away. My skin was instantly cold where his hands had been. "I'm going to turn around."

I let the gown fall to a puddle at my feet, the metal clinking against the wooden floorboards. I stepped out of it before grabbing from my wardrobe the gray shirt and shorts I usually slept in.

"Moonlight," Hal said, still facing my door.

His usual taunting demeanor was gone. His voice sounded tentative, almost shy. I halted everything at the sound. "Yes."

"This might be an insult, but . . ." He hesitated and shifted from one foot to the other, clearing his throat. "The color looked beautiful on you."

I clutched my gray shirt to my chest, where my heart ached. I stared at the wide breadth of his shoulders, tapering to a trim waist, and the muscled cords of his back, clear through the wet undershirt, the shade of blue identical to my gown. I couldn't process what that sameness did to me. I didn't want to.

"I'm going to shower." I needed to step away. I was too raw, exposed. I needed distance to piece myself back together.

"Right, I'll leave," Hal said, reaching for the door handle. I nodded, letting him go when the resounding *thunk* of the lock resonated, and the room plunged into darkness. The only light radiated from my golden wrist.

"Don't," I exclaimed, stretching out my arm, illuminating the room. "You can't leave."

Hal's entire body went rigid. "I need to go."

"You can't," I told him, quickly slipping on the gray shirt and shorts. "It's curfew. My door is locked and the door to the entrance won't let anyone in or out unless their MIND chip is authorized."

Hal raked his hands through his wet hair. "Are you dressed?"

"Yes."

"Good." Hal darted to my window, peering down before moving to the next window. He navigated the near dark easily.

"You aren't seriously thinking about going out the window, are you?" I asked, trailing him to the window near the bed. My eyes slowly adjusted to the dark.

"I can't stay here. You're in a contract."

"That's exactly why you have to stay, Hal. If you set off the door, I could be eliminated," I hissed at him, although it was possible I might be eliminated after my performance tonight if my family reported to the Illum how badly I had stepped out of line. Then finally Vincent might be happy.

Hal whirled around, coming face-to-face with me. "And how do you think," Hal shook his head, sending water droplets flying, "your Mate will feel about another man, a Major Defect, being in your room overnight?"

"I am hoping I never have to tell him," I confessed. "Look, I shouldn't have let you carry me up. I shouldn't have . . ." I paused, searching for the right words.

"Shouldn't have what?" Hal asked me, looking down at me. "Shouldn't have been human? Should have been able to withstand whatever they threw at you?"

"You don't know what happened tonight," I said, flustered.

"It doesn't take a genius to put it together. You were dressed in blue in High Town. I watched that Pod drop from the damn clouds."

I squeezed my eyes shut, hating how easily he read what I'd endured. Because the details didn't matter, did they? Someone had made my contract a mockery. Tears gathered beneath my lids, but I refused to fall apart. Hal stepped toward me.

I looked up at him. We were too close. Too close. I took a step back. "I'm in enough trouble as it is. I need you to stay," I admitted.

"Need me to?" he asked, and I could just make out a smirk in the dark.

"That's not what I meant." I fumbled over my words, my cheeks warm. "I meant you can't go. You are stuck here."

"So I am stuck here—with you all night—in cold, wet clothes." Each word set my heart careening. I gulped, and my eyes darted immediately to the bed.

Hal smirked at me. "I'll sleep on the floor. You still going to shower?"

The sweat and rain had crusted to my skin, and I nodded. I took a step but stopped. All of Hal's concerns were directed toward me. He hadn't mentioned himself once, not his work or what the run had done to him. "Will you get in trouble? For missing your shift?"

Hal moved in the dark. "Let me worry about that, Moonlight."

"Wait, what about your MIND?" I hadn't thought about the chip once. Did Collin already know Hal was here?

"It's taken care of," Hal told me, his voice closer. I looked up to find him standing before me. He held up his wrist, where a metal cuff encircled it. "The Majors have secrets. We can make ourselves invisible. For a while."

"How?" I asked, stepping closer.

"These scramble the chip and the Illum technology, not sure how exactly. Not my thing." Hal shrugged. "But the Illum don't watch us the way they watch you."

"I'm s—"

"Don't apologize," Hal cut me off. "I'll be fine. I am glad I was there." His eyes met mine.

"Okay, um, there's water from the sink. If you . . ." I had nothing else to offer him. "If you're thirsty."

"What, you finished all the chocolates?" Hal joked.

My cheeks flushed, my hands twisting the hem of my shirt. "I left the rest for you in my office."

Hal went still. "Why?"

"A lapse in judgment," I told him. I almost stumbled as those starburst eyes glittered at me in the dark.

I closed the bathroom door, blowing out a long breath. Hal was staying in my room tonight. I started the shower, grabbing my toothbrush as the water heated up. I brushed my teeth as I caught my reflection. I could just make out the smeared remains of Rose's work. Hal said I was beautiful in the gown, but I looked like I had almost drowned.

I stepped into the shower. Slowly, the hot water warmed the bone-deep chill from my run. My body ached in a way I barely remembered, limbs too heavy, legs already succumbing to the lactic acid accumulating. The water stung my feet; tiny cuts peppered them. It was a miracle I hadn't sliced them open. I lifted my face into the stream of water, washing it all away.

I pulled back quickly, but not fast enough, as the lens shifted before dislodging completely. I wiped my face, searching for it in the dark.

"Dammit," I muttered, resting my forehead against the tiles as the water cascaded down my back. "Dammit." I hammered my fist along the wet tile, the heaviness of the evening engulfing me. The water couldn't wash away my birth father's hatred or the Elite's desire to murder everyone they deemed beneath them.

And you wanted to save her, Helen.

Helen had wanted to save me. I still breathed so she must have been successful. I must have meant something to her at some point. Enough to whisper warnings but nothing else.

The glow of my wrist was the only light. The implications of my Procreation Agreement with Collin slithered in, unlocking something I had never let myself consider. The desolate part of my soul that had watched other Minors embrace their birth mothers on visiting day, devoid of any memories of maternal love, swallowed me as viciously as my panic had. How could she not want me?

Tears prickled in my eyes. Even alone with the water to conceal them I did not let them fall. I had always been fearful of my role. Terrified to carry an offspring. What if they were like me, defective and cast down? I couldn't let my offspring suffer as I had. I wouldn't.

A soft knock sounded on the door. "You all right?"

"Fine," I responded. "I'm fine."

I wasn't fine. Not even close. My birth family hadn't spent their whole lives isolated and alone. They were a family. Gregory's confession replayed in my mind. *I didn't believe them when they told me the girl in the sheer white dress was my birth sister. That I had a sister.* Members of my birth family hadn't known I existed. My twenty-seven years of solitude and pain—they had lived blissfully unaware of my existence.

Someone had dressed me in Major Defect blue and left me in my family's clutches. The only explanation was that it had been Collin. Despite my vehement declaration that I did not believe in happy endings, I had somehow allowed myself to become delusional. Thinking my Procreation Contract would somehow change my life. Allowing myself to believe my desperate dream was within my grasp. That that dream was enough. That the kiss and Collin's kindness might have meant something.

The thoughts were crushing. I scrubbed my face and washed my hair quickly, then shut the water and toweled off. I threw my gray shirt and shorts on and wrapped my wet hair with my towel.

I glanced at my reflection and was startled to see one blue eye and one brown looking back. I had gotten used to the lens—to brown eyes. I understood why people gawked.

I padded back into my room and froze, my heart beginning to pound.

Hal perched on the edge of my bed, clad in nothing but a pair of boxers and his cuff.

CHAPTER THIRTEEN

I stopped before him, staring unabashedly at his muscular body—his chiseled chest, broad shoulders, and strong legs. He was devastatingly handsome—and he looked at home on my bed. He was every bit as physically perfect as the Elite in the clouds, would blend in with their cohort beautifully. My chest tightened.

"So you really do like looking at me," Hal teased, glancing up at me. His gaze found mine in the dark, lens-free, and he stared at my defect greedily. "It's still mutual."

My heart did a stupid little dance at that. I took the towel off my head and chucked it at him, my wet curls falling all around me. "Don't be so full of yourself. Cover up."

"Not with this," he retorted, catching the damp towel and tossing it to the floor. "I took my wet jumpsuit off to warm up."

"So you're just going to sit here like that." I gestured to all of him.

"Unless you have something that will fit me?" Hal challenged. I took in his hulking frame. He smirked. "Take it that's a no. It's just a body."

"I've never seen a male body," I responded without thinking. My cheeks burned viciously at what I had just admitted. I turned quickly to hide my embarrassment. I hobbled to the sink, my legs protesting with every step, and downed a glass of water, then another. I refilled the glass a third time before hobbling back toward the bed. Hal watched me the entire time.

"Never?"

I shook my head. "Only in art."

"So do you want to talk about your findings of the male body or what drove you to execute a long-distance run you clearly aren't in shape for? Barefoot. In a gown."

I bit my lip, staring at the bed. My legs finally admitted defeat as they trembled under my weight.

"You can sit on your bed. I promise I won't ravish you," Hal drawled. "Unless you ask me to, Moonlight." He flashed a sinful grin.

I rolled my eyes, though my core tightened at the suggestion. "I won't," I promised.

"Shame," Hal tutted. I had to fight a smile that tugged at my lips.

I sat on the very edge of the bed, legs screaming, and a groan escaped me. My heart hammered helplessly at the proximity. I placed the glass of water on the floor.

"I had dinner with my birth family tonight. They are all Elite. As you can imagine, they aren't . . . they aren't proud to have a Minor Defect as an offspring. I had never even met my birth brothers." I swallowed, staring at the ceiling. "Collin was supposed to be there, and he couldn't come, so I went alone, in blue."

Hal shifted slightly, facing me, his expression serious. "Your dinner was with your birth family?"

"Yes. I don't know what I expected. I knew they hadn't lived isolated lives like mine, but they are a family. They have a life together." My throat tightened again, and I swallowed. "One of my brothers didn't know I existed. Maybe none of them did. I can't decide what is worse, being unknown or knowing I'm utterly alone in my loneliness." I looked at the ceiling, eyes burning. "I thanked a fellow Defect for bringing me water, and my birth father, he—he didn't like that." I took a steadying breath. "He said the Elite petitioned to have the Defects eliminated."

Hal didn't respond right away, and I continued. "I asked if he would have me eliminated. He said there's nothing he wouldn't do for the Greater Good. I don't know why I expected anything else, but I lost it, and I stormed out. I couldn't breathe in the Pod. So I ran."

I shivered. It wasn't entirely from the cold. I felt too bare from my confession. I pulled the covers out, working my way under them. I felt Hal's weight shift, moving until he sat beside me, leaning against the wall. I allowed myself to stare at his towering form, the darkness my ally. His jaw was set, making its hard line more pronounced. His legs were crossed at the ankle, hands folded in his lap. It should have been a relaxed position, but his shoulders were too stiff. He was too still. I found myself wanting to reach out and touch him.

Hal stayed silent for several minutes, our breathing the only sounds in the dark. Finally, he broke the silence. "My parents were both Major Defects. They fell in love." He raked a hand through his hair.

"Is it common for Majors to have offspring?" I asked.

"The Illum do not want Major Defect offspring to exist. So Majors do not speak about them," Hal told me. "Which was why my parents hid in the tunnels beneath the city for seven years. I had a family most don't. They loved each other, and they loved me with everything they had. That Act your father talked about, it was being discussed. Majors got scared. My dad was a brave man. A couple of other Majors went to the surface to get information on a way out. They were caught. The Elite Force broke in one night while we were sleeping. They got to my mom. I was too young to fight them off."

My hand flew to my mouth, horror rolling through me.

"They told me if I went with them, my parents would be forgiven for their crimes, that I was the cost of their decisions." I heard Hal take a deep breath. "I was too young to know what to do so I went. They implanted me with a chip, gave me an identification number. I was told I was going to the Minor Academy when an Illum named

Charles informed the men in white coats that two Major Defects had produced an Elite offspring." Hal loosed a bitter laugh.

"How?"

"Beats me. The Illum didn't like it. I wasn't meant to exist in the first place. I definitely wasn't meant to be Elite, but according to their chip, my genes were perfect," Hal spat.

"Hal, I'm so—"

"Don't be sorry for me, Moonlight. I made peace with those demons long ago." Still, there was an edge to how he said it.

"And your parents?"

"When I could, I went back. Disobeyed my MIND." Hal stared out the window next to the bed. Rain continued to fall, gently pattering against the glass. "The Elite Force killed them the night they took me away."

I reached out, grabbing his thigh.

He looked down at me. "I don't want pity. I have known love, and that is—" He paused, seemingly at war with himself. "There's nothing I wouldn't do for them. I told you so you would know what the Illum and Elite are capable of. Trust what you see and not what they tell you."

"If you're Elite, why did they put you in blue?"

Hal let out a sigh. "We can talk about it tomorrow after you've slept. It's a long story."

We sat in silence for some time, our confessions mingling. My blinks became longer as I wondered what exactly made a person a Major Defect. How had two Majors made an Elite? It didn't make sense. If they had love hidden in their tunnels, did that make the surface the place to fear? I had been taught to fear being cast down without really understanding it—that the worse possible fate, other than elimination, was to live outside of the Illum's light as a Major Defect. I felt sleep tugging on my mind.

"I'm glad you were there tonight," I murmured, eyelids closing.

The warmth of his body aligned with mine as one of his arms wound around my waist, pulling me in. Through the haze of impending sleep my stomach fluttered at the contact. I nestled back into him.

"Get some sleep, Moonlight," Hal breathed into my ear.

I smiled into my pillow at the nickname, too tired to fight it, to hide. My breathing became deep and slow. Sleep curled up around my sore body as dreams came out to play. I heard Hal mutter through the haze, or maybe it was my dream.

"I'd do anything for love."

There was no talk of sleeping on the floor as sleep claimed me.

CHAPTER FOURTEEN

I opened my eyes, immersed in warmth. The sky outside was still dark, but I couldn't focus on anything other than the sight before me.

Hal lay on his back, one leg intertwined with mine, an arm curled above his head, the other wrapped around my waist, tucking me into his side, as if he had held me all night, which maybe he had. His face was relaxed, his dark blond hair tousled. I thought of brushing it away as my eyes traced over his broad shoulders and sculpted chest that lay exposed. I drank in every curve of his muscles before landing on my glowing wrist on his chest, close to his heart. I bit my lip, staring at my hand against his skin, impossibly smooth and hard. I could lean closer and replace my hand with my lips. I startled at the thought, embarrassment and heat flushing through me. My heart picked up its pace. I should remove my hand, should get out of bed and put distance between us. I knew I should, yet I didn't move.

His breathing hitched, and I realized too late that he hadn't been sleeping.

I crashed into starburst amber eyes. The hand around my waist tightened, drawing me closer. I let Hal pull me in until my body was flush against his, my hand caught between us, no room to think of anything but him and the feel of his warm strength surrounding me.

Hal's hand dragged lazily up my spine, and I arched into him until his lips were inches from mine.

"You just going to look at me, Moonlight?" Hal whispered, his hand leaving goosebumps in its wake as he swept along my back, venturing lower.

"Emeline, Emeeelinnne."

Hal froze.

Thump. Thump. Thump.

I pushed us apart, heart racing. Had Hal's cuff not worked? Had my performance last night been too much? Had they come for me?

Thump. Thump Thump.

"For fuck's sake, Emeline," an exasperated male voice called from the opposite side of my door. Hal lifted a finger to his mouth before gesturing toward the bathroom. I nodded as he stood, the sheets falling off, clad in nothing but his briefs. My heart hammered for more than one reason as his sculpted back flexed when he bent down, grabbing his jumpsuit, undershirt, and boots before disappearing into my bathroom. For such a large man, he moved with stealthy efficiency.

I swept the room as he shut the door, ensuring nothing was left behind. I placed my glowing wrist under the scanner before I cracked the door to find Gregory staring at the ceiling.

"Fuck, finally." Gregory pushed past me without an invitation.

"What are you doing here?" I demanded, chasing after him, positioning myself between him and the bathroom door. Gregory took in my room, nose scrunched.

"You live here?" he asked incredulously.

"Obviously. What are you doing here?" I repeated, my heart refusing to slow. He was still in the wrinkled suit from last night. I could smell the wine wafting off of him.

"I seem to be tasked with fetching duties," Gregory drawled, looking around the room. "I can't believe people live like this."

My cheeks heated. "Fetching what, exactly?"

Gregory rubbed his temples. "You, obviously. Please tell me being a Minor doesn't make you dense."

"You're a horrible person," I seethed.

"Through and through." Gregory grinned at me. "You pissed a lot of people off last night with your performance. Which I loved, just so you know. I haven't seen Father that mad in a long time. Usually, it's directed at me." Gregory stopped, his head tilted as he took in the black boxes next to the counter. "What are these?"

"They bring me food and take away my trash and dirty clothing," I told him as he opened one of the doors and inspected it. "Where are you taking me?"

Gregory tore his eyes from the boxes, cursing. "Do you have some tea or water? Anything to stop the fucking pounding."

"There's water from the faucet."

"You're joking, right?" he demanded, pulling away from my counter. I crossed my arms, glaring at him. "Gross, you're serious. I'll wait. Here," he tossed a bag to me. "Get dressed and be quick about it. I'll be in the Pod. I can't stay in this hovel." Gregory gave my living quarters one more scrutinizing glare before making his way to the door.

"Oh, and bring the gown," he shot over his shoulder before leaving.

I shut the door behind him before sprinting to the bathroom. My legs screamed with each step. I wrenched the door open, coming face-to-face with Hal.

"Who was that?" Hal asked quietly, his jumpsuit and undershirt back on.

"One of my birth brothers. He's taking me somewhere." I twisted my hands together.

"Which one?"

"Gregory, the middle one."

Hal peered out the window at the Pod waiting below. I retrieved the bag to find a simple champagne-colored day dress, brown slippers, and a suede brown clutch.

"I'll be right back." I strode into the bathroom, quickly slipping on the dress. It had long sleeves, a fitted bodice, and a gathered skirt. I tidied myself up, taming my hair into a low bun. My stomach flipped at the blue and brown eyes reflected in the mirror. I didn't have a way to hide my defect. Collin hadn't seen me without a lens. I should be worried about the implications of Collin seeing me as I truly was, but I couldn't find it. Would they know Hal had stayed here? Had I endangered Hal? I could only hope they didn't know. They would know about last night. About the way I had stormed out. What were the ramifications of that? Did I care if the Illum had put me in blue? If Collin had put me in blue?

I strode out of the bathroom, my worries racing after me, to find Hal leaning against the counter, arms crossed.

"Moonlight," Hal began as I grabbed the blue dress off the ground, shoving it unceremoniously into the bag. I spun around, looking for my gold clutch from last night. "Moonlight—"

I grabbed it off the floor, fishing out my Comm Device. I had five messages. I hadn't thought to check it last night. I thrust it into the suede bag. I'd read them on the way. I swallowed, or tried to. My throat was bone-dry. I made my way to the sink, filling a cup with water.

"Moonlight, look at me. Do you remember what I said last night?" he asked, taking the cup and grabbing me with both hands, his eyes wide. "Trust what you see, not what they say."

I nodded, throat tight. I tried to reassure him but couldn't get the words out. "I have to go," I said instead. "My Mate, he's not Elite. He's Illum. I have to go."

"I will wait for you in your office," Hal said, stepping away. He didn't seem surprised at the revelation. A ding filled the room as food was delivered to the first black box. My HI turned on, and Hal walked over to the orb, messing with it until it quieted. How did he know how to turn that off? If I'd had time, I would have asked.

I opened the door as my stomach protested fiercely. "Here, I scanned so you would have something to eat."

Hal scoffed. "You're the one who needs it. You ran all that way."

"So did you. It's your night, right? You won't get food now."

Hal looked like he wanted to say something but stopped. "Thank you."

"It's the least I can do." I bent down, grabbing the bag with the blue dress and my clutch.

"I don't deserve it," Hal said.

"You do," I assured him as I strode out of the room, even though I felt I was leaving some crucial part of me behind.

The sky was still dark as I approached the lone Pod, stepping past puddles from last night's storm. My breath clouded in the cold morning air. Gregory was sprawled across one side of the Pod, mindlessly twisting a gold ring he wore. I scanned and sat across from him, and the Pod took off.

"Took you long enough," Gregory drawled.

I ignored him. I couldn't figure him out. He had turned his nose up at my living quarters and remained silent when Vincent had suggested the Elimination Act, but he had told me he liked me. He seemed unimpressed with our birth family. I grabbed my Comm Device, pulling up the first of five messages.

> Should be able to make it for dessert. Apologies for being held up.

> Phillip messaged me and told me you left

> Emeline, what's happened

All were sent before curfew while I was running. There were two from Lo.

> You going to be back in time to talk?

> Guess not . . . Can't wait to hear about it tomorrow.

Every warm feeling I had found upon waking slipped out of my reach. I didn't reply to Collin. Gregory hadn't told me where we were going, but I assumed Collin waited at the end of this ride. Dread filled me at the thought. I sent Lo a quick message.

> Last night was a mess. I'll have to tell you later. I hope your yearly went okay.

I rested my head against the glass as my thoughts skipped from one to the next, leaving me dizzy.

"Please don't hit the emergency button again," Gregory quipped.

My eyes flew to him. "How did you know about that?"

"Lesson number one, little sister: They are always watching you. They are always a step ahead." He stared out the roof, not even bothering to look at me. Had Hal gotten out of my living quarters unseen, or had the Illum found out? I could only hope that the metal cuff worked as well as Hal thought. Gregory's off-key humming pulled me from my downward spiral.

"Why are you here?" I snapped.

"Well, I'm bringing you to your dear Mate, of course. While he has taken you on as his charity case or whatever it is the Illum is scheming, he can't be seen in your area of town. Our baby brother is the biggest ass-kissing Illum lover there is, desperate to be promoted, so he couldn't step away from work. And Richard is following in the footsteps of our father, who would have you eliminated rather than have anything to do with you. Wasn't that what he said last night?"

I didn't deign to answer that. "And our birth mother?" I asked. "Let me guess, too delicate to handle seeing how Minors live."

"She isn't delicate. You don't know what she's been through," Gregory said quietly.

"Right, because life is so hard as an Elite woman," I countered.

"You're naïve and ignorant, so I will let that slide. For today."

I crossed my arms. "How can I *not* be ignorant when no one will tell me anything?" When Gregory didn't respond, I asked, "So why not send someone like me?"

"Like you?" Gregory asked. "Do you still think you're like the other Minors?"

"I've been called a dying breed thanks to my visual defect," I said. "But other than that, there's nothing special about me."

That's not true, a small voice whispered, one that sounded like Alice. She had made me feel special, as if together we could form our own way in the world.

"You are unlike any of us now, even the Elite. It is why Father is so livid. Well, that and the fact that you still breathe," Gregory said nonchalantly as he stretched his hand toward the roof. Was his mind still befuddled? "You're an Illum's Mate. Not just any Illum. The others stay locked away, ruling and judging from afar." My heart picked up its pace as Gregory carried on. "You are the Mate of the Illum they send into the Elite to carry out their judgments and punishments. He is their Enforcer. There is no one like you, little sister, because there is no one like your Mate."

"I don't understand," I admitted.

"I wouldn't plan on that changing."

I paused. "So . . . I'm not going to be eliminated? For my outburst yesterday?"

Gregory looked at me as though I had just sprouted another head. "No, Emeline. Quite the opposite. You are the property of the Illum, and someone has to pay for the mistreatment of you." The hair on the back of my neck stood on end, unease settling into my bones. The property of the Illum. A vessel and property. "As the family fuckup"—Gregory spread his arms wide—"I get to do the embarrassing groundwork." His eyes found mine, taking in my heterochromia. "Oh, sister, the horror."

I held his gaze. "The horrors do not hide beneath," I said, quoting his taunt from last night.

"Welcome to the family disappointment club," Gregory said, glancing back out the roof. Rain had started to fall again.

"There's a club?" I snorted.

"There is now. It had always only been me." I recognized the loneliness that laced his words.

"How have you been a disappointment? You're Elite," I scoffed.

"A story for another day, sister," Gregory told me. "Let's go see what your *kind* Mate has to say."

The Pod stopped at one of the seven identical megastructures, but there was no antechamber like the other buildings had. Instead, the Pod hovered at a balcony that jutted high above the clouds, defying gravity and sanity. The clouds were so thick, the ground lay hidden. As the doors opened, frigid air swept into the Pod, instantly chilling me to the bone.

Gregory rolled his neck as he stood and stepped onto the balcony and disappeared inside. I clung to my bag and clutch in one hand as I stood petrified. Uttering a prayer to any ancient forgotten gods who might still be out there—who might still care—I took a deep breath and followed.

The walk across the balcony was terrifying. It made the walk across the bridge in the Sphere seem like a pleasant stroll. The wind whipped viciously, the air so cold I felt like I would freeze before I reached the doors. I tried my hardest not to look at the unending sky. My sore legs wobbled, protesting with each step as I walked through the doors and into the unknown.

The room was warm and welcoming. I didn't know what I expected, maybe something formal or cold. Instead, I walked directly into someone's living room. The room was cozy, the walls primarily windows. The tiled floors led to a sunken seating area that faced the one interior wall, containing floor-to-ceiling shelves. There were books on them. I had never seen books outside of the Archive. I resisted the urge to open each one and smell the pages. In the middle of the bookshelves was a heating hearth, and above was a piece of art—a piece I *knew* I had reassigned at some point. I took a couple of steps closer, the books and art holding my fear at bay, dropping the bag as I made my way, entranced, to the art. There was art in an Illum's living quarters. Art with people in it.

It was a striking juxtaposition that stole my breath. Two figures stood in the painting. One, a fair-haired woman dressed in all white, looked outward as she walked away from the other figure in the painting. A man dressed in black stood by a tree, his eyes cast down, clutching his heart. A separation to them—a brokenness as the woman pulled away. Why was she leaving?

"Hi, Emeline" came a lovely voice, breaking the art's spell. A woman sat on the couch hidden among an array of pillows.

Her midnight black hair fell over her shoulder in a loose braid, and her fern green dress resembled mine. She was breathtakingly beautiful in a way I knew ancient humans would have tried to capture, yet would never have done justice to.

She patted the seat next to her, closing a book. "Come join me. They might be a while." She glanced behind me. I turned to find Gregory leaning against one of the windows, his hands trapped behind his back as he looked down at the woman, his face unreadable.

"Nora." Gregory nodded in her direction but didn't move.

"Gregory," she said, her voice like honey.

I slowly approached the woman as she stood. She was so petite and slender, her steps dancelike and graceful. She extended her delicate hand, and I took it. Heavy lashes framed her sapphire eyes, eyes I knew. "I'm Nora. It's nice to finally meet my brother's Mate."

"Collin is your brother?" I asked, flustered. It seemed obvious, as she said it: She was the spitting image of him.

"He hasn't mentioned me?" Nora placed a hand over her heart, her blue eyes alight. "How inconsiderate of him. I shall make him rue that choice." She winked at me, smiling wide. "Would you like some tea? Collin had your morning scan sent over. I believe your morning meal will be ready shortly."

"Tea would be nice, thank you," I responded. I wondered how

much power Collin had to have my morning scan already sent over this quickly. *There is no one like your Mate.*

I took a seat on the large sofa among tan pillows. A tea service sat on one of two identical rectangular taupe marble tables. Nora passed a cup to me before sitting beside me with her own.

The art captured my attention once again.

"It's called *Separation*," Nora said.

"I was unaware the Elite had art and books," I admitted, taking a sip of tea.

"The Elite don't really. The Illum do." She patted her worn book. It looked old, the pages yellowing, the leatherbound cover tattered.

"What are you reading?" I asked, unable to help myself.

Nora smiled. "Just a story about a man who desperately loved a woman."

A disgruntled sound filled the space. Nora's gaze sharpened, finding Gregory. "Why are you lurking, Gregory?"

"Don't flatter yourself. I'm following orders, Nora. I'm to stay," Gregory drawled from the window. "I'd like nothing more than to leave. Find my bed and a tonic for the pounding."

"Still drinking and partying then?" Nora sneered, cutting Gregory a vicious look. For all her ethereal beauty, she had a quiet ferociousness to her. I immediately liked her.

Gregory cast Nora a taunting grin, spreading his arms wide in a mocking bow. "Forever guilty."

"Deplorable," Nora shot back, sipping her tea. "Nothing's changed."

There was a gleam in Gregory's eyes as he sized up his adversary. He opened his mouth to retort, but quickly closed it, the picture of apathetic indifference, as Collin strode into the room, Phillip at his side. They ignored Gregory.

Phillip walked down the steps, clutching a stack of papers. Collin stopped on the cusp of the stairs, staring down at me, his glacial gaze intense and unyielding. They held my defective eyes.

Exposed, I steeled my resolve and awaited the consequences of my actions.

CHAPTER FIFTEEN

"Ah, there he is," Nora said. "Tell me, dear brother, why Emeline did not know about me."

"Nora, not now," Collin said. I stood as he descended the stairs, stopping in front of me. He looked dashing in rich brown pants and a white button-down shirt. It was strange to see him in something other than a black suit. My body and mind waged an unseen war in his presence. His magnetic pull tugged on something low and relentless, but my mind raged against it. I had worn blue. I'd had a Major Defect in my room last night.

I had not seen him since the Sphere. Since he had implored forgiveness before his lips met mine. Despite myself, my eyes lingered on his lips. Was I about to beg his forgiveness? I wasn't sure I wanted it.

"Emeline, are you all right?" he asked with real concern in his voice, and the war fell silent.

"Yes, I'm okay." I didn't mention how my muscles were still so sore that it was difficult to stand, much less walk, or how emotionally drained I felt.

His calculating gaze flickered between my blue–brown gaze, and I realized Nora hadn't commented on my heterochromia. She hadn't said anything, which had been a first. I glanced over my shoulder at her. She smiled at me, raising her teacup to her lips.

Collin gestured to the sofa. I took my seat as he sat on the table directly across from me. "Can you tell me about last night?"

I glanced over to Phillip, who shuffled through his stack of papers on the other sofa.

"Didn't Phillip tell you?" I asked, uneasy.

I didn't want to relive Vincent's words. I didn't want to tell a group of Elite what it felt like to be cast aside. That instead of accepting me, my birth family wished for me to be eliminated. My chest hollowed out at the thought.

"He told me his recount, that Vincent mentioned the Elimination Act," Collin said.

"He more than mentioned it," I choked out.

"Some of the older Elites still believe in it," Collin told me. I glanced at Phillip. Had he told Collin everything that was said? Collin made to continue, but I cut him off.

"Do *you*?"

The room fell deathly silent. The Academy lessons preaching obedience seemed very far away. I looked up, my mismatched gaze colliding with Collin's. I couldn't breathe at the wild look in his eyes. I wouldn't look away. If he thought people like me should be murdered, I would watch him say it.

"I do not," he told me, his gaze dipping to my lips. He cleared his throat, tearing his eyes from them. "We did not repopulate only to wipe out a good portion of our efforts. It would be counterproductive, as I have stated to the Press and in every meeting it has been suggested."

"What exactly is the Press?" I asked, one of the many questions I had boiling inside of me.

"A media source for the Elite," Collin said.

"It's a gossip column at best," Nora huffed, unimpressed. "It exists to entertain those in the clouds."

"We're getting off topic," Collin said. "After the dinner, your Pod had the emergency button pushed and then our cameras saw you take off on foot."

The floor went out from under me as fear surged through me, potent and heavy like my panic had felt last night. Had the Illum seen Hal? Surely he would have led with that. I was property, his property, if Gregory was to be believed.

"Your scans this morning are erratic at best, unhealthy at worst," Collin stated. Phillip passed along a paper, which Collin glanced at before handing it to me.

I scanned the entire photo. There was no sign of Hal—just me and my wild sprint. The metal cuff had allowed Hal to remain undetected.

"Oh, I love that dress," Nora exclaimed.

"Where is the dress?" Collin asked, looking toward the doors where I had dropped it. "Gregory, bring me the bag."

Gregory scooped up the bag, dropping it next to me.

"Gregory, didn't you want tea?" I asked.

"I'm fine," Gregory said before returning to the window. I watched him walk away. He was older than everyone else in the room, yet he stood on the outskirts, removed. I only heard his name as a summoning or a curse. Gregory stared at the blue dress Collin handed to Nora, his face unreadable.

Nora hissed. "Why is it this color?" It looked black in the photo.

"I don't know, but I want to find out why and who is responsible."

"You didn't make me wear it?" I asked, unable to stop myself.

Collin turned his head toward me, his face tense. "You thought I did this?"

"Of course I did. It came in a black box like my lens." I glanced toward my lap. "I was told the lens was from the Illum. That they sometimes send their—" The word *plaything* caught in my throat. "They send stuff to people like me. You said we should get the dinner with my birth family out of the way." I didn't look up to see how my birth brothers took that. "Then you didn't show. You left me alone with them. I thought it was a particularly cruel trial."

Collin leaned forward. "I intended to be there. My duties as an Illum have to come first. I have only sent you things I thought you might want and enjoy. I did not send you this."

"What else was I supposed to think?" All the hateful things Vincent had said my entire life twirled with the Academy's rules, spinning me lower and lower. "I am a Defect, a visual Defect. My own Elite birth family wants to eliminate me."

Collin moved closer, his long legs bracketing mine. I froze, heart thumping hard.

"Leave us."

A flurry of movement erupted around us as the others made to leave.

Collin didn't glance their way. "Maybe I didn't make myself clear in the Garden, so let me tell you again. I quit caring about the Elite's opinions long ago." Collin reached for me, then let his hand fall between his legs. "Emeline, you are an extension of me now." Slippers scuffed against the floor, lithe steps faltering. Collin held my gaze. "If someone hurts you, I take it personally."

Power churned in Collin's eyes as his jaw bulged. My pulse fluttered helplessly as all of him remained focused on me. Defect and all. Maybe I should fear the power I saw—the viciousness he directed at my birth family in the Sphere. How he could damn me to elimination with a breath. Instead, I leaned forward. The corner of Collin's lips tugged up, the power shifting into something else entirely, something I couldn't quite place as his gaze found my lips.

"You may speak plainly," he told me.

I knew that wasn't true. I had spoken too plainly and others paid the price. I didn't know who Collin was in the clouds when I wasn't around. Gregory had called him the Enforcer. I leaned back, away from his all-encompassing orbit I seemed afflicted by. Rose and Violet had been hurt. Hal had miraculously managed to remain invisible to the Illum. I swallowed my questions for their sake—Violet, Rose, and Hal. The cost of my curiosity was too much.

I looked to find the others congregating just outside the room. Nora leaned toward us, not at all inconspicuously, the blue gown still in her hands.

"Busybodies," Collin grumbled, disgruntled fondness in his voice, and surprise flashed through me. "Nora, do you recognize the gown?"

"Not off the top of my mind, but it fits her well in the photo," Nora called over, and they reentered the room. "Whoever made it had a good idea of her measurements." I swore Collin hid a smirk at her quick response. He hadn't even raised his voice to ask her, but when I looked again, his smile was gone.

"Have your seamstress look at it. See what she can tell us. Gregory, take the dress," Collin ordered. "Nora, are you and William free in three days?"

"I believe so," she said, gripping the dress tightly as Gregory approached her.

"Phillip, update their MINDs," Collin said. "Emeline and I will dine with them. At the Pond—is it still your favorite place, Nora?"

Gregory snatched the dress from Nora's grip, turning without a word as he walked out onto the balcony, undeterred by the frigid wind.

"Always," Nora said quietly. I didn't miss how her eyes had followed Gregory to where he stood at the balcony edge, the blue dress whipping wildly in the wind.

"Good. Summon a Pod for Gregory, Phillip," Collin instructed. "Add Nora's seamstress to his MIND. Begin running interference—last night stays close. Document Gregory's breach of curfew and be certain nothing befalls Emeline. Make it a trial or something." None of it made sense to me but it did to Phillip. He pulled out his Comm Device and began typing away.

"I—" I began but bit my tongue.

"You what?" Collin asked, turning toward me fully.

"What do you mean running interference?"

"And Vincent?" Phillip interrupted, his eyes on his device.

"You can leave that to me," Collin told him, his sapphire eyes cold. A shiver ran up my spine.

"Pardon, your morning meals are ready," an attendant stated before disappearing.

"We will meet you in there," Collin told Phillip and Nora.

I sat up straighter at his dismissal. A Pod came to a stop at the edge of the balcony, and Gregory disappeared from view. Nora turned away, looping her arm through Phillip's. They actually left the room this time.

Collin sat next to me. "Phillip is running interference to ensure the events of last night do not get out to the Elite collective, thus ensuring that the attendants at your parents' do not share what they witnessed. I also overrode the curfew by an hour, granting Gregory's MIND and yours access to move freely. I am calling it a trial so the rest of the Illum are not offended by my overstepping."

"The Defects?" I asked, shocked.

"Yes, it was not only your family in that room. The Minors witnessed as well. They could share the information if not persuaded to keep their silence."

"How will you persuade them?" I asked as fear twirled around my spine.

"Depends on the Defect." Collin paused, then said, "You ran last night, for quite a distance."

"I did." And I hadn't been alone. I swallowed, my throat tight, pushing Hal from my mind.

Collin looked conflicted as he adjusted his sleeves. "You are the first Illum Mate in a very long time. We have had several generations of Illum who have focused on societal advances and innovation rather than procreation. In taking you as my Mate, that has all changed."

"But didn't Tabitha tell you to take a Mate?"

"She did, and in being an extension of me, you will be watched more closely."

My stomach dropped. "What do you mean? Aren't they always watching?"

"The Illum cannot watch every MIND all the time. There are too many. They watch for outliers, MINDs that do not follow their rules. Anomalies. They will watch more closely if moments like last night happen again. It is a side effect of being my Mate. I understand Vincent upset you, but if you were to do that before other members of the Elite, it would create issues. Also, your yearly deemed running as detrimental to your Procreation Abilities. I have no test for you, nor am I judging you, Emeline. This mating will proceed." Collin's expression grew heavy. "If the Illum take notice, I will only be able to do so much."

"Why didn't you tell me this before?" I asked quietly.

"Truthfully, I didn't think it would be necessary. Forgive me, I thought being the Mate to an Illum would either be thrilling or terrifying enough to make my Mate follow the rules. As I said, you are not what I expected." Collin shifted.

"Being your Mate is," I admitted quietly.

"Which one?" Collin asked quietly, leaning toward me.

I stared into those sapphire pools, the depths treacherous—dragging me under. "I don't know yet." I didn't trust him and the Illum, not after the Starlings blamed me for what had happened to Violet. I was terrified. But there was something about the Illum before me—the power, the viciousness . . . I wasn't terrified of it, only how my heart raced in his presence—the thrill that ran through me when his lips met mine.

You just want to understand—figure him out, some small voice whispered to me. Even as my traitorous eyes landed on his lips.

Nora's tinkle of laughter floated from the room beyond, and my heart thumped wildly. I put distance between us.

"I do have one favor to ask of you. If something like yesterday happens again"—Collin cleared his throat—"if you feel you need to run from something, I ask that you run to me. You may contact me anytime, and I shall assure your safety."

He looked at me expectantly, and I murmured, "All right."

"We should join them. I assume you're starving." Collin stood, and I placed my glowing hand in his extended one, unsure what to say. His hand wrapped around mine, dwarfing it, as he led me up the stairs.

"You had something to say earlier when they were eavesdropping," Collin said, pausing at the top of the stairs. "You were biting your lip."

I released my lip I was once again holding. I wanted to know what had kept him away from the dinner, what it meant that he was the Enforcer. What had happened to Violet and Rose and whether he was behind it. I wanted to know about the Elimination Act, why the Elite hid so much from the Minors, and why the Majors weren't the monsters they led us to believe. I wanted to know more about the people's uprising. I wanted to know why he had chosen me with my defect when he could have had anyone. Whether the kiss had meant anything to him. If my hand in his had the same effect on him as it did on me.

My heart stuttered as his hand tightened around mine. "Nothing."

"All right," Collin said as he led the way. I swore that disappointment swam in his endless blue depths.

We entered a cozy solarium. From this height, on a cloudless day, Collin told me, he could see the entire city, all the way to Low Town. Right now, thick, heavy rain clouds whirled restlessly all around us, as tempestuous as my thoughts. Phillip sat at the black oval table, his back to the window, tending to the tea service set out, handing Nora a cup. She glanced our way, the ghost of a laugh still on her stunning face.

"There you two are. Emeline, they said this is all yours." Nora gestured to the spot in front of Phillip. I stared in shock at the four separate plates filled with food. "Exactly how far did you run last night?"

"Just over ten kilometers," Phillip answered.

Nora's eyebrows raised. "You did that on a whim in a dress and heels?"

"I did it barefoot."

"Your shoes are in my room," Collin said as he pulled out my chair and took the seat next to me. "Phillip brought them."

"Thank you," I muttered as I grabbed my tea.

"Do you like to run?" Nora asked. "I have never seen the point."

As an Elite with an Illum sibling and her life in the clouds, what could she need to run from? "I did when it was permitted."

Nora hummed appreciatively as she sipped her tea. "You make the best cup of tea, Phillip."

He smiled. It was the first time I had seen him do so, and he instantly looked younger. "After two decades, I'd like to think I can get it right."

"You'd be surprised. This one"—she gestured to Collin—"never puts enough honey in it."

Collin shook his head. "Most people enjoy tea with honey, not the other way around."

Nora rolled her eyes, leaning into Phillip, her head resting on his shoulder. The movement was effortless, like they had done it a thousand times. Phillip tilted his head toward hers. I stared at the two of them, the closeness.

Nora noticed, smiling as she sat up. "We've known each other almost our whole lives. We are the same age. We grew up together at the Academy." She scrunched her nose at Phillip.

The tea was bitter—like me. I set it down. "I didn't know how you take your tea," Phillip commented. He knew Nora, and I was a stranger.

"Were you guys ever Mated?" I asked. Phillip and Nora laughed.

"Never, could you imagine?" Nora said, placing a hand on Phillip's shoulder. Phillip shook his head, his curls bouncing. Collin downed his cup of tea, pouring another. "I used to joke that while I had a twin"—she pursed her lips at Collin—"I also had a brother."

Phillip and I locked eyes. Nora withdrew her hand. I took another sip of tea, hoping the heat would burn away the knot in my throat. I forced myself to focus on the aspect of her comment that didn't twist the dagger in my chest. The side of my leg grew warm as Collin leaned forward. He placed a spoonful of a golden substance into my tea without a word. I glanced down to see Collin's leg still warm against mine.

"Twins?" I asked, looking between Nora and Collin. Twins were unheard of.

They shared a look before Collin answered: "Yes, we were the first documented case in several hundred years."

"Your birth parents must be thrilled." I took a sip of tea, a sweetness there from Collin's addition.

Collin nodded, a shadow crossing his features. "They were."

A silence fell, and we turned to our plates. The taste of their food reminded me just how ravenous I was, and I tried to pace myself, the others all taking polite bites in silence. My stomach rejoiced.

Recognizing the gold-dusted chocolates, I reached for them, then hesitated. Was I allowed to eat them now? Was there a polite way to eat this much food?

"We are alone, Emeline," Collin said. "Eat the chocolate whenever you please."

My eyes went to Phillip and Nora.

"They do not count," Collin told me.

"That's rude," Nora claimed haughtily.

"You wound me," Phillip said as his hand found his chest.

"I've watched you eat an entire chocolate cake in one sitting, Nora," Collin retorted, taking a bite.

"I've seen her eat two," Phillip countered, smiling, staring at Nora like she was the only one there.

"I dislike you both," Nora insisted as she eyed the chocolates.

Phillip leaned forward, his curls swaying. "You'll change your mind in a few minutes. Your tea is almost empty."

Nora shook her head, stabbing her food. I snagged a chocolate, eating it before offering the plate to Nora. She grinned at me, taking one. I chewed the chocolate, trying to understand their closeness. It was all so informal. There were no Defects waiting on them.

"Is this your only residence?" I asked.

"What do you mean?" Collin inquired.

"I expected more grandeur for a member of the Illum," I confessed. While it was beautiful, there were none of the ostentatious displays of most of the other spaces I had seen in the clouds.

"This is my only residence," Collin told me. "This is my private floor. I created it for myself and those close to me. The floor below contains my formal quarters, which is what the outside world sees. It is every bit as grandiose as you would assume. The dinner will be held there."

The rest of the world seemed an exaggeration. The Elite saw it.

"Speaking of the dinner," Nora started—Phillip whooshed a breath, looking at the glass ceiling—"William mentioned at our last Courting that many Elite are becoming increasingly concerned with the frequency of the mishaps." Nora side-eyed me.

"William is Nora's current Mate," Collin told me. I wondered what he meant by *current*. Did Elite women switch Mates?

"My dear brother is kind enough to let me stay here during my Courting Phase," Nora told me before returning her attention to her brother. "Did you resolve everything last night? I didn't hear either of you return."

"Do you all live here?" I asked them.

"For now, yes," Collin explained. "Phillip is here until we move into our procreation phase. Nora is here until her own procreation phase. Elite women are housed by their relatives between Mates."

"Did you?" Nora prompted again.

"We handled it. It wasn't resolved," Collin informed her. He folded his hands on the table, his food only half eaten.

Phillip cleared his throat, glancing at me, and I felt the dagger twist again. "Is it wise to discuss this right now?"

"It's fine," Collin said. "They broke into our medical building containing our supplements. I was called away before I could resolve anything."

"Was the Reaper involved?" Nora asked, eyes wide.

Collin glared at her. "Do not use that name."

"Did you not call the Press a gossip column in the other room?" Phillip asked her.

"What? It's what the Elite are calling him," Nora told him unabashedly. "He has a reputation now, and I'm not gossiping. I'm asking you two. It's different; *you do not count*."

"Who's the Reaper?" I asked.

Collin turned, looking at me. "The person behind these difficulties. The Elite," he shot a severe look toward Nora, "seem to think he needs a name."

"What's he after?"

Phillip rubbed his neck. "We don't know yet. They raided a medical warehouse and might have taken vital supplements."

"Who do you think is behind it?" Nora asked, her food forgotten. "Besides the Reaper."

Collin stretched his legs. "That's what we have been tasked with figuring out. Possibly an Elite member trying to send the Illum a message. Possibly Defects attempting a rebellion. Regardless, sooner or later the Reaper will mess up and expose himself. The truth always comes out. When it does, the Illum will eliminate him."

Unease twisted deep in my gut. The Reaper wasn't the only one with something to hide from the Illum. But Hal visiting me in the Archives was different. Harmless.

And last night? a small voice whispered. The way it had felt when he called me Moonlight, trading secrets in the dark. I pulled my leg from Collin's as guilt settled in the pit of my stomach.

Collin stood, yanking me from my thoughts.

"Leaving already?" Nora asked.

"We need to get to the facilities. See what was uncovered overnight," Collin said.

Phillip downed his tea, squeezing Nora's shoulder in goodbye and nodding at me before leaving the room.

"You work too hard, brother," Nora expressed, sipping her tea.

Collin dismissed her concern and turned to me. "Nora will keep you company. Your Pod will arrive soon to transport you to work. Your lateness has been documented, and you will have your normal dismissal time. I have spoken with my fellow Illum, and you will receive a shortened workweek. Communications will be sending you a message about it."

I wondered briefly if Phillip was behind the communications. I cleared my throat. "I don't have adequate clothing."

"Wear this," Collin said, gesturing to my current dress. "I will see you soon."

I watched him walk out before returning my attention to Nora, who appeared lost in thought.

"Ms. Emeline, I have your morning supplements," a worker said, approaching me with a syringe on a platter. "Please raise your arm."

"My arm?"

"Yes, ma'am, for administration."

"Do you not take your supplements every day?" Nora asked, unconcerned.

"Yes, in pill form."

"How outdated. We take ours as an injection."

I held out my arm, trying to restrain my panic. A sharp pinch swept through me.

"Not so bad, right?" Nora said, smiling. "I assume your Pod will arrive soon. Shall we head to the sitting room?"

"Ms. Emeline, Mr. Collin asked that you receive this." The worker handed me a beautiful, rich brown knee-length coat. "Nora, today's Press issue."

Nora chuckled and grabbed the tablet from the man. "Bastard gave you my coat."

I followed her as she made her way out of the room. "I don't have to take it."

"No, I insist you do. It's just different. He seems concerned for you, considerate even." Nora perched on the edge of the steps that led to the sunken seating area, the tablet aglow.

I grabbed my clutch. "Does he not consider others usually?"

"He's an Illum," Nora stated. "He doesn't have to. It's different with you. Call it a twin thing."

"Is this 'twin thing' normal?"

"I wouldn't know. We are an oddity of sorts. An anomaly. I do know that Collin isn't heartless—he cares about work and duty above all else. It's why Phillip and Collin got along so quickly. That and their fervent desire to postpone mating for as long as possible, which is ridiculous. The male does very little. It's the female whom everything falls on."

I didn't want to think about that, the possibility of an offspring. Not again.

"Don't fret," Nora said. "I'll help you when it is time. I am a pro at this point." She smiled, but she looked sad. "It was wonderful to meet you."

Nora lifted the tablet. Her eyes widened before she flipped it down quickly, her cheeks tinged pink.

"What is it?" I asked.

"It's nothing. Just gossip."

"Can I see it?"

Nora looked between me and the tablet, then sighed and held it out to me.

Right there on the front page was a photo of myself and Collin, one arm wrapped tightly around my waist, pulling the sheer white fabric taut against my skin, and the other holding my face. My first kiss displayed for the Elite to see. Red-hot embarrassment and anger blazed through me.

"That happened the other night," I muttered, staring at the thing Collin and I hadn't discussed today. "Why—why today?"

Nora's fierceness flashed across her face like lightning. "There's power in revealing information at the precise moment it best suits the teller. When there is the most to gain. The Press—it is quite good at it."

She took the tablet from me but not before I saw the words above the photo.

YOUNGEST ILLUM SHOCKS ELITE WITH MINOR MATE: DO MINORS HAVE A PLACE IN OUR CLOUDS?

"I would ignore it," Nora urged as she settled into the spot I had found her in, almost entirely hidden by the pillows. She tossed the Press aside and grabbed her book. A Pod pulled up outside.

"Nora, who controls the Press?" I asked. The image burned into my memory as two words echoed in my mind. "It's the Illum, right?"

Nora stared at me sadly. "Yes."

CHAPTER SIXTEEN

Two words chased me through the swirling gray clouds. As the Pod plummeted toward the surface, so did my thoughts.

Forgive me.

They are always a step ahead.

YOUNGEST ILLUM SHOCKS ELITE WITH MINOR MATE.

If someone hurts you, I take it personally.

I used to joke that while I had a twin, I also had a brother.

If you feel you need to run from something, I ask that you run to me.

Forgive me.

Rule Nine: You are an obligation to your Mate. . . . His loyalty is to the Illum, not to you.

Do you still think you're like the other Minors?

He is their Enforcer. There is no one like you . . . because there is no one like your Mate.

Follow the Illum's protocol, abide by the rules of the Minor Defect population, and constantly seek self-improvement, and you will rise, fulfilling your use for the Greater Good.

And you wanted to save her, Helen.

Forgive me.

Had Collin known that the kiss would be captured? Had he used me to put on a show for the Elite and released the story today? Had he pulled away so quickly because he had achieved what he wanted? I was a desperate, lonely fool who had thought that moment had meant something.

I entered my office to find a familiar man in blue sitting in a chair, his head in his hands. I placed my MIND beneath the scanner, and the resounding beep sent Hal flying to his feet. "You're back."

"I'm back," I confirmed, walking toward the desk.

"And you're okay," he declared, more to himself. His hair was in a state, like he had raked his hands through it nonstop since we parted. Blue smudges marred his handsome face. Had he slept at all last night?

"I'm fine," I assured him. Shrugging off the brown coat, I took the vacated seat and logged in to the system. Hal flipped the trash can and perched on it as my screens came to life. "How are you? How'd you get out unseen?"

"I'm fine. Better now that you're here," Hal confessed unabashedly. "I used the chutes."

"The chutes?"

"Yeah, all buildings on the surface have chutes that lead to the Underworld so Majors can take care of the trash. Sometimes we use them for other reasons." Hal rubbed a hand down his tired face. "I'm going to stay for a while," Hal told me, exhaling deeply.

"Stay." I didn't want to be alone. "Who cleaned the office? Did you get in trouble for missing your shift?"

"A friend took it, but that's not important." Hal rotated my chair toward him, looking up at me. "Did they hurt you? Did he bring you before all of the Illum for breaking their rules?"

"No, Collin was the only Illum there and he wasn't angry."

"Did he question you?" Hal asked, leaning toward me.

"No. They had a picture of me running, though." Now that I was beneath the ground, I couldn't silence the questions of how he had done it. "How did you follow me unseen?"

"Their surveillance system is outdated. The surface is motion-based technology; you set it off. All I had to do was run outside the capture window. It's not hard to do."

My brows pulled in. "Why do you know so much about them?"

"Who do you think provides maintenance for their cameras?" Hal retorted, running his hand through his hair. "They have forced those they deem beneath them to run their city. They don't even realize the power they have given the Majors. They are complacent. It'll be their undoing."

Another question escaped my lips. "Hal, do you know the Reaper?"

"Did they discuss him with you?" Hal asked, surprised.

I nodded. "He's responsible for all the trouble, right?"

His starburst eyes gleamed. "More settling the score."

"They seem worried. They said the Illum will eliminate him when the truth comes out."

Hal smirked. "I'd like to see them try. Is that why you're upset? The Reaper?"

"What? I'm not upset."

"Yes, you are. You have been since you walked in. You wear your feelings for everyone to see. If your Mate didn't reprimand you, then what is it?"

"It's nothing," I told him. I didn't want to discuss the thing that was bothering me as those two words slithered to the front of my mind again.

"Come on, Moonlight—we've slept together." His knee knocked into mine, and my stomach somersaulted. I didn't want to think about how close we had come to crossing some unseen line.

"We slept *next* to each other," I clarified, biting back a smile at the nickname.

"That's what I said." Hal smirked, his dimple appearing. "I assume that remains our secret?"

"It does. Even though I don't understand how. They have cameras and yet you weren't captured."

"I know how to become invisible when I need to be," Hal assured me. Was he referring to the cuff he had worn? I glanced down to see his wrist bare beneath his sleeve. "Now, quit avoiding my question. What's wrong?"

"It's the Press," I muttered, my hands fidgeting with the sleeve of my dress.

"What lies is it throwing at the Elite now?" Hal asked, rolling his eyes.

"Collin kissed me at the Sphere and there was a photo of it," I blurted.

Hal went still, watching me. I counted his breaths in his silence. "Did you want the kiss?" Hal finally asked.

"There are rules I have to follow in a contract," I muttered. I glanced to the painting that waited to be sorted.

It was a striking image of a woman standing naked on a rock jutting from the ocean. She was seemingly in chains, her hands hidden behind her. On the other side of the rock was a tall man in black armor, looking at her. In the background was a city that met water. Was he freeing her, or did he put her there? *The Rock of Doom* was the title. My chest felt heavy. The painting was being destroyed.

"Right," Hal said. "I know their rules. I asked if you wanted the kiss."

"Why does it matter?" I fired back.

"Well, the Illum run the Press. Seems opportunistic, doesn't it? The Reaper is causing problems and suddenly an Illum is Mated to a Minor."

My chest burned like it had in front of my birth family. I stared at the naked chained woman. Hundreds, if not thousands, of years had passed since this was painted, before the Last War. The Illum said we had evolved from those ancient humans and their brutality.

But the golden glow on my wrist—was my shackle any different from hers?

I knew the cost of trying to break free. I knew what it cost Alice.

"I think it's bullshit," Alice, seventeen at the time, had hissed at me as we filed out of the lecture hall. We had sat for hours while the hologram illuminated our options for the future, drilling the rules of the Grooming into us over and over.

Welcome to the Grooming. For the remainder of your time at the Academy we will be instructing you on how to rise and serve the Greater Good. With our revolutionary advancements combined with the individual information gathered from yearly testing, you can overcome your defects. It is the Illum's deepest belief that every life has a role in the Greater Good. As you have learned from the history of the Last War, choosing oneself over society as a whole is destructive, a threat to our peaceful way of life. Your Role as a Minor Defect Female is simple yet vital to the Greater Good. Strive for obedience, and you will enter a Procreation Contract, and you will rise to the clouds. With fertile blessings, you will produce an Elite offspring and reenter the procreation phase. Produce a Minor or Major offspring, and your Procreation Abilities will be revoked. You will be condemned to blue. Follow the Illum's protocol, abide by the rules of the Minor Defect population, and constantly seek self-improvement, and you will rise, fulfilling your use for the Greater Good.

"Alice, they'll hear you," I urged.

"I don't care anymore. Explain to me how they can magically overcome our defects after telling us for our entire lives that they define us. It doesn't make sense, Em," Alice spat, her pale skin flushed with anger. Anger that had grown with each moon. Her plans had as well. Plans to ensure she didn't become an object. "And all of a sudden we're given to an Elite male, like some object, and have to pass their tests and put on a show for the Elite. Just to carry an offspring, and for what?" Tears welled in her eyes. "To feed their Elite population or become their damn servants? It doesn't make sense. They act like these saviors, telling us to blindly follow them and making us hate ourselves!"

Girls in gray came to a complete stop around us. I pushed Alice down the hallway.

"Alice, you have to stop. You can't talk like this," I had warned quietly. But her words resonated deep within me, in a long-buried, forbidden place.

"Em, I won't do it," Alice declared, wiping her face furiously. "I won't carry an offspring. It's too much. I'd rather be in blue than be their vessel."

Soon after that, Alice went to the headmaster's office and didn't return, and I never heard what happened to her—whether she had gotten her wish to be in blue and never carry an offspring or had been eliminated entirely. I hated that no one had ever told me. And I had gone on to be a coward, continuing with the Grooming, never stepping out of line for fear of the consequences.

I couldn't deny the part of me that responded to Hal's call for something better—a version of the world in which I had a choice, a version Alice had believed in.

"You still think he's different?" Hal asked darkly.

I turned in my chair to face Hal. "I don't know," I confessed.

He searched my face, his gaze lingering on my lips. "You shouldn't be someone's plaything, and he should have asked you." He leaned in until I could make out the ring of amber around his pupils.

My pulse fluttered wildly. "Asked me what?"

"If you wanted to be kissed."

Hal's lips looked so soft, a delicate pink that softened the harsh planes of his face. A distant alarm bell began ringing in the back of my mind. We were skating into very dangerous territory.

"Are you going to ask now, Moonlight?" His warm breath danced across my skin, and I shivered. Our lips were a heartbeat away.

A long whistle filled my office, startling me.

Hal groaned and pulled away, standing. "I have to go."

"Why? What is that?"

"An annoyance," Hal retorted, running his hand through his hair. "A signal from one supporter to another. It means Elite are present."

The whistle sounded again—impatiently. "You're a *supporter*? Why a whistle?"

"Their cameras don't recognize a person whistling. They register out-of-place movement. The person only whistles, and we know to find safety." Hal looked out the door before turning back to me. "I'll see you tomorrow?"

"Is it safe?"

"Yeah. I'm just late. I seem to lose track of time around you. I'll see you soon, Moonlight." Hal flashed a quick smile and slipped away.

I sat alone for the rest of my shift, sorting art and making notes in my report. Nothing I saw or typed took precedence over my racing thoughts. I wanted to understand. I was tired of being stuck in the in-between. When my screens finally went dark, I shuffled onto the elevator.

I pressed myself into the wall as the elevator slowly rose and more women in gray climbed on, staring at me. I had forgotten that I wasn't in gray.

I pushed through the doors the moment the elevator stopped and darted through the atrium, beelining for the Pods. Whispers accompanied the stares. *Her eyes don't match. How can she be in color?*

A buzzing filled my ears, my body too hot and cold at the same time. At some point I had begun to run, weaving amid the gray until I spotted sunshine hair. I skidded to a stop before Lo.

Shock radiated from her. "I don't mean to alarm you, but you're not in gray."

"It's a long story," I muttered. "I'll tell you everything. Let's just get out of here."

We worked toward the front of the line. People in gray stepped out of our way. I started to ask Lo about her yearly, but a whistle filled the air like the one I had heard in my office—a signal from one supporter to another.

I turned to find a man in gray staring directly at me. His eyes flew from my wrist before piercing me with a glare. He whistled louder, as if warning someone about my approach. My heart began to pound.

"Come on," Lo urged, pushing me onto the waiting Pod.

I recognized the way the supporter had looked at me. People were rising up against the Illum. The Illum controlled the Press. The Illum assigned roles, status, Mates. The Illum controlled everything. And I was an Illum's Mate.

He had looked at me like I was a threat.

✦ ✦ ✦

ONCE I REACHED THE SAFETY OF MY LIVING QUARTERS, I RESTED my head against the door, closing my eyes as tears attempted to gather there. The loneliness of belonging nowhere was crushing.

A soft knock sounded on my door, and I let in Lo, who carried a sad plastic mush container, but she was beaming.

"I'm approved, Emeline, I'm approved," Lo exclaimed, bouncing from one foot to the other.

"Lo! That's amazing. How do you feel?"

"Like I'm floating in the clouds," Lo gushed, spinning. "No more gray. I'm going to wear the most glamorous gowns and dance at balls."

I laughed as she waltzed around my room, the plastic tray her soon-to-be dance partner. Relief coursed through me. I wouldn't be entirely alone in the clouds. I retrieved my meal from the black box and returned to Lo, scanning my room. For one wild heartbeat, I thought Hal had left something.

"So where should we eat?" Lo asked. There were no tables or chairs. I had always assumed our rooms were bare due to shortages. Having seen the Elite's living quarters, I knew it was to deter us from this, from forming connections.

We sat on the floor, and I ate quickly, my body still screaming for sustenance after my run.

"Start from the beginning," Lo instructed. "I need to know everything."

I told Lo about last night. How one of the Starlings had gone missing, how Collin couldn't make it to the dinner with my birth family, the mysterious blue dress, how my father had told me he would eliminate all Defects if he could, to which Lo gasped in horror. My run and my meeting with Collin this morning. I told her about Collin urging me to run to him. How Nora, his twin, Phillip, and Gregory were there.

"Nora said Phillip was like a brother to her," I confessed, my appetite disappearing. "It hurt. My birth family has a life up there, and they have deep relationships."

"I won't pretend to know what that feels like," Lo said. "My birth mom was a Minor as well, and I was her only offspring. My birth father's an Elite, but I've never met him. He didn't want me when I was deemed a Minor. I was a failure. My birth mother ended up in the Sanctuary due to my defects. Then she ended up in blue after me. She told me I had failed her. I was her ticket up, and I messed it all up. Her last words for me were that she hoped I was Mated and my offspring was exactly like me so I would know the shame." Lo fell silent, staring at the floor.

Sadness and anger squeezed my heart. "Lo, I didn't know."

Lo shrugged. "I don't like talking about it. It's not fun being a failure before you ever got the chance to try, you know."

I did know. How many women in this building had the same story? Maybe we could find comfort in one another if they didn't pit us against one another from the beginning. If we were taught to be one another's allies instead of competition. How different would these halls be if we cared for one another?

"It's why a contract matters so much," Lo confessed, unwavering determination in her stare. "If I could just have a successful mating, then I can prove her wrong."

I looked at Lo, truly seeing her for the first time. I reached out, grasping her hand. "Let's show her what she missed out on."

Lo smiled at me, her eyes brimming with tears. "Tell me what to expect up there, Emeline."

So I did. We talked about everything I had experienced in the clouds, including the Press and the article, until it was almost curfew.

Lo stood, stretching, and made her way to the door. "Thank you, Emeline, for everything."

A confession slipped from me, halting her. "You were right, Lo. It is better to go through this together."

Lo smiled. "I knew you would come around."

After she left, I threw away our trash and collapsed in my bed, my mind unsure how to make sense of everything. So I did the only thing to quiet it, allowing sleep to claim me, stretching my glowing wrist out to the empty side of the bed.

✦ ✦ ✦

TWO DAYS PASSED. MY BIRTH FAMILY REMAINED AS SILENT AS they had been for the previous twenty-seven years, which suited me. I didn't hear from Collin. I didn't know if the Reaper had resurfaced. If that was why he had been silent or if he had achieved what he wanted with the Press and there was no reason to talk. Collin did send me flowers again, which sat in my office. I didn't bother to read the card.

I had two lessons with my HI, whom I had named Frida, after an artist that occasionally came up in the Archives. Both mornings, Frida announced that I had entered the luteal phase of my cycle, whatever that meant. My stats recovered after my run. Certain nutrients and minerals struggled, but my dopamine stayed elevated.

The first lesson addressed etiquette again before launching into my duty as a fertile vessel. My stomach twisted at how Frida's words echoed my time at the Academy, dragging up horrible memories that all ended with a freckled face disappearing from my life.

The next day, I started dance lessons. Frida would briefly describe the dance and then play a short video showing the dance before footsteps appeared on the floor for me to follow. I felt utterly ridiculous dancing alone in my room as the sun rose. Still, I let the music chase away any insecurities.

The music was beautiful, with peaks and valleys of sounds that I couldn't help but move to. I was left breathless and eager for the next lesson when the music ended. It wasn't the same as running, yet I felt that welcome calm take over as I danced.

Lo had brought her meals up both nights, claiming my floor was more comfortable for dining. We discussed her upcoming initial meeting. Thankfully, she had received a message stating that her first meeting would be in public tomorrow, the same night I would have dinner with Collin, Nora, and her Mate, William, at the Pond. Maybe we would truly go through this whole experience together.

While we discussed all things procreation, I kept Hal to myself. Twice, I almost told her about him, but fear stopped me. Perhaps it was more shame than fear. But those were thoughts I locked away.

Hal had come to see me both mornings. He didn't mention the Press or my Mate. He didn't mention the flowers' slow decay either. And I didn't ask about the supporter who had sent a warning whistle when he saw me. We talked about art, teased, and danced around the truth we both knew—that this, whatever this was, had an expiration date. It was approaching, and there was nothing we could do about it.

I thought of the painting of the couple embracing goodbye while I lay in bed alone. I thought maybe I was starting to understand their desperation. That terrified me, but like all things that scared me, I ignored it. Ran from it. We should have discussed it, but we didn't. Instead, we looked at art like we had all the time in the world. I stared at Hal like he was my own personal sunset. Let it captivate me, distract me, and make me appreciate him all the more because it was fleeting. I found myself unable to look away.

But, like the sunset, it must end.

CHAPTER SEVENTEEN

The next morning, on the day of the dinner, I found Hal sitting in my chair, his feet on my desk, staring at the ceiling.

"Hi." I grinned and scanned my wrist.

"Hey," Hal responded, dimple on display. He crossed the room toward the waste bin, his hand brushing mine. My body came alive at the graze. I sat in my chair and logged in to the system. As the first piece of art loaded, I turned toward Hal. He was limping, just barely, but it was there every time he took a step with his right foot.

"Are you okay?"

Hal flipped the trash bin upside down, grimacing as he sat. "Tired, but fine now."

My brow furrowed. "You don't look fine."

"Rough shift. Physical labor catches up with you," Hal said nonchalantly. "What do you think of this piece?"

The painting depicted a pregnant woman wearing a long dress decorated with golden circles and other colorful geometric shapes. Her breasts were bared, and she looked down at her rounded belly. Peeking behind her gown was a skull. At the bottom of the dress, three other women bowed their heads as if in mourning. I glanced at the title: *Hope II* by Gustav Klimt. My stomach bottomed out.

The women all seemed remorseful, as if the skull predicted the offspring's future.

"I don't like it," I confessed, wanting to look away. I hated that it depicted a warped representation of what might await any offspring I produced. That they would live my life, hidden and shamed for something they couldn't control. Something I gave them. It would mark the trajectory of their life—or death.

"Why?"

"Because only sadness and grief await those with offspring," I told him, shifting.

"Sad things can be beautiful too, Moonlight."

"I disagree." I looked away from the painting, glancing at the screen. "That's strange. They're reassigning it. Usually, they get rid of ones with people in them."

"Maybe they don't want to lose the idea that having an offspring is sad."

I couldn't look at the painting any longer. With a click, it disappeared. I released a long breath.

The next painting had a dreamlike, ethereal effect, capturing a city in the foreground and rolling hills that bled into the night sky. The stars swirled, and the moon glowed, the long brushstrokes mimicking the movement of light. It was stunning and unlike any night sky I had ever seen. *The Starry Night* by Vincent van Gogh. I was shocked that it was the same artist who had painted *At Eternity's Gate,* the despairing man with his head in his hands.

I bit my lip, lost in the contrast between the shadows and light.

"What are your thoughts?" Hal asked. I turned to find him staring at me.

"A person who painted such pain has also painted such beauty. I want to ask the artist which came first."

"What do you think?" Hal asked, leaning toward me.

"Beauty first. You can't come back from that kind of pain."

Hal chuckled, the sound pebbling my skin in its wake. But his eyes held a sadness. "Things are made more beautiful by pain. You see everything differently afterward. Not right away. It takes time, but knowing the darkest depths—" Hal paused. "It allows you to experience the highest peaks."

"I don't think I care to see the peaks if I have to feel the depths," I confessed.

Hal shook his head. "You do, Moonlight. I promise you do. They have just robbed you of it."

My Comm Device dinged several times. I turned, fishing it out of my bag.

"What news from the world above?" Hal asked. I read through the two messages, the first from Collin.

> Your work schedule has been updated. Look forward to seeing you tonight. I personally picked your gown. —Collin

The second was a formal message changing my workweek from every day to five days on, two days off. Starting tomorrow, I would have two days off.

"My schedule has been officially modified. I don't have work the next two days," I told him.

"So, things are progressing," Hal commented dryly. "Even with the Press article."

It was the first time he had brought up the Press since the other day.

Before I could respond, Hal rubbed his jawline and stood. "Guess I'll see you in two days."

"Don't do that," I urged, standing.

"Don't do what?" Hal crossed his arms.

"Walk out over something I didn't have a say in," I sputtered, frustrated.

"I'm not."

I reached out, grabbing his arm. "You are. You're trying to leave."

"It would be easier if I left," Hal admitted, looking over my shoulder at the painting. "One day you'll have the nerve to ask, and I don't think I'll say no." His eyes traced my lips before he stepped away.

I tilted my head back to stare into his starburst gaze. "What are you saying, Hal?"

"I was looking for . . ." Hal shook his head. "It wasn't supposed to happen like this."

"What were you looking for?"

"Not this," Hal admitted.

"Do you think I was looking for this?" I exclaimed, gesturing wildly between us. "I was happy down here with my life. Then you show up, and then the contract. I was happy down here."

"No, you weren't. You were lonely."

"You don't know that," I practically shouted, anger surging. "I was fine alone."

"Fine isn't a feeling," Hal said.

"It's better than this feeling. Why bother me if you're going to leave every time reality sets in?"

"I should have walked away the day I saw you staring at that painting like you saw more. I should have left you alone."

"You should have left me alone because I wear gray and you wear blue," I sneered. My anger turned into an ugly thing, vicious, the deluge of emotions and thoughts I had been running from breaking through my walls.

Hal fisted his hands at his sides, his posture rigid, and I knew I had crossed a line. "Yeah, you wear gray," he seethed. "It doesn't make you above me. It makes you a mindless vessel, one they use to achieve their whims. That's what your gray clothes get you. Do you think that Nora, Collin, or Phillip will ever accept you as anything other than a Defect? It's all an act and you just waltzed right into it, claiming he's different even as he uses you."

I felt like I had been doused in cold water. "I didn't tell you everyone's names."

He rolled up his left sleeve. On the inside of his wrist was a long, jagged scar. "I told you I was deemed Elite; they killed my parents and sent me to the Academy. I'm the same age as your dear Mate, his twin, and your brother. They were thick as thieves, swallowing every lie they were fed. Looking down on everyone else. Even after what they did to Nora"—my brows pulled in; what had they done to Nora?—"Collin stayed committed. The moment I left the Academy, I cut out that fucking chip. Most people die when doing it, but I lived. Faked my death and disappeared. I wore color and I gave it up!"

I know how to be invisible.

"You can cut them out?" I asked as too many questions ran through me. I felt blindsided, my heart beating too fast. "Who are you, really?"

"I'm whoever I choose to be."

My pulse roared in my ears. "Hal, are you—"

Footsteps sounded in the hall, and Hal moved quickly, sprinting behind the open door. I thought I might be sick as a man dressed in dark gray entered the room, holding a black velvet box.

"Ms. Emeline," he said, and I nodded, not trusting myself to speak. "Mr. Collin wanted this delivered personally to you. If I could scan your wrist." The man produced a small silver scanner. I thrust my arm out, willing it not to tremble, and he passed me the box. "Good day, Ms. Emeline."

I blew out a deep breath as the man exited the room. The box thudded on my desk as I reached for the doorframe, peering out to find a long empty hallway. I rubbed my hand into my chest, massaging my racing heart.

I knew one thing: If Hal was the Reaper, then the greatest danger to him was myself—the Mate of an Illum.

I turned to find Hal opening the velvet box. The insides sparkled in the light of the hologram.

"I'm going to go," Hal muttered, pushing past me to the door.

"Fine, go," I spat. "Everyone does, especially Elite."

"I am not like them," Hal growled, whirling toward me.

"Doing what you want, leaving when you want, giving half-truths, making me feel inadequate," I stormed, my chest aching as I did—begging me to stop. I didn't, because this was for the best and too many things were crammed away in the depths of my soul that were eating me alive. "Tell me, Hal, exactly how *you're* different?"

"Moonlight—"

"Don't. I've only known you a week anyway. Might as well say goodbye now."

"Whether I do it now or in three moons, you were always going to be a goodbye," Hal promised.

My eyes burned, but I didn't let the tears fall, clenching my fists so hard my nails broke the surface. "You're right. I'm a vessel, and that's all I'll be."

Hal stared at me, opening his mouth as if to say something, but a second later he closed it before turning and walking out. I gripped the door I never bothered to close, slamming it shut.

I threw myself into my chair. I was fine, I was *fine*. I chanted it over and over again until I leashed the mess that dwelled inside, shoving it all down until the buzzing from the lights overhead filled the room once again. My only consistent companion.

My chest felt empty. I had been no better than the Elite, throwing his status at him. Disgust twisted viciously as I looked at the open black velvet box. Inside was the grandest jewelry I had ever seen—an exquisite necklace that boasted large oval bloodred rubies surrounded by smaller round diamonds running its entire length, as well as a matching pair of diamond-encircled ruby earrings. The finery was grotesque in its beauty. Inside was a note.

    For tonight, something I hope you enjoy. —Collin

I snapped the lid closed, staring at the box unseeing as I waited for the ding to signal the end of my shift. Lost in self-hatred. For the ugly words. For not chasing Hal down. But mostly for being in this situation in the first place. I knew how to be alone. It was easier than this. In a week I had let my soul tether to others. Relying on them, wanting them, caring for them. It was a bad choice, one that put not only myself but others in danger. I needed to cut the tethers. With Hal, it seemed I had succeeded. It was safer for him to stay away from me.

The golden glow of my wrist was the one tether I couldn't sever.

I ran my finger down the inside of my wrist where Hal's scar had been. How had I missed it when he had sat exposed in nothing but his boxers? But he had been wearing the technology-scrambling cuff—why had he needed it if he didn't have a MIND? The question I never asked hung heavy all around me. The question I would not dare voice.

Was Hal the Reaper?

CHAPTER EIGHTEEN

After my shift ended, Lo and I scanned into the last Pod once the other Minors had cleared out. The Pod made its obnoxious announcement, and two different locations appeared on the screen. I would see the Starlings, and Lo would be tended to by someone else.

The Pod shot up, my stomach flipping at the quick ascent. Lo clutched her seat, her mouth clamped tightly shut like she might be sick.

"It's going to be fine," I said. "I told you everything I know, but regardless, he's going to love you, Lo. He'd be a fool otherwise."

She smiled tightly and didn't respond, and a tense silence fell. I watched the setting sun. Even as it burned my eyes, I refused to look away. It was fleeting, I reminded myself.

As the sun kissed the horizon its final goodbye, we reached Lo's destination. We hadn't yet passed the clouds, and I wondered whether the proximity to the surface meant anything. I felt a slither of unease.

"Message me when it's over?" I asked.

"Yeah, see you," Lo muttered as the doors closed. The Pod continued upward, breaking through the clouds.

I should have tried harder to reassure her, but I didn't know what to say anymore. We were powerless in this. Simply vessels. That was what Hal had said. Hal.

It was hard to believe it had only been a week since I had met him. Somehow, I needed to rearrange my life to what it was before Hal existed. But one week carried more weight than a decade. A foolish part of me fantasized that if I just got through the next forty-eight hours, I would arrive in my office to find Hal lounging in my chair. We would just go back and spend time together until . . . until I was active in the procreation phase, or until I carried an offspring of an Illum? Until Hal was caught and eliminated?

There was no scenario in which Hal and I could be together.

You were always going to be a goodbye.

It was good that it was done, I told myself. If one week caused this, what would have been the ramifications of three moons' time? This way, no one got hurt.

My chest protested fiercely. I rested my forehead against the glass as the sparkling buildings blurred together. There was a gap between two buildings, and I saw it. The moon looked at me, but it was only a quarter of it. The full moon was still a week off.

His voice echoed in my head. *I cut out that fucking chip. I'm whoever I want to be.*

Alone in the Pod, the moon my only witness, I wondered what I would do if I had a choice, who I would be.

The Pod doors opened to the familiar antechamber beyond, and the wish was swallowed up by the unending darkness of night.

"Ms. Emeline." Harold bowed his head before scanning my wrist.

"Harold," I said as we walked down the hall.

"The Starlings will be with you shortly."

"Both of them?"

He nodded gravely as the door snapped closed.

"Hello again, Fledgling," Violet's smooth voice called out. I turned and the air fled from my lungs, horror slamming into me.

Violet had been hurt. Badly. Her left eye was puffy, tinged a deep purple, and a barely healed cut on her lip reopened as she smiled, blood beading.

"What happened to you?" I whispered as Rose grabbed my bag, disappearing without a hello.

"It looks worse than it feels," Violet assured me.

"Who did this?" I demanded.

"The Illum," Violet said as she opened the door that led to the bathing chamber. "Don't worry. It would take more than this to keep me away."

Gregory's warning rang in my ears. *You are the Mate of the Illum they send into the Elite to carry out their judgments and punishments. He is their Enforcer.*

Had he enforced this? Who exactly was my Mate, and what did he have to do with what happened to the Starlings?

I followed Violet inside the steaming room, but I didn't feel any of the usual effects of the calming scent of lavender steam. Apprehension squeezed my throat.

"You know the drill. Clothes off." Violet reached for the jar of exfoliant and sucked in a sharp breath, her free hand flying to her side. What other bruises did she cover?

I stood naked before them as Violet and Rose silently began scrubbing me down. Violet breathed through her teeth as she turned to reach my back. Rose looked up from her crouched position, worry etched across her face.

"Please sit, Violet," Rose urged. "I can do it alone. Let yourself heal."

"They told me I was to return to my duties," Violet stated as she continued. It had been four days since I had last been here. How bad had Violet's injuries been if she looked like this?

"What did they do to you?"

Rose looked up, glaring at me. "You have caused enough trouble," Rose seethed viciously as she walked away, slamming her fist on the button. The showerheads came to life. Rose had barely scrubbed my lower half. She smiled brutally. "Some grime can't be scrubbed away no matter how hard you try."

"Rose," Violet scolded as she guided me to the showers. The scalding water assaulted my skin. I made my way to the other side, sputtering, trying to hear what the pair was arguing about.

"You will not."

"She has a right to know."

"Not at the expense of you."

"I am fine."

"I am not. I will not watch that again. I will not risk you."

I wiped the water from my eyes to find the two of them huddled close together. Closer than friends. Rose held both sides of Violet's dress as Violet cupped her face.

When the water shut off, they pulled apart. No one handed me a towel. I tiptoed over to the tub, dripping wet. They made their way to the tub's edge as I submerged. Rose helped Violet to her knees, her pain evident.

"I can wash my hair on my own," I said, desperate to avoid Violet's suffering. "Please."

Rose shoved my head beneath the surface, and water flooded my nose. She yanked me back up, my eyes streaming. "Why do you care now?" Rose demanded savagely, applying sweet-smelling soaps to my wet hair.

"I swear I didn't—"

Rose shoved me under again. I racked my brain for what I had said to Collin at tea all those days ago. He had encouraged me to speak plainly. Was it all so he could get information? I gulped air as I resurfaced.

"It could have come from another source. Someone *else* close to the Illum," Violet was saying. "She isn't the only one with ties to them."

"*She* wouldn't say anything," Rose retorted.

Violet clicked her tongue. "Rose, you don't know that. She's desperate."

I exited the tub when they finished, shaking from the near drowning, and took the warm towel Violet offered me. I watched as she walked out of the room gingerly. I just wanted to understand. I was so tired of being kept in the dark.

We entered the waxing room, where I dropped my towel unabashedly and crawled onto the table. They began their torturous application of the wax. I welcomed the pain today, letting it siphon some of the guilt and hurt I carried. Rose ripped a strip from a particularly sensitive area and I yelped, my eyes watering.

Tears slipped down my face. "Was the blue dress punishment?"

There was a weighted pause. "We already answered their questions about the dress," Rose snapped finally. "We had no part in it."

"I would understand if it was you," I told them, wiping my eyes. "I didn't mean to get anyone in trouble. I didn't mean for you to get hurt. I am sorry."

Violet laid a hand on my shoulder. "I never thought you did, Fledgling."

Rose ripped another strip from my skin, and I let out a small scream. "Slipped," Rose said. "You might not have meant to, but you did. You got my—" Rose shook her head. "You got Violet hurt."

"*Someone* got me hurt," Violet said plainly.

"But why?" I implored. "Does this have anything to do with the Reaper?"

"Shhh," Rose said, whipping her head like she half expected to see someone in the room. "Are you daft?"

"The Elite are the ones who told me," I explained.

They shared a look over my naked body, communicating in a nonverbal way that took true knowledge of another. Rose's mouth became a thin line as she shook her head, but Violet looked down at me.

"What do you think of the Elite?" Violet asked.

I caught my lip between my teeth. Violet nodded at whatever she read on my face.

"I don't think I need to tell you that what I am about to share doesn't leave this room," Violet whispered so quietly that I rose up onto my elbows to hear better. Rose began applying wax again. "A rebellion is coming, Fledgling."

People are rising up. My heart began beating faster and harder until each breath took effort. Was it fear, or was it my own battle cry?

"Does your Mate often confide Illum information to you?" Violet asked. "Clearly he's interested in you, judging from the photo in the Press."

"I don't know if he's truly interested, or if he's just using me."

Rose rolled her eyes. "There are many ways to kiss someone. Hands don't cling to obligations. Nor do polite kisses linger."

My face heated. "Who said it lingered?"

"Everyone. It's all the Elite have been able to talk about." Rose applied more wax. "Collin is constantly in the Press—giving messages on the Illum's new passings, the Reaper situation. Everything related to the Illum comes from him."

"And he's connected to you," Violet said quietly. "You are the only non-Elite with access to the Illum."

"What about Tabitha?" I asked. "Collin mentioned she has run the city for more than fifty years. Why isn't she in the Press?"

Rose grew impossibly paler. "We don't talk about her."

"We can't keep her in the dark," Violet protested. "He'll eat her alive."

"Better her than us," Rose responded bitterly, her eyes on Violet's bruised face.

"Rose," Violet began, a delicateness to her words. "We are all in this together."

"No," Rose declared, her voice cracking as she gripped the side of the table. "We aren't in this together because the walls have ears, and all secrets slither back to the mother's nest. And she is in that nest, soon to be in bed with one of them. I told you this is a bad plan, Violet. You overreach. Why can't this be enough?"

"Rose, the time of hiding is coming to an end. There is no going back. We will all have to pick our sides. You know mine." Violet held Rose's stare. Rose trembled, shaking her head. "No matter the cost. No matter the consequences."

"I need to find a new lens," Rose said, sniffling as she walked away.

"Tell me, Fledgling, are you tired of being in the dark?" Violet asked, ripping one strip.

"Yes," I said, and meant it.

"We need information, and you can get it."

I glanced up at her. "What information?"

"Information to help the Reaper." Violet tore the last strip from my skin, then beckoned me to follow her to the next room.

The Illum had always claimed to be dedicated to peace, but looking at Violet's ravaged face, that couldn't have felt further from the truth.

No one spoke as Violet styled my hair in a upswept low twist with pieces framing my face. Rose replaced my lens, painted my lips a bloodred, and left my eyes simple with long lashes. My nails were shaped into ovals and painted the color of rubies to match the jewelry I was to wear.

At last, we made our way into the final room. Violet passed me a pair of nude panties. I dropped my robe and shimmied into them before making my way onto the platform.

"Your Mate picked this dress himself," Rose told me.

They helped me into a wine-red, off-the-shoulder gossamer gown, with billowing sheer sleeves that hit just below my elbow and a boned bodice that ran up to soft cups. The skirt pooled on the floor, the thin fabric floating around me like a deep red mist. Rose finished lacing up the back of the gown and handed me simple black heels and a black satin bag.

Violet walked in a moment later with the necklace and earrings and fastened them in place. I stared at the girl in the mirror. She was beautiful, but all I saw was the violence Violet had endured, Hal talking about his parents' murder, Alice's fiery gaze that I would never see again. The necklace looked like drops of blood sparkling at my throat. Everything felt hideous. The brown eyes that had felt like a gift a mere week ago felt shameful, like I was hiding. A coward.

The Starlings walked me out. Violet placed a hand on the door that led to the hall, keeping it closed, and turned to me. "Which side are you on? Them or us? You must choose."

"I am an Illum's Mate."

"Precisely," Violet said. "Will you help us?"

"This is dangerous for you. I could let something slip," I whispered.

"Then I would die for something I believe in. But you won't." Violet leaned in, the intensity in her eyes searing me. "Remorse isn't something one can fake—not convincingly. I saw it when you saw my face. A better test than any I could give you. It wasn't fear staring back at me, Emeline. It was anger."

Goosebumps coated my entire body at her words.

"Take your time in the clouds to think it over," Violet stated, cracking open the door. "Are you content being his vessel, Fledgling? Or do you want power?"

CHAPTER NINETEEN

I HAD SEEN PAINTINGS OF WAR. DEPICTIONS OF VAST, ANCIENT-looking battles filled with blood and smoke. If the rebellion resulted in anything like that, Violet's injuries would be minuscule compared to the carnage of what was coming.

Suddenly, I desperately missed life before the contract. When everything was as I had been told it was. When the only problem I had identified was myself and my inability to follow the Illum's protocol. Before I had to contend with the Reaper and the Enforcer and an impossible choice that could mean life or death for me and anyone I cared about.

I didn't know what I was going to do, but either way, I needed to hold it together this evening. I buried the war that waged.

The Pod had dropped me off at the tall, thin building that housed the Pond. A large glass-encased half-moon observation deck jutted into the sky, where I now stood.

"Emeline, over here."

Nora stood with Collin and another man who must be her Mate. Her beauty took my breath away. A tight, high-necked emerald gown with structured shoulders wrapped around her lithe figure. She handed her Mate her bag, and the dress revealed her entire back. Her straight raven-black hair was tucked behind both ears, which were adorned with diamond-and-emerald earrings that curled around the entire shells of her ears.

Her Mate had a curious glint in his bright green eyes as he took me in. He had dark auburn hair and rich tan skin, like he too enjoyed the feel of the sun.

"Hello, Emeline," Collin said. As my eyes finally found him, I steeled myself. He was a pillar of strength and grace in a sleek black suit. His raven hair was perfectly styled. He was every bit as handsome as Nora was beautiful. Devastatingly so. "The necklace suits you," he told me, stepping toward me and taking my hand, its golden glow painting us. His power engulfed me, and a chill ran down my spine as his lips brushed against my hand. I hated myself for the reaction.

I traced the necklace weighing heavily on my neck. "It is beautiful. Thank you."

Nora nudged her twin, pushing him aside. "Yes, yes, she's beautiful. Now stop hogging her." Nora glanced at the necklace and then back at her twin. "It's nice to finally see it out of that box," she said quietly to Collin, to my puzzlement. "Emeline, I would like to introduce you to my Mate, William."

I bowed my head, and his emerald eyes had a devious look that left me too exposed. "It is a pleasure to finally meet the woman worthy of an Illum."

"Let's be seated," Collin interrupted as his warm hand found my lower back, guiding me into the antechamber, where an attendant stood behind a blue-green marble cylindrical podium that emitted a faint glow. The curtain of water behind the podium blocked any view of the room beyond, and water ran down the antechamber's walls as if we were inside a bubble.

Captivated, I hardly heard the attendant asking for everyone's arms for scanning.

"Emeline, your arm," Collin prompted. I hastily held my arm toward the scanner as another woman arrived.

A woman in a vibrant acid-green gown stepped into the antechamber with us. The dress had a high slit, exposing her trembling leg. Her sunshine hair cascaded in perfect waves, and relief shone in her blue eyes at the sight of me.

"Lo," I said, stepping away from Collin without thinking. "You look stunning."

Lo smiled sheepishly at me, making her look every bit her twenty-two years of age. "It's a very bright green, right?"

"Yes, but it suits you," I told her as she looked over my shoulder at the Elite behind me.

"Is that him?" Lo whispered, near silent. "Your Mate?"

I nodded, realizing I didn't want Collin or the Elite to know that we were friends. We were forbidden to have friendships as Minors and, more than that, Violet's battered face swam before my eyes. I would not let that fate befall anyone else. I glanced back to see Collin watching us curiously, and Nora looking at Lo's bright green gown.

"I'll see you inside," I whispered, ignoring her confused look and returning to Collin's side.

"Who was that?" he asked.

"No one," I said quickly. "Just someone I work with on the surface."

He didn't say anything, and the water parted as the attendant approached it, creating a path. A small *wow* escaped Lo from behind us as the pathway closed, leaving her on the other side. We followed the man over a black bridge, water flowing underneath, and Collin's strong hand once again rested on my lower back as we entered the main room.

I froze, my mouth falling open. Water cascaded from the curved windows, which soared several stories high, encasing the entire room with running water. Its flowing current obscured the sky outside. Ropes of white light hung precariously from the ceiling at varying heights, blurring the stars that peeked through the glass ceiling, illuminating oblong booths that, if I looked closely, were moving subtly in a slow dance. We stepped off the black bridge and onto a black-tiled floor, and I immediately felt unstable. I gripped Collin's arm, his hand flexing against my lower back.

Collin's breath caressed my ear. "The floor and tables move around the entire dinner. Not quickly. It is a slow progression." As we approached one of the booths, he held me back and asked, "The Defect in the entrance, how well do you know her?"

Rule Five: You are obligated to answer any questions your Elite Mate may have. The truth is expected at all times. Lying is not permitted.

I told him the truth—just not all of it. "She lives in my building."

"Are you close?"

"We are occasionally on the same Pod," I told him, capturing my lip. "Seeing someone like me up here was strange. That's all."

To my relief, he didn't press further. We approached the table where Nora and William were already seated. The booth was made of a smooth, dark wood and was curved inside, creating a sleek bench wrapped around an oval table of teal, green, and white marble that seemed to be illuminated from within.

I fluffed out my skirt once seated as Collin moved in next to me. From this vantage point, it was easy to see the booths moving, like tiny pebbles carried about by the ripples in the water. Glancing up, the rope lights could have been the sun's rays piercing the water. It was truly mesmerizing. It was art.

Nora beamed at me. "It is amazing, right? It's my absolute favorite place in the whole city. And on cloudy days, the water runs from the center of the ceiling, completely blocking out the clouds."

A part of me wished it was cloudy.

William laughed, putting his arm around Nora's shoulders. "She isn't exaggerating," he drawled. "She's made me bring her here three times in one moon. What is it about this place, Mate, that makes you unable to stay away?"

"I can see why. It is beautiful," I said.

"Oh, look," William said, craning his neck. "There's your Defect friend."

Lo walked behind the attendant, her vivid green dress hard to miss.

"She's just a woman from my building," I clarified, clasping my hands under the table.

"Tell me, do all the women below look so appetizing? Is there an entire treasure trove of beautiful options?" William watched Lo walk across the room, and I tried not to cringe.

I was saved from responding as Collin leveled him with a look. "You could have taken a Defect Mate, William. If I recall, you were rather adamant to have my sister."

William shrugged, his hand tracing long lines down Nora's arm. "I mean, I needed to see if the rumors were true."

I decided I didn't much care for William.

Nora didn't so much as move, but her throat bobbed as Collin's brows shot up. "Do tell me what those rumors of my sister are?" Collin whispered in a tone that made me sit up straighter. Viciousness emanated from every harsh line of him.

"It was but a joke," William said. "You know I have wanted Nora since the Academy."

Lo had stopped at a table with a man lounging in it. A man with brutally short hair.

"Ah, now your friend will be your family. That is your degenerate brother, right?" William chuckled.

Nora's eyes flew from the table to find Collin's, searching his face.

"His own brother suggested this," Collin told her as a Defect in gray placed impossibly delicate glasses of golden bubbling liquid on the table before bowing and departing.

"So while you and Phillip become Illum, the rest of us have to do what you both refuse to," Nora shot back, anger seeping onto her face, her fierceness making itself known and both twins exuding ferocity.

"I *am* an Illum," Collin stated, placing his drink back on the table. "I believe you have forgotten my Mate beside me—my Minor Mate."

I took a long sip of my drink and debated for a moment whether to down the entire thing. Did all families make eating together difficult?

Nora's cheeks flushed bright red. "Emeline, I am so sorry. That was so rude of me." She stretched her hand out, placing it on top of mine. "Please forgive me. I am thrilled with your mating. Truly."

"Of course," I said. I meant it. If I were Mated to someone like William, I would be angry at Phillip's freedom as well. I wondered how bad Nora's first Mate had been for her to choose to take on another.

"I always forget you and Gregory were close once," William remarked, swirling the contents of his drink as he stared at the potential Mates.

"We were never close," Nora stated, sipping her drink.

"He was Edward's best friend," William drawled. I racked my brain. Why did I know that name? A greasy feeling settled in my stomach. Right, the blond man I had encountered at the Garden when I first met Collin.

"Yes, my first Mate was friends with him," Nora said. I instantly understood why she would opt for a new Mate if her first had been Edward. I felt terrible for Nora. Edward and William both seemed like horrible Mates.

"Why did they grow estranged? The Press never covered it. They were inseparable," William said, taking a drink.

Nora glanced up momentarily, opening her mouth, but stopped as a worker distributed our food.

"I love that soup," Nora told me, leaving her food untouched. I reached for my glass, finishing the last bit of bubbles.

"Mate, I asked—"

"I can get more. I need to use the facilities anyway," Nora interrupted, tearing herself away from William.

"We can summon someone for more drinks," William said, placing his hand on her leg. Nora's eyes dipped to his hold on her. Collin shifted next to me, his leg bumping into mine.

"It's fine," Nora assured him, a smile appearing as her eyes went to the wall of water. "It is the least I can do for insulting Emeline." She pulled her leg from his grasp, waiting for him to move.

"Nora, get the one I like," Collin instructed. William glanced toward him as he begrudgingly rose from the booth, letting Nora leave. I took a small taste of my soup, and savory decadence burst across my tongue.

I watched as Nora walked away, grace in each of her steps. Most of the Elite watched her leave, several women whispering behind jeweled hands, but Nora seemed unaffected. I wondered what they could possibly say about a fellow Elite member with an Illum brother. The water curtain parted as she approached it; seconds later, it fell once more, and Nora disappeared.

Collin leaned in, dragging me from my thoughts. "How is the food?"

"It's delicious." I glanced toward his plate, where slimy, unappealing food sat. It looked disgusting. "Yours?"

"Would you be surprised if I said I enjoyed it?" Collin confided, eating another.

"So you don't like tomatoes, but you like that?" I asked, repulsed.

"You don't like tomatoes, Collin?" William inquired. "You know both are essential for procreation in males." William looked toward me. "I am one of the head members of the Health and Nutrition Department. I oversee the distribution of nutrients throughout the city."

While I debated asking him about the mush given to Minors while the Elite ate real food, Collin pushed his plate away. "I do not prefer them."

"Interesting. Do you know what else is interesting?"

I took another spoonful of soup, positive we were about to find out. I focused on my soup to avoid the eye roll that fought to be free. Collin's leg brushed against mine once more.

"These mishaps that keep happening and this Reaper everyone is talking about."

Unease found me, but so did my interest as my heart picked up its pace. Violet had said they needed whatever information I could get.

"What's interesting is the Elites' need to spread gossip that questions the Illum's capabilities," Collin said with quiet menace, his leg leaving mine. "The need to discuss a man who has already signed his elimination. It is only a matter of time."

William sat up straighter. "I fully support the Illum and know they will prevail like they always do." William cast me a look.

"And when was it decided that support meant gossiping?" Collin asked, an edge to his voice.

"I believe that occurred around the same time the Illum chose new ways of operating. It has left some of us uneasy. As loyal supporters, I believe they want answers. That is all."

I didn't need him to clarify to know I was the new way of operating. A Defect Mated to an Illum.

"New ways of operating?" Collin asked, tilting his head. I worked to swallow at the dangerous look in Collin's eyes. "Is that what they are calling it?"

William shifted under Collin's gaze, his survival instinct perhaps finally kicking in. "Like I said, they are simply curious and would like answers. Nothing more."

"You'll receive answers tomorrow at the dinner," Collin said. "Not that the High Council deserves them." Collin drained his glass of bubbling liquid.

"High Council?" I asked despite myself.

"A group of Elite who have shown unwavering support to the Illum. They present their findings for the Illum to pass judgment," Collin told me, his tone gentler.

"Your entire family is on it. Well, besides Gregory. Will your Mate grace the Elite with her presence?" William probed, watching me.

Collin leaned forward, his eyes dark. "It would seem you've misinterpreted a few things. Your contract with my sister doesn't offer you protection from the Illum's fury."

"My apologies," William muttered.

The attendant replaced our plates, including Nora's untouched dish, with our main courses. The waste sickened me. I had never seen an empty plate, besides my own, be taken away. Collin and William sat in silence in Nora's prolonged absence.

I looked around the room; our table was closer to the entrance now. But Nora was nowhere to be seen.

"I will go find her," William informed us, repetitively tapping his knuckles on the table.

"I would rather Emeline go. There are some things I need to discuss with you." Collin glanced at me, his voice softening. "If you're agreeable?"

"Of course," William said, tapping the table. "As the Illum insist."

"I wasn't talking to you," Collin told William without looking his way.

"All right," I told him. Sick satisfaction found me at the look on William's face.

Collin exited the booth, waiting for me. Slowly, moving the layers of red fabric, I came to stand before him. "Thank you," he said, nodding. A piece of his pristine hair fell out of place.

Without a thought, I tucked it back, brushing the shell of his ear. Collin seemed to hold his breath as he gripped my waist, the warmth heating my bare skin. Our gazes clashed, and I found his sapphire eyes wild. My traitorous heart slammed into my chest at the memory of his lips against mine.

Was that real desire in his eyes, or was this just another immaculate performance for the Press? He watched me, his eyes questioning—waiting.

Are you content being his vessel? Or do you want power?

Was this a game? All the questions I hadn't asked wedged their way between us.

A buzz rippled across the room. Words flew behind jeweled hands, but his eyes held mine as he ignored our audience.

"They are all watching us," I muttered. The same words I had said before he kissed me. Did I want that again?

"It is an unfortunate side effect of being mine," Collin said, releasing my waist, his thumb caressing my skin one last time.

Quickly, I stepped away from the table, away from Collin's magnetic field. Heads swiveled, following my every step, as did snippets of muttered conversations. "I am telling you I have seen her before"—"The Press"—"No, that isn't it—"

I ducked my head and finally reached the wall of water, which parted as I stepped through. The rush of water drowned out the noise of the Elite.

My skin remained too warm from the way his gaze held me. The heat in his eyes had certainly seemed real, but I had been fooled once before.

I glanced down a long, shiny teal tunnel. It seemed endless, with no obvious doors to be found. I had only made it a few steps when a male voice seeped into the hall, a voice I knew.

"Don't."

I peered around the glossy hall, but it was empty. I turned, but I was alone. Then I heard it again.

"Please," Gregory exclaimed, sounding desperate. "Don't even say it."

I heard a quiet female voice respond, but I couldn't make out what she was saying. My stomach twisted. Gregory was here with Lo. This was their initial meeting. All Lo wanted was a Procreation Contract, and Gregory was here with another woman.

"I will wait," Gregory growled. "I will never stop waiting for you."

I shouldn't be hearing this. Where was Nora? I spun around to retreat through the waterfall curtain when Gregory emerged from an almost invisible hallway door alone, locking eyes with me.

"Lost, little sister?" Gregory inquired. He leaned against the door, trapping the woman inside.

"I was looking for Nora."

"The very end leads to the prep area," Gregory informed me, pushing off the door and walking back toward the dining room.

"Your Mate, I know her. You're here with her."

Gregory looked at me and spat, "She isn't my Mate yet. I'm here because they told me to. I didn't choose this. I didn't choose her."

"Lo is a good person," I said, unable to stop myself.

Gregory walked away, looking over his shoulder. "You see, little sister, that's the problem; I am not." He left through the wall of water.

I walked to the end of the hall only to find a prep room with men in gray holding platters, who looked at me warily and claimed no Elites had been down that way. After ten minutes of searching, looking for more invisible doors in the hallway, I gave up. Nora wasn't here. I returned to the main room, scanning the slow-moving tables looking for ours. They'd all moved.

Gregory was with Lo again. He looked bored, a drink in his hand as Lo talked. I tore my eyes away, ignoring the looks as I searched for our table. Nora was there, William's arm around her again, all smiles. How had I missed her?

Collin let me into the booth, his hand grazing my lower back. William let out a low whistle, sipping his full glass of bubbles.

I froze at the memory of the whistle that had pulled Hal away, the supporter who had whistled, staring at me with hatred. William's whistle was utterly unlike those.

"Emeline, is something wrong?" Nora asked.

"It's nothing." I shook my head and took a long drink of bubbles. I wouldn't mess up again. No one else would meet the same fate as Violet.

"Are you certain?" Collin asked, searching my brown eyes.

"I'm certain," I assured them, then quickly changed the subject. "Where were you, Nora?"

"I think we just missed each other," Nora told me, taking a sip. I felt Collin's eyes on me. "I wish it was cloudy," she said longingly as she looked out at the stars.

I felt Collin's gaze leave me as he grabbed his glass. "But it isn't," he told his twin and downed the contents of his glass.

The rest of the evening was uneventful, the table chatting as if I weren't there, which suited me fine. My meal had been delicious, but the cake that followed was divine. Collin and I didn't exchange another word until he walked me to the Pod. Nora and William had hung back.

The moment the water fell, hiding the Elite from view, Collin turned toward me.

"You were quiet tonight," Collin observed. "Are you all right, Emeline?" He glanced toward the attendant. Without a word, the man instantly slipped away into a break in the water I hadn't seen, leaving us alone.

"Can I speak plainly?" I asked nervously.

"I would appreciate it if you always did."

"The Press," I said. "Is that why you kissed me? For them to publish it as a distraction for the Elite?"

Collin looked toward my lips. "Is that what you want it to be?"

"I want to know what it was to you."

"Selfishness," he told me. I stepped back. "Anything else?"

My nerves held me in a vise grip.

"You want to ask me about the Starlings, don't you? You saw them tonight—I assumed you would have questions."

Startled, my mouth dropped open. "I—I—" My eyes searched his.

"The Illum do not take lightly to anyone who spreads discord among the masses," Collin said quietly. "I told you they will stop at nothing to silence it."

My heart found my throat. "You questioned them. You're the Enforcer."

"I am." His calculating gaze took me in, something brewing in those blue depths. I half expected him to demand to know how I had learned his true role, but he stayed silent.

"Did you . . ." I asked, unable to finish the question. *Did you hurt them?* There was talking plainly and then there was stupidity, but I wanted to know what he was capable of.

Collin shook his head.

"You didn't?" I asked.

"It doesn't matter if I did or didn't," Collin said, walking to the waiting Pod outside.

"It does." It did. I had to know.

"It doesn't," he assured me as the Pod doors slid open. I opened my mouth to respond, but he cut me off. "You already believe I did. Good night, Emeline," he told me, dismissing me.

I closed my mouth, staring at the man I was Mated to. Unsure of what to say or believe, I gathered my dress and entered the Pod.

"Everyone has a role to play, Emeline," Collin whispered as I passed him, a shiver setting my skin on fire as his warm breath brushed my bare shoulder.

I placed my wrist under the scanner, turning to face him. "Do you enjoy your role, Collin?"

Sapphire eyes went wide as the doors shut before he could answer.

CHAPTER TWENTY

The next morning was my first day off ever, but at four-thirty, Frida's voice filled my room, jolting me awake from a restless sleep. What followed was a long morning of manners training for the upcoming ball. Eventually, she began to teach me a new dance that was faster than the one from the other day, and there were spins.

Exhaustion weighed on me—I had lain awake most of the night, repeating the events of the past few days—but I began to move in my oversize gray attire and bare feet. I lost myself to the sounds, the movements. My heart pounded, eager for each coming spin, arms extended toward an imaginary partner. The end of the dance was filled with even more turns.

For a moment, all the thoughts and fears emptied out of my head, and I relished the silence. Dripping with sweat, I lost track of how many times I practiced the dance, savoring each step and turn. But like all things I found comfort in, they took it from me before I could really enjoy it. The music stopped, the HI disappearing.

"Frida, play the song again, please," I begged through ragged breaths. Nothing happened. "Hologram Instructor play the song again, please."

Silence filled my room, and in the quiet all my thoughts began to come out of hiding.

"Dammit, play the song again," I demanded, walking up to the black orb. I flipped it over, looking everywhere for a button, but nothing. I slammed it down on the counter, stomping off to the clear area between my bed and counter. I began to hum the song, but it wasn't the same.

I gave up, throwing myself onto my bed, and checked my Comm Device to find two messages that I must have missed while I was dancing. The first was an official message from the Illum.

> F13463233, your presence is required by M17292834 at 8:00 this evening following your preparation appointment at 4:30. All travel information has been loaded to your MIND chip. A Pod shall be sent now. Fertile Blessings.

The second was from Lo early this morning.

> Gregory is your birth brother?! He's so funny. When did you leave? Let's talk soon.

I blew out a long breath. Gregory didn't want Lo, that much was obvious. He was seeing someone else, someone it had sounded like he cared for.

Everyone has a role to play...

What role was Gregory playing? What about Collin? Everyone else in the clouds? What role would I play?

I glanced at the time and sat straight up. Somehow it was already four in the afternoon. Time seemed impatient today. Begrudgingly I left my bed, bypassing all the beautiful gowns, and threw on my clothes before grabbing my Comm Device and bag.

I found a sunny spot outside, soaking in the warmth, until I heard a Pod approaching the Sanctuary across the street. I retreated several steps and pressed into the wall of my building as eight people exited the Pod, wearing helmets with shields that hid their faces and green uniforms that wrapped tightly around their muscular frames. Plates of the same color were fitted to their chests and backs. Each one had a thick belt laden with weapons and more strapped to their legs and backs. They could only be the Elite Force. For the first time, I watched the steel doors of the Sanctuary finally open as the soldiers entered.

The air was quiet, and a pit formed in my stomach. I stared at that open door, craning my neck to see what they hid inside. I could just make out the entrance to a building. Suddenly, banging filled the air, then silence.

And then women started to scream.

I pressed my back harder into the wall. The cries of young offspring joined the women. A part of me, the part that was concerned with self-preservation, screamed to run back to my living quarters, but I couldn't move. I was rooted to the spot as the screaming grew louder. The soldiers returned, escorting offspring out. Disbelief engulfed me.

Several soldiers restrained the birth mothers as their offspring sobbed. I couldn't breathe as the women dropped to their knees, their screams ripping at my soul as they reached for their offspring. None of them could have been older than four.

They were being taken away to the Academy.

I watched helplessly as one woman broke through two soldiers. She sprinted to a small boy, falling to her knees with a force that had tears burning my eyes. She clutched the boy to her chest, his small hands gripping her shirt.

"Please," she sobbed, "please don't take him."

Even the warmth of the sun couldn't pierce the chill that ran through my veins. My hands flew to my mouth in horror as one of the soldiers grabbed her by her hair, pulling her back.

"I love you, Albert, I love you. I'll find you, I love you."

"Control yourself," a soldier barked.

The boy trembled as another soldier pushed him into the Pod with the other offspring. A different soldier brought the end of his gun down on the woman's head—she fell to the ground with a resounding thud, unmoving. A gasp escaped me. Maybe it was a scream of my own. My feet set me in motion, toward the horror.

I was halfway there when a large masked soldier stepped in my way, a hand on his gun. "Do you have the authorization to be here?"

My eyes flew to the offspring wailing in the Pod as soldiers began filing in. Some of the mothers had grabbed the woman they had knocked unconscious and others stood still, staring at the Pod. Frozen.

"What are you doing?" I asked, my voice broken.

"Where is your authorization?" The soldier stepped closer just as a Pod showed up outside my building. "I suggest you get on that Pod, right now." He turned, stalking back to the Pod with the offspring and soldiers. The doors closed behind him, and the Pod took off.

I looked at the women. It wasn't desperation but undiluted devastation on their faces. The ones screaming and crying were difficult to watch, but there was one whose expression was a blank, unmoving mask of shock.

As I scanned into my Pod and it pulled away toward High Town, I knew her face would haunt me for the rest of my life.

The offspring were being taken to the Academy. I wanted to tell myself they would be fine, but somehow nothing seemed fine, nor would it ever be fine again.

I exited the Pod when it stopped, barely managing to nod at Harold as bile climbed up my throat. The Starlings began their routine, an exaggerated version that included a haircut. I didn't care—I didn't hear anything they said. Those mothers' screams replayed over and over again.

On the raised platform, fully dressed for the night, I looked at the woman they had created in the mirror. Violet had styled my hair half up, with the rest curled and loose. Large pear-shaped diamond earrings hung from my ears. The gown was more ornate than the ones before. It was sheer but had intricate gold-and-silver beading, tight, with a slit that exposed my left leg. It hugged my waist and bust before artfully wrapping around my neck and extending down my right arm. My left arm was fully exposed, my glowing shackle on display. I only saw the Illum and the disgusting things they stood for.

"Why are you wearing that face?" Rose squawked at me. "You're ruining my masterpiece."

It did not matter the image they created. It wouldn't conceal what was stolen from those women today. Being thrust into a room filled with the Elite and Illum, forced to perform for them, felt like torture.

"When I left my building, a Pod showed up"—I sucked in a shaky breath—"and men in green got out. They opened the Sanctuary doors . . . and took the offspring away. They took them away."

"The Parting," Violet stated as she drifted closer to Rose.

"The what?" I didn't understand why they were handling it so calmly. Maybe I should have explained the screams, the desperation and soul-wrenching pain. "You don't understand."

"We understand. She lived it," Violet said quietly.

"You what?" Disbelief filled me. They had lived it.

"We were in contracts before this. Rose successfully carried an offspring. What you saw we call the Parting." There was little space between Violet and Rose, who stood unmoving. "It's our reality in the Sanctuary. When an offspring comes of age, the Elite Force comes. They carry out the Illum's orders. They did this." Violet gestured to her healing face.

"It wasn't like that for me." I remembered little from my own journey to the Academy. Helen had given me up willingly. It had been a warm day. There had been no screaming, no soldiers in green.

"The Parting is only for the Minors in the Sanctuary," Violet said. "It happens unannounced, always when the other Minors are away for their workdays. There is no time for goodbyes."

"Do the offspring ever see their mothers again?"

"I didn't," Rose said, her voice small.

"And the Illum, they stand for this treatment?" I demanded,

thinking of Collin's power and viciousness. I had wanted to believe so badly in the kindness he had shown me.

Violet stepped closer to me. Her bruising had started to turn greenish, resembling those green uniforms. Rose grabbed at her quicksilver dress, like she needed to keep her close. "Have you given my suggestion any thought?"

"I have."

"And?"

I stared at my reflection in the mirror, then back at the two women before me, but I didn't see them. I saw that broken mother staring helplessly as her offspring was taken. I had run toward the screams, not away. I was done hiding in the dark. I didn't know the extent of this rebellion, but I knew one thing.

"I want power."

CHAPTER TWENTY-ONE

My stomach tied into knots as the Pod shot through the sky toward Collin's entertainment quarters. Violet's smile and parting instructions pulsed through the night air in time with my heart.

"What do I do?" I had asked.

"Tonight, pay attention. Be his Mate and pay attention. Try to gain his trust. We will talk when we see you next."

I tugged at the part of the gown that wrapped around my neck like a noose.

Which side are you on? Them or us?

It was safer to do what had always been done—to follow the Illum's rules. Adhere to the peaceful façade they had crafted. I had a litany of reasons to conform. But I ignored every single one of them.

The Pod stopped, its doors opening to a stunning antechamber. Fear latched onto my shoulders, threatening to pull me down, but I stepped into their clouds anyway.

A honeyed "Hello" floated toward me along with an overwhelming sweet floral scent. Nora stood beside a table and a large glass bursting with white lilies towered over her. Her sage green silk gown was so pale it looked almost white, with thin straps, a swooping neckline, a low back, and a high slit. I glanced at her clasped hands. Her left wrist was glowing. I realized I had never noticed it. She seemed to wear the glowing silver as an accessory rather than it wearing her.

"Your wrist is silver," I stated instead of hello.

Nora released a twinkling laugh. "I am the Mate of an Elite, not an Illum."

"Sorry," I mumbled, remembering my manners.

Nora sighed. "Please don't apologize. I'd very much like to be a friend in your eyes, not an Elite."

"We aren't allowed those down below," I muttered.

"The blonde, Gregory's intended Mate, is she not your friend?"

"Like I said, we aren't allowed friends below."

Nora didn't pry. "Well, treat me how you would want a friend to treat you, please." She stepped closer, threading her arm with mine. "You do have one up here."

"A what?"

"A friend, if you would like one," Nora said, leading me from the antechamber and into the room beyond.

Two sweeping staircases hugged the walls, meeting at the top of the grandiose entry room. Large glowing cylinders were suspended above us, connected by gold wiring, stacked precariously—like one huge balancing act.

"I didn't know if it was appropriate," I said.

"It is if you'd like it to be. You have days off now. I am free for two more moons."

I shifted my gaze to Nora as she looked at me. "Free?"

"Yes, I will enter my procreation phase with William. Things will be different then." Her tone was flat.

"I would like a friend."

Nora squeezed my arm excitedly. "Good—it makes my plan so much easier if you go along with it."

"What plan?" I asked as we ventured down a long hall.

"Making you my friend. It would happen either way. I'd make sure of it." She grinned and guided me past countless stunning spaces.

"I feel your plans usually work out."

"All but one," she informed me. "Welcome to the formal living quarters. Collin, sadly, never uses them."

"Why?"

"Some things are hard to revisit," Nora said quietly, her steps picking up their pace.

"What about for parties or balls? Entertaining friends?" I asked.

"Collin isn't a fan of either. He has work." We reached the end of the hall, stopping at the door. "And Phillip."

"And you, right?"

Nora smiled, laced with sadness once more. "I have been in contracts all my adult life. Before that, I was being prepared for one. I am usually with my Mate or offspring, while I get to be."

I glanced at Nora, her sorrow slipping past my walls. Her chin was held high, the picture of Elite grace, but her lips were pursed, her eyes heavy. A weariness blanketed her.

I saw the pain of the mothers from the Sanctuary in her expression. How did it feel to be without one's offspring? Ice slipped down my spine. I would find out for myself soon enough.

"Do you see your offspring often?" I asked.

"On visiting day, I see them all," Nora said, stopping at the door.

"Them? You have more than one?"

"I have three," Nora told me as she knocked on the door.

My mind raced. She was thirty-two. We had offspring every five years or sixty-five moons. A short Courting Phase, into procreation, into maternity. We then cared for the offspring until the Academy. Approximately five years for the entire process. The math didn't add up. "Did you produce twins?"

"Enter," came Collin's voice.

Nora shook her head before opening the door.

If Nora had three offspring, she had been Mated at seventeen. Disgust leveled me. Before she had even left the Academy. Why had the Illum done that? Collin would have still been in the Academy as well, not yet an Illum, I assumed. I couldn't fathom why he would want to join the group that did such horrendous things to his sister. I didn't get to ask anything else as Nora lingered at the door. She didn't balk from the shock radiating from me.

"We all have to do our part, Emeline," she said, then slipped away. I watched her go for a moment. Her lithe steps, her honey voice, her softness as others whispered and judged—they were the armor she hid behind. My heart ached.

"Good evening, Emeline." That powerful voice spilled into the hall, snaking down my spine.

"Hello, Collin," I responded quietly as I stepped over the threshold.

Sapphire eyes collided with my concealed defect, their depths churning, silencing my turbulent thoughts. He stood from his desk, dressed in all black again.

The ceiling soared. An angular chandelier hung directly above us, comprised of eight long gleaming spears connected at the top before brutally jutting out. Moonlight streamed through a wall of windows, outshining the spears, illuminating the cavernous room. The glow cast the wall behind his gray marble desk into relief—shelves sat empty.

He leaned against his desk, unrolling his sleeves and fastening the cuffs. Light reflected from the golden buttons.

A small black orb the size of a marble projected a labyrinth of tunnels into the air—paths that dipped and twisted, coming together only to shoot off in opposite directions.

He tracked my gaze. "Beneath."

"What?" I asked, straightening.

"The tunnels of beneath," he repeated. He tapped the orb, and the map shifted, going out of focus before settling again, the river that ran through the city now visible and the lone bridge that connected to Low Town. A blue circle glowed under the bridge.

"What is the blue spot?" I asked carefully.

"Work. Identifying weak entrances for the retaliation." My heart leapt, shocked that he had answered.

I hadn't realized I had ventured so close to the desk—to Collin. I stumbled back, sucking in a sharp breath, and his hand steadied me, pulling me forward to stand between his legs.

He's an Illum, my brain raged as I froze in his magnetic field. The vile things I had learned, had seen. The Parting still ringing loudly in my ears, haunting my every thought.

But Violet's instructions had been clear. *Be his Mate. Pay attention. Gain his trust.*

My pulse rioted under my skin as his hand lingered on my waist. There were no Elite in the room to watch, no one to pretend for.

A muscle in his jaw feathered as his warm grip left my side, yet I didn't move. I couldn't help myself. My eyes chased his hand as it found his thigh—his fingertips digging into the muscle like it had dug into my skin in the Sphere.

I stepped back. "What retaliation?" I asked, more breathless than I intended.

He turned from me, tapping the orb, and the plans disappeared. He slipped the object into his pocket.

"One that will cause problems," he told me plainly.

"Why?"

Collin looked at me, considering. "The Reaper has been too bold. He's killed Elite. Highlighted flaws in the system. The Illum does not tolerate chaos. They are adamant about sending him a message. One that will give him—pause."

"Do you think it'll work? This plan?"

"I do not know yet what the carnage of his people will do to him," Collin stated stiffly.

Carnage . . . Apprehension spun around me. "What exactly are you going to do?"

Power roiled in his sapphire pools. "My role."

"What exactly does that mean? What are you going to do to the Majors?"

"Whatever is required of me. Everything I do is for the Greater Good." Collin stood up straight, towering over me. "Everything you see tonight is for the Greater Good."

I refused to move as he walked to the door, holding it open.

"The Majors are people." My heart skipped a beat.

"They are waiting for us," he said as if I hadn't spoken.

"Why am I here? What is this dinner about?"

"The man who whistled at you, the reason you froze at the Pond. Did you tell anyone else about him?" Collin asked, power radiating from him.

My heart stopped. "How did you—what are you talking about?"

"Very little happens in this city that the Illum are not aware of."

"Collin, please, tell me why I'm here."

"You're my Mate," Collin said, his polished exterior gleaming, his face utterly impassive. There was not a single crack. "I'd ask you to trust me, but given our brief conversation at the Pond, that would be a waste of time."

I stepped back, his words hitting me in the chest. "Collin—"

He whipped his head toward me. "Tabitha does not handle being made to wait. She instructed we walk in together. Your questions have made us late."

Suddenly I felt the height of where I stood—how easy it would be to fall.

"After you," Collin said. There was no warmth to his voice. Violet's advice fell away at his austere tone.

"No beseeching my forgiveness tonight?" I asked. I wasn't sure why I did. Maybe I wanted to know that the man who had chuckled at my indecent sounds was real. That the kindness, the tenderness with which he had kissed me, weren't my desperate delusions.

Still think he's different? Hal's taunting voice found me.

Collin's hand tightened on the door, his knuckles bone white. He didn't meet my eyes as he gestured. "After you, *please*."

I bowed my head and headed out. His voice was so low I almost missed the words, but the coldness slithered beneath my skin.

"I'm not foolish enough to ask for something no longer obtainable."

CHAPTER TWENTY-TWO

Our breaths were the only sound as we headed toward whatever made forgiveness unobtainable. My heart ricocheted off my ribs, leaving me breathless. The heavy scent of lilies was overpowering as we made our way into an identical hall that led to two double doors, guarded by two soldiers in dark green uniforms, one impossibly tall. I tried not to cringe away from them. The masks made it impossible to tell whether they had been at the Parting. They bowed to us as Collin captured my clammy palm in his steady hand. The doors opened, and we entered the room beyond.

It was a tremendous dining room, double the size of my birth parents'. There had to be at least thirty members of the Elite standing around the table, waiting for us.

My stomach hit the floor. Vincent stood at the table directly before me. I lifted my chin as Collin led me to the far end of the room. Countless tiny chandeliers hung from the ceiling, like falling stars hanging over the length of the dark table. The walls were paneled, and there were two obsidian heating hearths.

The décor couldn't distract me from the faces I recognized. William and Nora. Phillip, Richard. I didn't see Gregory or Helen. Very few women sat among the Elite. I wondered briefly what they had done to have a seat at this table.

We reached the head of the table. Collin pulled out the chair to his right for me.

"Be seated," Collin stated. Chairs scraped across the floor. I took my seat, my spine painfully straight, the beaded gown too tight.

Halfway down the table, a man with long blond hair tied at the nape of his neck stood. Edward, the one who had approached us in the Garden—Nora's first Mate.

He held a glass of bubbles. "On behalf of all of the Elite here, I wanted to raise a glass to the Illum and to this peculiar mating. We know you have your reasons." Edward cast me a slimy smile, and several men chuckled around the table. "Many fertile blessings to the Illum."

People raised their glasses to toast us. Collin didn't. His hands remained folded on the table, staring at Edward.

Glasses hung in the air, waiting.

Collin finally grabbed his glass lazily, tilting his head at Edward like he was sizing up his prey. The contents threatened to spill at any moment. Collin flashed a dangerous smile before downing the contents and placing his empty glass on the table.

I reached for my drink, but without looking at me Collin shook his head just a fraction. I withdrew my hand. Phillip across from me hadn't touched his either. A few glasses sat on the table untouched. When everyone had replaced their glasses, Collin's eyes swept over every person who drank, marking them.

"Perhaps I misheard you. Peculiar mating?" The hairs on the back of my neck stood up. "Is that what you called this?"

Edward wrung his hands. "Yes, surely you understand. A member of the Illum stooping to a Minor contract."

"So I am stooping now?" Collin drawled, shaking his empty glass. A man in dark gray rushed over, refilling it. Collin took a long sip, then turned toward Edward, that viciousness in his eyes. "Was it stooping when you ogled my Mate so thoroughly in the Garden?"

"I—I meant no disrespect," Edward stuttered.

Nora took a sip of her drink like she enjoyed watching her first Mate squirm. Edward was clearly older than she was. How old was he when they had been Mated? He had been Gregory's best friend, so at least five years . . .

Collin sighed. "No disrespect? What did you mean then when you said I was forced to socialize with their kind?" Edward opened his mouth, but Collin continued. "You said it was barbaric. But if they look like this"—he gestured to me, my body going rigid as Collin's eyes lingered—"why not bring them out in public for some"—Collin tore his eyes from me as he stared down Edward with such intensity that it made me want to fidget—"entertainment."

Collin had remembered every insult Edward had given me. Was the anger radiating from Collin real? Was this *work*?

Collin leaned back in his chair. Edward again opened his mouth to speak but Collin interrupted. "You insult her, you insult the Illum. I do not forgive, nor do I forget the mistreatment of my things. Unless it is elimination you are after."

My head whipped toward Collin at his nonchalant suggestion. It was murder he was talking about.

Edward swallowed as he bowed. "I accept any judgment the Illum see fit."

"Be seated," Collin ordered, dismissing him. "Speaking of judgment, Gregory, did you receive the Illum's gift for the evening?"

"I did." Gregory strolled into the room from a separate entrance, a bored expression on his face. Shocked gasps rang out at the dark blue suit he wore, the same color my gown had been.

"Thank you for joining, so I can remind everyone here that every single thing the Elite at this table have is by the grace of the Illum." Collin's voice rang out. "With all the rumors circulating, perhaps this is the only thing that will silence you all. Failing to uphold the Greater Good is a punishable offense."

My eyes met Gregory's in sympathy, but he smirked at me. The family disappointment club, he had called us. Vincent and Richard refused to look at him, and Phillip only looked at Collin.

"All the rumors flying about the Illum's choices, yet not a whisper of the *Elite's* choices. My Mate went to dinner with her birth family last week. Someone impersonated the Illum. Sending a black box to the preparation appointment." Collin looked around the table. "People were hurt in the process. Perhaps it was just for someone here's entertainment." Collin stared at Vincent. "I didn't find it entertaining. Neither did Tabitha."

Everyone shifted uncomfortably as murmurs broke out along the table.

"Gregory, how does it feel to be the entertainment?"

"Honestly," Gregory started, dusting off a sleeve of the jacket. He glanced down the table, eyes gleaming as they lingered on our birth father. "You really wasted a great color on the trash of our society. I think it brings out the blue in my eyes."

My eyes volleyed between Collin and Gregory. I heard a glass break. Two men rushed over to clean up William's glass, its contents spilling onto the table. William grabbed the offered new glass, looking at Nora, who stared straight ahead.

"When I find the person responsible, they will find blue to be their permanent color. Am I understood?" A collective agreement rang out. "Be seated." Collin dismissed him.

Gregory spread his arms wide, giving an elaborate bow. "As you command."

A man brought in a white orb, like the one on Collin's desk, and placed it in the middle of the table.

"Which brings me to my next form of entertainment for this evening." Everyone sat up straighter, the room holding its breath. "There have been attacks. I am sure everyone here is aware of the man you all call the Reaper. My fellow Illum members have devised a plan to draw this pest out."

Around the table, approving chatter broke out. Collin held up his hand and silence fell instantaneously. "But before we discuss our plan forward, some entertainment for you all and a message to the ones foolish enough to doubt us. Tabitha?"

No one breathed in the room as the man in gray tapped the orb. A hologram projected above the table. Like my HI, the woman looked too solid, too real in the room.

Tabitha had short silver hair and a delicate face that seemed ageless. She wore a sweeping white gown. She didn't even stand in the room with us, and yet everyone stood at perfect attention. The woman they all feared. The woman who ran our city.

"Hello, loyal Elites," Tabitha began. Everyone bowed deeply. I followed suit. "I have joined this meeting to serve justice. Thanks to the help of Collin and his Mate, Emeline."

My stomach twisted, and I plastered a smile onto my face as everyone looked at me.

I glanced at Collin for one furious heartbeat, but he stared straight ahead, his jaw tight.

"We were able to apprehend a sympathizer with the Reaper's desire to destroy our peace and upend our prosperity and sacred way of life. His only goal is to spread discord among those with defects. Not all Defects are swayed by his empty promises. Emeline and many like her understand his threat to our life and have come to the Illum for help, as allies, as fervent supporters—seeking protection and justice." The woman turned to me like she could see me and smiled. "Bring him in."

I turned toward the doors as two men in dark green armor dragged in a man with hateful eyes, the same man who had whistled at me. My heart pounded painfully in my throat, suffocating me.

He had a cut above his left eye, and there was bruising along his jaw, which he held at an odd angle. The men in green dropped him to the ground.

"This Minor Defect insulted Emeline. Insulting an Illum's Mate is an insult to the Illum. Upon our investigation he was found guilty of passing information from the Capitol to the Reaper."

No. This couldn't be real. My pulse hammered in my ears. He had just whistled. I found those hateful eyes. *I didn't do it.* Cold sweat coated every inch of me. *It will be okay.* This was like Gregory. They were just sending a message. That was all.

"You would all do well to follow her example. Thank you, Emeline. The Illum are with you. Collin, you chose well. Proceed." Tabitha disappeared.

Collin would have the man taken away. He was going to threaten everyone and that was it. He didn't believe in eliminating Defects. He had told me he didn't believe in it.

Collin stood, the epitome of grace, that power and viciousness surrounding him. If there was an internal battle, he didn't show it.

Whatever is required of me. Everything I do is for the Greater Good.

"Eliminate him," Collin's voice rang out.

My pulse roared in my ears. I couldn't breathe.

The man didn't beg. He didn't do anything but release another low whistle before dropping to his knees. His eyes locked on mine as he began panting. Blood trickled from his ears onto the floor. I couldn't look away. It was the Parting all over again. I stood frozen in horror.

"The Reaper is coming for you all," the man rasped. "He will tear your buildings to the ground." He fell fully to the floor, gasping. A gurgling filled the air.

No one had touched him, but he was dying. His eyes began turning red. I felt the world tremble beneath my heels.

The man attempted to whistle again from the ground, but nothing came out. He tried again, unyielding in the face of death. Blood sprayed from his mouth with his last breath.

The blood from his ears pooled on the floor. The world shook again, like at any moment we'd all crash to the ground.

It wasn't the world, I realized. It was me. I couldn't stop shaking as some essential part of me, a piece of innocence I hadn't even realized I had contained, shattered for good.

Collin stood at the head of the table. "Does anyone else need any more entertainment for the evening?"

No one made a sound. I couldn't look away from the now lifeless body.

"No? Are we sure?" Collin asked, taking a drink. His hand didn't even shake. My legs shook so violently I thought I might fall into my seat. "Remove him and bring out our meals. Sit." My legs gave out.

Two men in green picked up the man; his now red eyes were open but unseeing. They carried him out and, with him, the part of me that had ever thought anything good happened in their clouds.

A hand touched my knee. I jumped as I found Collin looking at me. I couldn't read his expression or maybe I just didn't want to. He hadn't prepared me for what I had just witnessed. I pulled my leg out of his grasp, blinking. I felt stuck and hollow.

"Eat," Collin commanded.

The sounds of forks and knives filled the room. Slowly people began to talk. I heard laughter from the far end of the table. I mindlessly lifted my fork and knife, cutting into the meat. Red spilled onto my plate. My stomach turned. All I could see was the man's blood spilling onto the floor—the man Tabitha had said met his death because of me. I laid my fork down. I couldn't eat.

I couldn't think. Lightheadedness blurred my vision, and I focused on breathing.

I sat in the cacophony of the Elite, who ate like we hadn't just witnessed a murder.

Breathe. Again. Again.

A chair scraped against the floor as Collin stood. Distantly, I noticed our plates had been cleared.

"In two days' time, we shall ambush the underground community," Collin began, then called for ten members of the Elite to meet him in another room, including all the men of my birth family. I stood when I heard other chairs moving. Collin must have dismissed them.

Collin grabbed my hand. I made to pull away, but he gripped my hand harder, tugging it so I fell into him, his arm snaking around my waist. Everyone watched us. I didn't have the strength to push him away. I was utterly numb. "Nora will take you."

Nora's small hand threaded through my arm, linking with me. I let her guide me out of the room. With each step, the Elite bowed to us, to me. Nora sidestepped the pool of blood. It was all I saw on the walk to the private quarters. I tuned out Nora's calming words, the kind I assumed she would say to one of her frightened offspring.

Eventually, we were seated in the sunken seating area. I stared straight ahead at the woman in the art piece cloaked in all white, an innocence and purity about her—things I had just lost.

"Tea. The way you make it," I heard Nora say to someone. Heavy footsteps took off. Minutes, perhaps hours later, I had a warm cup of tea in my hands.

"How?" I asked, my voice cracking.

Nora leaned in. "How what?"

"How did they kill him without touching him?"

"MINDs all have a lethal dose of hemotoxin. It affects our blood. So the Illum can eliminate—"

"*Murder*," I spat harshly. "You all say *eliminate* like it means something different. That man is dead. Collin killed that man."

Nora didn't flinch. "Okay, murder."

I couldn't look at her. All I saw in her sapphire eyes was Collin. Instead, my eyes locked on the man in the painting. The hand clutched to his heart was red. Was it blood on his hands? Akin to the blood on Collin's. How could he do that? I had thought . . . I had wanted to believe in his goodness.

I sucked in a sharp breath. "I want to leave."

"You need to stay until Collin returns," Nora told me.

I didn't want to, but I didn't bother saying so. I had no rights up here. They had taken them from me.

I sat quietly and sipped my tea. It burned my throat viciously. The unmistakable smell of alcohol swarmed my nose. Someone had put alcohol in my tea. I relished the pain, taking another gulp as if it would burn away the image of the pool of blood. Blood that covered my soul, Collin's atrocities ruining me.

I didn't know how long we were silent before I heard voices. Collin and Phillip entered, and behind them was Gregory, still in his blue. Collin and I made eye contact. He broke away from Phillip, coming to stand in front of me. I didn't bother to stand. He took a seat in front of me on the table. He reached his hand toward me, like he might touch me. I pulled away toward Nora. His hand fell to his side.

"Leave us," he told them. They all began to rise.

"Don't," I begged. Everyone stood frozen.

"Emeline—" Collin started hesitantly. His calmness broke my restraint. "Look, I—"

"You what?" I demanded, turning toward Collin. "Killed someone, used me, embarrassed Gregory, who was innocent in my being in blue. Interrogated the Starlings—hurt them."

I stood abruptly, sloshing the last bits of my cold tea on my gown. I didn't care, though. It could be ruined, like the rest of me. "I want to go to my living quarters."

"You should stay here tonight," Nora suggested. "So you aren't alone."

I couldn't. I refused to stay in their clouds. I took a step, but Collin grabbed my hand, halting me.

"Forgive me," Collin whispered. "Emeline, please—" I felt the others go still at those words, but I was past caring.

"For which part?" I demanded. "What am I forgiving you for this time?"

Collin hesitated, his eyes finding mine. "For hurting you."

"Wrong," I growled. "I thought you weren't foolish enough to ask for something unobtainable." A cup shattered on the floor. "Imagine my surprise to discover you are, in fact, a fool."

"He was actively working against the Illum."

"So he should die?" I hissed.

"It's hard to understand."

"No, what's hard to understand is that you told me you didn't believe in killing Minors, but you just did," I fumed. No one else in the room mattered. I raged against that magnetic pull as his endless pools held mine—the sapphires fractured and dull. I searched for the man I had first met but before I could find him, Collin stepped back, turning away from me.

"That was before."

I shook my head as a cloud outside shifted. The light from the moon illuminated the room as if in answer to the questions swirling in my mind. *What role would I play?* Silence filled my mind. I needed to get to the ground. Because they didn't understand—living up here, they didn't understand. I didn't know what would become of my soul if I stayed here.

"I'd like to go to my living quarters, please," I said, willing myself to calm.

"Phillip, summon a Pod and get the Force ready for briefing. Gregory, make sure she gets home. We can't afford any more mistakes."

I whipped my head toward Collin, seeing him more plainly than ever before.

"I am going with her," Nora declared, marching up to me as I walked past Collin and up the stairs. Gregory stood by the balcony doors, waiting. Seeing him fully, he had been right. The blue brought out his eyes.

"No, you will not," Collin stated. "You will stay here."

"She shouldn't be alone," Nora told him, coming up to my side, grabbing my hand.

"Think of your offspring," Collin urged, a potency to his tone that ripped me apart.

Nora whirled toward Collin, a force. "You will not use my offspring against me," she seethed through her teeth. "You will not involve them. You will *never* involve them, do you understand me?"

"No," Collin said, holding his ground. "I won't. But we both know *they* will."

Nora took several steps back like she had been smacked. Gregory trembled, his mouth a thin line. He wasn't looking at me. All of him was directed at Nora. The confession I had heard at the Pond. The tinkling voice in answer. I had not been able to find Nora. How had I missed it?

"Arabella is almost of age," Collin said. "They will use her to get to you."

Nora released my hand as a single tear rolled down her face. "You wouldn't."

Gregory took only two steps when Nora locked eyes with him, and he stopped, his hands fisted tightly at his sides. His entire body shook like it took every ounce of willpower not to close the distance.

Phillip took a step back as he just watched. "The Force will be ready in twenty," he said quietly.

"I am fine, Nora. Stay here." I grabbed Gregory's arm, steering him toward the Pod that sat outside. "Let's go."

Collin grabbed my hand, stopping me. I let him, only to deliver the thing he had broken. "Speaking plainly, I wish you hadn't."

"Hadn't what?"

"Chosen me," I said, pulling my hand out of his. "You chose wrong."

CHAPTER TWENTY-THREE

Minutes later, I sat in the pod with Gregory. His eyes had filled with a sorrow I never wanted to know. "Thank you," he muttered quietly.

"I didn't have anything to do with you being in blue," I said. "I'm sorry."

"Don't be, little sister. It didn't faze me."

"How could it not?"

"It is just a color. It held no power until they told you it did. They told me to wear it, so I did." Gregory smirked, but it didn't reach his eyes. "Family fuckup, remember? It would seem it is just me again, now that you are the Illum's puppet."

"I am not." My plan gathered speed at his words.

"After tonight, in the eyes of the Elite, you are."

"I don't want to be," I said.

Gregory took off his jacket, tossing it to the ground. "If the Illum have taught me anything, it's that they don't give a shit about what you want."

"Any advice for me?"

Gregory stretched out over the seat, lying down, folding his hands behind his head as he stared at the night sky. "Yes. Never care about anyone. The less you care about, the less you have to lose."

"And if it's too late for that?" Because I cared. I cared about those offspring and their birth mothers. I cared about the man they had killed. I cared about Violet's injuries and her hidden love for Rose. I cared about Lo and her need to prove her mother wrong. I cared about Nora—about what they had put her through. I cared about Gregory. I cared about what the Illum had done to Hal. I cared so much, I felt as if I might break under the weight of it all. I cared about . . .

The Pod plummeted to the ground. I welcomed the drop, letting go of the last thing I thought I cared about, the plummet ripping any feelings for Collin away—leaving it among his clouds and the horrors I had found there.

Gregory looked right at me like he saw it all, devastation etched across his face. "Then never let them find out."

The Pod came to a stop, the doors opening. "You said they are always a step ahead."

"I did."

"So if they are, won't they find out?"

"Most likely."

"Then what do I do?"

"Only you can answer that."

"What would you do?"

Gregory gestured to his blue suit. "There is nothing I will not do, little sister."

"Do you love her?" I asked.

Gregory laughed, seeped in sorrow as he twisted the gold band he wore as the Pod stopped. "There is not a word I know for what I feel for her. She is"—Gregory swallowed, shaking his head as he stared at the stars—"everything, everywhere. The stars, the earth, the very air. She is everything. There is nothing I wouldn't do for her."

I wanted to know how it had happened, but I didn't ask. I stepped off the Pod as Gregory reached for the stars. The man who claimed he was a horrible person. He let them call him horrible names and acted the part, all for feelings he could not act on, all to protect someone he could not have. He might have been the most honorable person I had ever met, and no one would ever know.

I knew my next steps, but I didn't know their ramifications. My hand flew to the door, holding it open.

"What is it?" Gregory asked, coming to sit.

"You aren't a horrible person, Gregory." Our eyes met. I released the doors before he could respond, and the Pod took off.

My plan took shape with each step to my living quarters. I thrust my arm under my scanner before I made my way to my wardrobe.

My colorful gowns overtook the gray, all neatly hung up. I had been happy to see them every day. I had carefully displayed each one, the coordinating shoes and clutch neatly aligned with the dress. I treated them like sacred tokens from their beautiful world. They weren't sacred. They were guises, used to distract us from the horrors they committed.

I ripped off the beaded gown, desperate to be free of it—tearing at the neck until it came free, falling heavily to the floor, the beads scattering. There was a stain on the hem of the gown. My chest cracked open.

The man's blood had stained my gown. Hot tears of anger and despair filled my eyes, threatening to spill over. I wiped wildly at them, refusing to let them fall. My lens shifted.

I raised my hand to my left eye and unceremoniously removed the lens. I flicked it to the floor. I hung the gown beside the others. It wasn't a token. This gown was a beacon guiding me, pushing me toward this next step. I tossed on my gray shirt and threw myself onto my bed.

In my body's stillness my thoughts became mutinous as they tore apart my conditioning. Frenzied and crazed, those thoughts devoured the things that had left me okay with doing nothing.

Follow the Illum's protocol, abide by the rules of the Minor Defect population, and constantly seek self-improvement, and you will rise, fulfilling your use for the Greater Good.

I couldn't. My plan was dangerous. I ran my fingers over the chip hidden in my wrist. They would know where I was going. Maybe I would find one of those cuffs Hal had had before the Illum discovered me. Maybe I wouldn't. Somehow that should have given me pause. Collin had told me that if the Illum took notice, he would only be able to do so much.

The truth was I had enjoyed being with Collin. I had enjoyed the way his mouth felt against mine, the way he held me. I had wanted him to be different—to be that man in my immature dream of being twirled in a beautiful gown. I had wanted to be saved.

I'm not foolish enough to ask for something no longer obtainable.

I had ignored the viciousness and power that were always there. I had ignored what he was. He had killed that man, put Gregory in blue, and addressed the Elite in a way that left me feeling like the fool.

Collin hadn't been the only one to choose wrong.

I was the property of the Illum. I had no one to blame but myself and my desperate need for more, a foolish want that had sealed my fate. My self-pity greedily swallowed me whole.

Hal had been right, and I had pushed him away, spewed horrible things at him. I owed him an apology, but more, he needed to know that his people were in danger.

I had the day off. I didn't intend to waste it. The consequences be damned.

Alice had been right too. *I'd rather be in blue than be their vessel.* Maybe I would end up just like her. Perhaps I was okay with it. Sleep swept in and carried my inner chaos away.

◆ ◆ ◆

"TODAY IS THE EIGHTH DAY OF THE TENTH LUNAR CYCLE. Today will be rainy, with a high of thirty-nine degrees. You are currently in a Procreation Agreement with M17292834. In the Courting Phase."

Frida's voice filled the room. I shot up. I scanned my wrist before running to my wardrobe. I slipped on my usual gray attire, wishing I had something blue to blend in as Frida began her report.

Frida informed me I was still in the luteal phase and my cortisol levels were extremely elevated; thus my morning supplements were being adjusted to calm me—to alleviate my stress.

I froze on the last two buttons of my shirt. I was stressed because I had seen someone die violently, and it was my fault. What if I didn't want the stress to be taken away?

One of the black boxes dinged, my morning meal ready, but I ignored it. I attempted to tune her out while I waited for curfew to end, pacing before my door.

"Now, a message from the Illum."

I stopped. That was new. Why was I getting an HI message from the Illum? What did that mean?

"Good morning, loyal Elites."

That voice. Projected onto my far wall was that woman again. Tabitha. Bile crawled its way up my throat at the sight of her.

"I am here to address all the rumors that have reached us. There have been concerns regarding a man who has been named the Reaper. As of yesterday, we were able to apprehend a sympathizer of this Reaper. We obtained vital information before terminating the traitor. We will continue to root out this diseased way of thinking that threatens to destroy our peace and upend our prosperity and sacred way of life. To spread discord among those with defects. We can assure you, the Defect community is now under close surveillance and new restrictions and measures will be put into place to maintain the balance. Furthermore, anyone with any information is encouraged to come forth. Together we can put an end to this mishap. Any and all sympathizers shall be eliminated immediately. The Illum looks to you, loyal Elite, in this crusade to rip out this infectious threat before it takes root. To preserve our progress. We are one."

She carried on, each word anchoring me in disgust. Each word cleared my path forward. The mothers' faces, their desperate pleas, the crying offspring, gray eyes turning red, Violet's battered face, Gregory's love for Nora, and Rose holding on to Violet's dress.

There were many things I didn't know. Some things I didn't understand. Things I had not experienced. I had never felt an ounce of the pain those mothers felt. I had never felt the silent dedication Gregory carried alone in secret, or had someone cling to me, ready to strike down anyone who hurt me, the way Rose did.

I had never known love.

I had felt fear, though. The looks on those offsprings' faces. I knew that helplessness. That was a disease of its own. That was the disease I would end, even if it ended me.

I had been asked to do nothing, but I had never been good at following rules.

I didn't know what difference I could make or if I would even find what I wanted to find, but the Elite had bowed to me like I was one of them. It had snapped something in me. The Illum had used me. I took a steadying breath. I wouldn't make another mistake.

I walked into the bathroom. My makeup and hair were still intact from last night, and I still wore the diamond earrings. I yanked them off. I didn't look away for several minutes at my complete heterochromia. For the first time, I saw it. There was a beauty to it— in something different.

I grabbed my Comm Device. Five more minutes. I slipped my shoes on, turning my back to the video message.

Four minutes.

Your actions will bring peace.

Three minutes.

As long as there is life, we will fight to preserve our sacred ways.

Two minutes.

Eradicating this threat as one.

One minute.

We will continue our enlightened path forward.

Curfew ended.

We will eliminate anyone who threatens our progress.

I yanked my door open, dropping my Comm Device into my pocket. I saw no one on the elevators, and when I exited the building, there was no one on the street.

I was done doing nothing. I was going to the Underworld.

CHAPTER TWENTY-FOUR

The stone buildings were still quiet. With curfew ended I knew time was against me. Behind me the steel doors to the Sanctuary remained closed. My feet slammed onto the pavement as the ghost of those mothers' screams ran with me. The Illum would know what I was doing before long—my MIND would give me away. Running wouldn't change the consequences of going against the Illum. I could be eliminated for this. The sound of Pods rumbled in the distance.

I started to sprint. Sweat dripped down my neck.

Lungs screaming, I finally saw the bridge from Collin's map. The sound of rushing water welcomed me as I peered over the edge toward the current below. Two meters down sat a narrow ledge. It would be challenging to balance on it.

You could go back, a small voice whispered. I had no idea what I was actually doing. This plan seemed stupid.

You can't swim, that small voice warned me. This seemed like an inopportune moment for that knowledge to make itself known.

There was no one to witness me jump and no one to save me if I fell in.

Fear wrapped around my throat. I had too many reasons to push me off the edge of the walkway, and only fear to hold me back.

What scared me more? Drowning? Being a vessel? Being eliminated? Knowing I could have saved others from that fate and doing nothing?

I sucked in a deep breath. I knew my answer. I swung down. My body slammed into solid stone. The impact stole the air from my lungs. I felt skin break as my fingertips clung to the surface. I kicked wildly until I found purchase, my toes resting upon the narrow ledge. I gripped the edge above my head harder, the stone biting into my cut palms.

I had done it. I breathed in deeply. I had made it.

I looked toward the bridge and my seconds of relief from not plummeting to my death evaporated. I had thought I was close to the opening. From here it felt miles away. I couldn't see the entrance I thought I saw on the plans.

What if there wasn't an entrance? What if I was wrong and I was stuck down here?

I was on a ledge above rushing water. I couldn't swim. I was attempting to find an entrance I didn't know was there. Decisions that would ensure I was eliminated.

Fucking idiot. My hold became difficult as my pulse pounded in my ears.

"What are you doing?"

I squeezed the stone as my heart jumped out of my chest.

I turned toward the noise as much as I could. A woman stuck her head out of the wall. That must be the entrance.

"I'm trying"—I grunted, adjusting my grip—"to find someone in the Underworld."

"You're a Minor."

"Astute observation. Please, let me in." I moved at a painstaking pace, my racing heart leaving me unsteady.

"Fine," the woman conceded.

I shuffled along and reached for more ledge, only to realize it ended as it met the bridge. I couldn't balance without holding on. I rested my face against the cool, wet stone. I couldn't go any farther.

"Here," the woman said, thrusting out her hand.

"What if I slip?"

"You'll have to trust me." Her dry tone didn't evoke much confidence. "None of you ever have any trust." She rolled her deep brown eyes, one of her two braids falling through the opening. "What's it going to be, Minor?"

"Don't let me fall," I pleaded as I stretched my hand out. Her grip was firm.

"Let go, Minor, I've got you."

I let go, trusting—putting my life in the hands of—someone I didn't know.

"That's it," she coaxed as I took tiny steps toward the opening. When I reached it, her grip remained strong, anchoring me.

I hooked my left elbow and hoisted myself into the opening, bringing my other leg up, then shimmied through the entrance. "You can let go," I told her as relief flooded me. I finagled my legs around, scooting against damp stone before dropping out the other side. A musty smell hung in the air as my feet met hard stone. The tunnel was dark. The entrance was big enough for one person at a time but no more.

"Thank you," I panted. I glanced around to see a long stone tunnel. A ways down, small lights illuminated the path. I had made it to the Underworld.

"Turn around," the woman instructed, smirking. Her light brown skin was covered in freckles, and she wore a tight sweater, leggings, and boots. She was tall, I realized, with weapons strapped to her long legs. Nothing she wore was blue. She had a formidable strength about her I didn't realize a woman could have.

"Wait, I thought you said you'd help me?" I asked, confused as she tugged up my sleeves. A golden glow illuminated the tunnel. Cold metal clamped down on my wrists, and my left wrist throbbed wildly as she secured the restraints.

She stepped in front of me, staring at my mismatched gaze. "I said I wouldn't let you fall. Which I didn't. I never said anything about helping you. This might hurt."

Her triumphant smile was the last thing I saw as pain erupted down my neck and the world went black.

✦ ✦ ✦

"HOW HARD DID YOU HIT HER?" A DEEP ROLLING VOICE BROUGHT me back.

"I barely touched her," my supposed rescuer responded.

"Now, when you say *barely*, do you actually mean knocking her out cold?" another voice jeered. Warm hands gently touched my face.

"He is going to be pissed when he finds out," a calm male voice stated.

"*If* he finds out," the woman countered.

"He's going to find out, Bri."

"Not unless you tell him."

"What was the Reaper's one request yesterday?" the calm voice interjected.

"I wouldn't call it a request, more like a fucking order."

"No one touches her," that deep rolling voice stated.

What had happened? Were they referring to me and the Reaper? That didn't make sense.

I finally opened my eyes to find myself before four complete strangers. Bri stood bickering with a man with bright red hair. I blinked several times, adjusting to the dimly lit room. Everything around me was stone. I groaned at the pounding in my head.

"I still don't understand why the Reaper cares so much about her safety," Bri snapped. "She's in bed with the Illum."

"I could make a list of things I don't understand about the Reaper," the redhead claimed. "One—"

"It isn't for either of you to understand," the man with the deep voice said. "Her Mate killed Christopher last night. If the Illum kills more of our spies, we'll be in deep shit. We don't touch the Illum's Mate. We don't make contact with the Illum's Mate."

The voice belonged to a large man with long black hair, rich tan skin, and ink covering his exposed skin. My heart found my throat. The dinner. The blood. The impending ambush. I tried to stand, but the room tilted off its axis.

"Whoa, easy, Emeline," a man with dark brown skin told me, his warm hands gently grabbing my arms and steadying me.

They all fell silent, watching me. I tried to pull away. "How do you know my name?"

"Everyone knows the Illum's pet's name," the redhead shot.

"You are known in all areas of the city," said the man holding me. Black ink ran up his neck, disappearing into hair shaved close to his head. "I'm Gerald, that's Kane." He pointed toward the man with the long black hair. "That's Barrett." The redhead winked at me. "And you know Bri."

My eyes narrowed at the woman who I thought had been helping me.

"How are you feeling?" Gerald asked gently.

"My head hurts." I brought my hand to my head only to stop at the sight of the cuffs on my wrists. "Do these mess with the MIND?"

"They do, but not forever. How do you know about them?" Gerald asked.

"A friend. You're being nice," I said suspiciously.

"Your informant from up there making you soft?" Barrett teased.

Gerald rolled his eyes and ignored Barrett. "Do you mind if I look you over? There's debate on how hard Bri hit you."

I looked at Bri, who shrugged. "Force of habit. Surface walkers aren't welcome here."

"Forgive her, she's terrible at following directions." The redhead, Barrett, shook his long hair out of his face. Gold hoops on his ears glinted, as did his multiple necklaces.

"Is she okay? The quicker we get her out of here, the better," Kane said. "Who all saw you bring her in?"

Gerald flashed a light into my eyes. I squinted away from it.

Bri shrugged. "A few people. Rajesh, Tony, Bex."

"Follow the light, Emeline," Gerald told me. I tried to as my mind ached.

"He's going to fucking kill you," Barrett practically sang to Bri.

"Why does that make you happy?" Bri demanded, shoving him.

Barrett regained his balance, the necklaces around his neck swinging as he grinned toward Bri. "Finally say yes and I'll take the heat for you."

Gerald put his light away as he continued to watch me—like he was still looking for something.

"Enough," Kane commanded. "Let's figure out why the Illum's pet is here and get her to the surface where she belongs. We were told not to raise any suspicions and to lie low. This isn't lying low, Bri."

"She's the one who jumped off the bridge," Bri snapped.

"Yeah, to help you," I shot back.

Kane tilted his head. "How did you plan to do that?"

"You want to help us?" Barrett asked suspiciously. "Or were you sent here by them?"

"No one sent me. No one knows I came here. I wanted to bring information, to help. I risked a lot to come here. They watch my MIND. I told Bri I needed to find someone."

"Incoming," Gerald called out as footsteps sounded from beyond the room.

"Here we go." Barrett winked at me.

"East watch is clear. Cargo was successfully transferred. They said—" The voice cut off.

Hal stood at the entrance, still as a ghost.

"What is going on here?" he asked quietly.

"We were about to get to that." Kane crossed his arms. "Apparently the Illum's pet came down through the river entrance to help us. Strange, is it not?"

I stood, and Hal was moving as if ready to catch me. His hands found the cuffs around my wrists before brushing my curls out of my face. "How long?"

"Maybe twenty minutes," Gerald told him.

"She was out for most of it," Barrett said before groaning. "Stop hitting people."

"It's like you want him pissed at me," Bri seethed.

Hal's eyes ran over me in disbelief. "What do you mean by *out*?"

"Bri knocked her out," Kane stated plainly.

"She what?" Hal bit out, turning toward them.

"So, you see, what happened—"

"Barrett, I'm not in the mood for your damn word games at the moment."

Kane chuckled darkly. "Only certain games. It appears the two of you know each other. Why don't you inform all of us how you know the Illum's pet. We are *all* dying to know."

Hal turned toward Kane. "I don't know why that is any of your business."

"Is that so?" Kane said, walking toward us. I held on to Hal's arm. A vein in Kane's neck pulsed as he stared at my hand, before turning all that rage toward Hal. "You met her by chance?"

"My actions don't concern you," Hal snapped.

"So she's off-limits to everyone but you," Kane stated coldly.

"Does anyone care about what *she* has to say," I growled, and Kane glanced at me in surprise. As did Hal.

"We don't have time for this," Gerald interrupted. "We need to get her back to the surface. The quicker, the better. What did you want to tell us?"

"The Illum is planning retribution for the attacks. They want to send the Reaper"—I glanced at Hal—"a message. In two days, they said, they are going to ambush the Underworld community. I wanted you all to know. So you can prepare or run."

"No one's running," Kane said darkly.

"You were at the dinner last night?" Barrett asked, pushing off the wall.

I nodded. I could feel Hal looking at me, but I couldn't meet his gaze, not as the memories of last night pelted me.

"So you saw Christopher die," Barrett stated. "Did he suffer?"

I saw the man fall to his knees, gasping for air as his blood sprayed. I shook it away. "They used the MIND to kill him. I'm sorry. They are saying that I helped them, that his death is my fault, but—"

"But what?" Bri sneered, her eyes angry slits. "You're saying it isn't? You didn't run to your Mate about him?"

"I didn't run to him. It's difficult." I stepped toward her.

"Oh, it's difficult," Bri taunted, her hand coming to rest on the handle of one of her weapons. "Difficult for you, going to dinners and balls. Dressed up like some pathetic prize. I can see why a fucking whistle scared you."

"Briana, their women are only taught to be a vessel," Gerald told her. "You know this. That is not Emeline's fault. They don't give them any other option."

"Right, and how many people have we lost because they don't know any better? I'm tired of this. I'm happy I knocked you out," Bri spat at me.

Hal brushed past me. "Say that again."

"Guys, come on, is this how we welcome guests?" Barrett joked, edging his way between Hal and Bri. "She's going to believe all the horrible lies about us. I swear, we are usually much more welcoming."

"We all know the risk of this rebellion. This isn't news. We already know about their plans," Kane stated dryly.

"They have maps of everything. All the tunnels," I told them as Barrett pushed Hal lightly as he walked backward, taking Bri with him.

Kane sighed. "We know your little Mate's plans. I'm afraid if that's the only reason you came down here, you wasted your time."

"The entrance I used, it was circled on the map," I told them. They exchanged a look.

"Come on." Hal's hand found mine, but my feet stayed rooted to the spot. Gerald looked at our joined hands.

"Why did you feel compelled to risk yourself to come here?"

Gerald asked, looking at me like he saw something the others didn't. "You must know there will be consequences."

"I don't want anyone else to die," I confessed to them all. Barrett huffed a breath. "I am sorry about Christopher," I said, looking at him.

I let Hal pull me toward the exit as Barrett whispered, "You owe me twenty marks." I didn't know what marks were and I didn't hear what they had bet on.

"Hurry, I want to talk to you before I take you back," Hal told me quietly as he picked up his pace. Loud music filled the tunnels as we turned into a large, cavernous room. People danced with reckless abandon. It was nothing like the dancing I practiced with my HI. It was captivating, and on the walls of the room were countless canvases, many of which I recognized as having been assigned for destruction.

I moved toward the art, but Hal pulled me to an exit. I glanced over my shoulder at the dancing one last time. There was an intoxicating pull to it.

"I'll take you sometime," Hal whispered as we made our way down a long tunnel.

"There's music and art down here," I said more to myself than to him. "Why didn't you tell me?"

"Would you have believed me if I did?" Hal asked. He had a point. I had only ever been taught to fear people who wear blue. "I told you someone has to take out their trash. No one here is interested in erasing what makes us human."

We weaved through tunnel after tunnel. Each one looked the same. Silence found us as he turned down another tunnel, and another. "There are so many tunnels. How long has this been here?" I asked as we turned again. Hal navigated them like it was second nature, undisturbed by the dark.

"The tunnel system is ancient. Some of it was built before the Last War. When the war ended, all remaining humans lived down here."

"What?"

"Yeah, they don't teach you that at the Academy." We turned again. "After the war we all lived beneath as equals. The nuclear warfare set off something called a nuclear winter, and no one could survive aboveground."

"What changed when we resurfaced?" I asked.

"I wish we knew, but something horrible took root," Hal said, turning again, down another tunnel identical to all the others.

"How do you not get lost?" I asked as he made another turn.

"You get used to it, and there are tells if you know where to look."

We entered a tunnel that was wider than the others. A round opening glowed dimly in the distance and Hal came to a stop, looking around. We were alone.

"I want you to have this," Hal said, extending a knife toward me. It was small, the handle simple.

"Why do you want me to have a knife?" I asked, holding it awkwardly.

"Seeing you in there today, with them . . . I might not always be there if you're in danger."

"Was I in danger today?"

"Yes. But not just from them. Emeline, your MIND tracks you. You shouldn't have come. This was dangerous." He shook his head.

"*Hal*, I watched a man die, and the Illum said it was my doing. I saw the Parting." I gripped the sheathed knife, my frustration mounting. "Bri is right. I'm a vessel who isn't taught anything. I am tired of living in the dark. I chose to come down here because I am tired of doing nothing. I told the Starlings I wanted to help because—"

"You what?" Hal asked, stepping back.

"The Starlings, they support the Reaper. I told them I would help. I told them I would get information on the Illum for the Reaper."

"Did they suggest you come down here?" Hal demanded.

"No, they told me to do nothing. Do you know them?"

"The Reaper's network is wide. You should have listened to them," Hal exclaimed, dragging his hand down his face. "This is dangerous."

"I know that. I came anyway. I came down here to find the Reaper. I came down here to find *you*."

Hal tipped his head toward the ceiling. "Moonlight, there is a reason I said goodbye. You are the Illum's Mate. You can't do this."

My Mate. I tried to feel guilty for coming down here, but I didn't. Collin had chosen wrong. He had killed that man. "You were right, you know."

"What was I right about?"

"Everything. About me. About the Illum and Elite." I worked to swallow, my next sentence choking me. "He isn't different."

Hal stopped, turning toward me. There was no vindication in his eyes at my confession. No pride. "I'm sorry I was right." He stared at me, and my skin felt too tight.

"I should have listened to you."

"Truth is never easy. Plus, I wear blue, and you wear gray, right?"

I grabbed his arm. "Hal, I'm sorry. That was a terrible thing to say. I was angry. I shouldn't have said those things. I didn't mean them. I also thought I was protecting you."

"I've been called and told much worse. Protecting me how?"

The air between us became thick as questions pressed against my skin. "Hal . . ."

He stepped closer. "What is it?"

"Are you the Reaper?" I whispered.

Hal just stared at me until my skin was too warm. Did I want to know? Had I not run from Collin for taking a life? The Reaper was also killing people.

Hal shook his head. "That wasn't the question I was hoping for." He raked a hand through his hair. "The Reaper didn't rise to where he is by giving away his identity. There is power in people not knowing who you are, even those close to you. Just as there is a vulnerability to everyone knowing who you are."

"That wasn't a no," I told him, stepping closer.

"It wasn't a yes," Hal stated, matching my step. "I thought I wouldn't see you again."

"I thought so too. What did you want me to ask?"

"You know the question, Moonlight."

One day you'll have the nerve to ask, and I don't think I'll say no.

I retreated a step. My breaths were too shallow, his presence engulfing me, sweeping away everything. Hal took another step closer, and my breathing hitched as he brushed a curl behind my ear. I looked into his starburst eyes, and time slowed down for just a moment.

"I need to get you back," Hal told me, but he didn't move. "Unless you have something to ask."

"Yeah, you've said that," I said breathlessly, my eyes taking in every line and curve of his face. The way his amber eyes drank me in, defect and all, his dark blond hair that fell into his face, the tension in his jaw.

"Because I do," Hal breathed, his mouth inches from mine.

"I have another question," I murmured.

"Then ask it, Moonlight."

"Kiss me?" I whispered, damning myself.

His hand brushed my cheek with such gentleness, his thumb tracing my bottom lip before cupping my chin. My eyes fluttered closed from the warmth, each breath bated. His lips met mine, and the world, my world, shifted.

Hal pulled back, a slight tremble in his hand before sliding it to cradle the back of my head. I opened my eyes to see him staring at me. He shook his head just a fraction before he surged forward, his lips crashing into mine.

His hand snaked into my hair, pulling me closer until every inch of me was pressed against him. His other hand grabbed my hip, holding me against him as his tongue traced my lower lip, and I opened for him.

Hal took advantage, and his tongue swept into my mouth, tangling with mine. A groan escaped him as he pushed into me, my back colliding with the stone wall, all of his rugged strength meeting every supple curve of mine.

A firestorm of desire hollowed me out and yet filled me to the brim all in the same breath. The yearning, the aching, the countless emotions of the past week—all of it caught in the hot tempest that threatened to consume me.

I couldn't get close enough to him. I ran a hand through Hal's soft strands, while the other gripped his knife tightly as I hooked it on his shoulder, tugging him closer.

Hal's hips ground into me, and a breathless moan escaped me. A pulsing want I had never felt before took root deep in my core, demanding more. My hips rolled to meet his as I burned from the inside out, heat pooling between my legs. Hal's hand traveled down my hip, gripping my thigh, pulling my leg up.

"You're playing a dangerous game," Kane's voice sounded to my left.

I felt like I had dived into the cold river. Hal pulled away from me, but his hand remained in my hair. "I didn't ask for your opinion earlier, and I don't need it now."

"Those cuffs only scramble her chip for so long," Kane barked, stepping closer. Hal released my leg, guiding it gently back to the ground. "Her Mate is killing people. We can't afford to make mistakes."

"I'm going," Hal said, grabbing my hand. He didn't look at Kane as he led me away down the tunnel.

"Find me after," Kane shouted. I turned to see Kane's glowering frame, fury staring back at Hal and me. I shivered at the rage in his gaze, burning into my back as we walked away.

CHAPTER TWENTY-FIVE

Hal and I remained silent the rest of the journey through the tunnels. The energy between us had shifted. For better or worse, I didn't know, but he didn't let go of my hand. As we approached the round entrance I had come through, he led me to the corner, his calluses scraping against my hand. There was a gap in the stone that was almost undetectable.

"Through here, come on." Hal entered the gap, pulling me with him. My shoulder brushed against the cold stone before it opened to a spiral staircase.

"Where are we going?" I asked, the temperature dropping as we descended.

"Under the river, there's an entrance on the slum's side," Hal told me as we entered a long, damp tunnel. "You really came down through the river entrance?"

"It's the only entrance I saw on the plans. I wanted to make sure you knew about the ambush. I can't swim," I admitted. "I panicked, but then Bri found me. She helped me in before knocking me out."

Hal shook his head. "I can't believe you did that."

"I didn't know how else to find you. I didn't think you were coming back."

Hal paused, turning toward me. "I only did that because I thought it was safer to leave you alone. Clearly, I was wrong, since you've taken to careening off ledges."

I yanked my wrist from Hal as an electrical current shot through my arm. Hal looked between me and the cuff.

"We need to hurry," Hal said, grabbing my hand and picking up his pace. "Your MIND is about to be active again."

I glanced down at the cuff. "How do these work?"

"Honestly, I don't know. That's Gerald's thing. I want you to keep one, though."

We reached the top of the stairs. There was a wooden door to the right. Faint sunlight from the surface trickled in through the crack. My grip on Hal's hand tightened, and his thumb brushed the back of my hand reassuringly.

"Will the Illum know that I came down here?" I whispered, thinking of the last thing Tabitha had said. They planned to eliminate anyone who helped.

"They shouldn't," Hal reassured me.

"But if they do?" I asked, because it wasn't elimination. It was death, and there would be no coming back from that. On this side of things, that was a different kind of fear.

Hal's hands came up to cradle my face. "Then I will come for you." I trembled in his arms at the resolute determination reflected in his starburst gaze. He tucked me into him. His steady heartbeat was a song of its own, one that was quickly becoming the sweetest sound.

"Will I see you again?" I breathed into his chest.

I felt his lips brush the top of my head. "Yes, there are no more goodbyes," he said into my curls. "It will be a while, though. We have to handle this threat."

"You will be safe?" I pulled back to see something I didn't know how to register reflected in his eyes.

"Don't worry about me. Here." He pressed two buttons on the cuff on my right hand before moving to the left, my wrist engulfed in his grip. "Don't come back to the Underworld, do you understand?"

"But—"

"Promise me."

I nodded, even though I didn't want to.

Hal pressed the two buttons, and the other cuff released. "Take this one. If you think they are coming for you, put this on and come to this house."

I opened my mouth, ready to retort, but his lips met mine. The kiss was quick, over before I could truly register it. "Go, and head straight back to your living quarters. I'll come to you as soon as I can."

"Is Kane going to be mad at you?" I asked as he yanked the door open.

"Kane's always mad. He forgets his place here. Go—your chip will start tracking in less than a minute, and you need to be on the other side of the river. Hurry!" Hal pushed me through the door, looking me over one last time. "I'll see you soon. Do whatever they ask, and don't draw attention to yourself."

The door shut.

I was alone. I didn't give myself time to think about what I felt in my chest before I made my way through the small, dingy sitting room and out the main door. It opened onto a street on the opposite side of the river. I shoved the cuff into my pocket and put my dagger in my waistband. Different types of trinkets from beneath, not above.

I began to jog toward the bridge, the city looming from the other side. I had always been in awe of the spindly structures, at the life in the clouds, but as I approached it from this angle, I didn't see the impressive feats or the view they provided. We had all been beneath the surface together. When we had resurfaced, something sinister had broken free.

I crossed to the other side of the bridge, walking toward the spot I had swung down from, when a shock rippled up my arm from my left wrist. My MIND must be activated again.

I walked back to my living quarters, my mind ricocheting from one thought to the other. A few beeps later, I found myself in my room. My Comm Device dinged, and I grabbed it out of my pocket. I was shocked to see it was still only eight-thirty in the morning. It felt like I had been gone for ages, but it had only been a few hours.

Perhaps it was the loud music and dancing—the life below and how no one had acted like a day was just starting. Everything had been in full swing. Clearly, the rumors about the Major Defect community being nocturnal were accurate. The accuracy ended there.

I had expected some dark, decrepit place—the type of place that awaited those too defective to live above the ground.

The Underworld wasn't that at all. There was more life in that one room than in any room above the surface. I thought of the Garden, the Sphere, and the Pond—all beautiful places—but I thought of how the Elite acted. Gossiping and staring as others walked by. The uptight rigidness, following protocols and procedures without question. The spaces were all so alluring: the gowns, the food, sparkling jewels, and lights. Everything bedecked in finery—chattels to their comforts. I had never seen a single person happy.

A façade.

A beautiful façade to hide the hideous truths, beguiling the viewer into thinking all was well.

It wasn't. The people weren't. None of them were actually living. They were just pawns for the Greater Good. Performing, pretending that everything was well so others wouldn't know.

We all bought it from the ground level. Sought to obtain it. Idolizing the Elite and their life in the clouds, fighting for a way up. Twisting and contorting ourselves until approved. Made to hide our inadequacies and deficiencies in the pursuit of a contract.

I had believed my visual defect was too damning to be accepted and lived in shame until they covered it.

I had not been naïve; I knew the constant monitoring and stats stripped us of some essential part of ourselves. I knew it was wrong, and I still fell victim to it—too afraid of the unknown.

Below where they danced. Where they wore a variety of colors. Not miserable, not defective.

They didn't hide the Majors to protect us from their defects. They hid them so we wouldn't discover the truth. That we were the ones in pain, and they—they were free.

Collin allowed this. Enforced it.

I looked at my Comm Device to find a message from Lo. Lo, who wanted more than anything to belong in the clouds.

Hey, checking in. I never heard from you. Are you okay?

She had messaged me about Gregory, and I hadn't responded because I thought finding Gregory talking to another woman had been too much. It seemed trivial now compared to everything else.

Hey, I'm okay. I have so much to tell you. Come here after work.

How could I tell her anything I had discovered—about Gregory, the Elite, Hal? I sent it before sinking to the floor. The sound of metal filled the air as the cuff slipped from my pocket. I glanced down at the cuff Hal had given me as the dagger handle dug into my hip. I pulled the blade out before retrieving the cuff from the floor, placing them between my legs.

I stared at them, running my fingers down the covered blade. I pulled the knife from its sheath. The blade was simple. I had no idea what to do with it. Gray eyes flashed, turning red. I sheathed it as my hands trembled. I wasn't sure I would ever use it.

The inside of the cuff had grooves running through it to a rectangle. I wondered if the chip embedded in the cuff matched the one hidden under my skin. The outside was a matte gray. I looked at the gowns in my wardrobe before clutching the cuff to my chest. It felt like the most precious thing I had. I took the knife and the cuff to my wardrobe, placing both in the white clutch that had gone with the cloud dress, and closed the doors.

I showered and spent the rest of the day lying in bed, thinking of our kiss. The way my body had felt alive. The feel of Hal's body against mine. It wasn't long until a different kiss filled my thoughts—the one in the clouds with Collin. How at the time I hadn't wanted it to end. I pushed the thought away. There was no comparing the two. Collin had kissed me because he needed to, for the Press. Hal had kissed me because I asked, because I had wanted to kiss him, despite my contract and the consequences. Hal saw me; there was a freedom in that, which I knew I would never find with my Mate. The shadows around my room shifted, and the sun began to descend in what felt like no time, prompting me to pull myself from the confines of my bed.

A soft knock sounded. I shoved my wrist under the scanner as I opened the door. Lo made her way into my room.

"I'm happy you messaged me. I got worried," Lo said, sitting cross-legged on the floor. "What happened to you the other night? I didn't see you leave that Pond place. It's weird how the tables move, right? Gregory went to the restroom and couldn't find our table on his way back. You were right about the food. I had this thing called soup. It was so good."

"Yeah, the food was really good," I said absentmindedly as my black box dinged and I retrieved my meal. I sat next to Lo on the floor. "Tell me about your initial meeting," I said, desperate to get Lo talking—to focus on something other than my own thoughts that bled into one another with no delineation.

"Well, I went to some older woman named Mary for my prep appointment. She wasn't creepy like your bird ladies. She was fine, very chatty. Talked about some upcoming dinner the Elite were all in a tizzy about. She sorta rushed me so she could tend to her other clients, I think. I also think she messed up on my gown. She said my proposed Mate noted he loved green. But Gregory commented that my gown was very bright."

I bit my tongue, hard. The *bird ladies*, who had told me to do nothing, just get close to Collin. What kind of tizzy were the Elite in now? How many knew about what Collin had done? The elimination. And Gregory liked green, just the green of another woman's dress that night.

"But the dinner went well, I think. I made him laugh. I thought he got bored since he was gone for so long, but like I said, he just got lost. He said the room always confuses him. But he can't help coming back for the view."

The view of someone, I was sure, who told me that was her favorite place in the whole city.

"Anyway, I haven't heard anything from him yet. I hate to ask, but can you find out if it went well? I know he's your birth brother, but he's so hot. His blue eyes. It's a shame your eyes aren't both that blue. His are so dreamy. Also, why aren't you wearing your lens?"

The lens that represented what the Illum demanded of me, something I couldn't avoid forever. I caught my lip between my teeth, the lip Hal had licked as he held me against him.

"Emeline, hello?" Lo waved her hand before my face. "Are you listening to me?"

I shook my head. "Sorry."

"What's wrong? Did something happen?"

Yes, so much had happened. I opened my mouth but stopped.

We will eliminate anyone who threatens our progress.

I couldn't tell Lo. Even if I wanted to, and a part of me desperately did, I had made my choice to go below. That didn't mean I had to drag her down with me. I wouldn't risk her safety.

Lo's warm hand pulled me from my thoughts as she laid it on my knee. "Emeline, are you okay? You can tell me whatever it is."

I took a deep breath, meeting her blue eyes.

"There was a dinner last night," I told her. I wouldn't tell her everything, nothing that would endanger her, but like Violet had said, we were in this together as Defects.

"Do you think the dinner is why Gregory hasn't reached out?" Lo asked, scooting closer to me.

"It's highly possible. A hologram of an Illum named Tabitha was there. And so was Collin."

No one had told me to keep the events to myself. The last time I shared information, Violet had gotten hurt. Badly. That was me telling an Illum information a Minor had told me. This was different. I was warning a Minor of what the Illum and the Elite were up to. This was protecting my own—not seeking information from above.

I blew out a big breath, my eyes finding her wide blue eyes.

"Don't repeat what I'm going to tell you."

Lo's spine straightened. "Okay."

"Lo, the Illum are looking for Defects who are working against them. They're going to be watching us. Whatever you do, don't go see Becca."

"Okay. But who would work against them?" Lo asked, leaning toward me.

"People who are unhappy with how things are. People in the Underworld."

"The Underworld?" Lo asked, her brows knitting together.

"Where the Majors live. They don't live in Low Town, they live underground. Listen, they captured a sympathizer, the guy who whistled at me before we got on the Pod that day. You remember him?" Lo nodded. I took a steadying breath. "They killed him."

Lo shifted, leaning back, away from me, as her hand flew to her hair, twisting it. "Did you tell them about him?"

I shook my head. I hadn't and yet Collin had still found out and Christopher was now dead. "The Illum told the Elite I was helping them."

"Are you?" she asked, her eyes wide.

"No, I'm not helping them. They killed a man. The Elite have this group of men who wear green, called the Force. I saw them the other day outside the Sanctuary."

Lo looked at me, twisting her hair wildly as she whispered, "Did they take offspring away?"

I nodded. "Did that happen to you?"

"Yes," Lo said, her voice small.

"Lo, I am so sorry."

"I don't want to talk about it. Is Gregory helping the Illum?"

"I don't know, but Gregory isn't a bad person, Lo," I assured her. I didn't think he would ever care for Lo truly, but he seemed like a good person, despite what he said. Lo had a good Mate.

"Okay," Lo said again. "I think I am going to get some sleep."

After Lo left, I climbed into bed. My hand stretched out to the spot where Hal had slept all those days ago, and I thought about Hal's safety, the people in the Underworld, Lo, Nora, Gregory, my contract, and someone out there who might be waiting for Christopher to come back.

I didn't get much sleep.

CHAPTER TWENTY-SIX

"Today is the ninth day of the tenth lunar cycle. Today will be cloudy, with a high of thirty-eight degrees. You are currently in a Procreation Agreement with M17292834. In the Courting Phase," Frida began the following morning. I stood by the boxes waiting for my meal, dressed in gray, exhausted from the dreams that had plagued me. "According to your most recent scans, you are on day twenty-one of your menstrual cycle. In your luteal phase. I have adjusted your nutrients accordingly to provide the best nutrition for your luteal phase."

Frida droned on about my nutritional deficiencies and overall inadequacy but congratulated me on my optimal dopamine and oxytocin. I tuned her out while I ate my meal. I dumped the supplements into my hands, tracing the outline of each one.

Yesterday Frida claimed they had been altered to calm me. Why had the Reaper attacked the building containing them?

My oxytocin and dopamine levels were elevated, but I hadn't taken the supplements yesterday. It didn't make sense. What were these supplements really for? What did the rebellion know?

I turned them over in my hand as Frida finished her report. She didn't mention anything about my MIND going off the grid yesterday. I breathed a sigh of relief. The lesson was another dance, but I was so distracted by what might be happening in the Underworld that I found it hard to enjoy it. After the lesson I threw on my coat, and with it, my anxiety returned.

Lo and I sat together on the way to work; for once, she was quiet. I wondered if that meant Gregory still hadn't reached out, but I didn't ask. At work, no one in dark green barged in to take me away for going to the Underworld. Collin didn't message me. Hal didn't show up. I went home at the end of my shift, but there was no news, and my nerves were in tatters.

Lo came up, and we discussed contracts a bit before she left. She seemed distracted, but so was I. I checked my Comm Device, but still nothing.

I dreamed of a long dark tunnel with a light at both ends, eerily quiet. I was running toward the light, yet never getting closer. My ragged breaths were the only noises until I heard my name whispered in the darkness. I ran harder, my footsteps reverberating through the tunnel, my name getting louder, *louder*—

I awoke drenched in sweat, utterly alone.

✦ ✦ ✦

A WEEK PASSED IN A BLUR. I REMAINED IN THE DARK, NO WORD from either side, and fear was eating me alive. Each day, I returned to my living quarters at the end of my shift, and anxiety crawled in bed with me each night. Lo kept her distance, claiming she was tired, which suited me fine. I was in no mood for company. Sleep provided no reprieve from my fear. My exhausted mind urged me to bed each night only for the black tunnel to swallow me whole, my whispered name a haunting that left me reeling. I had hardly been able to eat or even focus on pressing the *delete* button at work, any relief that I usually found from the art eluding me. I could only spiral, wondering helplessly whether the Illum had been successful in their raid of the Underworld, or if the rebels had indeed been as prepared as they had said. Even if they were, I knew the Illum would be as well. My wrist still glowed gold, so I supposed that meant I was still in the contract, and Collin was alive.

The only deviation in the monotony of my existence had been several lessons preparing me for my menstrual cycle. The supplements discontinued our cycle while we waited for contracts. Once approved, our cycle returned. Frida had made its impending arrival sound insignificant. She had been wrong. I spent my two days off huddled in a ball while my cycle's return leveled me, the cramping in my guts unbearable.

On the sixteenth day of the tenth lunar cycle, I turned the corner to my office. I was still in the menstrual phase, no longer doubled over from cramps, thankfully.

"Hey, Moonlight."

Starburst eyes sparkled at me. Relief flooded me, finding Hal in my chair, his dark blond locks disheveled, falling into his face. He half-smiled, revealing his dimple.

The dark cloud that had followed me all week finally lifted. I dropped my bag to the ground, moving toward him, but stopped as he gingerly made to stand, grasping my desk.

"Hal! Are you okay?"

"I'm fine," he said, but remained bent over, bracing himself on my desk.

"Sit down," I commanded, grabbing his free arm and directing him back to the chair. "What happened?"

"Nothing," Hal said again.

"It's not nothing, you fucking martyr," came an exasperated voice behind me. I whipped around to find Barrett half hidden behind my open door, dressed in a black shirt and dark green pants. His red hair was pulled back, exposing a fang earring. He had stubble on his chin and dark circles under his emerald eyes. Weapons were strapped to his legs and on a harness over his shoulders. His golden chain necklaces winked at me. "Hi again. You need to be more aware of your surroundings," Barrett told me.

"I told you, Barrett, that you could only come if you kept your mouth closed," Hal growled from the chair.

"Right," Barrett scoffed, pushing off the wall, "and like I told *you* when I found your sorry ass trying to hobble all the way here, you wouldn't make it if you didn't have help. So you're welcome." He paused at the door. "Make it quick. Things aren't like before."

"Thank you," I told him before he could leave.

Barrett nodded. "Don't forget what Thea said, Hal. No physical activity at all for at least another week. Afraid you'll have to keep this reunion more subdued than your last one." Barrett's eyes flashed mischievously. Hal rumbled next to me as Barrett chuckled the entire way out.

I perched on the edge of my desk, my cheeks red. "You told them?" I asked, embarrassed.

"No, Kane did," Hal said, clutching his side and taking a deep breath, the pain evident on his face.

"You shouldn't have come, Hal. You should have rested."

"You sound like Barrett now," Hal said, rolling his eyes.

"Maybe he's right."

"Don't let him hear that. It'll go straight to his head."

"Too late" came Barrett's amused voice from the hall.

Hal dragged his hand through his hair, huffing something between a laugh and a growl. "I thought you said you were leaving."

"I said no such thing. I just left the room. You can barely stand. I'm not leaving you alone. Thea is already going to kill me for bringing you," Barrett said. I glanced back at Hal to see his lips tugged up in a half smile. He was in a white shirt and gray sweatpants. I couldn't see any weapons on him.

"What happened?" I asked again, leaning toward him. Hal rolled the chair toward me until I was between his legs on the desk. His hand found the outside of my thigh, and warmth seeped into me, chasing away the uncertainty of the last week. "I have been so worried. I thought . . . I thought horrible things."

"It's why I came," Hal said. "I didn't want you to worry."

Our eyes met for a moment. "Tell me what happened, and who's Thea?"

"Thea is our best healer," Hal said. My brows pulled in. "A healer is someone who takes care of injured and sick people. They used to be called doctors. Majors get hurt from the manual labor a lot."

It was strange to think of the body getting hurt. It was unheard of on the surface.

"The Force attacked the Underworld like you said they would," he continued. "Thankfully they don't know the extent of the tunnel system like they think they do. We cut all the power below. They weren't ready for that. Not all of them had night vision. They came during the day, thinking we were all nocturnal. Gave us an advantage. So did you telling us about the river entrance."

"Really?"

"We had planned to smuggle some supplies out using the river. Our scouts saw a small Force Unit there the day of the attack. We had to scrap the plan. It's unfortunate and puts us behind, but the supplies weren't harmed or confiscated. We owe you."

"Did anyone get hurt?" I asked, catching my lip between my teeth.

"More of them than us," Hal told me, his left thumb rubbing absent-minded circles on my thigh.

"Your friends?"

"They are all okay. Gerald needed a couple of stitches. Bri, Kane, and Barrett came out unscathed."

"Unscathed?" Barrett's outraged voice floated in. "I dislocated my pinky finger on my trigger hand. I would hardly call that unscathed."

"And the Reaper?" I asked.

"He's fine."

I paused. "And you?"

"I'm fi—"

"Oh, for fuck's sake," Barrett erupted, walking back into the office. "Your little hero here pulled some of our guys out of the way of an explosive that sent a metal barrier hurtling into him, pinning him between the barrier and the tunnel wall as they swarmed in, causing several broken ribs and internal bleeding. If Kane and Bri hadn't been there—"

Hal had stopped rubbing my thigh as he glared at Barrett.

"No one asked for your input," Hal barked.

"Hal, you do her no justice keeping her in the dark," Barrett protested, and gratitude surged in my chest.

"I can decide that," Hal said.

"I think it's the wrong call."

"Hal, tell me," I said quietly.

"No." Hal gently gripped my thigh. "I can't tell you, Emeline. Not now. The less you know, the better. If they question you, you won't be able to answer them. I will not let them take another thing I care for." My heart swelled as my stomach dropped. *Care for.*

Barrett stood by the door, his mouth a thin line, but his eyes held a sad understanding. He didn't push Hal.

"Hal, I told the Starlings I'd help them. I *need* to help." I didn't know how I would get through being around Collin and the Elite otherwise. How I'd be able to live with myself.

"That was before the Reaper deemed you off-limits," he said.

"Fucking birds," Barrett mumbled at the same time.

"Can't you just change the Reaper's mind?" I asked.

"I'm not willing to consider it," Hal told me, and I looked at him, hard.

Before I could push further, Barrett turned to Hal. "We should go. We can't stay."

Hal hung his head, breathing more heavily than normal. I ran a hand through his hair, unsure if it was appropriate or the right thing to do. When Hal didn't react, I did it again, lightly scraping my nails on his skin. A low groan escaped him. I glanced over to see Barrett pointedly staring out the doorway. Hal pushed the chair back, sucking in a deep breath. His knuckles were white as he gripped the edge of my desk to stand. I ducked under his shoulder to help, and he leaned into me as he panted, his pain filling the room. My hands flew up to his arm and chest, unsure where to touch him without exacerbating his pain. He buried his head in my neck as his breathing settled, and before I knew it, we were embracing. His usually steady heartbeat was replaced by a furious pounding against my cheek.

Guilt washed over me. He shouldn't have come. I heard footsteps as Barrett made his way toward us. There was no cunning or mischievous gleam in his eyes as he approached, just worry.

"We need to get back, Hal," Barrett said quietly. Hal didn't move.

"I'll come back soon," Hal promised me, pulling away.

"Just get better first," I whispered.

"You're not wearing your lens," Hal stated quietly. Barrett stepped closer to Hal, as if he were ready to catch him at any moment. How much was Hal downplaying his injuries? "Why not?"

"I haven't seen anyone from the Elite or Illum since that dinner."

Hal released a breath, from pain or relief that I hadn't been with Collin, I didn't know.

"I used to see it as my chance at life," I said. "Now . . . now I don't."

I looked up to find them both watching me. Shock radiated from Barrett. I couldn't breathe around what swirled in those starburst eyes—something completely foreign to me.

Barrett made to help. Hal tried to shrug him off. Barrett growled, "There's no one to impress here. Just take my damn help, you stubborn ass."

Hal grumbled but leaned into Barrett, who was shorter but easily held his friend up. I followed them out, watching them walk down the hall before turning right. Hal didn't say goodbye. I was starting to think I would never be able to say goodbye to him—glowing wrist or not.

✦ ✦ ✦

THE REST OF THE DAY, I STARED AT THE HOLOGRAMS AND WORried about Hal: the pain he was in and how I could do nothing to help. The first few paintings were landscapes that went quickly. After my midday meal, I pulled up the next piece and instantly felt paralyzed.

A woman with dark, free-flowing hair and a unibrow stood topless, white bandage-like wrappings above and under her breasts and twice around her midsection. The background was barren earth and an indigo sky. Her face looked determined, but the thing that held my gaze was the tear down her middle, revealing a fractured column where her spine might be, ripping her in two. I looked closer to see countless small metal nails piercing her skin. An involuntary shiver snaked up my spine. *The Broken Column.* I felt transfixed by the woman's evident pain, the impassive glare in her eyes that confronted the viewer, the gaping hole for all to see. I just sat with her for a long time.

The usual ding signaled the end of the day. I tore my eyes from her and hit *delete*. I typed some notes in my report before I gathered my things and resurfaced. My anxiety trailed behind, lurking. The sun was close to setting as I exited the atrium.

I found Lo alone by the Pods. "Hey," I called out, making my way to her. I hadn't seen her in almost a week. "Are you okay?"

"I haven't heard anything," Lo mumbled as we moved forward in line.

"Do you want to ride back together?"

Lo shrugged. We stood next to each other in line, an odd silence between us.

We scanned our wrists as we boarded the Pod. I sat beside her as the Pod took off. Lo sat staring blankly ahead, leaving her hair in a plait. Was she that stressed about Gregory?

In seeing Hal, my thoughts had quieted, and unease settled within me as an eerie silence blanketed the Pod. None of the women looked at their Comm Devices. No one talked. They all stared blankly ahead like Lo.

I turned toward Lo, fully taking her in. Her blue eyes looked glazed, her sunshine hair was haphazardly braided, pieces falling out, and her clothes were wrinkled. I had never seen her look so unkempt. My unease thickened.

Everyone around me had the same glazed look, and I realized what had happened to the Minors.

I had been so distracted with what might be happening underneath that I hadn't paid attention to the surface. The balance Tabitha had preached entailed sedating the Minors into submission.

I grabbed my Comm Device and pulled up Collin's name. I began to type but stopped. Collin hadn't reached out since the murder, after I had told him he had chosen wrong. I wanted to ask him about it, but he could be behind this.

I deleted the message, noticing the gold light that filled the Pod in the dark. My mating was on full display, but no one whistled. No one even looked.

Except one, a woman wedged between two drugged Minors. Her hair was pulled back in a bun. Her eyes locked with mine, alert and assessing. She looked down at my wrist and then up at my mismatched gaze. She smiled, winking at me, and every hair on my body stood on end.

The Pod stopped at our living quarters. Two Minors and Lo exited without a backward glance. I hurried after them but froze on the threshold.

"The supplements."

I whipped my head toward the woman with the clear eyes, but she stared straight ahead. "Does *he* know?" I whispered, afraid to say the Reaper's name aloud.

"Of course he does. Now run along, pet. They're watching you."

The reason for their behavior slammed into me almost as hard as *pet*. I was so stupid. I hadn't been taking the supplements, but they all had. My HI had said they planned to alter my supplements to calm me. None of them would have gotten the same information. This was more than calm—they were drugging the Minors.

I chased after Lo, slipping between the closing doors of the elevator. The woman's other statement burrowed into my chest. I was being watched, but which side was watching me? Both of them? I had never seen her in the transportation Pods before. Suddenly, Hal's declaration that there was a vulnerability in being known sent my mind spiraling. How many spies did the Reaper have? How big was this operation?

The doors opened and Lo walked off. I followed her down the hall and into her living quarters. It wasn't until the door fully closed that I approached her. The room was smaller than mine, facing Low Town.

"Lo, listen to me. Are you taking the supplements daily?"

She didn't blink. "Of course."

"Lo, you have to stop taking them. They did something to them."

"We have to, Emeline." Lo gazed over my shoulder. "I have to make this mating work."

"This is more important than a Mate. Don't take them," I urged.

Lo grunted as she scanned, and the automated voice filled the room as she walked to her wardrobe filled with only gray. She stripped, throwing on gray leisure clothes.

I glanced toward her black boxes and counter space to find trays and empty stimulant cups everywhere. "I'm going to pick up." I gathered the trays and consolidated them as the first box dinged. "I'll bring it to you."

I crammed the trays into the second box before I opened the first box and grabbed her tray of mush and supplements. We were never given supplements with evening meals. I snatched the supplements from the tray.

Someone from the dinner had gone behind the Illum's back. Someone had told the Reaper about the Minors before I could. My head started spinning again.

The Reaper knew. Why hadn't he already stopped this? Perhaps because he was injured—barely able to walk . . . I didn't know anymore.

I handed Lo the tray. She stared at it, then ate three bites before dragging her feet to her bed and falling into it. I followed her over. "Lo, in the morning, don't take the supplements. Can you hear me?"

Lo opened her eyes, finding mine. Behind the haze, desperation stared at me. "Why . . . what did I do wrong, Emeline? They said—you . . . why Gregory won't give me a contract," she finished incoherently.

"Lo, I don't know. It's not important. Right now, I need you to tell me you won't take the supplements. They put something in them to make you like this."

"Not important . . . you have Illum. Your future set," Lo slurred groggily, her blinks becoming longer.

"No one's future is set. Look, Lo, we can figure out Gregory, but you have to stop taking the supplements."

She mumbled something incoherent before her breaths began to even out. Part of me wanted to stay with her to ensure she was okay, but I needed to scan. I didn't want to draw attention to myself—to her. I would come up right after curfew ended tomorrow. Hopefully, she wouldn't have had her morning meal before that. I tossed a blanket over her sleeping form before I left.

Sleep evaded me as I tossed and turned in my bed, my thoughts infecting me with fears, until the unknown won, distorting my grip on reality.

I searched for my old dream of spinning in a pretty gown in the arms of an Elite man that would save me—desperate for its simplicity, the hope it had once given me. The more I dug, the more out of reach it became, solidifying its fragility and deceit. It didn't exist—it never would. Too much had changed in the world—in me.

Sleep claimed me and with it came a dark tunnel, my whispered name—a haunting, urging me onward or trying to hold me back. I didn't know.

In what felt like minutes, I awoke to Frida prompting me to scan. I made my way over to the scanner and dragged myself toward the three black boxes, hopping onto my counter and resting my head against the wall as Frida began her report. I wished she would tell me when this whole menstruation thing would end, but she didn't. I didn't trust the supplements anymore, but I missed the ones that kept my cycle away. I sighed, closing my heavy eyelids.

"Your levels are all improving dramatically, Emeline."

I whirled toward Frida. She was smiling.

"I am pleased to see our plan is working for you. I will contact the Illum with this wonderful news." *Please don't,* I thought. "Enjoy your morning meal, and then I will begin our lesson."

The black box dinged, and I retrieved my meal, scarfing it down. I ignored the container of supplements. I hadn't taken any since the day before the dinner.

"Today, we will review several of the dances we have learned. Enjoy, Emeline."

The rest of the lesson flew by too quickly, each step and spin siphoning my frustration and clearing my head.

The lesson ended with the dance that was becoming my favorite. The dance was faster, with bigger swells in the music and countless spins. When the music ended, I was sweaty and panting, but for a moment I felt lighter.

I opened the container of supplements, staring at the various shapes and colors of the pills. I would never take them again if I could help it.

I could give Hal the supplements. Maybe he would know what was in them.

I dumped the supplements into my white clutch, alongside the cuff and the knife.

CHAPTER TWENTY-SEVEN

The day below passed at a slow pace. I received no messages. I didn't really expect Hal to show up, not with how much pain he had been in yesterday, but a part of me was still disappointed each time I looked at my doorway and I didn't find him leaning against the frame, half-smiling at me. I reminded myself he was injured and needed rest. Still some part of me just assumed he would always show up regardless of the consequences.

When my shift finally ended, I found Lo in the atrium and was relieved to see that her complexion had more color. She had dark circles under her eyes, but her gaze was clear and her hair was clean and braided neatly.

"How are you feeling?" I asked. She hadn't answered my knock this morning, and I hadn't seen her on the way to work, and I had worried about her. Around us, Minors in gray scuttled about, their gazes dull.

"Much better. I'm actually hungry," Lo said, and her smile reached her eyes before fading. "They're actually drugging us," she whispered, shaking her head. "How did you figure it out?"

"I didn't realize at first. I stopped taking mine after the dinner. My HI said something about changing them to calm me. I thought initially it was only mine because of what happened at the dinner. Yesterday I figured it out."

"So no one told you about them, not even Collin. Neither did your birth brothers?"

"No, our relationship isn't like that."

"But you didn't have any of the effects I had?"

"No, I didn't," I said. "What happened this morning? I knocked on your door."

"I woke up in the middle of the night. Felt really shaky. Started throwing up. This morning was rough. I sat in my shower for a long time. The moment curfew was done, I left to find Becca. Her shift ends around curfew. Found her and begged for a stimulant drink, hoping it would make me feel better. Can't hurt, right? It's not like Gregory has reached out."

"They're *drugging* us," I stated, repeating her words. "Isn't that more pressing?"

Lo shook her head. "No, I need a contract more than ever. They aren't being drugged up there."

They did receive their supplements as injections. There was no way to determine what might be in them. I couldn't see them drugging the Elite. They didn't need to. The Elite followed the Illum blindly up in their clouds.

I sighed. "Lo, I am sure he has his reasons. I can ask Collin the next time I see him."

"Have you talked to him?"

"Not since the dinner." I quickly changed the subject. "You shouldn't have seen Becca this morning. What if they notice you left the area?"

"If I'm eliminated, I won't have to worry about a contract."

I grasped her arm. "Lo, don't talk like that."

"Fine, fine." She patted my hand, and I released her. "Why do you think Collin hasn't reached out?"

"I'm sure he's busy managing all of this," I said, gesturing to the Minors staring into space. "He's an Illum after all. This came from him."

"Emeline, thank you for getting me off those supplements. I'm sorry I didn't say it sooner."

"Of course. I know you'd do the same for me."

We exited through the tall glass doors. I tilted my head toward the sun's dying rays when a panicked gasp escaped Lo, her face pale as she looked toward the Pods.

"The Force is here. They have weapons," Lo whispered, her voice quaking.

Slowly, I tracked her gaze to see dozens of green-clad men with guns walking around the women in gray. "Let's get to the Pods."

"Why are they here?" Lo asked, barely audible.

"I don't know. Let's go. Don't look at them."

I stared at the ground as we joined the line to the Pods shoulder to shoulder, Lo's fingers brushing mine. The footfalls of heavy boots thudded in my ears.

My Comm Device dinged, and panic seized me.

"Whose device is that?" a voice rang out. The crunch of boots against the pavement drew closer. Dread squeezed my throat as my Comm Device dinged again.

Lo's fingers flexed next to mine. Tighter surveillance, that's what Tabitha had said in the Illum video. Apparently, drugging the Minors into submission was not enough. They had called in the Force.

"Look, come forward, and things will be nice and easy," the soldier said, closer this time.

A man laughed. "I'd rather it be hard. Easy is no fun."

"They won't fucking hear you," another drawled. "They're not really there."

"If one of them does, we'll have bigger issues."

"They'll be the one with issues. The Illum is giving out promotions for finding Minors disobeying."

If I said something, I'd reveal I wasn't taking the supplements, but Collin was still my Mate. I was an extension of him, of the Illum. I alone might have some protection. Or would I be scrutinized further? Regardless, I needed to buy Lo time to get into the Pod. I gripped her hand and then released it, my heart beating furiously.

"It's mine," I said, stepping away from Lo. I heard her sharp intake of breath but refused to look over.

Three soldiers in dark green prowled toward me. They wore the same uniforms as at the Parting, their faces completely covered by intimidating helmets. They stopped in front of me, guns gleaming in the evening light.

"Why are you receiving messages at this hour?" one Force soldier demanded.

"It is likely from my Mate, a member of the Illum."

The words tasted like ash on my tongue.

One of the other soldiers snorted. "All that time underground making you imagine things?"

Shock sent my heart beating harder against my ribs.

"Give your bag to me," the soldier closest to me instructed.

They would find the white clutch, filled with supplements, the cuff, and the knife. True terror grabbed me.

"I won't ask a second time," the first one warned, stepping closer. Over his shoulder, another soldier trekked toward us as Minors moved in the direction of the Pods.

"Why are you just standing there?" the soldier demanded. I looked up. He was talking to Lo, not me. Cold sweat slid down my back.

Since my approved mating, I had put myself in many stupid situations. This was the dumbest of them all.

The soldier directly in front of me moved his head. My mismatched eyes reflected back in the shield covering his face. My clear eyes.

The large soldier approached, looming over the other three. "Look at her fucking wrist," the man barked at his comrades. I swore I knew the voice. I held up my glowing wrist for them to see.

"So what?"

"It means she is, in fact, the Enforcer's Mate, you fucking idiot."

"Shit, Fredrik, are you serious?"

The large soldier nodded his head. "Yes."

The other soldiers stumbled back, heads swiveling between me and the large soldier, Fredrik I supposed. I heard light footsteps. I didn't turn to confirm Lo had walked away, but relief still found me.

"Why didn't you say Enforcer?" the one closest to me spat.

"You didn't seem inclined to believe me," I retorted. The large one chuckled deeply, walking off.

"Get going," the other soldier barked.

I didn't need telling twice. I fled, searching for blond hair, my breaths shallow. I spotted Lo near the Pod, staring at her feet. I rushed toward her.

"I'm sorry I left you." She was near-hyperventilating, her face white.

"Don't be. Next time, run immediately. Collin's status can spare me. I don't think it'll stretch to you." I grabbed my Comm Device. I had one official message and another from a number I didn't recognize. I shoved the device into my bag.

"Emeline, what's happening?" Lo asked, terrified.

"I don't know. I'm going to find out. Get on the Pod." I checked over my shoulder. There were so many soldiers in green.

"Come with me," Lo insisted, trembling.

Unease cloaked me. I knew I was being watched.

"It was an official message. When I scan my wrist, the Pod will make an announcement. I don't want you here for that. *Go.*" I pushed her into the throng of Minors.

She boarded the Pod, and our eyes locked, her jaw tight. *Be safe,* she mouthed. The doors closed and the weight of terror lifted as the Pod took off.

The back of my neck prickled, and I whirled around to find the large soldier watching me nearby. I clambered onto the last Pod, shoving my wrist under the scanner.

The announcement filled the air. I took a seat, the doors closing. The soldier tilted his head as he watched me, like he was sizing me up. I felt the air leave my lungs as the Pod shot up, the weight of that stare searing me the whole way.

CHAPTER TWENTY-EIGHT

Did you make it to the living quarters? I messaged Lo.

I clutched my Comm Device to my chest. It dinged seconds later.

Yes, are you okay? Let me know when you get back.

I'm fine. I will.

Fine was easier than trying to describe the chaos raging in my heart. I was pretty sure I knew where I was heading. Only one person ever summoned me like this, and for once, I was okay with that.

The Pod stopped at the edge of the balcony of his private living quarters without visiting the Starlings first. I was in gray, my defect visible, but I couldn't care less as I stormed across the balcony. After everything that had happened, I had no idea how I would face Collin, but I had questions for my Mate.

I entered the sitting room, the memory of the last time I had been here after the dinner crashing into me. So much had changed after that night.

"Can you tell me why the Elite Force was patrolling the Pods?" I demanded as I walked toward the sunken area, only to find Nora waiting for me instead of Collin, the same worn book in her hand.

"Hi, Emeline," Nora responded. "I don't know why they were there. I can contact Collin if you would like. He would know."

"No," I said quickly. "I mean, isn't he the reason I am here?"

Nora closed the book gently, as if the seams might split at any moment, before standing, her evergreen long-sleeve dress shimmering in the dim lighting.

"Actually, I summoned you," Nora said.

"*You* summoned me?"

"Yes, I did. I hijacked your evening. I bullied Phillip into it. Collin said he was giving you time, but I think you've had time enough. Not everyone likes to suffer alone. But you seem to have questions for Collin, not me."

What answers could Nora give me? I crossed my arms, running my hands down my gray-clad arms.

"Are you upset? I can summon a Pod to take you back if you—if you don't want to be here."

"I'm in gray," I muttered. It was a pathetic excuse. I liked Nora, but when I looked at her, all I saw was Collin.

"I don't mind, Emeline. Collin had some clothes sent over from the Starlings for occasions like this. I can show you if you'd like." Nora threaded her arm through mine. "Come on, you can change so you're comfortable."

We passed several doors before she took me into a stunning bedroom. Floor-to-ceiling windows sat on the far wall, letting the night sky spill into the room. A chandelier with crystals resembling delicate flowers cast playful light throughout the space, which was covered in soft ivories. A plush bed faced the windows, laden with cream pillows in various textures. It would be a dream to fall into it. A large vase of white peonies adorned the nightstand closest to me.

We walked into a dressing room, bigger than my entire living quarters, laden with exquisite fabrics in all sorts of colors. In the center of the room was a large pouf. The back wall was filled with clutches and shoes of varying heights.

Nora handed me an amber, long-sleeve gown, much like the green one she wore, and selected a pair of matching satin slippers. I held the dress and shoes awkwardly. The color reminded me of starburst amber eyes. I bit my lip, staring expectantly at her.

"You can change here, I don't mind, but if you want privacy, that door"—she gestured to a door leading away from the room—"leads to your bathing chamber."

My brows raised. "*My* chamber?" I had assumed these were Nora's quarters.

"Of course," she said. "This is your room, Emeline. All of this is for you, for when you are in the procreation phase, which we will have to avoid discussing for the entirety of our friendship. I do not wish to hear about my brother."

In the beginning, I could picture procreation with Collin. After the kiss, a part of me had wanted it. Now, seeing what he had done, his role as the Enforcer . . . I couldn't fathom how I was supposed to go forward with the contract. Violet's words rang through me: *You are the only non-Elite with access to the Illum.*

Nora noted my silence. She stepped closer, placing her delicate hand on mine. "But we can talk about it if you need. I know it isn't easy the first time. Sometimes not even after that, but it is our duty to the Greater Good."

I gritted my teeth. There it was again. The Greater Good.

"Emeline," Nora began, pulling me from my thoughts. "Collin isn't an evil man."

I opened my mouth to protest. I had to do a better job of not wearing my emotions on my face.

"No, listen, I won't plead his case, but give him a chance. Collin can come across as cold and removed, but he doesn't do anything without a reason."

"Is there ever a reason to murder someone, to use someone?" I blurted.

Nora took a deep breath and perched on the edge of the pouf, smoothing her skirt. Her eyes burned like brilliant sapphires, so like her twin's.

"Offspring are the funniest thing," she said. "They change you so fully and quickly that you don't have a say. They take all the beliefs you thought you had, all those preconceived notions, and wipe them away. It leaves you quite vulnerable. You see, before my offspring, I thought I knew right from wrong. At the Academy it all seemed simple. But the moment they placed Arabella in my arms . . ." Nora smiled. It was the fiercest yet saddest smile I had ever seen.

"Everything became unimportant. The world consisted of only her. I realized there was nothing I wouldn't do to protect her, no line I wouldn't cross. Then James came along, and then Eleana. I thought my heart would shatter with my third, to split myself so many times. Without fail, whenever I have welcomed another offspring, a part of me goes with them. I fear what this next one will do to me." Nora rested a hand on her stomach, and then she met my gaze. "But I face it for them. There is no evil I wouldn't face to save them and no evil I wouldn't become to spare them."

Fierceness shined so bright in her crystalline eyes, it could pierce the unending dark of night. A chill snaked across my skin, coiling around my heart, leaving me breathless.

"Why are you telling me this?" I whispered.

"What you want to know is not so simple. Should someone ever do those things? No. But no one is all good or all bad. Each person has their breaking point, their line in the sand. Maybe find out Collin's before you write him off completely." Nora stood. "Get dressed. I'll meet you in the sitting room."

"Nora," I called after her, "did Collin put you up to this?"

She stood in the doorway. "No. In fact, he'll be outraged when he finds out. He detests meddling."

"I won't tell him," I assured her.

"Collin always finds out. This is just one friend looking out for another."

I watched her leave, her fierceness disguised by delicate trappings. What could a person become, having a mother love them the way Nora loved her offspring? Did all mothers love their offspring quietly? Was that the only way they were permitted to?

And you wanted to save her, Helen.

Was I wrong about my birth mother never caring about me, or had my status truly stifled any love from her?

I walked into the bathroom and gaped in awe at the large tub, enormous marble shower, and white vanity laden with bottles like Rose and Violet always used. On the counter sat another item they always had.

A lens.

I placed my bag on the counter next to all the beauty items. It felt safest to leave it there, considering what it contained. I changed quickly, slipping on the amber silk dress. The flowy sleeves cuffed at my wrist, hiding the gold, and the skirt hit below my knees. I donned the slippers and released my tight bun, hair spilling freely over my shoulders. I looked at the lens and, taking a deep breath, put it in.

Nora sat near the heating hearth, a tea service on the table. The tray was laden with a teapot, two teacups, two glasses of the bubbling liquid in delicate glasses, chocolates dusted in gold from the Sphere, and a spectacular cake covered in chocolate frosting embellished with glittering flowers.

"Oh, good. I wasn't going to be able to wait much longer." Nora patted the seat next to her. "Tea or bubbles?"

"Can I say both?" I inquired, sitting beside her.

Her grin lit up her face. "I am delighted I decided to make you my friend." Nora handed me a glass of bubbling liquid and cut into the chocolate cake. "So, you said the Force was out today?"

Surprise rippled through me. I thought she would avoid any topic related to the Illum. "Yes, patrolling the Pods where I work. They were armed."

"William did say last night that the new measures would begin now that they had time to put their plan in motion," Nora said, taking a bite of the cake. "You don't like him, do you?"

"I didn't say that."

"I just handed you a piece of the best cake in the whole city, and your nose is scrunched up like I offended you," she finished, taking another bite.

"Fine, I can't say I was impressed. Do you like him?" I asked, before taking a bite of cake. A moan escaped me despite myself. It was the fluffiest cake I had ever had. I blushed. "Sorry."

"Don't be, it's good cake," Nora said, taking another bite. "It isn't important if I like him."

I paused. "How can you say that?"

Nora put her empty plate down, grabbed her bubbles, and downed almost all of it. "Because I am not interested in my Mate outside of my duty. It was the same with the others."

"Others?" I felt like I was missing something.

"I always forget you don't know all the gossip of the Elite. What a gift." Nora smiled sadly. "William is my fourth Mate."

I placed my fork down. "Why?"

"I am to be bred to spread my genes into the population. I get a new Mate right before my offspring's fourth birthday."

Disgust blanketed me. "Collin allows this?"

"Collin can only do so much," Nora said quietly.

I glanced around the room, ensuring we were alone. "And Gregory?"

"I thought you might have figured it out. He hasn't been careful lately. He's angry. We were both up for new Mates again. I was matched with William, while Gregory was assigned a Minor mating. Then he found out about you and Collin. I have never seen him so angry. He wanted to know why you and Collin could be matched but we weren't." Nora poured us both tea.

"You've known one another since your first mate?"

Nora smoothed out her dress. "Yes, since Edward. Gregory was

Edward's best friend throughout the Academy. A troublesome pair. Nothing serious, but they were always up to no good. When I bled, the Illum decided I should be Mated. I was sixteen at the time. I was Mated with Edward. My immaculate genes, as they called them, would further our society. He was five years older than I was. We were all so young. We attended a few balls that the Illum said we should. It was all fine and good—the dancing, gowns, drinking." Nora stared out the windows behind me like she was lost in the memories.

"Then, it was time for the actual procreation. I had seen the videos. I knew what was coming, but I was terrified. I couldn't do it the first time. Edward wasn't pleased. He raged and broke things. When I missed our procreation window, I told him I would be ready the next moon, but he changed. Became cruel. I think a part of me did too. When the second moon came around, I couldn't bring myself to lie with him." Tears welled in Nora's eyes as she met my gaze.

"He didn't take that well. We had all been together that night leading up to it—me, Edward, and Gregory. Gregory had noticed the change in his friend. When I told Edward no, he became physical with me. Gregory heard and broke into the room. He—it was a mess. He beat Edward, badly, and carried me from the room. He stayed with me those next few nights. He kept Edward away." Nora took a shaky breath.

"Nora, I am so sorry."

"It is okay."

"It isn't." My heart ached at what she had been through, at hearing more about the kind of man my birth brother was. "So, you've loved him since that night?"

Nora shook her head, a tear falling, "No, I loved him long before that moment. It happened in stolen moments on the dance floor, in the middle of the night, with only the stars to see. I told him a dream I thought only I could see, but he saw it too. The moment, it doesn't matter when. I know deep down that I loved him long before I met him. I will love him in this life and whatever comes after it."

"Even if you can't be together?"

"Yes."

"What if there was a place you two could be together?" I pressed on.

Nora's eyes went vacant before shaking her head. "Emeline, such a place doesn't exist."

"What if it did, in the Underworld, where the Majors are?"

"Emeline," Nora warned.

"But it isn't the same as up here. It's different." This was dangerous territory, but my heart wanted to know that two people who loved each other could be together.

"I don't know why you know that. I don't want to know," Nora told me. "But even if it were an option, I wouldn't take it."

"How can you say that?" I demanded.

"They have my offspring at the Academy. I will undergo anything they ask to keep them safe. They will not fall victim to my selfish choices."

I paused in understanding. "What about Gregory?"

"Gregory would never ask such a thing of me. He—" Nora fell silent, looking over my shoulder toward the breakfast room.

My heart beat fiercely against my ribs. I knew what I would see before I even turned.

Collin walked into the room, holding a glass of amber liquid in his left hand. He was dressed in a black suit again, the image of Illum nobility, his midnight hair styled perfectly. His huge frame moved toward me with lethal grace. Power emanated from him, as if he were death incarnate.

"Sister," Collin greeted. "Mate." His eyes raked over me.

"Brother," Nora responded, tipping her head toward him, her brows pinched. "I thought you said you were working late."

"I was, but—"

"But Phillip is a dirty little snitch," Nora interrupted.

"Phillip works for the Illum. He was obligated to tell me. You should know better than to change my Mate's MIND," Collin told Nora.

"I thought someone should check in on *Emeline*," Nora replied, "which I believe I have told you every night." She took another forkful of cake, smiling sweetly. Masking everything we had been talking about.

"I'd like a word with my Mate," Collin stated, crossing his arms. "Alone."

Nora looked at me like she wouldn't leave unless I was okay, and my chest warmed at her protectiveness. I couldn't avoid Collin forever. I nodded. She stood, tucking her book under her arm, and grabbed the cake stand and her fork, scrunching her nose at me. "Wouldn't want this to go to waste. I'm here if you need me, Emeline."

"And if I want more cake?" I challenged.

"Then you're out of luck," Nora remarked. "I'll bully them into a weekly informal tea for us. No one should be alone. Good night."

"Good night, Nora. Thank you for everything," I told her, and meant it. She waltzed from the room, her tiny frame carrying the massive cake a sight.

"She's always eaten desserts like that. I tell her she's lucky she's Elite, and our supplements make it so it doesn't affect her," Collin commented.

"Lucky, hmm?" I said mildly. I didn't know if you could call it lucky after all the things Nora told me she had suffered as an Elite.

His eyes pierced straight to my core, as if piecing together what Nora and I might have discussed. He didn't press further, though, and instead looked to Nora's vacant seat before seemingly thinking better of it, perching on the edge of the table instead.

"She is right, though." Collin stared into his glass of amber liquid. "I should have reached out. I should have checked in on you before now. I thought . . . given what you expressed the last time we were together, that perhaps you would want your space from me. Then I got the report that your levels are optimal." Collin took a long drink. "I assumed that meant I had made the right choice. However, we do need to maintain our public appearances. The

Press and Elite want to see you more. See who you are to me, to the Illum."

"I think the Elite know what I am," I said deliberately. He raised a brow at me. "They bowed to me after you told them I sent the man to his death."

"Tabitha wanted to send the right message."

"The right message," I echoed incredulously, my anger clawing its way up my throat. "That what? I am subservient to you and the Illum?"

"Everyone below the Illum is subservient to them, including the Elite," Collin shot back. "Well, everyone except you." He stood, and I ground my teeth as my anger engulfed me. He shrugged off his jacket, tossing it aside as he slowly made his way to a bottle of brown liquid that sat on his bookshelf. He poured another glass, his back to me as he continued. "I got another report about you."

Dread roared through me, my heart twisting viciously in my chest. Willing myself to calm, I grabbed my glass of bubbles and took a sip. Collin remained silent as he took a drink.

"I did tell you, very little happens in this city that I am not aware of." His voice was pleasant, but terror pulsed through my veins. "I told you when it comes to you, I am aware of everything."

"What report did you receive?" It was more breathless than I intended it to be.

"You took a run to the river the morning after the meeting," he stated, a dangerous edge to his voice. "You stayed there for some time before returning to your living quarters."

"The dinner was unsettling," I retorted, clutching my glass to prevent it from shaking, from giving me away.

Collin turned slowly, finally looking at me. I couldn't read his face. "Your heart rate was elevated several times. *After* you stopped running."

I worked to swallow, the feel of Hal's lips on mine swarming me. Had my MIND registered that? Or was it from me hurtling myself off the edge? How much did those cuffs scramble?

"The message from Tabitha was off-putting," I said. "I enjoy running, and the water is relaxing."

"Must be. Your oxytocin and dopamine levels were elevated when you returned to your living quarters." He tilted his head. "Why do you think that is?"

"The water is relaxing," I repeated dumbly, panic rising to a feverish pitch.

"So you said. Relaxing by Low Town where the cameras are outdated," Collin mused, his eyes dipping to the glass in my hand.

I willed it to remain steady. "Seems like a poor place for your cameras not to work. I'd have thought the Illum would want to watch the Majors."

"Tabitha agreed with you when it was brought to the Illum's attention that my Mate was in an unapproved area."

There was no hiding my shaking now, and I placed my glass down, lacing my fingers together tightly.

"So instead of leading the retribution I planned, I was sent to fix a flaw you found while simultaneously coming up with a valid reason for why you were there."

"Sorry to take away your chance to hurt more Majors," I spat.

Collin rolled his shoulders. "They seemed to manage well enough without me. The Majors were more prepared than the Illum anticipated. Rumor is the Reaper got hurt in the process and bailed." Collin threw back his entire drink.

The Reaper had gotten hurt. My mind whirled.

"The cameras by Low Town now work, and the Illum have a new spy to give them feedback on Minors."

I didn't miss the bitterness in his voice. It left me off-balance. "Who?"

Collin locked eyes with me. "You."

I shot to my feet, choking on shock. "Excuse me?"

"You went where you shouldn't have without warning me," Collin bit out. "It was the best I could come up with for why you were where you weren't supposed to be."

"So being your pet wasn't enough?" I barked, stepping toward him. "Now I have to be your spy?"

"I never called you my pet," Collin gritted, his eyes flashing. His anger tangled with mine, electrifying the air between us. "It would be so much easier if that's all you were."

"What does that even mean?" When he didn't answer, I snapped. "Fine, don't tell me. I might as well be your *pet. Mate, pet,* what's the difference?"

"Is that what you want to be to me?" Collin asked, stalking toward me.

"None of this is what I want. I'm a vessel that has to be subservient to you."

He towered over me, and my pulse grew louder in my ears. "I have never asked you to be subservient, Emeline. It would be nice, however, if you could just try to follow their rules. So I wouldn't have to worry all the damn time."

"You act like they're different things. Their rules make me your property." My tether on everything I shoved down snapped completely.

I darted from the room into my soon-to-be quarters, slamming the bathroom door behind me.

"Emeline," Collin called. I snatched my bag off the vanity. "I just meant we could make this pleasant for both of us. This mating doesn't have to be like this. I understand this isn't what you want, but could you just stop fighting me and trust me?"

Trust what you see, not what they say. I took a steadying breath. I saw a man who murdered Defects and somehow asked me to forgive and trust him without telling me anything.

I reentered my quarters to find Collin to the right of the bed, his hands fisted at his sides. I took him in, his shirt slightly unbuttoned, exposing the top of his sculpted, tanned chest. The windows behind him, the night sky surrounding him as if it belonged to him. My traitorous heart raced at the sight. He was a vision.

I understood why I had gotten swept away. Collin was everything the Elite held sacred. He truly was beautiful, and if beauty was all that mattered, he would be right. I could envision it. It might even be more than pleasant.

I thrust my hand into my bag, finding the loose supplements. I withdrew a fistful, walking into Collin's magnetic pull.

Maybe I was digging my own grave, solidifying my demise. Maybe, like all the art they destroyed, I had revealed too much of the things they tried to keep hidden. But I knew one thing: I had felt more alive beneath than I ever had above. Maybe I was okay burying myself alive.

"Here, my *spying*," I said, my heart in my throat as I held out my hand. Collin's brows knitted together as he reached out. A shiver wrecked me as his hand brushed against mine.

I dumped the supplements into his palm. His eyes flew from the supplements to me.

"Does anyone else know you're not taking these?" Collin asked, his sapphire eyes wide.

"Does it matter?"

"Does anyone else know?" Collin demanded, closing the space between us as he bore down on me, his warm breath caressing my face.

"Strange that now that I stopped taking them, I'm optimal."

"It isn't pleasant what happens to those who don't follow the Illum."

"You mean don't follow *you*," I spat, our breath mixing. My heart slammed into my ribs. Something twisted deep in my core, but I ignored it. "You know what's unpleasant? Being drugged into a shell of yourself against your will." I shot past him, ripping away from his magnetic field as I stormed toward the living area.

I heard his footsteps not far behind me.

"I am doing what's best," Collin growled, that polished exterior cracking as I heard the supplements scatter across the floor. I spun to face him.

"The best for who, Collin?" I yelled back, marching up to him and poking his massive chest. "The best for you? The best for the people in the damn clouds? What about the people down there? What about me?"

"What about you?" Collin bit out, grabbing my hand from where, I hadn't realized, I was touching him, wild storms raging in his eyes. "Tell me, what's best for you, Emeline?"

I froze as his eyes dipped to my lips. My pulse skittered across my skin, leaving a wildfire in its wake beneath his gaze. He stepped closer until his muscular chest grazed mine. I should step away from him. I shouldn't want him near me.

My feet remained rooted.

"I—" I began breathlessly as he dragged his eyes back to mine. I couldn't step out of that pull of his.

"You," Collin murmured, lowering his face until the tip of his nose grazed mine. "You are unlike anything I have ever known." His voice was a deep whisper. "You're maddening, consuming, unwilling to follow any of their rules. I have a role to play and yet I spend my time thinking about you."

If I leaned forward an inch, our lips would meet. His heart thundered against my chest, as untamed as his eyes.

His eyes held mine, a need there I had never seen.

"Thinking about how to make sure I'm obedient?" I rasped.

His lips found my ear. "You have only ever listened once. Rule Ten." He breathed in the scent of my hair, and I shuddered, warmth pooling traitorously low. The feel of his lips in the Sphere slammed into me.

Beneath the storm that raged through my veins, I remembered.

Rule Ten: You are not permitted under any circumstances to tell your Mate no regarding public appearances, attire, or desires. If your Mate asks, you are to oblige him.

"Would you say no to me this time, Emeline?" Collin asked, dragging his mouth away from my ear until it hovered above mine. His eyes searched me desperately. Looking for something. "If I told you to kiss me," he said, his lips brushing against mine with each word. The touch featherlight, a mere whisper of what could happen. "Knowing every terrible thing I am capable of. Would you tell me no?"

I couldn't breathe around how his eyes held mine. My core tightened. I would tell him no. I didn't want this. An Illum.

But my body betrayed me as his arm swept behind my lower back, pressing me against him, and I welcomed it. Arched into him. My hips flush against his, my hands finding his chest, his heart thundering beneath my touch. I told myself it was to push him away.

"Tell me no," Collin breathed, his lips lingered before mine. Was he begging?

My eyes fluttered closed, my breaths too shallow. "I can't."

Collin went unnaturally still. "Can't, or you don't want to?"

I leaned in.

"Oh," a small voice squeaked. I whipped my head to find Nora in a cream robe behind Collin with her cake stand.

I ripped away from him as reality found me.

"I want a Pod now." I felt as if my body were on fire. I covered my searing lips.

"Of course," she muttered, her eyes flying between us once more before she rushed to her room.

Collin stared at me like he had never truly seen me. I watched as he re-formed that polished exterior, the storms in his sapphire pools winking out. He pulled away to fetch his empty glass and refilled it from the bottle on the shelf. Collin downed the liquid before filling the glass again. He stalked over to me.

"The other rules should be followed. I am a member of the Illum, and you are my Mate," Collin told me, thrusting the glass into my trembling hand. "Therefore, you have to adhere to their rules."

"And if I don't?" I whispered. Those sapphire eyes gutted at my question.

"The consequences won't be pleasant." Collin spoke quietly, stepping away again, his hands in fists. The space between us grew. "Nora will secure you a Pod. The ball is in two weeks. I shall see you then. Good night."

"What of the public appearances?" I asked, my chest empty as something that resembled disappointment crept in.

Collin halted. "There's no need. You can just be my pet at the ball."

My spine went rigid at the way he said *pet*. The knot in my throat choked me. I downed the drink to burn it away. It didn't work.

Without another word, he left, as if he couldn't escape me quickly enough.

Alone, I stared at the painting above Collin's heating hearth once again. What made the woman walk away? I hated that I would never know. At the man's feet something grew—maybe a flower, bloodred as if his agony had given it life. The woman walked away all the same. But a tendril of her blond hair flowed behind her, a connection to the man and his perpetual sorrow. As if even in leaving him she remained tied to him. Forever.

CHAPTER TWENTY-NINE

Harold greeted me the night of my first ball. "It's been some time. The Starlings are ready for you."

I had spent the last two weeks almost entirely alone. Lo was once again my only companion, but even she was distant. Gregory hadn't approved their mating yet. Even with clear eyes, she was withdrawn. Most mornings I would find her stuffing an empty stimulant drink into her bag, surrounded by the other still-drugged women. Was she sabotaging her contract, or did she no longer care in Gregory's silence? I never got to ask her, thanks to the soldiers who now rode on the Pods with us. I didn't know if Gregory's silence was due to whatever was going on with the supplements or his displeasure that, for all Lo was, she would never be Nora.

I didn't hear from Nora either. Her determination to bully Collin for an informal tea seemed unsuccessful. Or perhaps she had heard our argument and decided against being my friend after all.

Hal hadn't returned to my office. I assured myself that it was due to his healing and that I would hear from someone if something was wrong.

My office, which had provided the two of us refuge, became a cell again, the buzzing lights my only company. I looked at art, my mind bouncing from intrigue to wishing I could discuss it with someone to wondering if the pieces I sent to destruction found their way into the Underworld. One of the paintings they destroyed stuck with me—a man led a woman by the hand, but the woman was pale and looked upset and lost. Was he taking her away? Were the people among the trees mourning her leaving? *Orpheus Leading Eurydice from the Underworld.* Had there been an Underworld before the Last War? I didn't know. I never would. The lights never talked back, so I sat alone with my thoughts, staring at all the things the Illum were determined to destroy. I couldn't bring myself to look too closely at that last clash with Collin—the line I had very nearly crossed, one I never would have forgiven myself for.

I followed Harold into the room, where I waited for the Starlings. Collin's voice echoed in my ear.

Knowing every terrible thing I am capable of. Would you tell me no?

The look in his blue eyes haunted me almost as viciously as how my body had moved toward him instead of running. Instead of saying no.

You're maddening, consuming, unwilling to follow any of their rules. I have a role to play and yet I spend my time thinking about you.

I could have listened to the boundaries and obeyed. Allowed my Academy training to win—be a suitable Mate. Adhered to my role in this society they had built when we resurfaced after the nuclear fallout.

But that would mean I must ignore the injustice I had seen. Overlook the blood on my beaded gown and the person it had belonged to. Forget Violet's battered face. Disregard the mothers' screams at the Sanctuary. Let go of the Majors' life beneath. Brush off the way Hal had kissed me.

Tell me no.

And yet I hadn't.

"Hello, Fledgling," Violet's silky voice cooed at me, startling me back to the present.

I turned to face her, relief flooding me to see her healed and unmarred face. Her eyes were clear. "Hi," I said, and smiled.

"Come, we have a long appointment," Rose said, holding the door open to the steaming bathing room.

Within minutes, I was stripped naked, and they scrubbed every inch of me. I was pelted by the hot shower before I plunged into the tub.

"We thought you had messed it up," Rose commented with forced nonchalance, working her hands through my hair. "Your other two appointments got canceled."

"You didn't listen, Fledgling." Violet *tsk*ed. "You did not do nothing."

I sucked in a deep breath and honesty slipped out. "I couldn't."

They shoved my head under the surface to wash my hair.

"Let's move on," Rose prompted. I heard her walk away. I left the tub to find Violet waiting for me with a towel. Her eyes danced, and a chill snaked down my spine.

"Come," Violet said as she steered me to the next room. She leaned in. "I do not condone you disobeying orders. It's stupid and lives could have been lost. Still, I admire your dedication. My brother saw you brought in below."

"Who's your brother?" I asked.

"Rajesh. He was phased out of the Academy. He found me five years ago. I thought I had lost him."

"Wait, he was phased out? What happened? Do all phased-out offspring end up in blue?" I asked as red hair and freckles flashed before my eyes. Was Alice below?

Violet shook her head. "Not all of them make it to the Underworld. Many are eliminated."

My stomach turned, and I thought I might be sick. They eliminated young offspring?

I cleared my throat. "How did he make it?"

"He does not talk about it," Violet told me gravely. "I am just glad he lives."

"Is he why you picked their side?" I asked in a hushed voice. Violet gazed ahead at Rose, who was gathering supplies in the corner of the room. The way she looked at her, the need, left me reeling. "Among other things," Violet confirmed, grabbing my towel and tapping the bed for me to lie down.

The two of them worked together in silence as they stripped my body of hair, then lathered my skin until it shimmered. I threw on my robe and followed them.

Rose attacked my nails while Violet dried my hair. Finally, the dryer was put away, and Violet's hands were crafting my hair into one of her artful swept-away updos.

"You don't have a lens in," Rose commented while painting my nails. The chipped red paint was replaced with a shimmering silver. I flicked my eyes to my reflection. I had forgotten exactly when I had decided to remove it in the two weeks I had spent alone. It had begun to burn so I pulled it out.

"There was no reason for it while on the ground," I confided, catching my lip between my teeth. Violet and Rose had clear eyes even though they wore their variant of gray.

Rose tutted. "Without it, you are easily recognizable. You are the Illum's Mate; sticking out might be ill-advised." She had a point, but then again, all the Minors were still drugged and wouldn't recognize anything.

"What do you want to say, Fledgling?" Violet prompted, staring at me in the mirror as Rose finished my nails.

"The Minors below, they aren't right," I whispered.

They shared a look. "Did the shackle on your wrist or your wits spare you?" Rose inquired.

"My wits. My Mate certainly didn't warn me. Why aren't the Minors in the sky drugged?"

"Our jobs require more wits than yours," Violet said. "We wouldn't be able to service them. We are being watched, though. Minors in the sky are quiet now."

Rose replaced my lens and began painting my face. I asked the question that had found me over and over the past two weeks. I had heard nothing about the Reaper.

"Is the Reaper going to do something about it?"

Violet opened her mouth. "We shouldn't, Violet, please," Rose interrupted desperately. "She didn't listen. You can't trust her."

Violet shook her head, pain painted across her face as she turned to Rose. Her next words were spoken like a lover's. "Dear, I am fighting for us. Do not ask me to stop."

"You said he sent the message to leave her out of it," Rose pleaded.

"I am not asking her to do anything. I am simply giving her information. What she does with it is her decision."

Rose shook her head.

"Yes, he is making a move soon," Violet said. "We don't know what, just where not to be."

"When?"

"Within the next few days."

"Have you met the Reaper?" I asked them.

Rose tutted at me, sniffling. "Don't move so much."

"We haven't. The Reaper is not known by many," Violet told me, leaning against the vanity, handing Rose different items as she painted my face.

"How do the Elite know him then?"

"He has a style to him," Violet said in a hushed tone.

I raised my brows at her, and Rose swatted me. "If you can't sit still, you two cannot talk." She shot Violet a stern look. Violet raised her hands, conceding as she smiled. A reluctant smile tugged at Rose's full mouth in response.

"What's his style?" I asked.

"Being an efficient killer," Rose said tersely, as if his methods bothered her.

Violet added, "He's very lethal, capable of taking down twice as many men as anyone else, but he leaves a message every time."

"Close your eyes," Rose told me.

"If he has time, he cuts the chips out of the Elites' arms."

I kept my eyes closed as the hair on the back of my neck stood on end.

I only knew one person who had cut out their chip.

"What does he do with them?" I asked, voice trembling.

"No one knows. Some say he is making his own chips, others say it's just to send a message, and some say he's taking their MINDs and raising the dead to take down everyone in the clouds."

"How do you raise the dead?"

"He's reusing the cutout chips to grant access to his followers."

"I don't understand."

"Your Defect MIND isn't allowed in the clouds unless the Illum approve it, but the MINDs of the dead Elite are allowed to move freely in the clouds. Scan that MIND instead of your own and suddenly his army is in the sky."

"Army?"

"Don't move your mouth for a moment. I know that will be difficult for you," Rose said.

I grumbled as I closed my mouth for her. Violet continued, "Yes, army. It spans from Beneath to Above."

Rose finished painting my lips, and I immediately asked, "Why kill the Elite, though? Why not just take their MIND chips and leave them?"

"Because they weren't stupid when they inserted our chips. This right here"—Violet took my glowing wrist and tapped a bluish vein under my skin—"that is called a radial artery. The chip is right by it. If you aren't extremely exact when you cut it out, and you hit that, you'll bleed out. If you want the chips, then the owners have to die."

"So he kills them for the chips or just to kill them?" I asked. I needed to know.

"I don't know. You would have to ask the Reaper. They kill us. Marginalize us. Why shouldn't we retaliate?" Violet seethed viciously.

But if we killed each other endlessly, how would the cycle of murder stop? Which side was right? There were good people in the clouds as well as bad. Status alone didn't determine who should be saved.

As if reading my thoughts, Rose shook her head at me. "You thought there was a good guy and a bad guy, didn't you?" Rose scoffed. "How naïve." She left the room, and Violet stared after Rose's swishing hips before the black room beyond swallowed her.

"Why do you know so much?" I asked Violet now that we were alone.

"In this world, I cannot have her, so I looked into our options. Majors have tried cutting the chip out. Very few survive."

I followed her into the final room, where Violet handed me a pair of high-waisted black underwear. I dropped the robe, slipping them on, and stood on the podium as Rose brought over a pile of sheer black fabric, cradling it like it was an offspring. As I looked at the fabric, I realized why they had added extra steps to make my skin shimmer. There would be a lot of it on display.

"Come down here. It'll be easier," Rose instructed.

I stepped down, and the two finagled me into the delicate fabric.

"Back up now," Rose cawed.

I looked at myself on the podium. The gown was not of this world. The midnight black was featherlight against my skin. Delicate satin buttons connected the thin fabric at my wrist, snaking up my arms before plunging into an impossibly low V that ended just above my belly button. Artfully placed lace appliqué provided a shred of modesty. The dress fell to the floor, and a slit on my left side made the dress move with the slightest breeze. The skirt danced around me like the clouds that thunderstorms rolled in on.

My hair was swept into an intricate braid around my head, with small glittering pearl pins woven in the folds. Wisps of hair fell around my face. Rose had kept my face fresh and my own. My eyes were lined and my lashes black. My lips had a rosy pink to them. My shimmering skin beneath the dress reminded me of the stars in the night sky, peeking through the endless black.

I tore my eyes from the mirror, looking at them. "You are both so talented," I told them in awe.

"The fabric wrinkles easily. Don't sit unless you have to," Rose instructed me, brushing off the compliment while fluffing the skirt. "Give me a spin."

I spun for them. The slit in the sheer skirt sent the fabric flying all around me. Rose clutched her chest and preened as the material moved, and Violet rested her cheek on Rose's shoulder, watching me.

For a second, I felt a spark of joy. Of excitement. Not just because of the otherworldly beauty they had made me into, but because of the two indomitable women who had carved a place for their love in this world.

"Exquisite," Violet whispered to Rose. "You amaze me. Every time I think you have done your best work, you outdo it." Rose glanced down at Violet, the woman who had chided and snapped at me gone. In her place stood a woman beaming with pride and adoration—a woman helplessly in love. I glanced down to see their hands intertwined between the folds of their quicksilver dresses. I turned to give them a moment.

Violet was fighting for them, but why would they risk anything? They had found a way to be together in the Illum's world. They had each other here, safe in the clouds. If I were in their shoes, would I fight or stay where they had put me? If I did fight, would I fight for others or just run? A part of me screamed to run away from it all, but I had stepped toward the Parting. So would I?

"Here." Violet interrupted my thoughts, handing me an oblong leather clutch with a golden clasp. Rose wrapped a tight black belt around the narrowest part of my waist before she bent down and slipped black heels on my feet.

"You should be able to dance in these," Rose commented as she stood, fluffing my dress again.

"You're a vision," Violet said as they looked me over.

"Oh, the earrings," Rose exclaimed, running from the room. She returned a moment later and fastened them. "Now you're finished."

Black diamond earrings glittered at me, adorned with hanging teardrop pearls.

"You should be going," Rose said, pushing me out. "Also, try not to mess anything up. It will be a shame if your dress for the next ball goes to waste. The time I have spent placing each crystal . . ." Rose blew out a breath.

Violet chuckled, smiling. "I'll take her." We made our way into the black receiving room, and she grabbed the handle on the door leading to the hall. "Are you ready to be back in their clouds, to be his Mate, Fledgling?"

"No," I confessed.

"Are you afraid?" When I nodded, Violet said, "Good."

"How is that *good*?"

Violet leaned close to me. "Because it is normal to be afraid of doing something that matters. Power is a frightening thing. It's even more terrifying to do what is right when they would all applaud you for doing what has always been done—to be his vessel. Even if it is wrong." She pulled open the door.

"Now go, little Fledgling," she whispered. "And good luck."

I stepped into the hallway, and the door clicked shut.

"Your Pod is here, Ms. Emeline," Harold said.

"Thank you," I responded absentmindedly.

"Fertile blessings."

I nodded at him, crossing the threshold, staring at the stars beyond the glass. They twinkled magnificently, not a cloud in sight, and with the moon's absence, they painted the sky with a glittering display. The doors behind me closed, but I didn't care as my gaze didn't leave the stars above the glass ceiling. They looked so free, so unencumbered by rules or restrictions. Shining without fear.

A noise to my right caught my attention, and I realized I wasn't alone.

"Hello, Mate."

CHAPTER THIRTY

Collin lounged in the pod, his ankle propped over his knee. If I glittered like a star, he was the darkness that blanketed the night sky. My breath caught as my body grew too warm. In the space of a heartbeat, the memory of his body against mine heated my skin. His sapphire gaze drank me in, from the sheer skirt of my gown to the plunging neckline, like maybe he was plagued by the same thought. I shook it away, standing tall.

"So it's *Mate* now?" I asked instead of saying hello. Something about him made me unable to be proper. I wanted to shatter his control, find out who he really was underneath his polished exterior.

"It is what you are," Collin informed me, his eyes traveling up the sheer bodice of my gown, "and it is less personal."

He met my gaze. The Pod lurched forward, and I flung my hand out against the glass, attempting to balance myself, and widened my stance.

He perched on the edge of his seat as if ready to catch me. "Do you intend to sit?"

"I was told the fabric wrinkles easily and not to sit unless I have to," I told him. "You wouldn't want your pet to look unkempt, would you?" I smiled innocently.

An exasperated sigh escaped him, and he rubbed his temples.

"To what do I owe the pleasure of arriving with you?" I asked.

The stars and buildings swirled around us as we made our way through the clouds.

"We need to discuss our situation before this ball," Collin said. "I told the Illum that you have been actively spying for us the last two weeks, and that is why we didn't have any public appearances. That you felt it would hinder your ability to get information. You need to sell that story to the Elite."

"And what information did I supposedly give you?"

"You don't need to worry about the details. The Elite, while nosy, know their place. Just act the part."

I huffed. "All about appearances."

Collin's jaw bulged. "This is not about appearances. You could be eliminated for your actions. Do you comprehend that? Do you understand what it feels like to watch people be eliminated?"

"Thanks to you, I do," I snapped.

Collin leaned back in his seat, away from me. "Just follow their rules and the narrative."

"What do I tell them about not being drugged by you?" I asked viciously.

"Many don't know anything about the surface," Collin told me.

"So you lie to the Elite too," I spat.

He stared at me, and I fidgeted under his gaze. "Think of it as selective truth."

I paused. "My HI said my supplements were altered to calm me after that night when you . . ." *murdered someone.*

"Yes, as a kindness to lessen the shock of seeing that. But your supplements were never to be altered like the others. I wouldn't let them drug you, Emeline."

"Why not?" I asked. "Why treat me differently than the other Defects?"

The Pod shot up into the sky, sending me off-balance. I grabbed uselessly at the glass. Collin was behind me in an instant, his firm hands at my sides, steadying me. His warm grip burned straight through the thin fabric. The Pod slowed at a line of Pods hovering ahead, depositing Elite into the sky.

Collin released me quickly, putting space between us. "Does it matter? You wouldn't believe me."

"What reason have you given me to trust you?" I fumed.

"Just play the role or whatever you have decided to call this." I opened my mouth, furious, but Collin continued. "I know you will not do it for yourself. You clearly place no value on your life."

"Who taught me not to?" I demanded, stepping toward him.

"If you can't do it for yourself, and you damn well won't do it for me, then do it to prove your birth father wrong," Collin told me as he straightened his jacket.

A sickening panic stuck to my skin. "What does Vincent have to do with this?"

"He's been telling anyone who will listen that you will be the Illum's biggest mistake and downfall, among other things." Collin's voice was deathly quiet.

Vincent placed far too much faith in me if he thought I alone would bring down the Illum. Still, an ache as old as my very bones throbbed wildly in my chest. "And what did you tell him?"

The doors to our Pod slid open. "He values his life enough not to say such things to me."

Collin ran his hands down his jacket one last time, rolling his shoulders before he extended his hand toward me. I ignored his hand.

"Just take it," Collin ground out.

"Fine." I placed my hand in his, and I trembled slightly as we crossed the threshold. If Collin noticed, he didn't say.

I found myself awestruck as we approached a grand staircase leading to a dance floor below. I had been so distracted by Collin that I hadn't noticed where the ball was held. A translucent ceiling soared above us, and the night spilled in. The room was stunning, everything a shiny black infinity mirror that reflected the night above, blurring the line where the sky ended and the ballroom began. From this height, it felt like we were among the stars.

I wished I could dance alone like I had done in my room this past moon—to turn and spin until I became one of those stars and all my worries fell away.

Collin cleared his throat, and the dream floated away into the unending darkness. "We must descend," he whispered.

We stood at the edge of the grand staircase. Everyone below gazed up at us.

Collin leaned into me, and I fought a shiver. "I know you detest me, and you do not trust me, but I am not a danger to you in this room. Some of the Elite down there, they are. They would love to watch you plummet to the ground for the insult of being my Mate. So I am asking a favor of you tonight."

"What favor?" I breathed.

"Do not fight me. Not here."

Collin pulled back, but his scent lingered around me. He smirked at me like we had shared a secret. I attempted to match it. "Ready?"

I nodded, not trusting any of the words that might come out.

We began to descend the long staircase as every Elite in the room watched us. With each step, the sheer gown felt suffocating, the belt around my waist too tight. My palms grew clammy in Collin's hand. He gave no indication that he felt my fear and anxiety.

I looked over the heads of the Elite for as long as I could, but then I saw him. There in the crowd, he didn't smile. His lip was curled back. Vincent looked at me as he always had. Like I was filth.

I felt my body shake as the knot in my throat grew. Collin's gripped tightened, and Vincent looked away.

Out of the corner of my eye, I saw Phillip, who stood alone in all black, share a look with Collin, and then Phillip was in motion.

I watched as women began to lean in, conversations uttered behind jeweled hands. A woman in a sleeveless red gown that hugged her curves glared at me with such disgust that I felt it to my soul.

As we neared the bottom of the grand staircase, Collin muttered under his breath, "We will be going directly onto the dance floor."

Music poured into the room, and the Elites cleared the floor. My heart pounded as I broke out in a cold sweat. There were too many eyes, too many people, focused on me.

"Why?" I asked.

"It is what's proper. You know the dances, correct? You have been practicing?" Collin asked as our feet met the bottom step. A fellow Defect raced forward, taking my clutch before disappearing.

"Of course I have," I hissed back, frustration chasing away my nerves.

"Forgive me, seeing as it isn't Rule Ten, I did not know if you felt obliged to follow or not," Collin said so quietly, only I would hear.

I glowered at my Mate as he led me to the center of the room. The Elite gathered to watch.

"Look up," he whispered to me.

The noise from the Elite and the music faded into the background. Above us the stars seemed to fall into the dance floor, some illusion or trick of the light. Yet I felt comforted, like they were winking, cheering me on as they danced around me.

"Now bow," Collin instructed. I did as he said.

A new song began, and shock filled me as Collin bowed—to me.

It was the first time Collin had ever done so. An Illum was bowing to a Minor. Every single person stared, eyes drawn to us, unable to look away. A buzzing spread out over the dance floor as whispers flew.

"Ready?" The sapphire pools of his eyes reflected the falling stars, almost turning them silver, and I focused on nothing else.

It was a slower dance, the steps simple. I had never paid much attention to it, preferring the ones that were more physically exhausting. But as I grasped his shoulder and he pulled me close by my waist, capturing my other hand with his, the dance transformed into something else entirely.

Collin began to move, leading us across the floor. Like everything he did, he moved with grace. I fell into his rhythm. The spectators became a blur as I released Collin's hand and spun. The sheer skirt billowed and rippled all around me, refracting the starlight in a dazzling display. I couldn't help but smile, wishing Rose were here to see her creation in action.

Collin traced my breathless grin with burning eyes.

My breathing quickened. I told myself it was from the exertion.

Following the training, I turned until Collin was behind me, my hand outstretched. Then I felt his hand on my hip. The other dragged along my outstretched arm, making me gasp at the closeness, the intimacy of the move. I didn't remember that part from the video. I felt Collin chuckle behind me more than heard it before he spun me again to face him. We were back in the Sphere when his lips had found mine. I was too warm, something traitorous pulsing in time with the musical beat.

He smirked at me, clasping our hands above our heads. It was the man from those first dinners who danced with me, the version of Collin I had desperately wanted to believe in.

"Different from dancing alone?" Collin whispered as we continued to move around the floor.

"Yes," I breathed, and he turned me again, my back against his front. I was ready this time as he trailed his hand along my arm, but my body shivered against my will as I felt his breath hit my neck, heard his inhale as he breathed me in.

"You dance very well," Collin commented as he spun me to face him. The music began to build, the end approaching. "You enjoy it."

It wasn't a question, his sapphire eyes assessing me. "I do. It quiets my mind."

"Is your mind often not quiet?" Collin asked, his gaze piercing.

He spun me a final time, the music swelling and crescendoing, until again, joy sparkled through me.

The music down swelled, and his right hand held my left above our heads, our bodies pressed flush together, my chest heaving against his. We were in his living quarters; he was begging me to say no. I clamped my mouth closed, my gaze on his lips. The moment dissolved with the music.

Collin released my hand, stepping back from me. Without the music, I realized my heart was carrying its own frenzied beat. My cheeks felt warm, but there was a lightness under it all that only music and running had ever given me.

"Would you like another dance?" Collin inquired. The next song started, dozens of Elite couples joining the floor. It was a faster-paced dance with more spins and passing partners.

My heart begged for another go, but I said, "I would love a drink."

Collin looked away as he nodded, and his firm hand guided me from the dance floor. I forced myself to look ahead even as my body protested, desperate to join them. Collin pushed to the outskirts as Elites bowed. The suffocating feeling returned.

Everywhere I looked, brightly colored gowns met me. I wondered if I could ever look like them, the simpering smiles. Their insipidness was as foreign to me as this ball—a part of me content with that never changing. My black gown was a glaring mark to their cheerful display. I was not the stars at all but the unending darkness, threatening to suffocate their Elite light.

An attendant appeared, holding a silver tray with bubbles. Collin grabbed two delicate glasses, handing me one. The man disappeared.

Collin took a long drink, looking over my shoulder, and he shook his head a fraction.

"What?" I asked.

"You will wish you stayed on the dance floor in a moment," Collin whispered. "Remember what I told you."

"Collin," I heard behind me.

"Do not bow to them," Collin muttered under his breath as he gently turned me. "Alan," Collin said, any warmth dissipating. The Elite man had short, dirty blond hair and piercing gray eyes.

"So, this is your Mate everyone has been talking about, the one worthy of you," Alan said, sweeping his eyes over me before bowing. I placed my hand in his and he placed a small peck upon it. "Charmed to meet you, Ms. Emeline. I think this union will be beneficial for us all and our storied peace."

Flustered, I looked at Collin, who smoothly said, "Yes, we both feel the same." I attempted a smile before taking a sip of my drink.

"I won't pretend there weren't many Elite prospects eager for the role as your Mate, Collin. But there is always your next mating."

My insides hollowed out. His next mating. I hadn't really thought about what my life would look like beyond the next four years.

"We shall see. I have no intentions for a second mating." Collin looked straight ahead, avoiding my gaze.

"Ah, well, I daresay your sister can carry on with the distribution of your genes within the Elite population. It is her duty to the Greater Good," Alan said.

I took a sip to hide my disgust.

"You both must be thrilled to have entered your second moon cycle," Alan continued, grabbing a glass from a passing tray.

A shock ran through me. We were in the second moon cycle. One moon cycle closer to our procreation phase. My days down to sixty.

"An Illum offspring will be a blessing. There hasn't been one in my seventy years of life."

This time, I didn't hide my shock. The man didn't look past forty.

"We are delighted to have the first Illum offspring in over a hundred years for the Greater Good," Collin said.

Once again, my mind reeled, desperate to know why he would choose me for something so important. A warmth touched my lower back—Collin, reminding me where I was.

"To the Greater Good," Alan said, raising a glass. I downed the rest of my drink. "The Press published a wager on how many moons it shall take you two. Given her disposition, the most popular guess is two moons. Surely no one would fault you if you decided not to wait, Collin. Give those of us who wagered only one better odds." The man winked at Collin.

"Glad to know we can provide the Elite with needed entertainment," Collin stated. I felt like a prized breeding animal.

Two more Elite members joined our conversation. I missed their names as Collin grabbed my empty glass, replacing it with a full one. I took a sip immediately, washing away the revulsion.

"I have to say," another male said to me. I didn't dare guess his age this time. He had jet-black hair and brown eyes and a pompous smile. "It is honorable for you to continue to live among the Minors on the ground to help our cause in this ridiculous Reaper business."

"Yes," Alan agreed. "Your commitment to root out this evil is most commendable. We, the Elite, find ourselves surprisingly in your debt. The Illum chose a worthy vessel."

What exactly had Collin been telling them? I took another sip, resisting the urge to throw it in Alan's face.

"However, it would seem the Reaper received your message from the dinner, Collin," Alan continued. "He has been quiet for some time now."

"Scared, I'd say," another man sneered.

"As he should be." Collin's hand sprawled on my lower back. I felt nauseous.

"Does she not speak?" the other man asked.

"Would that be a bad thing?" Alan chuckled. "Is there any use in her words?"

"Elite manners are the great distinguishing factor between a civilized mind and a defective one," the other added. "Perhaps there is weight to the debate of whether Minors are capable of being reformed."

I opened my mouth as two things happened: Someone said my name and Collin turned me away from the men.

"Emeline," Nora greeted me smoothly. She wore an off-the-shoulder golden gown, tiny chains crossing her exposed back. It was eerily similar to my blue gown. She curtsied before linking her arm through mine. "There you are. If you'll excuse us," Nora said with a honeyed smile, "but if I do not steal my soon-to-be sister now, I daresay my brother will hog her all night."

"For obvious reasons," one of the talking heads joked.

"I promise to return her for a dance soon, brother," Nora told Collin, who simply nodded at her before he captured my hand and placed a kiss upon it, and that magnetic power tugged on me.

Nora pulled me away as I heard one of the men say, "There is no way you make two more moons."

"It will be a testament to my willpower if I do." I felt Collin watching me as we walked away.

Nora leaned into me. "I am sorry I didn't come sooner. I just saw Collin's signal."

"Collin's signal?" I asked as we stopped on the opposite side of the ballroom.

"Yes, to rescue you," Nora said, grabbing a glass. A golden ring with a large emerald gleamed on her finger. "Like my dress?" Nora asked, swishing golden fabric about. "I was inspired."

"I like the color," I told her.

"How have you been? I am sorry we haven't gotten together. I wanted to reach out, but I had my visiting days for Arabella and James. Eleana's is next week."

"How are your offspring?" I asked.

"They are healthy and well cared for." Nora smiled sadly. "Still, the goodbyes seem to get harder. I usually find it difficult to leave my bed afterward. It's why I didn't reach out."

"I assumed you heard my argument with Collin and decided against being my friend."

Nora tilted her head. "Why would you think that?" She waved over a man in gray carrying a tray.

"Well, he's your twin," I stated, like it should be obvious.

Nora shook her head, grabbing several sweets from the tray and handing them to me before taking some for herself.

"Don't go far," she warned the man before eating a delicate dessert. "I am more than aware of how enraging he can be. I do not fault you. Collin has always acted first and informed later," Nora said, rolling her eyes.

"But Nora, I am a Minor. Why would you want to be my friend?"

She smiled, her eyes traveling over every inch of me. "I do not see a Minor. Even with your eyes, Emeline. I see a woman who has been treated unfairly."

I remembered the day I had met her. My defect had been exposed, and she hadn't said anything.

I took a bite of the food, praying it would carry the knot in my throat away. The drinks had left me dizzy. Or maybe it was the conversations or the incessant noise of my thoughts. I didn't know anymore.

I glanced up at the stars, my thoughts and feelings as endless as the sky above. Was that why I was always at war with myself—perpetually enraged by the depth I always carried? The peace it stole from me?

"I can see you discrediting yourself," Nora said softly. "I will not try to dissuade you. I know better." She searched the dance floor. I was sure she was seeking out a certain man with brutally short hair. "If any of my offspring had been deemed a Defect at birth, I would love them all the same. We women, regardless of status, are all vessels in the procreation system. We are all alike if we care to see it."

"You believe that?"

Nora turned toward me, her eyes burning with the fierceness she sometimes showed. "With everything I am. I hope one day we're more. Arabella is almost of age—I cannot stand the idea of one of these men with his hands on her."

The music changed, an upbeat song replacing the slow, melancholy one. Nora's face shifted as she bounced on the tips of her toes, looking wildly around us. "I told William I would meet him on the dance floor for this song. It is my favorite."

"Go," I told her. "I'll be fine."

"Are you sure?"

"Yes, go," I assured her.

"I'll find you after," she exclaimed as she pranced to the dance floor, ditching her glass with one of the many men in gray.

I watched her meet William, smoothing her dress, before a quick curtsy and the song began. I stood mesmerized as she danced, her joy lighting up the entire room. Her lithe steps shined upon the dance floor.

She switched to another partner, staying in his arms for just a moment, and her smile spilled into the sky above. Gregory held her, spinning her. He smiled too—a real one. Time slowed. I swore even the stars halted their celestial dance as two souls held each other.

I stood in awe of this one moment they had in front of others, their true feelings on display. A private moment disguised by the masses as nothing but a dance. No one saw the way Gregory's fingers dug into Nora's back, the desperation there.

I wished I could capture this, immortalize what they had, that their love existed in a world that told us it couldn't.

Gregory released her, and Nora spun away, landing in William's arms, her smile shifting as the moment ended, and the stars filled the room again.

"Emeline," a hesitant voice said to my left.

I turned to find my birth mother staring at me as she had in the Sphere, as if overwhelmed by my presence. I looked for words to say to her, but nothing came as the air thickened around us.

"I am glad to see you here tonight. It is nice seeing you in the clouds." She came to stand beside me, her long-sleeve purple gown spilling around her.

All I heard was her parting advice. *Look down, Emeline.* I lifted my chin.

I would never look down again. I stood in silence, my words too tangled with my anger. It snaked up my spine until my skin crawled.

Regardless of how she truly felt about me, she had still made a choice—still chosen my birth brothers over me, never deigning to even visit me in the Minor Academy.

"He seems happy, doesn't he?" Helen stated carefully. I tracked her gaze to Gregory, who spun Nora once more.

"If you say so," I stated, watching Gregory's face fall the moment Nora left his arms.

"Are you"—she cleared her throat—"happy, with your Mate, I mean?"

My chest burned viciously. I twisted the button on my sleeve. "Does it matter? No one cares for my happiness, Helen." The word *mother* caught on the immovable knot in my throat. "It's not what I was made for."

"I care," Helen whispered. I whipped my head toward her.

Helen met my gaze, her blue eyes heavy. "Emeline, I—" Helen turned quickly, her words dying as clipped footsteps sounded. Her gaze became vacant.

"Helen, you are needed elsewhere," drawled a voice, "with the retired women."

Very few memories remained from before the Academy. Somehow the sound of my birth father's voice was a vivid one—carved into the very fiber of my being.

"Of course," Helen stated before she walked away. "Good night, Emeline."

Vincent watched her walk away before turning all his attention to me. "You disappear for two weeks, not a word of you, no sightings, and then you are here."

"I was somewhat occupied." I dug for what Collin had said in the Pod.

An ugly chuckle filled the air. "Collin can spread all the lies he wants about you furthering our cause, but you have done nothing but threaten the Greater Good from the moment you opened your eyes. When the truth comes out, you all shall meet your downfall."

Unease filled me as Vincent watched Gregory dance with Nora once more, the song coming to an end.

"Collin is a member of the Illum. To insult me is to insult them." The false bravado rang hollow.

"It's not. He is young. In time he will see his mistake in choosing you, if the Illum do not eliminate him for his failings." Vincent turned toward me, his voice turning malicious and quiet. "Never question my commitment to the Illum again. My loyalty is absolute. The only insult I have ever given them was you."

His words slammed into my chest.

"What did I do?" I demanded, because hidden underneath it all was a young girl who wanted to know. I needed to know the reason for his hatred for me.

"Our ancestors built this city after the Last War. They helped create all of this. We had a flawless lineage and unwavering loyalty. Always beside the Illum, almost one of them. Then you ruined everything. My abilities were questioned because of you."

"Is that why you put me in that blue dress?" I looked at him, wanting to see the answer.

Vincent smirked maliciously at me. "I didn't send you that dress, but my unending gratitude to whoever put you in the color you earned at birth. The despair it brought your mother to see you in the color she fought so hard to keep you out of."

"She what?" My breathing became difficult.

Vincent chuckled. I detested the very sound of it. The way it found every crack in the walls I had spent my life building, crumbling them in an instant. He smirked like he knew.

"If she hadn't intervened, the moment I saw your eyes you'd have been in blue or worse. You breathe today because she was too spineless. My reward for my moment of humanity was to be stuck with the woman who gave me you. They removed me from the program and blamed my genes, not hers. I would never be assigned another Mate." My ears rang at the declaration. Helen had cared. Vincent's vicious tone sliced through the ringing. "Even if you pop out some Elite offspring, you will return to where you belong. But mark my words, when you fail, which you will, you will destroy everything Collin worked for. Either way"—his brown eyes found mine, and I hated that our gazes matched with the lens in—"I will enjoy watching you fall and the chaos that ensues."

I fought off the stinging in my eyes. My heart stilled in my chest.

A warm hand rested on my lower back, and Vincent's features changed. "Collin, nice to see you this evening. I was just telling your Mate how stunning she looks."

Collin stepped into me until his front was almost fully pressed against my back. I didn't fight the comfort I found in it—I might have even leaned into it. "Now, we both know that isn't true," Collin bit out with that quiet fury. His hand found mine, pulling me away, before he paused, turning back to my birth father. I collided into him. "Vincent, the Illum truly are getting impatient. You should have had answers by now. It was a task beneath your intelligence. That's what you said." Collin's sapphire eyes looked like chips of ice as he glared at Vincent. His hands found my hips, steadying me. "If that were true, one would think you would have delivered by now. You more than anyone understand the ramifications of disappointing the Illum. Now, if you'll excuse my Mate and me—we are expected for another dance."

A new song started, though I could hardly hear it over the broken beat of my heart as we reached the dance floor.

Collin stepped away from me and began to move, and the training kicked in. I tried to find the quiet dancing brought me, but shame clung to me, burrowing under my skin.

Collin held his hand out. I placed mine in his, and he spun me until I was dizzy. I released the breath I had forgotten I was holding. Collin caught me, steadying me.

I continued to move, being led by Collin, trying to ignore the one thing Vincent had said that had left me too exposed, that had altered everything.

I tried to stay one step ahead of the words that fed my fire. The crescendo swelled, and I prepared for the final two turns.

The song paused, shorter than a breath, before the finale. Vincent's confession roared in my ears as Collin spun me once.

The despair it brought your mother—

Twice.

—to see you in the color she fought so hard to keep you out of.

I care.

My throat tightened, the air too thick. Collin disregarded what was proper and spun me again.

My shock loosened my thoughts' grip.

He spun me a fourth time.

I saw his mouth tug up on the side before he spun me a fifth time. Finally, I landed in his arms.

He gripped my hip as his other hand ran down my spine, and in his magnetic pull, my mind quieted.

The music faded, but Collin didn't release me. My eyes locked with his.

A new song began and the whispering of others filtered in. I felt their pelting stares and heard someone titter, "Oh, the Press is going to *love* this."

The reminder of the roles we were playing felt like a slap in the face. Once again, I had lost myself around him. I forgot how his work was hurting people—destroying everything beautiful and different. My body couldn't see what my Mate stood for.

Not looking at him, I stepped away, quickly curtsying, and beelined for an attendant holding a tray of delicate glasses. I grabbed a glass, downing it immediately before grabbing another. I drained a second when Collin stood beside me, holding his own glass.

"Too many of those will befuddle your mind," he said under his breath.

"Maybe I want to be befuddled," I shot back.

"I would advise against that, given the audience we have."

My face grew warm, frustration coursing through me at the constant need to be aware of the Elite.

"What was that on the dance floor, the extra spins and the—the touching?" I sputtered, hating how my body had reacted to it instantly.

Collin took a sip from his glass as I ditched my second, grabbing a third. "I was attempting to distract you. To quiet your mind." Collin stepped closer, putting himself between me and the Elite—who still watched us.

"I didn't ask you to do that," I muttered furiously. I brought the glass to my lips, but it was pulled away.

Collin held my glass, his jaw tight, face inches from mine. "I'd like a word."

"And *I* would like a drink," I stated, diving far past speaking plainly, landing in dangerous territory.

"Come with me," Collin bit out, passing off our glasses as he steered me toward a wall, practically pushing me from the room. Two men in dark gray opened a set of doors. A shock ripped up my left arm, my MIND having a strange reaction to something unseen, as we crossed the threshold into a comfortable sitting room.

I didn't even take in the room before the doors clicked behind us, and Collin was towering over me.

"What was the one favor I asked of you?"

"Not to fight you."

"And yet you are fighting with me. Nora had one job," Collin growled.

I stepped toward him. "So I'm a job?"

"When you refuse to be sensible. When you refuse to think about the consequences of your actions. Yes—you are a job, Emeline," Collin fumed. "I am an Illum. They are all watching—"

"Exactly, they are all watching while you do whatever *that* was on the dance floor."

"You're my Mate. It isn't uncommon for Mates to occasionally show affection. Would you rather I let everyone see the power you let Vincent have over you? Would you rather I let all of the Elite see you like that, paint you as the weak Minor?" Frustration laced every word.

"I would rather not be here at all." The words flew from my lips. "I would rather be on the surface."

"You cannot have that now," Collin said, his voice falling flat.

I whirled on him, everything from the night ripping through me. "Because you took it from me. I am now stuck in your damn clouds surrounded by my birth family while Elite men discuss me as if I were your *property*. You just stood there."

"What would you have me do instead?" Collin whispered angrily, stepping to me—power and viciousness spilling from him. "Would you have me throw them in blue? Eliminate them completely because they disrespect you? No, not that, you didn't like when I had to eliminate someone. Would you have me upend everything that is proper?"

"I don't need any more blood on my hands because of you." My vicious tone matched his.

Collin's breaths sawed out of him, his polish corroding. "What do you want from me, Emeline?"

My mother's confession collided with that stupid dream of what I thought I'd find up here. My unending loneliness engulfed me and, in my petulance, I admitted too much. "To be cared for. To be saved."

My hand flew to my mouth.

Collin stepped away from me as if I had shoved him. His crystalline eyes shattered and his composure slipped for a breath before he rolled his shoulders. The youngest Illum formed before my eyes.

"I am your Mate. Not a savior," Collin said, his tone flat.

The doors opened, and Phillip entered the room.

"Tabitha has requested you. There's an issue."

Collin glanced at him. "How long?"

"Not long at all," Phillip said, completely ignoring me.

"Lead the way," Collin said. He didn't look my way as he told me,

"I'll find you for the last dance. You can stay here. No one will come in."

The doors clicked closed. My heart filled the empty space, frantically berating me. Maybe I *was* befuddled. When had talking plainly morphed into stupidity? Why was I determined to destroy myself in his presence? I hid my face in my hands, attempting to pull myself together.

"Tell me, does he always talk to you like that?"

I whirled to see the last person I expected entering through one of their concealed doors. A tall man dressed in dark gray, with a dimpled half smile and starburst eyes that crinkled at the corners.

Hal.

My heart exploded in my chest, and I blurted, "What are you doing here?"

"Working. Seeing you is an added bonus." Hal smirked.

"What do you mean *working*? You shouldn't be here," I exclaimed.

"Just pushing the boundaries, testing how complacent the Illum are in their clouds," Hal told me, leaning against the wall. His eyes raked over me—a hunger there.

"Collin could come back at any minute."

"He won't. Turns out they aren't that complacent here. The Illum are having a rough night."

"What did you do?" I asked breathlessly.

"Sent the Illum on a chase. How's your night been?" Hal asked, crossing his arms like we were in my office rather than at a ball with hundreds of Elite on the other side of the door.

"Someone could see you or track you," I said as fear ripped through me.

"Once you put on gray, no one really sees you. Plus, I don't exist, remember?" Hal held up his wrist to flash his jagged scar.

"Someone could still see you. Gray won't protect you."

"You didn't notice me when you danced with your Mate," Hal informed me. "You dance incredibly well."

"Thank you, but—"

"Your Mate seemed to enjoy it," Hal said too quietly.

My breath quickened at his tone. "Are you jealous?"

"Of an Illum? Never."

His head whipped toward the door as the soft clicking of heels headed our way. He extended his hand toward me.

"I heard you're looking for a savior."

I looked toward the doors as the heels stopped and the clink of the handles sounded.

I wanted to be far away—from my obligations, the judgment, my thoughts. The way Vincent's words pierced my soul. My mother's presence but lack of words. The way my mind and body waged a war over Collin.

Maybe it was seeing what Nora and Gregory shared, the envy it filled me with.

Maybe I didn't care about my life.

Or maybe I wanted the simplicity of that dream and the way Hal was looking at me like he saw me. Maybe it was never an Elite who was meant to save me. Maybe it was someone in blue. Someone more dangerous.

"What's it going to be, Moonlight?"

I placed my hand in his.

Hal smiled as the doors began to open. He pushed against the hidden door he had entered from, and I swore I heard my name. But we darted down a quiet hall and into a small closet.

As the door snapped closed, we were plunged into darkness.

CHAPTER THIRTY-ONE

I BUMPED INTO HAL, INSTANTLY TOO AWARE OF HOW THIN the fabric of my dress was. It sparkled in the low light from my sleeve-covered golden wrist. "Sorry."

"Shhh, they're coming closer," Hal whispered, his warm breath caressing my cheek, and my heart galloped.

Heels clicked, then paused.

"Emeline," I heard a honeyed voice call out. A voice I knew. I gasped, but Hal's hand clamped over my mouth, pulling me back against his chest.

Had Nora been sent to rescue me once more? She called my name again before the sound of her heels clicked away.

Hal lowered his hand from my mouth as I faced him, our chests meeting with each breath. My body uncoiled and awakened as if he were siphoning the tension from me.

"This is dangerous," I muttered.

My eyes had adjusted enough to the dim light to see a smile tug at his lips. "I know where the Illum's attention currently are," he said. "You look beautiful tonight, Moonlight."

"The Starlings did a good job."

"You looked beautiful in your office that first day in gray and no lens. You are beautiful, not the gown." Hal ran his hand up the side of the dress, leaving sparks in its wake, then ran a finger along my jaw. "Or the makeup." He traced the shell of my ear, grazing the diamond earrings, then caressed the column of my throat, where my pulse fluttered wildly. "Or the jewels." His hand gripped my waist. "Just you, Moonlight."

I lifted a hand to his chest, his heart steady beneath my palm. My breathing became difficult as he held my gaze. His entire face had a golden glow, as did his hair.

Heat flooded my cheeks at the reminder of reality. Hal captured my wrist before I could pull it away.

"Don't," Hal told me, bringing my wrist between us.

He let go of my waist to slowly unbutton the delicate cuff of my dress, then gently tugged the sleeve up until the golden glow fully illuminated our small closet.

"You don't have to hide anything from me," Hal whispered as he brought the outside of my wrist to his mouth and kissed the glowing skin. "You don't have to pretend." He turned my wrist. "I want you, contract and all, Moonlight."

His mouth found the inside of my wrist where the chip glowed brightest. A soft moan left me.

"Tell me you want me too," he whispered. He trailed kisses up my arm. His other hand snaked around my waist again, tugging me into him. I went willingly, my pulse a wild thing, demanding more as it began to burn beneath my skin.

His lips found my neck, and my body ground against his in a plea for more. The last of my sanity reminded me of his injuries.

"You're hurt," I practically panted, grabbing his shirt.

He growled against my neck, and my body responded. My head tilted to the side without a thought, giving him better access.

"I'm fine," he said roughly, his voice deeper than normal.

"But Barrett—" I began, and rational thought fled as Hal kissed along my exposed neck. I gripped his shirt tighter.

"I don't want to talk about Barrett right now," he said, his gaze searing me. "Do you want this?" His grip on my waist tightened.

I nodded my head, the screaming need extinguishing all sanity. I wanted more.

"I need you to say it, Emeline. If you want me to stop, I will. You can leave and head back. It's the smart thing to do."

He was right. Logically, I knew that. His hold on my waist loosened, and my body wailed in protest.

"I'll let you go," he rasped.

An ache had grown deep in my core that I couldn't ignore. I knew what awaited me out there, but in here . . . I didn't know what this was or where it would lead, but I wanted to know. I wanted to just be me. I wanted it so desperately, I was consumed by it.

"You want me," I whispered. I swallowed, my heart banging against my chest to get to him, "and I want you, Hal."

Hal came unleashed, body trembling. His lips collided with mine, tongue tracing my lips instantly. I opened for him.

I ran my hands through his hair, pulling him into me until our bodies crashed together. I heard him suck in a deep breath.

I pulled away, worried, but he tugged me back in, his mouth claiming mine as the hand on my waist slid up to my breast. Another moan escaped me as Hal dragged his hand along the underside through the thin fabric before cupping me, tracing the tight peak.

"Hal," I begged.

I didn't know what I was begging for, just that if I didn't have more, I would explode.

Hal spun us quickly. I found my back pressed against the wall as Hal spread my dress, the high slit exposing my legs and panties. He traced the arc of my hip bone, his calluses scraping my skin. The ache in my core throbbed, demanding more. Hal dipped his hand lower, stopping at the edge of my underwear, and I arched my hips toward him.

Hal took me in, gaze locked on me. "Do you want me to stop?"

"No." I gripped his neck and pulled him to me, my lips finding his.

Hal traced the edge of my panties. This time, he didn't stop. His fingers dipped between my legs. Hal's mouth swallowed my gasp as he began tracing my center through the soaked fabric. Heat scorched me.

He groaned into my mouth. Everything that weighed me down let go. My conditioning slipped away, as did my contract and the rules I had been force-fed my entire existence. The games and roles disappeared. Until it was only Hal. His mouth against mine, the hard planes of his body pressing against mine, and my burning need for more.

This was everything I wanted. This was everything I needed. He nimbly pushed aside the thin fabric of my underwear. The feel of his rough skin against my most intimate part left me undone.

His thumb pressed against the bundle of nerves. A moan ripped from me.

"Shh, Moonlight, they'll hear what I do to you." Hal breathed into my neck as he cupped the apex of my thighs, rubbing slowly. Another moan escaped me—there was no hope containing it.

"If you can't be quiet, I'll have to stop," Hal hissed, tracing tight tantalizing circles until my core began to tighten. "You don't want that, do you?"

I tried to tell him no, but it was lost—hidden under another aching moan.

A glimpse of a smirk lit Hal's face before his mouth found mine again to drink in my ecstasy or to quiet it. I didn't know. I didn't care as my tongue met his stroke for stroke.

I wanted more. My hips undulated against his hand, the added friction mounting something within me. Growing stronger, consuming me.

Hal moved his hand against me and pulled his mouth from mine, staring at me.

"Let go."

I felt my body tremble at his command, his hand increasing

slightly in speed and pressure, and his mouth found my neck, kissing and nipping in encouragement.

One of those fingers dipped into me. I was consumed by the foreign sensation. He moved inside me, and I couldn't breathe as everything went taut and hazy with cresting desire. I couldn't contain it, couldn't stop.

He slipped a second finger in with the first. My head rolled back, resting upon the wall as I panted through the intrusion, the fullness stretching me as his thumb rubbed tight circles over the bundle of nerves. His mouth found my neck again and his teeth grazed over my heated skin. It was all too much. I couldn't have stopped the desperate moan he coaxed from me if I wanted to as my core throbbed—all-consuming.

"Let go, Moonlight."

That name on his lips unraveled all I was. I let go. I couldn't breathe. Couldn't do anything but grip desperately onto Hal as my pleasure shattered apart. He didn't stop. Fingers moving as waves of pleasure racked my body.

Everything I was fractured around us as his movements began to slow like he knew my body needed the reprieve. It was the closest thing to divinity I had ever known.

I opened my eyes to find Hal staring at me greedily.

He withdrew his hand, wrapping it around my waist, careful of my gown. He held me tightly to him, his need for me pressed into me as I attempted to put myself back together, gasping.

"You're beautiful when you let go," Hal whispered into my hair. I sighed into his embrace. My hand found his chest, an exploration of my own beginning. Hesitantly I dragged it down his chest—searching.

I met his waistband, tentatively dragging my finger along it as a nervousness filled me for all I didn't know. I fumbled with his button. Hal groaned but his hand closed over mine, halting me.

"Please," I whispered, desperate to explore—to make him come undone like I had been.

His hand found my chin as he tipped my face toward him. "Not tonight. Tonight was about you," he told me. "You have to get back. They won't be distracted forever."

I hated that he had spoken it out loud. His words like a key that opened the door to all that waited for me on the other side. A deluge of reality that trampled the bliss. Those sane, rational thoughts I had lost trickled back in.

"Tell me there's a time when it isn't like this," I whispered. "Tell me there's a place where I dance with you."

Hal smiled sadly down at me. "I don't know when or where, Moonlight, but I will fight to find it. The place where we don't say goodbye."

I blinked rapidly. "Hal . . ."

His eyes held such tenderness as he looked at me like he knew.

"We have to get you back," Hal said, letting me go.

"When will I see you?" I asked as cold air flooded all the places that had touched him.

"It's been a while since I've seen some art." Hal tucked a curl behind my ear. "If tonight goes well and the plan goes forward, I'll be seeing you very soon. But you have to get back."

Hal pulled the door open before I could ask about the plan as hurried footsteps filled the hallway outside our hiding spot. Hal snapped the door shut, shielding me behind him. Terror left me paralyzed. Had Collin found me?

CHAPTER THIRTY-TWO

"Quit being an idiot and just accept the contract already," a male voice rang out.

"Why don't *you* accept a contract already?" the other male snapped back.

The footsteps drew closer. "I promise you should be thanking me for rejecting my last contract, Gregory. You think you're angry now. Emeline and her brother were an excellent match. One would assume, given that we share fifty percent of our genes with Emeline, that one of us would match to Nora."

There was a scuffle. Someone slammed against the wall near our hiding place. Hal pressed me farther into the wall behind him.

"You," Gregory spat venomously. "They matched her with you." Fury and panic filled the hall.

"Yes," Phillip replied, his voice strained. "I rejected it. But maybe I shouldn't have. You seem incapable of hiding it anymore."

"I do not care if others talk."

"You should, and she will," Phillip shot back. "If they go after her offspring, she will never forgive you. You are being selfish and they will notice."

"Only if you or Collin open your mouths."

"Collin does not wish his sister ill. It is why we are having this conversation. I daresay our sister is keeping him busy enough as it is."

Hal's grip on me tightened.

A growl ripped from Gregory's throat. "That's rich, seeing as Collin has stood by as Mate after Mate has taken his sister. One would think *that* is wishing ill. I thought he would stop it."

"Collin cannot control everything."

"Only you, little brother, only you."

"You are to enter this contract with the Minor, Gregory."

"People do not enjoy being told who to be with. I cannot do it again." Gregory hissed a breath between his teeth.

"It is either that or lose her completely. Others are noticing. They will not allow it. They will never allow it. They will not give you something you care about. You know this. You have to let her go."

"I will never let her go."

"If you love her—" Phillip began, but the sound of a fist colliding with a wall rang out. I jumped from the impact.

"If—" Gregory shouted. "*If?* Do not question something you have no idea about. You have never loved anything, Phillip. All you have ever done is climb your way up. Don't ask if I love her. I have given everything to her." Gregory's voice shook with a fury I felt.

"Then you doom her," Phillip threatened. He didn't even raise his voice.

My hands grew clammy. I swore I could feel Gregory's fury break as pain slithered through the door.

"Accept the contract, procreate with the Minor, and protect her. She accepted William," Phillip continued, his voice quiet like he felt Gregory's pain too. "She didn't even hesitate when the contract was presented. Think of Timothy."

"He's at the Academy now. You know Katherine wants me nowhere near him."

"You have to let this go. Your contract will be official and approved by dawn. A public Courting and cohabitation. Accept this. Don't neglect your role again."

There was no cordial end to the conversation, just footsteps leading away. Hal and I waited in silence, making sure they were gone. Hal finally opened the door.

"You should go out alone. Go down the hall and back into the room," Hal whispered. "I will come by your office soon. Go. I have kept you for too long."

Before I could protest, Hal gently pushed me out of the closet.

I stood in the hallway, suddenly feeling cold and completely alone. I debated going back into the closet and never leaving. Hal was right, though. I had been gone too long. I took a steadying breath, shoving all the conflicting emotions away. It seemed Lo would have her contract, but I found no joy in being able to tell her.

"Little sister," Gregory drawled from the shadows. I whipped my head to find Gregory leaning against the wall.

"Gregory," I exclaimed. "What are you doing here?"

"I could ask you the same thing," Gregory said as he dragged his eyes over me.

"Collin told me to stay here. I found the Elite to be too much," I told him.

"In a hidden hall? That leads to a service quarter?" Gregory pushed off the wall, crossing his arms. "Was it all the Elite, or just some of them?" Those blue eyes flicked to the concealed door behind me. "Or do you miss your kind?"

"I don't know what you're talking about."

"Hmm, it would appear I am not the only family fuckup after all," Gregory drawled. "I assume it isn't Collin in that closet. Doesn't seem his style."

"I don't know what you're going on about," I repeated, my heart racing. I prayed Hal stayed put. "I have to get back. Collin said he would find me later." I stepped toward the ballroom doors.

"Before you do, you should probably fix your lipstick and your hair." My hand flew to my hair. "Even then, I think the gown is a lost cause," Gregory practically taunted from behind me.

I looked down. The sheer skirt of my gown was devastatingly wrinkled. Panic hit me hard as I whirled to Gregory.

"Gregory, I—I—" I stammered, attempting to smooth my skirts.

"What are you doing?" I demanded as he pulled out his Comm Device. "Gregory, what are you doing?"

He finished typing a message and put his Comm Device away. "The only way out is through the ballroom, up the stairs."

"I can't go in there like this," I sputtered, terrified.

Gregory moved closer to me. "Emeline, it will be okay. May I?" I nodded mindlessly. Gregory rubbed his thumb quickly along the side of my mouth and chin. "Okay, that's better. Don't move." He slowly and expertly adjusted pins and tucked curls away. "Wear your hair down next time."

My heart sank at why he knew that as he stepped away.

His Comm Device dinged, and he quickly read a message. "Okay, Phillip got a Pod. I told him I found you upset and intoxicated. I am going to put my arm around you, and we will walk quickly through. Do not stop for anyone. Phillip is telling Collin I am getting you home. Ready?"

"Why are you doing this?" I asked, the knot in my throat returning.

"Because we cannot help who we care for." He looked behind me. "I did not know I had a little sister for too long. This is what a brother should do." He put an arm around my waist to pretend to hold me up. "That and pummel whoever the fuck didn't think about your damn safety."

Blinking away tears, I choked out, "You're a hypocrite."

A chuckle rumbled through him. "Yes, well, I cannot be perfect. Let's get you out of here." I leaned into Gregory as he whispered, "Don't look up."

Time collapsed upon itself as Gregory guided me through the ballroom. My frantic heartbeat drowned out the idle chatter of everyone around us.

I glanced up only once to see Collin with a woman in a red dress standing close to him, her hand on his chest. My stomach filled with lead as shock ripped through me. When had he returned?

Gregory ushered me into the waiting Pod as footsteps hurried after us. I looked up to see Nora holding my clutch. I had forgotten all about it. I looked down again as Gregory turned to intercept her.

"Is she okay?" Nora demanded. "I looked for her but couldn't find her. Eve is all over Collin. The Press is having a field day."

Eve. The name sounded vaguely familiar, but I couldn't place where I had heard it.

Nora attempted to push past Gregory, but he didn't let her pass. "Why won't you let me see her?" she demanded.

"I was told to get her to her living quarters, no theatrics. I have her." Nora stopped fighting him as music swelled from the other room. "The last number is next. William will be expecting you. Thanks for the clutch." Gregory turned, stepping into the Pod and sitting beside me. Dismissing Nora.

The doors closed. Right before the Pod took off, I looked up to see Nora wipe wildly at her face before turning away.

Gregory scooted away from me, sighing as he lay back.

"Why do you always do that?"

Gregory remained quiet for a moment. "Because it makes the stars look different. You should try it. You don't have to worry about ruining your gown anymore." I glared at him before moving to the Pod's other side to lie down.

He was right. The stars swirled like the *Starry Night* painting as the Pod shot through the sky.

"Do you want to tell me who matters so much that you are willing to risk your life for them? Collin is an Illum. Not just any Illum, Emeline. Your choice is stupid."

"Do you want to tell me what you're going to do about Nora?" I shot back, frustrated.

"So, you heard that?"

"Yes."

"Should I be concerned about who you were with hearing that?"

"No, your secret is safe." When Gregory didn't answer my question, I hesitated. The Pod dropped before shooting onward. "Who's Timothy?"

"My offspring. He's five. At the Academy. My old Mate hates me, not without reason. She has kept him from me as much as possible." I glanced over. His right hand hung off the bench. His knuckles were swollen and bloody.

"Tell me about Lola," Gregory said as he watched the stars.

"Lola?" I repeated, confused.

"The Minor, my intended Mate," Gregory clarified. "She said she knew you."

"Oh, Lo. She desperately wants this contract to work. She has dreamed about it since I first met her. She's funny, intense, and beautiful. She's a good person."

"Hmm," Gregory mused.

The Pod came to a stop outside my building. I stood, grabbing my clutch.

"Thank you," I told him, leaving him to his vigil with the stars.

"Emeline, if you care about the person you were with at all, never see them again."

Our gazes met. "You, of all people, have no room to talk."

"You will regret it," Gregory warned, coming to sit, his eyes haunted. "You will regret loving someone you cannot have. It will destroy you. You will spend your entire life fighting. Fighting to keep a secret. Fighting to hide your feelings. Fighting for someone you cannot have. You will never find peace; all you will have are fleeting moments in secret. The goodbyes will lurk and ruin you, cutting you down each time. And the Illum will find out, and they will not allow it. They will ensure you never get it."

"And what will you do?" Because I didn't want to talk about me.

Gregory looked at the building behind me and then the stars again. "Whatever it takes to keep her safe."

"You'll let her go?"

Gregory laughed. It was humorless and raw, seeped in bitterness. "All I have ever done is let her go. It is as known to me as breathing. Good night, little sister."

CHAPTER THIRTY-THREE

Later that night, I tossed in bed, staring at my ceiling. I couldn't get one lesson from the Academy out of my mind.

Centuries ago, the world was unrecognizable. Conflicting ideologies caused discord until the earth was left in ruins. This year, your education will focus on the history of the Last War and the ever-present risk to our peaceful way of life.

Destruction is but an option for an uncivilized mind. For destruction lacks intelligence, needing little effort. The civilized and evolved mind knows that rebuilding is the actual battle. To build as the Illum have done, creating our great society, takes real power.

Our world is only made possible by the sacrifices of the Illum and now yours. Human life is vital to our society's future; while Elite genes create the ideal offspring, there is a purpose for you. As a member of the Minor Defect population, your defects provide the Illum with the ability to learn from and eliminate detrimental genes in the greater population by providing a wider pool, but that is for your later education.

Prosperity of Peace is the cornerstone of our great success. This can only be achieved by eliminating all threats physical and mental that cause discord. The Illum's persistent endeavor of complete eradication of these anomalies protects our way of life. As long as there is human life, the Illum shall defend it with their own. Let us prosper in this era of peace by learning from those primeval humans' mistakes and selfishness. As always, follow the Illum's protocol, abide by the rules of the Minor Defect population, and constantly seek self-improvement, and you will rise, fulfilling your use for the Greater Good.

They wanted to eliminate "anomalies," with no definition of what that entailed. They sorted us into Minor and Major Defects based on genetics, but then cast people down if they stepped too far out of line. Why? What qualified as an anomaly?

I thought of what I had done with Hal, of my trip to the Underworld. All the art I destroyed. The way Rose loved Violet. The way Gregory held Nora on the dance floor. The mothers grabbing for their offspring. Nora's declaration that she would become any evil to protect her offspring.

Where did it end? What would remain if they succeeded in destroying it all?

I had thought Collin had chosen wrong because of his role but maybe I was wrong. Was I not the exact thing the Illum wanted to eliminate?

Why choose something destined for destruction? The Illum would defend human life with their own . . . All human life or just the ones who conformed for their era of so-called peace?

You will regret loving someone you cannot have. The Illum will find out, and they will not allow it. They will ensure you never get it.

Would I regret it? Was I past caring if I did?

I fell into a fitful sleep. I was dancing with Hal, dressed in a white gown, but I turned, and he morphed into Collin. His hand ran down my spine before I turned again, the dress becoming heavier, and it was Hal. Then Collin again, the gown too heavy. Collin smiled, spinning me, and I searched for Hal, but the dress had been nailed to the ground, and I couldn't move. The room went black as I fell through the floor.

Then I was running again, my ragged breaths the only sound until someone whispered my name. Was Hal urging me on or was

Collin calling me back? I didn't know. I couldn't get enough air. I couldn't find the light. I was alone.

I spent the next day by myself, lost in my thoughts after oversleeping. Frida hadn't woken me up for some reason. I had awoken to quiet and sunshine. Hal didn't come by the office, and I didn't hear from Collin. I remained alone until that evening when a soft knock sounded on my door.

I opened the door to find Lo. She smiled sheepishly at me. Right, Phillip had said they would be approved by dawn.

"I'm approved" burst from her mouth as she barged in. "Emeline, I can't believe it! The paperwork arrived first thing yesterday morning. He offered cohabitation rights. I thought I had messed it all up." Lo danced around my room.

I donned my nightclothes before grabbing my meal and sitting on the floor, where she joined me, practically glowing.

"You know this means we will be sisters," Lo exclaimed.

"For the procreation and cohabitation periods, but that's only four years," I told her, taking a bite of food. "Our friendship will outlast that."

Lo smiled at me. I tried to return it through my bite before taking another.

"Emeline, is everything okay?" Lo asked, leaning toward me, her blond hair tumbling over her shoulder. "I thought you'd be more excited about dancing with Collin. You said you loved the lessons. I thought you'd be happier for me."

I glanced at the wardrobe, which I had left ajar as I hurried out the door. My eyes snagged on the hem of the beaded gown. The blood coated my thoughts.

"What if it isn't better up there, Lo?" I asked quietly, placing my food down.

"Don't be ridiculous. Of course it is," Lo retorted, her brows high. "They have balls, gowns, and real food. They have everything up there."

"What if that isn't enough?"

"Emeline, you have an Illum Mate. If that isn't enough for you, what is? Most Minors would kill to be in your place. I imagine most Elite would as well."

"What if he isn't what I want?"

Lo shook her head. "This isn't about what we want in a Mate, Emeline. Collin and Gregory are our way out of this. Do you really want to stay down here? The Minors are drugged. We have no rights."

"They are the ones drugging Minors. How is that better?"

"Because they have the power and are spared. Anything is better than this," Lo declared.

"What if the Underworld is better?" I asked, my voice small.

"Funny, Emeline."

"I'm serious. What if there's something more down there. Haven't you ever asked Becca?" I whispered.

"Of course not. She wears blue." Lo scoffed, tossing her hair over her shoulder. "What could be better down there?"

"Freedom."

"Freedom," Lo exclaimed, her brows disappearing. "Freedom in living hidden underground, taking out the garbage? That's not freedom. That's prison."

The Illum were smart—convincing all the Minors there was nothing below, so we only ever looked up. It was enough for most of them, but it had never been enough for me.

"And if Gregory never cares for you, if you never care for him? What if you are a horrible match and only ever tolerate each other?" I pleaded.

"Then I will tolerate it with a smile in a gown and jewels around my neck. I will not become my mother. You said you find Collin attractive; focus on that." She grabbed my hands. "We are doing this together, just like we wanted. It's almost curfew. Let's talk tomorrow."

She released my hands, making to leave. She hesitated, her hand wrapped around the doorknob. "You know, for someone who says they want to stay down here, you say *Minors,* not *us.*"

"What?" Her statement pulled me from my despair.

"You don't say *us* anymore. You say *Minors* like you aren't one," Lo said, her blue eyes piercing me.

"I say *Elite* and *Majors* too," I countered.

"Right, so where do you belong if you don't align with any of us?" Lo asked, then left.

Where did I belong? Certainly not among those following rules to become a vessel. After last night there wasn't a place for me in the clouds. Collin might have been forgiving before but surely he would eliminate me if he found out about Hal. Even if he didn't—I couldn't . . . I couldn't continue with our contract. Something buried deep down, the same thing that left me unable to untangle my thoughts and my body's reaction to his presence, protested. I buried it deeper. I had seen an end to it—to him.

Beneath? Did I belong in blue in the Underworld? Would my life have been better if I had been assigned to blue from birth? If my mother hadn't intervened, would I have landed among my own? My chest ached viciously. If I belonged below, would I ever find out how she truly felt about me or what she had endured? And what of Nora, Gregory, the Starlings, Lo . . . Could I walk away from them all?

I'm whoever I choose to be.

My fingers toyed with my wrist, where the chip hid beneath the glow. Would Thea, the healer Hal mentioned, know how to remove it without me dying?

The choice felt impossible.

CHAPTER THIRTY-FOUR

In the archives I stared at a painting of a thin woman in a pale pink dress crawling in the grass toward a house in the distance. The painting seemed sad, the colors muted. I hadn't heard from or seen anyone since the ball two days ago, and my thoughts had endlessly circled around what my next move would be.

"What do you think happened to her?"

I spun to see Hal leaning against my doorway. "Hal!" I exclaimed, moving toward him.

"Moonlight." He wrapped his arms around me.

"That's enough, you two," drawled Barrett, making his way into my office. He looked at the painting. "Isn't it obvious? She's unable to make it home."

"Do you think she actually wants to go home?" I asked.

"We don't have time to pontificate about ancient art," Hal told us.

"Another time," Barrett commented, winking at me.

"Why are you here?" I asked Barrett.

"I have an unending affinity for bad decisions," Barrett teased, his eyes finding the art once more.

"We have to go," Hal interrupted.

"But you just got here."

"I mean all of us," Hal clarified as he strode toward the door.

"What? Why?"

"Because our plans are moving forward. We are about to shut down the grid."

"I think the term *we* feels a bit wasted. It's *my* ass that's shimmying up that chute," Barrett interrupted.

"You volunteered," Hal said, rolling his eyes.

"I'm the only one who can fit. Wouldn't call that volunteering," Barrett retorted, his weight shifting from one foot to the other—a restlessness to him.

"Bri would have fit," Hal countered.

Barrett froze. "Like I said, I'm the only one who can fit."

"Suit yourself. We need to go. I don't want you above the surface." Hal took my hand.

"Wait, why are you shutting it down?" I asked, looking at Barrett.

His gear resembled the gear the Elite Force wore. Thick plates lined his chest and, like always, he had weapons strapped up and down his muscular body. His hair was pulled back tightly. No necklaces were visible today.

"You're in Elite Force green," I stated.

"Guilty. The grid is going black because the Reaper is ready for justice."

I whipped my head toward Hal.

"We have to go," Hal repeated, pulling me from the room. "Leave your bag."

Our footsteps echoed down the hall as I stayed close to Hal. Questions fought to break free. The sound of metal on metal reverberated in the hall. Barrett grinned at me from behind, his gun at the ready.

Hal began to jog as we rounded the corner, heading to the right. I kept his pace, my heart gaining speed with each step. We approached a hallway door and Hal pulled me through the doorway. Barrett ran to the corner of the room, grabbed a bag and helmet, and checked his watch.

"Thirty seconds go, Hal," Barrett urged. "Wait until you hear the sound. If you don't hear it"—he looked between the two of us—"it's your call."

"Come back," Hal told Barrett. They grasped hands quickly, their foreheads meeting for a moment.

"I will," Barrett answered. "Or I'll wait for you on the other side."

They broke apart. Barrett donned his helmet and left the way we had come without a backward glance.

Hal pulled me away, knocking on the far wall of the room. A door opened and we slipped in, leaving the surface behind.

"Damn it, Hal, when you two asked for my help, you didn't say it involved the pet." My eyes adjusted to the dark. Bri stood there in all black, her hair in braids. "Kane is going to lose it."

"Tell me something I don't know. You should go." Hal paused, then said roughly, "And come back."

She shot us both a glare. "I will so I can yell at you, or I'll wait on the other side to fucking yell at you there. Either way, I'm fucking yelling." Bri shook out her braids before she pulled on her helmet. She grabbed a gun strapped to her leg.

"I'll be waiting," Hal told her, his palm sweaty in mine. They nodded to each other before she turned and took off down the hall, the darkness swallowing her.

Hal released a shuttering breath as he began to pace restlessly.

"Are you okay?" I asked.

"I'm fine."

"Fine isn't a feeling," I said, drifting into his line of pacing. Hal halted, blowing out another breath. His hand intertwined with the bottom of my shirt, pulling me closer to him as he leaned against the wall.

"Fair enough," he exhaled. "I should be out there with them."

"But you're stuck here with me instead."

"I don't mean it like that. I was going to get you down here one way or another. I wouldn't have been able to focus knowing you were above. I have never sat out a mission with them."

A loud whining sound echoed above us. An endless groan.

"What's that?" I asked as the sound droned on until there was a loud thud and then utter silence.

Hal released my shirt, grabbing my left wrist. He pulled up my sleeve. My wrist wasn't glowing. I gaped, looking between my wrist and Hal.

"It worked," Hal marveled, turning my wrist over. "Come on, let's get out of here," Hal said with a smile.

"How'd they do it?"

"Gerald would have to break it down for you. Even if he did, it's complicated."

"Why now?"

"Because the chase was successful the other night, and the Minors have been drugged long enough."

"Are they going to harm the Elite?" I asked as I thought of Gregory and Nora.

"Only the ones who get in the way," Hal told me. I came to a halt. "Why, do you have Elites you care about above?"

"If I do?" I challenged.

"I'd be relieved they haven't destroyed your humanity yet. Even if none of the Elite deserve your concern."

"I disagree," I told him as we followed the way Bri had gone. "So why aren't you with them?" I asked as we wound our way through the network of tunnels.

"Thea claims that while I feel better, my internal injuries aren't healed enough for combat. Everyone else felt inclined to agree." Hal snorted.

"Are you still in pain?"

"Not like I was," Hal confessed, raking his hand through his hair.

Music pounded ahead. "Are people dancing while this is going on?" I asked in disbelief.

"Of course," Hal said as we came to a room. It was the same room from my first trip down.

"Aren't they worried?"

"Probably."

"Shouldn't they be helping?"

"Doesn't work that way down here. They have a choice."

"I don't understand," I said, captivated by the moving bodies, the beat of the music thumping against my skin.

"For some, life down here is enough. It isn't a ball, but want to go out there?" Hal inquired, watching me.

"Your friends," I stammered, thinking of their quick goodbyes. Hal stood still, a tension to him he never had. Perhaps he needed to quiet his mind.

"I could use the entertainment."

"And I'm the entertainment?"

"Today you can be." Hal grabbed my hand and dragged me into the middle of the swaying masses. The crowd smelled of sweat, the energy contagious. I watched, frozen.

Hal spun me, coming up behind my back, his warm breath tickling my neck. His hands found my hips, engulfing them in his grip. "There's no right way, just let go," Hal whispered.

My body went taut at the words, at how I had felt the last time he had told me to let go. His hand drifted lower on my hip like he thought of it as well, before returning. I hesitantly moved my hips as Hal guided me.

Hal moved his body fully against mine. My breath caught. "Stop thinking. No one's paying attention to you."

Slowly I lost myself to the beat of the music and his hands on my body, a stronger effect than any glass of bubbles I had ever consumed, my thirst for it unquenchable.

We moved together, each beat rolling seamlessly into the next before I felt Hal's lips against my neck, and my head rolled back onto his chest. His hand sprawled out across my lower stomach, pressing me closer, until his hips cradled mine, and I could feel the effect I was having on him, the pressure making me ache. I spun toward him, and he held my gaze, eating up the need there. His thigh slid between mine, and I ground down, panting into his ear.

Wordlessly his hand found mine. We weaved through the crowd and into a stone tunnel. I didn't pay attention to the turns as Hal dragged me by the hand, my desire a force threatening to consume me. After two turns, Hal came to a stop abruptly. His eyes met mine for a single breath before he pounced, crashing his lips onto mine.

He devoured me as he answered my need. He grabbed my ass and scooped me up, pinning me between the wall and his hard chest. My hand ran through his silken waves, scraping down to his shoulders, and he groaned.

I wrapped my legs around his waist. I sucked in a quick breath as his hard length found my core, and he ground into me. I whimpered at the pressure. Hal tore his mouth from mine as I looked to where he pinned me. He watched me before he wrapped his hand into my hair, drinking in my mismatched gaze like it was a lifeline.

Hal's mouth found mine again briefly before trailing along my jaw and down my neck, his hand leaving my hair and drifting down to my breast, caressing through the fabric. He pulled at the shirt, a button giving way.

His name left my lips, intertwined with my moan.

"Get a room," someone snickered. I whipped my head in the direction to see several people in blue waltzing by, laughing.

Hal huffed a laugh. I began to unwrap my legs, red-hot embarrassment flaming my face.

Hal grabbed my thighs. "Don't. They're already gone."

"This isn't very private," I muttered.

"You want private?" Hal's eyes flashed wickedly. Before I could answer, Hal lifted me over his shoulder, a yelp escaping me.

"What are you doing?" I demanded as Hal laughed, taking off down the hall.

"Finding somewhere more private. Stop fidgeting. I'm injured, remember?"

"Exactly. Put me down!" I said, even as a laugh escaped me.

"Absolutely not," Hal responded. I could hear his smile as he worked his way through the tunnels.

"Hal," I demanded, laughing, the blood rushing to my head.

At last, Hal came to a stop, placing me on the ground. He held my face between his hands. "I would risk injury daily to hear your laugh, Moonlight." He placed a quick kiss on my lips before pulling me into a room.

We entered a living area. Four threadbare sofas were facing one another with a large wooden table in the middle. Guns, daggers, cups, and papers littered the table. There were three doors leading from the living area, and in the far corner, there was a mat with what looked like fresh blood on it, as well as a round target with small darts sticking out of it. A paper was tacked to the wall next to it with tally marks under each of their names. Gerald, it seemed, was the best.

"Sorry about the mess," Hal said. "They were in a hurry when they left. No one slept last night. Welcome to my home."

His nerves seemed to be returning, gaze darting from one thing to another. It tore at me, his concern for his friends.

I could be his entertainment—whatever he needed right now. I swallowed, approaching him. He stood still, watching me. I wondered if he breathed as I came up to him, my hand landing on his chest. I rose onto my toes, my mouth finding his.

I kept my eyes open as my tongue traced his lip, watching his eyes close as he deepened the kiss. His arm snaked around my waist, but I grabbed his shirt, tugging him into me, stepping back toward the sofa.

Hal broke away, his breaths ragged. "Not the sofa. There's not enough room and Bri stashes her daggers in it."

"Wait, she what?"

"Later," Hal said, his lips claiming mine again as he picked me up and carried me into his sleeping quarters. He placed me down quickly. A loud scraping noise followed as he pushed two of the beds together. "I'm sorry it isn't more," Hal told me.

It was a simple room, three beds and a few personal items, but with Hal standing in the space, it was the most breathtaking place I had ever seen.

"I don't care."

I meant it. With him here, I didn't care. It had never been about appearances or roles with him. I didn't have to hide. There were no games here. No rules.

He smiled at me, his eyes darkening as he stalked toward me. His hand gently lifted my chin as his mouth met mine. Within seconds the need that had taken over in the tunnel slammed back into me with a force that left me breathless.

I tugged impatiently at Hal's shirt. Hal chuckled and broke the kiss, pulling his shirt over his head and tossing it to the floor.

I looked at him, the perfectly sculpted muscles and planes of his stomach, and my head emptied out. His mouth found mine again, trailing his lips and tongue down my neck to the tops of my breasts as he undid my gray shirt. It fluttered to the ground, followed by my bra a second later. His gaze roved hungrily over me.

Hal lowered me onto the bed. He stood before me as he gently tugged on my pants until they too found the floor, and I was left in nothing but my panties. My breathing hitched at the rawness—the vulnerability.

"You're beautiful," Hal breathed, his gaze traveling over every bare inch as he climbed on top of me. I felt it in my very being—I felt beautiful here with him. His mouth found mine, but it wasn't frenzied and desperate like before. It was slow, gentle, like he knew. His fingers slipped between my legs, and he pushed aside the thin fabric, his touch light against the wetness gathered there. I arched into his hand, and he slid a finger into me. I moaned against the fullness as he moved. It was blissful, but it wasn't enough.

"Hal—" I rasped. He broke the kiss, his starburst eyes finding mine, and he froze above me, his hand stilling.

I trembled because it wasn't enough. I wanted him. All of him. Here. With the grid down—with all of us free for a limited time. In that freedom, I chose him.

Maybe there wasn't a world where I danced with him in a fancy gown. Maybe there wasn't a world where we could be together.

Maybe allowing myself this—allowing myself him—would be something I would pay for. Maybe every moment I ever spent with Hal would be laced with secrets and goodbyes.

"What is it, Moonlight?"

My heart swelled. I would pay any price. I would protect our secret, and I would bear the weight of every goodbye, for this moment. This choice. I wanted this for me. For us.

"I want you."

Hal swallowed, his throat bobbing. "Are you sure?"

"Yes," I said, pulling at his waistband with shaking hands. He covered my hand with his own, gently removing it as he stood and pulled down his pants. I glanced down at his obvious need for me. Nerves twisted around my desire as he joined me on the bed again.

"Have you ever . . ." he began.

I shook my head, afraid my voice would fail me if I spoke.

Hal pulled off my underwear. I lay naked before him, and he ran his hand along my breasts, down my stomach, before dipping between my legs. I arched my back, pushing the wetness there into his hand again.

"It'll hurt for a moment," Hal told me, nudging my legs apart and settling himself between them.

I wanted this. My first time. I didn't want the Illum to take it from me.

"Moonlight, look at me," Hal coaxed, hovering above me, and I did. "Are you sure?"

I nodded.

"I need to hear you say it. I need to know. We can stop," Hal said gently.

I took a deep breath and grabbed his face, pulling him to me. "I want you, Hal. I want you to be my first."

And if the world weren't so cruel, my only.

Hal kissed me as he reached down, dragging himself up my core. Once. Twice. I moaned, gripping his taut forearms. He lined himself up, and I felt him nudge against my entrance. He slowly pushed in before he paused, giving me time to adjust to the new sensation, then he retreated.

His starburst eyes stayed on mine as he eased in again, a bit farther this time, then retreated. He did it again and again. Easing himself in inch by inch. Slowly working himself into me, his eyes never leaving mine. Until I felt he could go no farther.

He pulled back, hesitating for the span of my frantic heartbeat before he thrust again, seating himself fully as burning pain ripped through me.

I couldn't get a breath in as I dug my nails into his shoulders. I closed my eyes, panting against it. Hal froze, buried inside me, letting me adjust until the fullness outweighed any discomfort.

"Look at me," Hal whispered above me, planting a tender kiss on my forehead. "Are you okay?"

I took a steadying breath, finding his gaze. "Yes."

He sighed as his lips found mine and he began to move again, the pain less demanding with each thrust. Pleasure slowly took its place as he undulated against me, grinding against the bundle of nerves at my apex.

He flexed his hips again, eliciting a moan from me as well as that need for *more*. On his next thrust, my hips rose to meet his. My hands wove into his waves, pulling his mouth back to mine.

Hal groaned into me as his thrust became deeper, quicker. I met his thrusts, and we fell into a rhythm until my body began to tighten, a pressure building deep within, burning me from the inside out. My legs wrapped around his hips, wanting him closer, deeper.

"Moonlight," Hal groaned, his lips crashing down on mine as he drove back into me.

The pressure deep in my core built higher, consuming me. I trembled against his next thrust. Hal moved deeper, harder, like he sensed it, his mouth finding mine like he could consume my pleasure.

There was no prompting this time. There was no need for it as he thrust again, his mouth on my neck and release crashing through me.

He drove into me again—drawing out wave after wave of pleasure until I was shattering around us, dragging my nails down his back. He groaned against my climax until he shuddered and withdrew completely. I breathed him in, holding him to me. My chest swelled—heavy, an ache taking root at the thing I couldn't deny any longer.

Hal placed a kiss on my forehead. "Are you okay? Did I hurt you?"

I shook my head, too afraid of what words might come out. At the emotion pulsing through me.

I took in the man before me. I felt it—this sweeping thing that had awoken in me, expanding wide, eating up all the space in my chest. Something foreign, the depths terrifying and unknown. The thing that had evaded me my entire life waited for me. All I had to do was fall into it.

"Are you sure?" he asked, grabbing one of the blankets and wiping away his mess before placing another kiss into my tangle of curls.

"I'm sure," I whispered as he tossed the blanket to the ground.

He reached over, grabbing the remaining blanket, pulling it over us before tugging me into him. We lay there for several moments, my head on his chest, listening to the sound of his heartbeat.

"I don't think we have much time left," Hal said, breaking the silence as he reached over to check a clock that sat on a rickety table. He turned back toward me, the scar on his left wrist visible. I reached my hand out, dragging it along the scar. The life he'd left.

I glanced down at my own wrist. It would glow again. I would be bound to Collin. Hal seemed to follow my train of thought. He captured my wrist in his hand and brought it up to his mouth, placing a kiss right above the chip that was hidden within.

"Hal, what if I just stayed?" I whispered. "What if I cut it out like you?" *What if I fell into that expansive thing. Chose it.*

"It's too dangerous."

"You survived."

"I shouldn't have. I survived because Barrett found me bleeding out," Hal told me. "I didn't do it right. If it hadn't been for his quick thinking and Thea's help, I wouldn't have made it. We can't risk it," Hal said, running a hand down my back.

"But, Hal—" I began, the weight of the world above crushing me already.

"I don't want to risk your safety. Thea won't cut them out anymore. Too many casualties. And she is the only person I would trust to do it."

"Do your friends all have chips?" I asked. I was curious how many had freedom.

"That's not information I can share. Those who are free don't discuss it. Everyone fears being found out and having a chip reinserted."

"How long have you known them?"

"A long time. I met Barrett right after I left the Academy. Then I met Kane and Gerald about a year later. I met Bri two years ago. She used to be with my bunkmate."

"Does she actually put daggers in the sofa?"

Hal chuckled against the top of my head. "Didn't forget that? Yeah, she does. They're sheathed, but she constantly tells Barrett she's going to leave one unsheathed when he annoys her. We've all taken to checking the couches before sitting. She also"—he moved some pillows to the right of us and pulled out a lethal-looking dagger—"sleeps with one under her pillow."

"Why in the world does she do that?" I demanded, shocked.

"Says it lulls her to sleep," Hal said, shrugging, putting it back. "She'll kill me if she finds out I touched it. It's our one bunk rule."

"Wait, you share a room with her?"

"Yeah. She moved in a couple of moons ago when"—he paused—"when her old place didn't work for her, and she's involved enough that this suited her."

"Why doesn't she stay in the other room?" I asked as jealousy coursed through me.

"Barrett snores. We drew straws, and I won. I used to have two male bunkmates, but"—he stopped himself, raking his hand through his hair—"they aren't with us anymore."

"And you two never . . ." I began quietly.

"No, never."

I swallowed. "But there were others?"

"Is this really what you want to discuss now?"

I shrugged.

"Yes, there were. There hasn't been anyone in some time."

I nodded into his chest, that knot in my throat throbbing.

"I'm a moon closer to the procreation phase," I muttered. "If I can't stay here, then that means I have no choice but to go back to . . ."

Hal blew out a breath. "I know. Two moons left."

It warmed my heart that he knew. I pushed off of him, coming to sit beside him. "Hal, I don't want to give this to him. I can't stand the idea of allowing them to take anything else from me. I want a choice. I want to be more than a vessel. I want . . ." I shook my head at all the things that rushed to be voiced—at all the wants I had spent a lifetime ignoring.

"To help," Hal finished for me, pushing himself off the bed.

I pulled the blanket up, covering myself as I took in Hal's naked body. "Yes, I do."

"It's dangerous."

"You say that about everything."

"Because it is."

"I can't spend my entire life doing this," I stated, gesturing to myself. At what their conditioning had failed to achieve. I couldn't be content like Lo. I couldn't ignore the injustice. I couldn't conform. Down here—down here I might be able to do something else. Something more. It was dangerous, but so was giving in to what they had raised me to be.

I might die from this choice, but had I not been slowly dying this entire time?

"Hal, if I can't remove my chip, let me help," I almost begged. "I want to do something. I can't go up there and be with him. I need to do something."

Hal bent down to retrieve his pants. He slipped them on as he said gruffly, "Then be his Mate."

"I am his Mate. How is that doing anything?" I came to my knees, knuckles white where I gripped the blanket.

Hal stared at the wall. "He is clearly affected by you. He might even care. You could use that to your advantage."

I shook my head. "You're confused. He only cares that I don't make him look bad."

"Perhaps, but the Collin I knew at the Academy was stoic. Unflappable. He failed at nothing. He was never goaded into a fight, into breaking a rule. He didn't miss a step when they pulled Nora from the Academy. Told everyone it was an honor. He isn't like that with you."

"That is one argument," I countered. Hal was wrong. Collin just couldn't stand my inability to listen.

"So he's never been like that with you any other time?" Hal asked, shrugging on his shirt.

Heat rushed through my body at the memory of Collin.

You're maddening, consuming, unwilling to follow any of their rules. I have a role to play and yet I spend my time thinking about you.

"He's only like that because I don't follow the rules. I mess up the role he plays," I assured Hal. Or was I assuring myself?

"I saw the photo," Hal said quietly.

Suddenly I was aware of how naked I was—how exposed.

"It was a just kiss for the Press," I said, attempting to brush off the warmth I felt in my cheeks.

Hal shrugged. "If you want to help, just be his Mate and use his lack of composure to our advantage. Gain his trust."

It was Violet's same advice. "What would I do once I had it?"

"He might let slip information on the Illum. Once we know you have his trust, we could feed false information to the Illum," Hal said. "Just something to think over. How much are you willing to do to help?" His eyes locked with mine. "Who are you willing to hurt?"

I bit my lip as my thoughts picked up speed. What if I didn't want to hurt anyone? I wanted to help those mothers. I wanted to help the crying offspring. I wanted to help the drugged Minors. Violet and Rose, Gregory and Nora—I wanted them to have a place to belong.

Not everyone in the clouds deserved to be destroyed. It wasn't that simple.

"Before we started this conversation, I was going to tell you I got you something. Stay here," Hal told me, a gleam in his eyes.

"Okay."

Hal smiled at me. It was one of the most beautiful things I had ever seen. Hal smiling, despite all the darkness that surrounded us. I wished I could capture it. To hold it forever. He darted from the room.

I stretched out but quickly retracted my legs. Soreness shot through me from a choice I had made all on my own, and a grin spread wide on my face. Something they couldn't take from me, even if I couldn't stay. I threw the blanket off and shimmied gingerly into my clothes and shoes before heading into their living area.

I glanced around the room, every corner, every surface radiating life. People lived down here. I walked to the dartboard. Tallies sat by every name. Countless games had been played. I sidestepped the mat and its blood and headed to the sofas. They were worn in and ripped, the likes of which would never be found above the surface. Cushions lay permanently sunken from holding the people who dwelled here. Even in the disarray, life shined through.

The table was laden with bottles of something that smelled sour, some almost empty cups of that drink Lo always had. Papers and weapons were sprinkled throughout.

I was surprised they had any weapons left behind after how many Barrett and Bri had strapped to their bodies. A rusty, ancient-looking gun lay on the table. A word caught my attention—a word scribbled on a piece of paper, poking out from beneath the gun. *Moonlight.*

I smiled to myself, wondering why the nickname was written

down here for all of his friends to see. I gently moved the weapon from the paper, pulling it toward me.

It wasn't just a paper, though.

It was a folder. As I lifted it, several pages fell to the ground.

A ringing began in my ears as I looked at the first paper. My heart hammered harder with each page, and my hands shook.

Pages of thorough information on me, on my job, on my birth family, my defect. Information that had been collected over a period of time, longer than the few weeks I had known Hal. I leafed through page after page. My pulse thundered in my ears, blocking everything out.

Images of me standing, waiting for a Pod.

Images of me walking into the Capitol building.

Images of me with Lo.

Images of me in my office.

My breaths became sharp, shredding everything in my chest.

That one word.

I felt like I had been drenched in ice-cold water, a chill gripping my bones. Notes were scribbled in the margins in a sloppy, slanted scrawl.

Likes art. Stares a lot. Learn about art.

Has no friends. Alone.

Hates her eyes, make her like them.

Make her care. Easiest way to manipulate.

About 90 moons until procreation.

I stared at the words. That warm, wonderful feeling that had unfurled in my chest ruptured, shattering all the things I thought I knew, all the things I thought I wanted.

I was acutely aware of the door opening as I shut the folder. Hal was saying something, but I couldn't hear him over the roaring in my head, the word written on the folder taunting me. I turned, the folder clenched in my hand.

"Moonlight."

CHAPTER THIRTY-FIVE

THAT WORD. MY EYES SLAMMED INTO HIS STARBURST GAZE. He looked between me and the folder. His smile faltered. He held a painting in his hands.

"Moonlight," he said again, slowly lowering the frame. This time it sounded like a plea. "Where did you get that?"

I couldn't get the words to come out. I couldn't ask. Because I knew that once I did, once he voiced it, this would be real. I pointed to the table.

"Moonlight, I can explain." Desperation tinged his voice as he rested the frame against the sofa.

"Do. Not. Call. Me. That," I bit out.

Hal took a step toward me.

I retreated. I needed to get out of here. I dropped the folder. I needed to get away from everything. Everything I had begun to trust, everything I had begun to rearrange my life around. Everything I had given away. To him. I needed to run—as far away as possible.

Hal moved toward me again, grabbing at my hand.

I yanked it away. "Don't touch me."

"I can explain, Moon—Emeline," Hal begged. "I can explain. It isn't what it looks like."

I had risked so much, bent rules and lied for what I thought had been real. I had given myself to him. Walked right into his plan. I felt my heart crack open under the realization that both sides seemed to have a role for me—a need, not a want.

I had chosen wrong—again.

"Emeline, I can explain," Hal pleaded, coming to stand in front of me.

A ghost of a laugh escaped me. My chest hollowed as the remains of my heart seeped out, contaminating the room. The knot in my throat gagged me as my eyes stung.

"Did one of those papers tell you to sleep with me?" I choked out. "Or was that just for fun?"

I stared at those starburst eyes. The eyes I had seen a future with. Eyes I had been willing to risk everything for. I stared, needing to see the truth.

"Moonlight." I flinched at the word. "Emeline, listen to me. Let me explain."

"Explain what? That you knew exactly who I was before you showed up in my office, that none of this was by accident. That I was researched so you could find out how best to manipulate me." My fists clenched at my sides. "*Make her care.* You succeeded, Hal."

"It's not like that. We thought—"

I didn't hear the rest of his statement. His use of *we* sent me reeling as I was assaulted by all the things I had missed.

"They were all in on this?" I asked.

"Yes. I mean, no—not everyone was for it, but we got sick of waiting," Hal said, running his hands through his hair.

"Waiting for what, Hal?"

He remained silent, a look in his eyes I had never seen before. Helplessness.

You met her by chance? Kane had asked Hal when I first came to the Underworld. *You do her no justice keeping her in the dark,* Barrett had told Hal in my office. Gerald had known my name. *You owe me twenty marks,* Barrett had said. I hadn't known I was what they were betting on.

Each revelation felt like a battering ram to my heart. They had all known. I was a fool.

Make her care. But it was more than that. What I felt for Hal—I had been running from it for a while. I had known in that closet. That beautiful expansive thing in my chest I had contemplated falling into collapsed on itself. An endless chasm, hollow and desolate. I slammed into it, sucked into its incessant depths until it swallowed me whole. My chest broke open, and emptiness slithered in. It had all been a lie.

"Look, I wrote all that before I ever met you. We found out that you might be the Illum's Mate several moons ago. I thought you could help us work from within. Get us information from Collin. The Illum have been impossible to infiltrate."

"By making me care about you? By manipulating me?"

"By making you agreeable to the cause," Hal clarified—like it meant something different.

"Because I was someone you were willing to hurt," I said, repeating his words from only minutes before.

"Emeline, you were a job."

Collin's words crashed into me. *Yes—you are a job, Emeline.*

"I fully intended to go through with it," Hal continued, "but then I got to know you. I realized you meant something to me. I couldn't lose another thing I love."

His declaration sat between us—too big for the room. "You love me?" I whispered.

"Yes, I do. That wasn't part of the plan." Hal stepped toward me. "I fell in love with you."

I hated that words that would have meant everything to me moments ago only served to break me now.

"That's why you didn't want me involved, why you kept telling me it was dangerous, why you told everyone the Illum's Mate was off-limits?" I asked, watching as Hal closed the distance between us.

"Yes. I didn't want you involved. I needed you away from this and safe. If Collin found out you were helping us . . . the things they might do to you . . . I didn't want to lose you. I couldn't lose you." Hal cupped my face gently.

"Why did you tell me to be his Mate after?" I asked, willing my voice not to break.

"You seem determined to help. Nothing I say—nothing I do—stops you. You wouldn't listen to me. Just being his Mate mitigates the risk while letting you help. If you do what he wants, you're safe."

My hand came up to the hand upon my face as I looked at the man before me, truly. I interlaced my fingers with his—squeezing. I clung to him for a moment longer.

"So my safety matters to you?"

"It is everything to me."

I squeezed his hand one last time before I pulled it from my face, stepping away. "Except when you have something to gain from me breaking their rules, when my risk benefits you physically."

"That's not true. I have been protecting you."

"Protecting me," I hissed, my hand finding my empty chest. "Protecting me how? By keeping me in the dark? Is that your idea of protection? Was it protection when you left me to walk out in front of all the Elite with my hair and dress destroyed? So it was obvious what I had done. You knew the Illum were there. If I hadn't run into Gregory, I could have been hurt or eliminated."

I suddenly hated the way my very skin felt. The wrongness of it—of me. I stared at Hal. "I have been lying, protecting you. I was willing to cut out my chip for you. I risked everything for you."

"Like Collin hasn't been lying to you too," Hal spat.

"He's an Illum, Hal. The consequences aren't the same. Maybe I wanted to trust him at first—"

"Is this where you defend him? Tell me he's different again?"

Anger speared through me. "No, that's not what I'm saying."

"Then what are you saying, Emeline?"

I didn't know. When it came to Collin I didn't know how to hold both truths: that the man who could show kindness and apologize for my birth family's treatment of me was the same man who ordered Christopher's death.

"I saw the way you looked at him on the dance floor. He's a fucking Illum and you stood out there in front of everyone like you wanted it—wanted him," Hal snarled, and I winced. "The Illum are killing people."

"So are you," I whispered, admitting the truth I had attempted to ignore. "Did you ever think to just ask me to help? To tell me the truth. To give me a choice. Or did you think we were all too brainwashed above the surface to be capable of helping?"

Hal stared at me, the truth there.

"You did, didn't you?" I said, stumbling back—the weight of that truth pulling me under. "So, who does the Reaper actually plan on saving? Only those in blue?"

"Mostly, they're the innocent ones," Hal told me.

"No one on the ground or in the sky is innocent?" I asked.

"Not the ones I've met."

"I'm one of those people, Hal. Am I not worthy of being saved?"

"You just defended an Illum," Hal said coldly.

I laughed, but it came out defeated and cruel—my brokenness permeating everything. "I thought the Reaper was a brave man. I thought he was better than the Illum. He isn't. There are good people up there."

"You're wrong," Hal said. "He—"

"When everyone above the surface believes everyone below is uncivilized and defective and you all believe everyone above is immoral and self-serving, who wins? How can anyone win when you all hate one another?" I asked. Hal said nothing. "How are you any different from them?"

The door blew open as Gerald hurtled into the room.

"What is it?" Hal asked, whirling toward him.

Gerald vaulted the sofas, sprinting through the room, coming out with several Comm Devices. "Shit," he said, his fingers flying.

"Gerald, what is going on?" Hal demanded.

"It's not holding," Gerald told him. "We need more time. They're still in there."

Our fight fell away as Gerald's panic filled the room. "What do we need to do?" I asked.

"*We* aren't doing anything," Hal growled. I ignored him.

"There's a shaft on your floor that leads to an old tunnel. I need to get this cube there, now. I'm too big. I won't fit. I need to get there right now. We have less than ten minutes." Sweat beaded across his brow.

I looked from the papers to Gerald. For once, no one's voice filled my head other than my own. I didn't look at Hal as I said, "Tell me what to do."

"Emeline, you can't do this. If you're caught—"

Gerald nodded at me and held out his hand. "We're going to run."

My heart quaked at words I had waited my entire life to hear.

"Gerald, you won't involve her. You have orders," Hal interrupted, grabbing my arm.

"You're not the only one afraid of losing people," Gerald said, his hand finding mine.

I yanked away from Hal, bumping into the frame he had brought in. It fell to the floor.

The mismatched woman with the book sat there, in all her beauty. Her broken form. The painting I had seen beauty in despite her fractured image. I hadn't been able to see it in myself until Hal helped me find it. Only to destroy it.

Another onslaught of torment rampaged through me. It only served to solidify my decision.

"You can't go, Emeline," Hal stated. "He'll kill you if you're caught."

"That's my decision to make." I turned to Gerald and said, "Run. I can keep up."

CHAPTER THIRTY-SIX

"How hurt is Hal still?" I asked through labored breaths.

My lungs burned as Gerald held my hand tightly, pulling me left and right as we sprinted through the dark tunnels, each step tucking the hurt away, burying it somewhere I wouldn't be able to find it.

"He punctured a lung when he got hurt. He can't keep up," Gerald told me, turning at the last second. I blindly followed him.

"Good," I grunted. I didn't want him to follow us.

A ding sounded from Gerald's pants pocket. "Fuck. Fuck."

"What?"

"Messages mean the lower systems are rebooting. We're running out of time."

"Run faster," I urged. Gerald didn't look back. He began to sprint, his hand sweaty in mine.

My recurring dream found me as we ran through the dark, our footsteps thundering through the tunnels, the only sound besides our heavy breaths, the pace too demanding for conversation.

His Comm Device sounded again as we skidded to a stop outside the door I had entered from.

He punched a code into a panel on the wall. The door slowly began to move.

"I was really hoping that wouldn't work. Help me," Gerald panted as he forced the door open.

I threw my weight into the door, and it inched open enough for us to slip through. Gerald released the door and pulled me in after him. The room was empty. A golden flash filled the room, but when I looked down, my wrist was dark again.

"Come on, we're almost out of time," Gerald commanded.

I followed, too out of breath to talk as Gerald darted down the hall and into a room on the opposite side, near the elevator. A panel lay on the floor.

A small circular hole sat exposed, revealing a narrow crawl space. Gerald stuck his head in. "Barrett," he called. He whistled in a song-like way.

No one answered.

Gerald thrust a black cube into my hand. "Keep this safe. Climb the chute, then take the middle tunnel. Go straight. When it dips, go slow. You're going to get to a circular room. Do not leave the tunnel. There's a huge metal device in there. It powers the chips. Toss this onto the device. Then get out quick so I can activate it."

Gerald knelt before the opening, his hands outstretched, waiting to help me in. A million questions raged. Why was this here? Had they always known about it? Why put something so vital on a floor with Minors? What did the cube do? How did Gerald know how to work it?

"Emeline, look at me." I turned toward him. "I can't answer your questions right now. We are out of time. If the power grid comes back up, everyone out there could be lost, those with chips tracked. The rebellion will fail. I need you to do what I said or move so I can try. I promise I will come back and answer your questions. Just go. Please. I need your help."

I tucked the cube into my pocket and put my foot in his hands. Gerald hoisted me up. Adrenaline rioted through me as I began to climb.

"Middle tunnel, do not go into that room. The moment that cube hits the device, shout to me and get the fuck out of there. I'll do the rest. *Go!*"

I didn't look back as I moved. My sweaty palms slipped against the sides of the tunnel. I didn't stop even though my body urged me to. I pushed against the sides and my thoughts that waited, ready to drag me down.

I had wanted to help, not by being a Mate or being used. This was what I had wanted. I didn't agree with the Reaper fully—more than those beneath deserved to be saved—but the Illum were wrong too. This wasn't peace.

The chute leveled out to reveal three openings barely visible in the dark. I crawled through the middle one, my eyes trying to adjust. A low humming sound filled the tunnel.

"Emeline, hurry." Gerald's voice echoed, urging me on. I swore I heard him say something else, but I couldn't make it out over the humming.

I picked up my pace when the floor suddenly dropped, and I slipped. The descent was too steep. I tumbled down.

I kicked my feet out helplessly, clawing at the sleek metal sides. My heart sat in my throat, my thoughts rolling free with me.

Follow the Illum's protocol, abide by the rules of the Minor Defect population, and constantly seek self-improvement, and you will rise, fulfilling your use for the Greater Good.

I didn't believe in the Greater Good anymore.

I wouldn't mess this up too. My fingertips attempted to dig in to abate my fall, scrambling for purchase. A sickening squeal of flesh on metal filled the tunnels as my fingers burned viciously and my shoulder slammed into the side.

My foot caught on the edge of the chute, bringing me to a halt. My heart refused to slow even as my body came to a stop.

I dug my hand into my pocket, scrambling for the cube as I took in the sight before me.

I had never seen anything like it. Metal wrapped around the sides, caging in a massive pulsing device the length of several Pods. Gears slowly moved around the edges. The hum came from a central bluish light.

My name echoed down the tunnel. I tossed the cube, and it attached onto the device as if it were magnetic. I glanced down to see hundreds of black cubes, varying in size, upon the floor. How many times had they tried this?

"It's on," I yelled.

"Get out," Gerald shouted.

A ringing started. I turned and fled, moving up as fast as my body would let me. My sweaty hands stuck to the metal. I released a long breath as I reached the top.

"Gotta activate now, cover your ears," Gerald called up.

I crouched down, covering my head as hot air whooshed through the tunnel. The groaning sound from earlier was deafening from this distance.

"You good?"

"Yes," I called, my head aching. I shifted my body until I slid down the chute, my feet colliding with the floor.

"You did it. Systems are down. The black hole wasn't that strong. It won't hold forever. Maybe ten more minutes, but that should be enough." Gerald checked his silent devices. "Thank you."

I nodded at him. "I have questions."

Gerald blew out a breath, a knowing smile etched with relief upon his face as he took me in. "You're not deterred easily, are you?"

"No."

"I may not have all the answers, but the ones I do have are yours." Gerald placed his devices in his pocket.

"And you won't lie to me?" I demanded.

"I don't lie," Gerald assured me in that calm voice. "If I cannot give you the truth because it endangers those I love, I won't answer, but I will not lie."

It was better than anyone had ever given me.

"Why don't you lie?"

"That's your first question?" Gerald asked calmly, assessing me. "We have limited time."

"It's unheard of."

"It's simpler. Oftentimes the lies cause more damage than the truth."

"What was that cube?"

"We call it a black hole. It's complicated to explain. It's the same technology as the cuffs. That's what we based it off of. Most rudimentary explanation: It interferes with the tracking technology, but on a larger scale, by absorbing the energy."

"Did you invent it?" I asked.

"No, but I altered it to make it effective for our purposes."

"Do you believe in the Reaper's cause?" I asked.

Gerald's jaw flexed as he nodded. My heart found my throat. I needed to know.

"Have I met the Reaper?"

My name filled the hall.

Gerald froze, and my eyes went wide.

"I thought you said he couldn't run?" I whispered.

"It's not Hal," Gerald said confidently. I swore his shoulders sagged. "Someone must have gotten the elevator to work when the systems were coming back." He quietly put the panel on the wall.

"Emeline." Footsteps sounded outside the room, but they carried on toward my office.

"Our questions are done for now. Go."

"What about you?" I whispered as a door creaked open.

"I'm relying on you to keep him distracted so I can get back," Gerald said.

"Are you not afraid of who might be out there?"

"No, your Mate would only send one person to get you, and I don't fear him. Go. Your brother is waiting for you."

I wanted to ask him why he knew that, and why he didn't fear my brother, but I heard my name again. I turned and left Gerald behind.

The hall was empty when I entered it. I had only taken three steps when a head of curly hair poked out of my office. Phillip stepped into the hall, holding my bag and Comm Device. His hair was a mess, his cheeks pink like he had run here, his clothes wrinkled. I had expected Gregory.

"Where were you?" Phillip demanded.

I ran a hand through my hair, sure my curls were equally as disastrous. "I was looking for a way out."

"You shouldn't have left your office." Phillip took me in. "You're a mess. We have to go. We can talk in the living quarters. They're bringing the grid back up now."

Nerves snaked down my spine. Had the ten minutes been enough for everyone out there? Wherever *there* was? I suddenly felt I had missed a vital question: What had they actually been doing?

"Why did Collin send you?" I asked, my nerves on fire as we walked past the door Gerald was behind. Phillip's device dinged. He stopped, taking it out. "Don't we need to go?"

I swore Phillip looked at the door, and I reined in my panic. "He was needed elsewhere. You're an Illum's Mate. A rebel might go after you to get to him and the Illum."

He kept moving until he came to the elevator. He lifted a wrist to the scanner, but nothing happened.

Phillip typed quickly as his words began excavating the things I had buried on that run. In the silence my broken heart thudded pathetically. How did I tell him a rebel named Hal already had?

"What happened?" I asked, holding the assailment of emotions at bay.

"The Reaper staged an attack on one of the buildings containing the supplements. I don't know the damage yet." He looked up from his device as a loud grinding noise filled the hall until it morphed into a hum and the elevator doors opened. "Collin hasn't contacted me yet. He's still out there."

"Out where?" I asked, surprised. I had expected Collin to be safe in the clouds.

"On the ground, managing the attack," Phillip explained as we stepped into the elevator.

My body trembled as the elevator shot up, my breathing unsteady. Thoughts sprinted around my mind, blurring one into the next. I clawed at all the emotions threatening to undo me, wrangling them into submission as the doors opened. My battle ceased at what waited on the surface.

The usually quiet atrium was a flurry of frantic movement and shouts. Six Elite Force soldiers waited outside the elevator doors, one taller than all the others.

Phillip nodded at them.

"Let's go," the tall one yelled, coming up behind me as the rest encircled us. I recognized his voice but couldn't remember his name. He hit a button on his arm, and we set off.

"Phillip, what's happening?" I asked, panicked as the soldiers bumped into me. "Phillip," I called again, unable to see past them and their armor.

"Just follow them, Emeline," Phillip called out somewhere behind me. I had no choice, my heart in my throat as we made it outside, where smoke filled the air.

What had the Reaper done?

"Jog," the soldier in the front shouted. I moved my feet at a quicker pace, keeping up.

A Pod sat waiting and the soldier in the front began shouting at someone or something. I couldn't see past the circle of Elite Force soldiers escorting me, but I could hear people moving about, running as if for their lives. Sweat dripped down my neck as my fear held on tight. Tighter than it had in the tunnels.

One of them grabbed my arm. "Get in, go."

"Systems up enough for this thing to get into the air?" the one behind me barked.

"Here's hoping," Phillip responded.

I felt myself being pushed and pulled until I was shoved into a Pod, Phillip right behind me. His wrist went to the scanner, and the doors shut.

I fell into the seat as the Pod shot straight up, slower than normal, leaving the pandemonium below as his Comm Device began to ding rapidly. Did that mean the grid was fully back?

Phillip stared behind me, shock etched across his face. I turned, only for panic to seize me. The destruction that sat in my chest was nothing compared to the destruction before me.

The surface was in flames.

CHAPTER THIRTY-SEVEN

"What happened?" I whispered.

"I don't know," Phillip admitted, typing again. "The Reaper has been targeting that building for a while."

I couldn't look away. Near the Wastelands, at the edge of High Town, a fire raged, shooting giant plumes of thick gray smoke into the sky.

"Collin's down there?" I asked.

"Yes. The Illum sent him."

"You haven't heard from him?"

"He'll be okay," Phillip stated.

How could that cube give anyone enough time to escape that? How many people had my interference trapped down there? The Pod ascended into the clouds, blocking out the horror.

"Why aren't we down there helping?" I demanded.

"We aren't authorized to help. Our MINDs won't take us there."

"Change them. You do it all the time."

Phillip met my gaze. "This time I can't."

The Pod slowed outside a familiar balcony. Phillip exited, and I chased after him, the smoke choking me. Phillip and Collin had gone to a building containing supplies weeks ago. How long had the Reaper been planning this?

I entered Collin's living quarters, and Phillip shoved my items into my hands. "Here."

I pulled out my Comm Device, typing a quick message to Lo, asking her to tell me when she was safe. "Where's Nora?" I asked, tucking my device away.

"Unbelievable," Phillip bit out, picking up a lacy black bra from the floor. "I will never understand how we are brothers." He turned on his heel and headed toward the sleeping chambers.

A forgotten book, ancient and tattered, lay open on the sofa. I hurried after him, putting the pieces together. "Phillip, just leave them alone."

"No," Phillip spat before banging on the door, the bra clutched in his hand. "Gregory!"

There was movement behind the door, then it swung open. Gregory stood shirtless in the doorway, his pants slung low on his hips.

"Little sister," Gregory greeted me, nonplussed. "Phillip." I heard a flurry of movement behind him.

"What do you think you're doing here?" Phillip demanded.

"Do you want to know the specific positions or just the gist of the events?" Gregory drawled, crossing his arms.

"Our city is under attack, and you are meant to be at the Capitol, not here."

"No," Gregory said simply.

"No? What do you mean *no*? Those were your orders."

"They weren't. If the world is about to end, I am right where I am supposed to be, regardless of the consequences."

Nora came up behind him, tying a green robe around herself. "Phillip, please understand."

"How many times have I understood, Nora?" Phillip fumed.

"I would do the same for you, you know that," she urged.

"But you cannot," Phillip stated, an ugliness to him, "because you both lack the wherewithal to obtain the power to do so."

Gregory's body shook as Nora's hand found his arm.

"Please cover for us one last time, please," Nora begged.

"*Last time?* There is no last time with you two. How many times have we been here? How many times have I cleaned up your mess?" Phillip demanded. "You can't keep doing this. You will be caught, and you will pay. It won't just be undesirable Mates. They will kill you. Collin cannot keep saving you, Nora. Think of your offspring."

One moment Gregory stood by Nora. The next, Phillip was pinned to the wall, Gregory's face inches away.

"Bring her offspring into this again, and it will be the last thing you do," Gregory seethed.

"Gregory, stop. *Please.* Phillip is only looking out for them." Nora pulled on his arm. I stood frozen.

"Someone has to," Phillip choked out, staring daggers at Gregory. "I'm blocking your MIND from here."

"Then I will find another way," Gregory shouted.

"Gregory, Gregory, stop," Nora pleaded, pulling Gregory back. "Stop. He's right."

Gregory stilled, looking at her, his anger morphing. "What do you mean?"

The look on Nora's face. I wanted to run away at what I knew was coming. At what I knew I was about to hear.

"We have to stop this. He's right. Others are noticing. William knows, and Arabella is almost the same age as when"—Nora swallowed—"when I was Mated. I can't watch her go through what I did."

"What are you saying, Nora?" Gregory trembled, forgetting about Phillip and me. All of him focused on her.

"You know what I'm saying," she muttered, tears welling in her sapphire eyes. Gregory shook his head like he could make this stop.

"You do not mean that," Gregory insisted.

"I have to."

"Then say it," Gregory demanded. My heart cracked as grief

leaked from him, so poignant that it sucked the air from the room. "Say it, Nora."

A tear rolled down Nora's devastated face. Gregory stepped into her, his thumb wiping it away.

"I'll say it then," Gregory whispered. "That was the last time. We can't do this anymore." Nora's shoulders shook harder as Gregory's hand ran along her face. "I won't come back. They'll be safe."

Nora watched him walk away, choking on a sob before she ran after him. "Gregory, there's a"—she sobbed, her voice breaking. She stood, clutching the green robe like it was a lifeline.

"I know, love" was all he said before he turned away from her, grabbing his shirt and shoes before walking out onto the balcony. Nora fled to her room and snapped the door closed.

I stood alone with Phillip as he pulled out his Comm Device again.

"Would it be the worst thing in the world for the Illum to just let two people who love each other be together?" I asked.

"Yes, it would be," Phillip admitted hollowly as he turned and left. I slipped into my future living quarters.

I shut the door, sucking in deep breaths. The sky outside was an ominous orange as the smoke from the fire choked out the blue, blurring the time of day. I beelined for the bathroom. I cranked the hot water knob in the tub until the temperature was close to scalding. Maybe it would burn away the feel of Hal on my skin. I caught a glimpse of myself in the mirror and froze.

I looked the same as I did this morning, yet I did not recognize the woman in the mirror. I turned away, unable to look at myself, at what I no longer had, at what I had fallen for.

I couldn't get a breath in, the feel of him a brand. I yanked my clothes off, throwing them to the far side of the bathroom.

I submerged in the tub even as the water scorched my skin, turning it pink. I welcomed the physical pain. My fingertips burned viciously. I turned them to see blisters from the chute. Tears threatened to spill.

Hal's hands on me. His mouth against mine. The feel of him inside me. The file. The broken woman with the book. The chute. The humming device. Gerald answering my questions. The fire. Gregory and Nora breaking before my eyes.

A sob snuck past the knot threatening to suffocate me, unraveling me. I had thought giving myself to Hal would give me love—a choice. I thought siding with the Reaper would give us freedom—a future.

I have been protecting you.

But Hal hadn't protected me, not in that closet, not today. What were the ramifications of our choices today? I'd be eliminated if our actions beneath resulted in something that wasn't meant to exist. I hadn't cared because I thought this thing with Hal had been real. It wasn't.

I had been a mission. An assignment. A job. Selected. Researched. How far did that assignment go? All the things I had confessed—how much had he already known? How much had he pretended to go along with while I thought it was a real connection? While my foolish heart thought it was more. I was so desperate to be loved, I hadn't bothered to look too closely. Desperate to not be alone anymore. Hal had known. Yet here I was.

Alone.

They destroy everything beautiful and different. Hal had said that about the Illum and the Elite.

I couldn't accept that he had as well.

I couldn't stomach the betrayal.

I couldn't handle the destruction.

I couldn't breathe.

I couldn't.

Panic rose in my throat. I sucked in all the air that I could and went under, the water washing away the tears I held at bay as the world went quiet.

I stayed in that quiet, trying to banish Hal with each beat of my heart. My lungs began to burn.

Still, I pushed against the need for air.

Only when small stars burst before my eyes did I admit defeat. I emerged, gulping oxygen as a heaviness fell over me.

My heart hadn't taken him away.

I mindlessly dumped soap in my hands and washed my hair and body, scrubbing every inch before dunking again to rinse away the soap. I started again, washing everything away. But no matter how I scrubbed, I didn't feel clean. I couldn't get back to the woman I once was.

Collin would return from those flames, and I would be his Mate.

A heaviness blanketed me. I didn't fight it. I closed my eyes.

I was back in the tunnels, running. Sprinting for my life, but I was alone in the dark. I wouldn't make it.

A dark form shifted to my left, my name piercing the dark. I ran to the voice frantically. I couldn't breathe.

And in the darkness, I let go.

CHAPTER THIRTY-EIGHT

Firm hands pulled me up, and I burst to the surface, spluttering and coughing. Water sloshed over the sides of the tub.

"Are you all right?" a deep voice asked.

"I—I fell asleep," I gasped. The room had grown dark. How long had I been in the tub? Midnight hair came into view. My stomach plummeted to the ground below at the sight of my Mate. "You made it out?"

Collin released my arms. "I did."

"What are you doing here?" The acrid smell of smoke radiated from him.

"Phillip said you had shut yourself in your quarters. I knocked. You didn't answer, so I came in to check. You were asleep in the tub. I didn't plan to wake you, but you began thrashing around and went under, so I pulled you out. I have seen enough death today."

Collin leaned against the counter. The soft sound of water dripping from his green-clad arms filled the room. For once, his hair was disheveled. Soot marred his face. I wrapped my arms around myself.

The attack. The raging fire. I felt my anxiety returning with each breath—clutching me in a choke hold. "Is it bad?"

Collin nodded, staring at his wet hands. My arms tightened around me.

"I will give you privacy. There's food." Collin turned toward the door, his heavy gear shifting as he did.

He looked so at odds with the Collin I knew in suits. I took him in, the polished exterior shed for something more real—more lethal.

"Why are you in that gear?" I asked.

He stopped at the door. "I was in the Elite Force before I became an Illum. The role I have for the Illum . . . it's because of this." He gestured to the gear.

"You never told me that."

"You never asked," Collin said over his shoulder as he left.

Several minutes later I stood in front of the mirror, taming my wild curls. I wore black silk pants and a matching long-sleeve top. The colors and options had been too overwhelming, and the dark simplicity soothed me.

My eyes were blue and brown. There was no lens in the bathroom. I closed my eyes, sucking in a deep breath.

I had spent my whole life hating my defect. I finally embraced my difference, and now . . . now all I saw was him. *Hates her eyes, make her like them.*

I walked away from my reflection and headed to the living area, barefoot. Cold tea sat on the table alongside the device Nora had used to read the Press.

I picked it up. Would they already be reporting on the attack? It lit up, but there was no image of the fire. Instead it was an image of Collin dancing with a woman in red at the ball. The woman was smiling at Collin. Her name was Eve, I remembered distantly. The caption read: ILLUM MATE'S EARLY DEPARTURE FROM BALL RAISES QUESTIONS: ARE MINORS BEYOND REFORMING?

I placed the device down. I didn't want to read anything anyone had to say about me. I had read enough today.

The sky was dark. No clouds floated by, only large plumes of smoke so thick they blocked the stars and moon. In the distance, still burning, was the fire.

Footsteps sounded behind me. "Are the Illum angry?"

"Furious," Collin confirmed.

I turned toward him. He wore one of his customary black suits, his hair wet but in place once more. His eyes traveled over me. We hadn't spoken since the ball.

"And you?" I asked. "Are you angry?"

"Are you referring to the attack or the ball?" Collin asked, coming to stand next to me.

We both stared at the flames—our reflections shining back at us. "Both."

"The ball should be forgotten after this. It wasn't ideal for you to run off. But then you do not seem to be a fan of ideal scenarios," Collin said, looking straight ahead.

Memories of Hal in the closet assaulted me. I closed my eyes. "It was stupid of me. I was stupid."

"Emeline, we are in private. You may rage at me all you'd like."

I searched for it, that inability to maintain myself around him. I couldn't find it. Everything felt hollow.

"It won't happen again," I told him quietly.

"I am sure that won't be the case," Collin said, staring at my reflection.

I couldn't return his quip—couldn't fight. I stared at the glowing orange flames in the distance. "Why?"

"Why what?"

"Why would the Reaper cause this much destruction?" I asked. There had to be a better way.

"Desperation has a way of causing things to get out of hand," Collin said, shifting next to me.

I knew that—too well. "Is the Reaper desperate?"

Collin's reflection adjusted his sleeves. "Yes. The Illum are figuring him out too quickly."

"Because of you?" I asked. That was what he had been tasked with figuring out all those days ago.

Collin straightened his jacket, staring at the fire. "Yes, because of me."

"Will the Illum retaliate?"

"The Illum survive because of their ability to retaliate."

"More people will die." It was a statement, not a question. Somewhere underground, when I handed over my innocence, I lost that naïveté as well.

There was no good or bad guy. There were no saviors, just varying shades of morally corrupt people with different lines in the sand.

"We are closer to war than ever before."

I nodded, tired.

"I have already been gone for too long," he said. "Your friend Lo made it back to her living quarters. I saw her when I left the area. That part of the city is still dark. You won't hear from her or be able to reach her."

Sapphires locked with my defective gaze in the glass. "Thank you."

"I know you will demand to return to your living quarters, but I would like for you stay here tonight." Collin stepped away from the window, as if he could leave quickly enough for me not to push back. To fight.

"All right."

His brows raised. "There's food and a scanner on the table. Everyone left. It is just you and Nora. Help yourself to anything that you need or want. What's mine is yours. I will check in sometime tomorrow."

"Okay," I said.

"Okay," Collin repeated, assessing me, his puzzlement obvious. I could tell he had expected a fight. "Also, going forward, the ball, the running, the rule-breaking"—he tilted his head—"that ends now. Things will be very different."

"Fine."

"Well, good." Collin walked toward the balcony, but he paused.

"Are you okay? Did something happen?" he asked quietly. Concern thrummed in his usually powerful voice, and it threatened to break me. I couldn't take his kindness. Not tonight.

"I am tired," I told him. My soul felt too heavy. I was tired. Tired of everyone's secrets. Tired of roles. Tired of pretending.

"I will be back tomorrow. You have my information on your Comm Device if you need anything . . ." He trailed off like he knew that even if I did, I wouldn't reach out. "Right. Good night."

"Do you ever just want a way out?" I stared at the outskirts of our city, beyond the fires, to the world the ancient humans had destroyed. I could barely make out the overgrowth beyond the smoke. In all my time in the clouds, I had never really looked.

"All the time," Collin murmured. "Maybe then my mind would go quiet."

I turned toward him fully. Collin held my broken gaze for a single breath before he turned to the balcony for a Pod.

I watched him leave until the thick smoke swallowed him and he disappeared into the night. I didn't go looking for food. I crawled into the bed that was as soft as a cloud.

The sound of a door opening and shutting echoed through the empty quarters.

I closed my eyes against the stinging, refusing to let any tears fall. When I went to sleep, I didn't dream.

✦ ✦ ✦

I AWOKE TO SUNLIGHT AND QUIET. MY COMM DEVICE DINGED as Nora walked in, wearing a simple cream dress and holding a cup of tea.

"I was coming to wake you. How are you?"

"Fine. You?"

"Horrible," Nora told me, even her sad smile absent. "More so now that we've been summoned."

"What do you mean, summoned?"

"All of the Elite have been. There's a ball tonight. It's mandatory for Elite to attend. The Illum will be there."

"Is that normal for them to do something like this?" I asked.

"No," she said, her expression grim. "It most certainly is not."

CHAPTER THIRTY-NINE

Within an hour, I found myself in the glossy black cage waiting for the Starlings. Two Pods had pulled up to take Nora and me away.

"Be safe," she had said before climbing into her Pod.

On the way, I observed the surface. The fire had been extinguished, but billows of smoke still swarmed the city, obscuring the view, blending the divides between the different parts of the city until it was one gray blur.

The door creaked open, and Violet and Rose entered, their faces solemn.

"Has your Mate given any details of the fire?" Violet demanded immediately. "Any idea of casualties? The network is down."

"The grid is fully up," I told them. It was the only other thing Nora had told me this morning.

"I am talking about the network between supporters, not the Illum's grid. I haven't heard from Rajesh." Bags sat under Violet's eyes.

"My Mate didn't say. Only that the Illum are furious. People died, but I don't know how many casualties."

Violet sucked in a deep breath, her hand finding her chest.

Rose clutched her arm. "Vi, it was a Reaper-led attack. He would have done everything he could to protect his people. Rajesh is trained for this."

The fog in my head lifted at her statement. "The Reaper wasn't down there."

"Of course he was," Violet stated. "This was his plan."

I bit my lip. "He wasn't. I was with him."

They fell silent, watching me. Rose recovered first, opening the door to the bathing room, steam swirling. "We must hurry."

"You were with him?" Violet asked incredulously. "He identified himself to you?"

I nodded.

"That cannot be right," Violet said. "He would never stay behind for a woman. Nor would he reveal himself to someone tied to the Illum. You're wrong."

"I'm not," I assured her.

"No," Violet protested. "This is his first successful attack since the Last War. He bested the Illum. He wouldn't stay behind."

"He's still injured," I confided.

Violet crossed her arms. "He isn't injured. That was a farce."

"It isn't. Also, his success came at the expense of innocent people's lives."

"That is a necessary by-product of the cause," Violet said.

"A by-product?" I ejected furiously. "A by-product? They are *humans*."

"You support him."

"Maybe I don't believe in the Reaper's methods now," I said plainly. "Maybe I don't respect him anymore."

Rose watched me, her body tense. Did she agree with me?

"Respect him? Fledgling, he is taking down the system. He is giving us power."

"What is the cost of that power? Is the power worth Rajesh?" I demanded. "Is it worth Minors' lives who had the misfortune of having chips placed in their wrists? He's hurting people, Violet."

"So are the Illum!" she seethed. "What is the cost of keeping things the way they are, Fledgling? Women as vessels?"

"That doesn't make it right." Why didn't anyone else see it?

"Rajesh would give his life for our freedom."

"Would you? Is the freedom worth it if you lose those you love?" I demanded, staring at Rose.

"In this world, in their world, we aren't permitted such things," Violet spat, stepping in front of Rose. "If I have to destroy my soul to change that, then I will."

"It doesn't give Hal the right to stoop to their level!" I declared, my anger bursting through.

Violet fell silent. "What about Hal?"

"He—" I stopped myself.

"That's who you were with yesterday?" Violet asked, her dark eyes wide.

"He's the one Rajesh talks about, right?" Rose whispered. "Wasn't he the one behind the dress?"

"What?" My voice trembled. "The blue dress?"

Violet stared at me, her eyes slits. "Yes. He brought it to level the playing field, then played the hero, apparently."

My anger winked out. It had been a game all along.

Rose grabbed my hand and led me into the steam room. "We have wasted too much time. We cannot be late tonight. The Illum are up to something with the ball. We all know this. We must hurry."

In what felt like seconds and yet a lifetime, I found myself on the podium, fully dressed for whatever awaited. No other words were spoken during the rest of the appointment. An air of tangible dread followed us room to room.

The gown was a work of art and a labor of love. I was unworthy of it. The off-the-shoulder dress was utterly sheer and nude, bedecked with thousands upon thousands of crystals. All of me on display.

My eyes burned from the beauty of it, so at odds with the ugliness I felt plagued by. I spun, looking over my shoulder at the back, the crystals artfully placed. It was as if Rose had captured the stars I had once wished to be.

All the beauty, and I felt none of it.

Violet stepped onto the podium, fastening the large oval diamonds to my ears as I felt a tug on my dress.

I glanced down to see Rose crouched on the ground, attempting to add more crystals.

"Leave it," Violet urged. "No one will notice it isn't done."

"They notice everything. There are supposed to be more crystals. I was supposed to have another ten days." Rose added another crystal toward the bottom of the gown. "The Illum will be there, and it isn't done."

Violet grabbed her arm, and Rose came to stand. Violet pulled her in close.

"It is time. I will see her out," Rose said. Violet didn't fight it as she released Rose and left the room.

"I ask—no, I beg you, do not betray us to the Illum. Please, I love her." Rose glanced back at Violet. Tears fell as she confessed, "It isn't worth it to me. Freedom. Without her, it isn't worth it."

I didn't remember leaving. I didn't hear Harold's goodbye or what the man in dark gray said as I arrived in the antechamber I knew had a large glass vase of white lilies. Collin's entertainment quarters.

The doors beneath the stairs stood open, the Elite conversing beyond, but I turned right. I wasn't aware of where I was going until I found myself in a two-story office filled with moonlight. I walked to the windows and stared at the moon through the lingering smoke. The stars were hidden.

"Emeline," a honey voice called.

"Nora," I stated, turning to where she stood beneath the spear light fixture dangling above her like a cage. She wore a black silk gown with an asymmetrical draped neckline and a high slit. Her midnight hair was braided around her crown while diamond-and-gold earrings snaked up her ears.

"I am aware of why I am in mourning, but why are you?"

I had spent my entire existence quieting the questions I always had. Now I found myself unable to hide them. "Did you mean it? Yesterday, with Gregory?"

Nora looked at me sadly. "I must. Phillip was right. I need to think of my offspring. If there were something I could do to keep him, I would. Something to make it different this time."

"This time?" I asked. How many times had they gone through this? How did she have the strength to keep going?

"Yes, but he will come back despite common sense and reason. He always comes back when I cannot remember."

"Do you believe in the Greater Good?" I asked.

Nora methodically rifled through several papers on Collin's desk. "I have always hated this office. I don't know how he stands it." She pushed the papers aside and perched on the desk, staring at the empty shelves, but they weren't empty. The moon's light reflected off small orbs strewed on the shelves. Nora looked toward me. "That depends on which Greater Good you're referring to. Theirs or ours."

"There is more than one?"

"Of course. It's all just a matter of perspective, Emeline."

Unease found me, but I pressed on, asking the question I really wanted to know from the only person I had ever met who saw people, not status. Who had told me we might be more alike than different. Who had seen my defect and embraced me. The only person I had ever known who seemed curious.

"What do you think of the Reaper?"

Nora looked from me to the windows and back, idly messing with the edge of a paper on Collin's desk.

"Some days I think the Reaper has the right idea," Nora whispered so quietly I had to lean in to hear her.

"You saw the fire."

"Yes, but I have seen other things too. Evil flourishes when no one stands up to it. It isn't heroic to confront it. It is horrifying. I think the Reaper is tired of being told who to be and watching everyone around them be told the same. I think the Reaper is willing to destroy themselves if it saves others."

"Do you support him?" I asked quietly.

"It's all just lines in the sand, Emeline. Given the right motivation, people cross them. We should head in before Collin sends Phillip to come and fetch us. I don't need another lecture from him." Nora hopped off the desk and waited for me by the door, her arm outstretched.

I approached her, my thoughts spinning. "Nora, you never called the Reaper a man."

She threaded her arm in mine as we left the office. "Who says it has to be a man? Maybe a woman is tired of being a vessel."

I stared at her, eyes wide, questions pressing against my skin.

Nora pulled me into the ballroom before coming to an abrupt halt. I tracked her eyes to the dance floor. Gregory turned Lo, a beaming ray of sunshine in a pale pink strapless gown. How had she gotten into the clouds so quickly? She looked at home among the Elite. Gregory spun her, and she locked eyes with me, smiling. I attempted to smile back.

"It's quick, is it not? Her being in the clouds?"

"Are you okay?" I asked Nora.

"It doesn't make sense. She shouldn't be here yet."

Unease churned in my stomach. "Where is Collin?" I asked.

"Wherever the Illum are. He is here as one of them tonight."

"Where are your keepers this evening?" a voice drawled to my left. I turned to find Vincent standing before us.

"You forget your place, Vincent," Nora said quietly, her fierceness ablaze.

"Perhaps my place has become of higher value thanks to the information I have given the Illum. Such an insignificant task turned out to be quite fruitful." Vincent followed Nora's gaze. "A good pair, are they not? He is where he belongs for the Greater Good."

Collin appeared at my side. "Vincent, sister," Collin said, his jaw tight.

"Collin, what a wonderful ball you have put together."

He inclined his head at my birth father, then whispered to me, "We are expected to dance now."

"Right now?" I muttered. "The crystals on the gown are heavy."

Collin rolled his shoulders, taking my hand. "It wasn't an offer."

Collin steered me onto the dance floor as a new song began. I recognized it immediately. It was my favorite, the one with the most spins and changing partners.

I looked to my left to see William and Nora dancing as well, and to my right, Lo and Gregory.

My heart raced as I bowed to Collin. He barely moved his head in a bow to me before he grabbed my hand. His other hand found my waist as we began to move. The man who considered a way out wasn't before me. Cold, calculating power held me.

My brows knitted together as he spun me once before capturing me back in his arms.

"You're a spy," Collin stated, an absoluteness to his words as he led.

I tried to talk, but the words never came out. Which spy was he referring to? Was he seeking confirmation on what the rebellion had asked of me, or reminding me of the role he had told everyone in this room?

"It is the reason you are in this position right now," Collin said under his breath, something too cold to be anger lacing each word. His hold on my hand tightened. "You breathe because of it."

A movement behind Collin's shoulder caught my attention, but as Collin spun me, I lost sight of it. My breaths sawed out of my chest.

He pulled me back in tightly, his voice dropping low. "I did tell you it isn't pleasant what happens to those who don't follow the Illum?"

"What?" I asked, my covered defect colliding with churning sapphire pools.

His grip tightened on my lower back. The countless crystals dug into my skin as the music swelled. I was spun to the man on my left. Collin tracked me as he danced with Lo.

"You look lovely this evening, Emeline," I heard William say. "The Illum's sparkling jewel."

I mumbled a thanks, unable to look away.

William chuckled. "One more spin, and you will be back with your dear Mate."

I spun, landing back in Collin's arms. "Why couldn't you value your life?" he said at my ear in a deadly whisper.

"Collin, I don't know what you—"

"The act is up, Emeline." He spun me again, this time right into my brother's arms, my fear now a tangible thing, a cold sweat coating me. The voices from the Elite surrounding the dance floor seemed to grow louder.

"Are you okay, little sister?" I looked between Gregory and Collin. My skin too tight—the crystals too heavy. Gregory leaned in. "Talk quickly."

"I messed up," spilled from my trembling lips. "I didn't listen to you. They're a step ahead of me. They know, brother." It was the first time I had used the word. The room was moving too quickly, the brightly colored gowns and jewels a blur.

"Find me after this dance." The words floated with me as I spun back to Collin.

Collin held me firmly, the crystals a million tiny knives on my skin. "The crystals, it hurts," I breathed, arching my back.

Collin took advantage, leaning in. To any spectators, it looked like a lover's embrace—two people who needed to be close.

"You do not know pain yet, Emeline." His lips brushed my jaw. "But you're about to, and I cannot stop it."

The music swelled. I knew the series of spins were coming. The final moments of the dance.

The Starlings had said to be on the lookout. To stay alert.

"What about a way out?" I breathed desperately.

Collin shook his head. "There is no way out. It's what I've been telling you this entire time."

He spun me. My head whipped around. Again. Again. Again. Again. Again. Ag—

Chaos erupted off the dance floor. On my final turn, I landed in Collin's arms, and we spun toward the commotion. The music had stopped.

Voices filled the room.

What is going on?

It's the rebels.

"You're a spy, Emeline," Collin whispered in my ear. His arm wrapped tightly around my waist. "It is not only your life that relies on it."

They've got the Reaper.

Don't let the others get away.

I couldn't breathe. Several people lay on the ground unconscious or worse—I didn't know. Two members of the Elite Force wrestled one of their own to the ground. Others rushed to help.

A knee slammed into the person's gut.

I couldn't breathe. I couldn't breathe as one of the soldiers removed the helmet.

The world tilted off its axis as my heart hurtled to the ground forever below. Starburst eyes met mine.

"Act, *Moonlight*," Collin warned. I sucked in a sharp breath.

I stood paralyzed, my heart no longer in my chest, as they dragged Hal from the room.

CHAPTER FORTY

Collin's arms remained wrapped tightly around me, preventing me from lunging forward. Elite Force swarmed the room. His breath was warm on my neck, but his voice in my ear was emotionless. "You're a spy, Emeline. I need to let go of you now."

Numbly, I felt Collin's arms leave me, and his hand captured mine in a death grip. He pulled me toward the door Hal had been taken through, stopping only briefly in front of Nora.

"Go home and do not leave there," Collin commanded before he pulled me from the room into a hallway and up a set of stairs.

I heard voices that interrupted my silence. A group of men and women dressed in black and white stood on the landing before a set of double doors. The Illum were always talked about as one entity. It was strange to see varying heights, skin tones, and hair colors. Seeing them as individuals—as humans—felt wrong.

I tried to pull away as I saw Tabitha. Collin's grip on my hand tightened, tugging me into him.

"Our hero of the evening," Tabitha stated, looking at us.

I didn't know if she meant me or Collin. He came to a stop, bowing slightly. I hurried to follow suit. As her gaze found me, she closed her eyes for a fraction too long to be a blink, as if she couldn't bear to look at a Defect. When she opened her eyes, she looked to Collin.

"We shall address the Elite, and then you are to take Emeline to the Capitol so we can discuss our next move."

"You would like my Mate to join?" Collin asked.

"Oh yes, we have so much to discuss, your Mate and I." Tabitha smiled, then turned toward the double doors that I hadn't bothered to notice. "Bring him," she called.

Terror closed my throat as two Elite Force soldiers dragged Hal forward. His face was bleeding profusely. He didn't look at me. My heart pounded viciously.

"Come, little lamb," Tabitha beckoned, reaching out her hand as the double doors opened. "We must tell them of our victory. The rest of you may leave us. Except of course Collin and Charles." Tabitha watched Collin as she said it. The others in black and white left.

Collin pushed me forward, and I followed Tabitha onto a small balcony above the dance floor. The Elite gathered below. A cold sweat slicked my skin.

"Our dear Elite," Tabitha began. The room quieted. "I would like to celebrate this moment with you. We have apprehended the Reaper."

Below they gasped, and my breaths quickened. The soldiers slammed their weapons into the back of Hal's legs, sending him to his knees before them all. Tabitha turned her head toward me, breathing deeply like she could sense my brokenness.

"There is so much to be thankful for as we restore our peace—to you all for your unwavering dedication. We are thankful. Without your cooperation, the Reaper's plan for chaos might have been successful, upending our order. Your presence here has shown your allegiance. The same cannot be said to any Elite who declined this offer. They are being eliminated as we speak."

I couldn't breathe. I stumbled back, colliding with the youngest Illum. Collin's arm snaked around my middle as his hand sprawled across my stomach, digging into the crystals.

"We elders also thank our youngest Illum for this brilliant plan. As well as his Mate, Emeline. Her unwavering dedication is admirable. In unprecedented times, sometimes unprecedented measures must be taken. Unwavering loyalty is a gift. Before you all, the Illum have decided to do something that has never been done. We grant Emeline full Elite status. Effective immediately."

Was that my heart or Collin's that thundered through me as the declaration hung in the air? The silence in my mind leaked into the room as the Elite all fell quiet. Hal didn't look my way.

Tabitha stepped toward the railing, peering down at the Elite—waiting. Applause began instantly. She grinned.

"Yes, yes, so rightfully earned and deserved. Emeline has been dedicated to our cause. Spying, gathering intel, and socializing with the defective. She deserves your respect and thanks. Without her, we would not have captured the Reaper." Tabitha turned, locking eyes with me. The coldness in her stare hollowed me out. She drank it in. "His elimination is her doing. Hers alone."

Collin's fingers dug in hard enough to bruise me, but I didn't care. I fell apart from the inside out, his hold the only thing keeping me upright. My legs trembled as Tabitha's words crushed my heart in a vise grip.

"Not today, though," Tabitha clarified. "Soon, in front of you all. Until then, dance. Enjoy this victory. It is as much yours as ours, faithful Elite." Tabitha raised her hands. "To the prosperity of order." She turned as music filled the room, drowning out the crowd below.

They hauled Hal away again. Tabitha beckoned to Collin and me as a man with a long black ponytail trailed after us. My eyes focused only on those dark blond locks. Where were Kane, Barrett, Bri, Gerald? They took down an entire building. Where were they now? Who was coming for Hal? He was their leader.

"Take her to the Capitol. I shall be with you shortly," Tabitha ordered Collin. "Oh, but first, bring him forward."

They dragged Hal over. He didn't fight them as they sent him to his knees again at my feet. He didn't look up. The doors behind us closed loudly. Tabitha stepped forward as the man remained to observe.

"Don't you want to look at her?" Tabitha cooed at Hal. My knees threatened to give out—to join him on the ground. "No? Are you sure? She can't stop looking at you. Lift his head."

The soldiers pulled Hal up by his hair. Those starburst eyes met mine. I stared at him, heartbreak, sorrow, terror, and rage blazing through me. There was no fear in his eyes, just resolute acceptance.

"Show her his wrist," Tabitha demanded, still smiling. Somehow it was the cruelest thing I had ever seen. His left wrist was thrust forward. There was an angry red mark near the scar he always covered. "He fought rather hard, but he has a chip again. Isn't it wonderful?"

"Tabitha, stop playing with your food," the man with the ponytail said gravely.

"That is rich coming from you, Charles," Tabitha claimed, walking away. "Cuff him."

The soldiers holding him placed large metal cuffs on Hal's wrists before yanking him to his feet as Tabitha and Charles walked away. Hal's eyes drank me in, taking in every detail like he was committing me to memory. He held my gaze until he couldn't as they carried him away.

I took a step toward him but was pulled back. Collin pushed me out, down the stairs, into the foyer, and onto a Pod. The calmness he had maintained flew into the sky. A cold fury leaked from him.

There was a familiar beep. The doors closed and, with them, all of Collin's composure. Collin turned toward me, his polished exterior as shattered as my heart.

"Explain yourself, Emeline," he demanded as my knees finally gave out. I fell into the seat.

"You organized tonight?" I asked as the crystals stabbed into me.

"I was told to host the ball. They had organized most of the plan while I was away," Collin confessed. Away making sure I didn't drown.

"I don't believe you," I said.

"I do not find that shocking with the lies you have told me." Collin moved toward me. "Who knew about your involvement? Did you plan to join their cause?"

"Why would I tell you?" I responded.

"Did you plan to join?" Collin growled as the city proper engulfed the Pod, sending lights swirling past the glass at a dizzying speed. Collin remained standing, unaffected.

"My involvement with the Reaper is none of your business," I snapped.

"It is entirely my business," Collin seethed, as wickedly as they all claimed him to be. "So, what was the plan? Let me guess—spying on me to get information on the Illum? Infiltrate the Illum from within?"

"I don't have to answer you."

"I am your Mate. You do answer to me."

"I won't."

"You will, but not to me. You have to answer to the Illum now. To Tabitha. You have no idea what you have gotten yourself into."

"I don't care," I shouted, my rage matching his.

"She will make you care. It is your life we are talking about. Not just your life but the lives of those you care about. They will know about all of them. They will destroy them to destroy you. I have watched them do it, Emeline," Collin thundered, stepping toward me, his anger encasing me.

"You mean *helped* them. You are an Illum," I spat.

Collin stared at me, his face unreadable. The Pod stopped—and his exterior re-formed before my eyes. As the doors opened, Collin turned, grace and strength wrapping around him until he became a picture of power. Collin offered me his hand like he hadn't just screamed at me. I hesitated, momentarily wondering what would happen if I didn't take it. His sapphire eyes flashed as he grabbed my hand and led me out.

Six soldiers waited just inside the door. Collin crossed the entrance, making his way to the door across the hall.

"Updates from the Capitol?" Collin asked the tallest soldier.

"The soldiers have entered the building," he responded in a menacing voice I knew. "All of them."

Collin nodded to him as he stood quietly. It grew too quiet. My gown suddenly felt too heavy as my mind became restless.

"She approaches," the soldier said, breaking the silence.

"Which members of the Illum will be joining us?" Collin asked, blocking my view of the door.

"Charles isn't with her. She comes alone."

Collin's shoulders sank for the space of a breath as the doors slid open and smoke slithered in.

"Tabitha," Collin drawled. "What is the update?"

"The rest got away. We might have injured a few. The Force was following the blood trail, but it stopped abruptly." Tabitha looked at me, half hidden behind Collin.

My heart squeezed as both disappointment and relief flooded me. It halted, though, as I looked at her white gown, blood spattered on its front.

"I am sure with some persuasion, we can convince the one to lead us to the others," Collin suggested.

"Oh, I do not doubt it. We have all the persuasion we need." Tabitha smiled at me, her perfect teeth gleaming, and it horrified me. She stepped closer. Everything inside me screamed to run.

Collin nodded. "Excellent. Shall we enter?" He turned to grab my hand. "There is so much to discuss and celebrate."

"No, only her. As we speak, her living quarters are being emptied, and her belongings worth saving are being moved to your living quarters. You are to go oversee that," Tabitha instructed. "Now."

Collin hesitated, his eyes flickering between us. "As you wish. Shall I return to retrieve her?"

"Oh no, that will not be necessary, Collin. I will personally make sure your property makes it back to your living quarters in one piece."

"Of course." Collin turned, his eyes scanning my face. "I shall see you at our living quarters soon, Mate."

"Collin," Tabitha called, but she looked at me. "The one who actually informed us of the Reaper. She deserves an award. They shall fill you in on the way. You will oversee that. Ensure she gets what she wants. I daresay she's been trying to achieve it for long enough."

"It will be done."

Dread filled me. My heart began to batter my insides relentlessly. Tabitha drank it all in.

"I understand your fondness for this Defect," Tabitha mused. "She is rather reactive, is she not? How entertaining."

"*Fondness* is generous. Like I have told you, she is an interesting specimen."

"She is. As I was saying, while we will publicly acclaim your Mate, she shouldn't be forgotten. If not for her, we wouldn't be here. Well, your Mate did give us some insight with her spying."

I grasped at the remains of myself. I refused to fall apart. Not yet.

"Of course." Collin bowed. His hand seemed to hesitate for a fraction of a second, and he was gone.

I stood, staring at Tabitha. The doors opened.

"Come," Tabitha ordered, walking in front of me. I followed, even as everything told me to run.

CHAPTER FORTY-ONE

I felt I might be sick as I entered the tearoom. Once, I had imagined having my tea on a beautiful flower-adorned table and chair, drinking from a delicate teacup. Before me was everything I had once wanted. A full tea service on the table with a large pyramid of gold-dusted chocolates.

The Illum will find out, and they will not allow it. They will ensure you never get it.

"Please, sit." Tabitha took a seat at a small table before pouring the tea. "You prefer bubbles, but we should keep our wits about us for this." She smiled, winking at me. "Come, sit. Now."

She didn't even raise her voice, but the command had me moving. The crystals on my gown dragged heavily across the floor and dug into my thighs as I took my seat, but I let the pain anchor anything left of me.

"Please, drink and enjoy." She gestured to the tray of chocolates. "These are your favorite, right?"

I nodded, my gaze locked on the blood on her front.

"I apologize," she said, gesturing to the gown. "I forget how they bleed. He wouldn't give me the information I wanted. It took some persuasion. Have a chocolate."

I reached out, grabbing one. I didn't eat it. I wasn't sure if I would ever feel hungry again. What had they done to Hal to cause so much blood?

"I have to admit, I found myself"—she paused—"disappointed when Collin decided not to have a trial for you. He expressed his intense desire to capture the Reaper for me instead. Said that putting you through the paces would be a distraction for him. It was a waste. The Elite need entertainment, you see. You are an anomaly in the clouds. You are of the utmost interest to everyone. Your treat is melting."

The chocolate was gooey beneath my sweaty fingers. I placed the chocolate on the table, staining it, unable to stomach it.

Tabitha tilted her head as she continued. "It felt wasted until I realized I could conduct my own trial for you while Collin chased the Reaper. It would be creative. You excelled beyond even my expectations, all while being blissfully unaware."

My brows shot up.

Tabitha smiled at me. "F13463233. You will restore our peace. You have primed us to destroy everyone who is standing against us. And how beautiful of a view you will have as you watch us dismantle this rebellion. Because, if you even attempt to help them, M13672314, or Hal, as I believe you call him, will be eliminated. Your spying has ended."

I couldn't breathe.

"Finally, a trial from Collin. I agreed with it, incredibly clever. He said you were extraordinarily obedient."

I couldn't make sense of her words, my thoughts too quick, ever changing, swirling around me until I couldn't pick one out from the other.

"Don't look so morose. The other Illum, Charles in particular, had petitioned for your instant elimination now that we have the Reaper. No foresight, men." Tabitha chuckled, and it felt like nails gouging down my body. "If I were to eliminate you now, it would be a mercy to you, and I would lose the leverage on the Reaper and his pathetic followers. We cannot have that. Plus, there is no fun in it. Death is so quick. I learned that the hard way the first time."

"He will not help you," I said. Hal would *never* help them.

"But he will. You see, we have tried to show you all that these emotions make things messy. We provided you with roles, Mates, sustenance. We maintain stability through these resources. Everything you could need to survive. We have given you order. But it isn't enough for you." She smiled viciously at me, her tea untouched. "It is never enough. You insist on letting these emotions dictate your lives. So we capitalize on your inability to see reason. M13672314 told us you were just another faceless Minor. But then I pulled your chip and ordered them to eliminate you. Oh, it is a shame you missed the way he begged. How quickly he fell apart. Pathetic, really, to ruin my fun so quickly." Tabitha shook her head. "The rumors were true—a woman had derailed the rebellion. The Reaper had fallen in love."

That couldn't be true. She was wrong.

"Do you like games, Emeline?" Tabitha asked.

"No," I whispered.

"That is too bad, because I have a game for you. You will help me now."

I shook my head as horror rolled through me.

"No, you will. If you don't—if you fight—I will eliminate him. He will help me because if not, I will eliminate you." Tabitha grinned, savoring my fear. "The game is simple. Who loves whom more. The winner lives and the loser dies."

My hands shook. She noted it. "The other part of my trial was Collin. You are creating the most splendid Illum member. Eradicating the little humanity, hope, and kindness he had left. Leaving him capable of capturing his true power and strength. The suggestions he gave us last night . . . they were quite creative."

This all couldn't be true. I had thought I was choosing my own path. A side I believed in.

"I don't understand." My pulse rammed against my skin.

"Of course you don't. You are all so shortsighted. Drink your tea, and I shall illuminate things for you."

I raised my shaking hand, taking a sip.

"And another."

As I did, she took the plate of chocolates that were arranged in a high pyramid.

"Power, people think the strongest get it. They would be wrong. You see, power is a balancing act. For those who cannot maintain the balance, the power is gone before they even have a chance to use it. Please take a chocolate from the bottom of the pyramid."

I did as she said.

"You need many on the bottom to hold up the top. When you take a single piece from the bottom, just one, the power isn't affected. But we need a reason to keep those at the bottom. They have to believe in their roles."

She gestured to my tea. I took another sip.

"So we chose you, our little sacrificial lamb. You had an obvious defect, so the ones below would see you as flawed but still chosen because you listened, helped, and adhered to our way of life. Or that's what they saw." She smiled, indicating my tea. I took another sip.

"Everyone always thinks fear keeps the balance. They are also wrong. You cannot have fear alone. You must also have hope. Duality. The Defects saw you in color, saw you succeed. Believing they too could become more than they are, they became more compliant and more eager to uphold our peace. Because maybe they too could be saved." She laughed, and goosebumps coated my skin.

"It worked so well, how quickly they sought us out. F17443485 came running to us the moment you got your contract. Desperate not to be left behind."

Left behind. The floor fell out from under me, my heart thudding pathetically.

"We knew she might when we synced your work schedules, but—you've figured it out. I see it in your eyes." Tabitha grinned like I had given her a treat. "You call her Lo, correct?"

I hadn't seen it. Her need for details. Her desperate desire to be included.

"Lola is her given name, but she didn't tell you that. Among other things. The secrets she was willing to share for her contract, and what she handed over for her cohabitation rights . . . That is power."

Lo had betrayed me. *Tell me everything, Emeline. Tell me what's wrong. Tell me what happened. Tell me.*

Delight lit Tabitha's eyes. "Where was I? . . . Yes. Also, in choosing you, your presence struck fear into the Elite. Fear that they were replaceable. Unimportant. Especially after so many saw you without that lens in. Saw how defective you were when he didn't cover you up. It didn't matter what we had taught them for years—seeing you and it was all forgotten. Knowledge thrown away for a different kind. They became desperate and compliant as well. To maintain their position, their naïve idea of power. You wouldn't believe how many slithered back to us, desperate to give us information. Creating the perfect balance."

"And the Majors?" I choked out, reeling.

"I admit, the balance has been off. We let too many from the bottom think for themselves. Act on their own. You have to, you see. They have to have some freedom. Something to stay down there for. We don't force supplements and meals. There is no need for constant scanning. They are all rotten anyway." Tabitha picked away the chocolates from the bottom one by one, the pile becoming unstable. Teetering before my eyes.

"How to control them then? How to keep them down there?" She tossed another chocolate to the floor. The grin upon her face would be scarred into my mind forever. "Offspring. You see, offspring are such a glorious way to cause fear. Almost all mothers will do anything you ask when you hold their offspring. But why bother with the Defects' offspring? The Majors all happily stayed beneath with their defective offspring. I allowed it while they behaved, but now that changes. They have lost them."

Shock rippled through me.

"Did you not know there are offspring down there? They do not tell many. Especially those who go down from above." Tabitha looked at me.

How much did she know about my time below?

"They keep them hidden, sacred. As we speak, the Elite Force is finishing the raid on the ground, taking all the offspring, regardless of age."

Tabitha removed one final chocolate, and the pyramid collapsed. Chocolates went scattering across the table, spilling onto the floor.

"And I have you to thank for the perfect entrance. The one you used when they shut down the grid. No one would think twice about a large group of Elite Force being stationed at the Capitol building, especially after their attack. The Elite Force wouldn't ask questions either. So when the time came to carry out the raid, any in the Force with loose lips wouldn't have time to tell anyone."

An involuntary shudder worked through me at how far ahead of us they were.

"Brilliant, right? All the Minors were in their living quarters for curfew. The Majors at their shifts. The Elite all in one place for a ball. Leaving only the rebels to deal with. That's where you came in. While you were *spying* the other day, you were seen. That information got back to Lola, and she came running."

Breathing became difficult. My heart gave no distinction between one painful, frantic beat and the next—just one endless rolling procession.

"So, how would I flush those rebels out?" Tabitha began, leaning onto the table. "You."

"Me," I whispered.

"You and those worthless emotions. I planted a story that your disloyalty had been found out and you were to be eliminated in front of all the Elite. They came running. Now I have their offspring. I have the Reaper. And I have you. The Illum again have the power."

"You can't hurt the offspring. They didn't do anything. Keep me instead." I was the reason for their capture. I had ruined everything the Majors were working for. I had messed everything up.

"Foolish child, I already have you. We wouldn't harm the offspring. We will indoctrinate them. Make the Majors adhere to our peaceful life. You control the youth, you control them all. We would only hurt them if the Majors don't fall in line, and they will. They always do."

The tea sloshed in my stomach. I felt sick.

"You will help us rebuild the pyramid."

"Why me?" I felt dizzy from the information.

"Drink more tea, and I will tell you." Tabitha smiled as I drained my cup. The room felt unstable.

"No matter what, you were defective, Emeline. Even if your eyes matched. You have free will. You failed every single test at the Academy. You wouldn't conform. You wouldn't obey. Which interested me greatly because, well, I do love a challenge. A wonderful tool you are."

I gripped the table as the room spun violently. I looked at the tea Tabitha had handed me. She hadn't touched it. She tracked my gaze, smirking.

"You feel it now, don't you?" Tabitha stood, walking over to me. I felt like I couldn't breathe. She pulled my head back gently by my hair until she swam above me—all her faces.

"I shall relish breaking it, Emeline. Breaking you and the Reaper." She released my hair. I swayed violently, any semblance of balance gone as my chair slipped out from under me. I went flying to the ground. No one caught me. No one saved me as my face collided with the tile floor.

"I look forward to our next little chat. Take her."

Hands grabbed me, pulling me away. I couldn't fight it. I couldn't win. My mind became a jail as I was dragged away.

There was scraping and thuds, a cluster of sounds with no home. I felt the ground hit my face again. Then I felt the familiar pull of a

Pod taking off, or maybe it wasn't. I couldn't see properly. A part of me hoped the Pod never stopped.

"Fuck. Emeline, Emeline, can you hear me? Fuck."

The voice sounded very far away, somewhere above me.

"Hang in there."

I didn't want to. I tried to let the blackness win for a moment. But gentle hands jostled me.

"What did they give her?"

Another voice sounded, or was it the same one?

"Emeline, we have you. It'll be okay."

It wouldn't be okay. I wouldn't be okay.

"I have you."

I found no comfort in that. I didn't know if there was anything left of me to have. I was ruined to the core. The darkness wrapped me in its clutches. I didn't fight it. I let it take me away.

I had fucked it all up.

EPILOGUE

The cuffs on my wrists chafed against my skin. They were too tight. My head fell back against the rough stone wall. How had my life come to this? When had I lost control?

Mismatched eyes flashed before mine, afflicted with disconcerting curiosity. I was a captive from the first time I saw them. Her left eye was the clearest blue—an insistent thirst for knowledge, for understanding. Set against her right eye, the depthless brown—her dreams of fairness. A representation of her duality. The destruction that dichotomy created in her mind, unseen and unknown to everyone around her. I saw it immediately—knew it.

Her. It had been Emeline who had brought me here. She had been a step in a plan, just a step. Until she wasn't.

Then I had seen her break before my eyes, while I had stood helpless, something in me severing at the sight.

A jolt shot through my left arm. I took a steadying breath.

While my hands were tied, the others' were not. Their grid might have been restored, but not before it had been modified, a ticking time bomb set. The supplements had been successfully funneled to those in need. My supporters and spies in the clouds remained my secret alone.

I wasn't leading a rebellion. That ardent drive in my soul burned brighter, stronger. This was a revolution. I would upend everything. Their buildings in the clouds would crumble.

Footsteps sounded, light and gentle. I let the mask I had crafted slip into place, washing away anything besides what I had become all those years ago. The ones I loved, their safety. The things the Illum had put me through at the Academy—the things they had taken from me. The mask settled and everything, everyone, fell away.

But my love for her clung to me—as stubborn as she was. Even if she would never return it, the mask it fought against the very thing that made her hate me. It was safer this way.

I buried it—her.

The footsteps stopped.

"Imagine my delight in knowing you are here," the owner of the footsteps said, her voice victorious.

I didn't take the bait. I stood silently, head against the wall, eyes still closed.

"Tell me, Reaper, are you ready to talk now?"

They had broken me once. I wouldn't break again.

"That depends," I drawled, opening my eyes.

"On what?"

"What you want to talk about." I looked at the figure before me.

"I always wondered what would break you."

The woman's smile gleamed in the dark.

ACKNOWLEDGMENTS

For someone who has moved as often as I have, spent most of her life standing on the outskirts of tightly knit groups, and often felt alone, the number of people I need to thank still shocks me.

However, before I thank the people who played an integral role in getting this book into your hands, I would first like to thank you, the reader. A book without a reader is just words on a page. The reader always brings those words to life and carries the story beyond the pages. Wherever this book may go from here, it will mostly be owed to you. So, thank you for breathing life into this world and these characters I love so dearly. I cannot wait to see where you take *Conform*.

Now, to all the wonderful and powerful women who had a hand in this book.

To Jenna Hager, your unwavering belief in my stories, the stories of countless other authors, and the light you shed upon them, is a gift. Thank you for your emphatic support and enthusiasm for *Conform* and my lofty trilogy of trilogies. You are a force and the very best cheerleader! I'd also like to thank Hal for being George's friend and that playdate I almost forgot about because I was writing. A "Sorry, running late got caught up writing" text grew into something far beyond my wildest dreams. It will forever be one of the best text messages I have ever sent. I am honored to be one of the Thousand Voices.

To my wonderful agents at UTA, Christy Fletcher and Rebecca Gradinger, for guiding me through every step of the process and supporting the unconventional way I saw this trilogy of trilogies. Rebecca, thank you for helping me with that first rewrite and the all-caps, passionate back-and-forth, for having my back, and for allowing me to believe I might actually be a warrior princess. Christy, thank you for juggling it all, for all the football talks, and for believing in me and telling me, "Just because it hasn't been done, doesn't mean we can't do it."

To Team *Conform* at Ballantine Books. To Kara Welsh for the crew you surrounded me with to make this book what it is today. To Jennifer Garza and Brianna Kusilek for tackling, and holding my hand through, all things Publicity. To Taylor Noel and Emily Siegmund for your creativity and cleverness in the marketing landscape. To the talented Regina Flath for all the time and iterations of art. You captured the ethereal essence of *Conform* and created a beautiful book I adore. To Francesca Baerald for the stunning map of the city you created from a very poorly drawn one I provided.

To Natalie Hallak, my brilliant editor. I cannot express enough how much your dedication and wonderful insights shaped this story. From countless hour-long phone calls that always went off topic in the best way to your honest opinions and help with all the kerfuffles that arose to your genuine and contagious enthusiasm for this novel and this world, *Conform* shines the way it does because of you! Thank you for making a daunting experience so enjoyable!

To my UK team for bringing *Conform* overseas. To my UK agent, Cathryn Summerhayes, for helping me land with such a wonderful Publisher. To Tor Bramble and the excellent Gillian Green, for your keen eye and ability to guess the plot! I am so thankful for your belief and so excited to see *Conform* in the UK.

I want to thank my sisters and friends: Sara Harris, Laurie Riley, Laura Sullivan, Alex Robinson, Lindsey Collin, and Anna Kupp, who read the raw, unedited words, often in episodic chunks of chapters, which arrived via countless emails titled: "No, wait, not that one, this one." Your early belief in a story I was still telling myself is the reason *Conform* is where it is today. I am so lucky to have women like you in my life!

To Katie Borquez, beta reader extraordinaire, co-president of the SYDS club, fellow moon lover, and dear friend. I had no idea a conversation while drinking water in an underground trailer-park-themed bar in San Diego would lead to this. I was fielding rejections and had just decided to rewrite the entire manuscript, and you offered your help. Your support in querying, reading each chapter of my rewrite and every chapter I have written since, and your heartfelt notes guided me and Emeline. Thank you for loving her as much as I do.

To Krista Howard, platonic soul mate, smutty-book-loving queen, and my first-ever reader, there aren't enough words to adequately describe what your friendship and support mean to me. Nor do I know how to put into words how they have forever changed me. However, I have eight more books in this series; perhaps I will find the right words along the way. Thank you for all the things I cannot say.

To my mom for a phone call during the pandemic that led to you moving in with me, John, and the boys. This decision provided support and broke apart the way I perceived family dynamics. Most important, it gave the two of us space to know each other as women and as friends. Thank you for showing me it is never too late to relearn or chase something new and for displaying the quiet strength and the power in that. I love you.

Now for my boys.

To Harry and George, for reminding me of the magic of imagination, reteaching me the art of play, and embracing the inner child in me. You two are the reason I do everything. I love you both to the moon and back. I love being your mother more than any other role I have, or ever will take on.

To Harry, thank you for showing me the best things often come when you are not ready for them. You are a testament to tackling things even when you are scared. Thank you for allowing me to see how you unabashedly share all your emotions regardless of the connotations attached to them, your love of deep conversations, your unending kindness, and the way you say, "I'm scared," but do it anyway. I am so lucky to know and love you. You were almost six the day I shared that I was writing this book. I doubted whether I could, and you asked me fiercely, "Why can't you do it? You can do anything you believe in. You're Mom." I love you, H.

To George, thank you for teaching me the ultimate lesson in perseverance and faith. You are the embodiment of what awaits someone who does not give up. Thank you for allowing me to witness your enthusiastic, unwavering tenacity for life, the bravery you show as you tackle anything life throws your way but still hold my hand to fall asleep, your curiosity and desire to understand everything, and your soul-deep understanding and acceptance of who you are and the way you honor that. You were worth the wait and all the losses. I love you, Georgie.

To my husband, John, for listening to me talk about the world in my head for countless hours even when you were utterly lost, for holding space for me to pursue this dream, but mostly for reminding me of the power I always had when I was certain I had lost it. Thank you—for all of it.

Lastly, I want to thank the countless storytellers who have enriched my life, made me feel seen, and validated unspoken fears in a way only art can. Whether the story was told on a canvas, in a song, or on a page, these artists' expressions of vulnerability and authenticity were the foundation for this book and where my love of writing was born. So thank you to the artists I will never meet who made a perpetual new kid feel less alone. And to the places like Hogwarts, Neverland, Narnia, Middle Earth, Wonderland, Lands Beyond, and many others that gave me a home during those years when I felt I didn't have one, from the most broken parts of me, thank you.

ABOUT THE AUTHOR

Ariel Sullivan lives in Connecticut with her husband and two sons, as well as their two French bulldogs. Growing up a military brat, Ariel moved every two years and was a perpetual new kid; she often observed from the outskirts, where a deep love of reading was born. When she isn't writing, Ariel loves to read everything from poetry to psychology, bake with her sons, listen to live music and travel. *Conform* is her first novel.

Instagram: @arielhsullivan